A JANUARY KILL

Paul Toolan was born in Yorkshire but now admits to being a southern softie living in the West of England. After a successful career teaching and managing in Further Education and Universities he wrote book/lyrics for musicals before 'turning to crime'. *A January Killing* is the sequel to *A Killing Tree* and a chance to re-visit Inspector Zig Batten and the cider-country settings of Somerset.

Like Zig, the author enjoys walking, fishing, gardens and the occasional whisky - but unlike him, he appreciates cricket and the taste of mushrooms, and loves travelling to sunnier climes, Greece in particular.

A JANUARY KILLING

Paul Toolan

Published by Paul Toolan

Copyright © 2015 Paul Toolan

All rights reserved.

This is a work of fiction. Names, characters, places, and incidents are products of the author's imagination or are used fictitiously and should not be construed as real. Any resemblance to actual events, locales, organisations or persons, living or dead, is entirely coincidental.

No part of this book may be used or reproduced in any manner whatsoever without written permission, except in the case of brief quotations embodied in critical articles and reviews. For more information e-mail all enquiries to: paul.toolan1@gmail.com

A JANUARY KILLING

PART ONE
Frost							1

PART TWO
Ice							27

PART THREE
A Veil of Snow						115

PART FOUR
Equinox						219

PART ONE

FROST

One

Superstore, faceless, second of the day. Eighty miles from home. Ice-white envelopes from this one.

A pack of cheap white paper, bought from the first, lay locked away in the old van. Shadowy, the van. But paper and envelopes of pure white. *To some people, white is not a colour.* Hmph. White is the *only* colour. It is chosen.

Gloved fingers made their selection. Silky envelopes, but cheap paper. Confusion for the recipients.

Three recipients, first. Man. Woman. Man.

Random items in the basket, to blur the drowsy till-girl's meagre memory. Then pay, in old coins of course, and to the van. Invisibly parked, a long way off, despite the frost.

Care. The essential exercise of care.

The pure white virtue of preparation.

Two

'Cold enough to do *what*?'

'To freeze your monkeys, zor.'

Batten worked out what his Sergeant meant. Had plenty of practice.

'*And*, zor, it's a good excuse for this.' Sergeant Ball pointed at his pint of cider, fortified with brandy as the Wassail tradition dictated.

'Since when did you need an excuse, Ballie?'

'True, zor. In which case, 'Waes Hael!" Ball lifted his glass and glugged a throatful. Even outside the copshop, in his own front room, he still called his Inspector 'sir' - and he couldn't even say that properly.

'Drinc Hael!' Batten replied, raising his glass too - but only sipping. His short sojourn in Somerset had taught him hard lessons at the hands of vintage cider. Di Ball, his Sergeant's wife and head to foot a Somerset girl, topped up his glass regardless.

'Why does a Wassail have to use Old English?' Batten asked. 'Why can't I just say 'Good Health', or 'Drink Well' - or plain old 'Cheers'?'

'Oh, you can', she laughed. 'If you want to sound even more like an incomer than you already do, *Inspectuh*.'

He'd lived in Somerset for over a year now, but still took gentle stick for his Yorkshire accent. Not that the Somerset burr was immune to ridicule.

'Aaargh, waal. Oy'll troy, moy luvver.'

'No human throat has ever before coughed up such a noise, zor,' his Sergeant said. 'Hearty congratulations - and Waes Hael!'

Ball would have said - and drunk - more, but his mobile rang. Di Ball said it for him.

'You're *unique*,' she chuckled.

Zig Batten didn't feel unique, but he did feel welcome - fortified cider and the deep red flame of a log fire said so. His Sergeant's house was necessarily warm. Outside, it *was* cold enough to freeze the balls off a brass monkey, and how much colder would it be tonight, when they all trooped out in the pitch-dark to the apple orchard, for the Wassail ceremony? The things I do for love.

He sat back in the soft armchair, twiddled his toes at the fire and gazed up at the ceiling's old oak beams. Beyond them, in the Ball's spare bedroom, Erin Kemp felt welcome too. She and Batten had been an item for nine months now, a gestation period unlikely to become literal. Despite being the right side of forty, Batten had no desire for children, and in any case Erin had a thirteen year old of her own. Sian was also upstairs, with mum, adjusting the hem of the traditional fur cloak worn each year by the Wassail Queen.

The day she was chosen to be Queen, Sian began to prepare - she joined Instagram, and tripled her presence on Facebook. Erin's job as business manager of a local cider farm was a factor, though Batten told Sian her rosy-apple cheeks had clinched it - and the fact that she was beautiful. But thirteen year olds test you.

'More beautiful than mum?'

'Er...'

'Or *less*?'

His diplomacy was improving. Plenty was needed to bridge the north-south divide - and to forge a relationship with a divorcee whose thirteen year old daughter was going on twenty six.

'Well, she *is* your mum. Stands to reason you'll *both* be beautiful, doesn't it?'

'What, exactly the same beautiful?'

'Exactly the same. Photo finish. A dead heat.'

Sian Kemp smiled knowingly. Mum had told her about good lies. And the difference between a fact and a truth.

A passionate re-cycler, Jean Phelps peered over her spectacles at the fat bundle of bumph that lay on the hall carpet like a lumpy paper doormat. However hard she tried to discourage the love affair between junk mail and her letterbox, their troth showed no sign of un-plighting. She flopped onto a chair by the waste bin whose sole purpose was to store unwanted mail. Once a week, she took a trip to the re-cycling centre and dutifully fed unwanted bumph into its welcoming jaws.

Today's bumph actually included *real* missives: a bill from the plumber, which she was in no hurry to pay; a Greek Islands travel brochure which she would soon gobble up with the aid of Columbian coffee and a touch of Mozart; a delegate's pass for her required attendance at a Senior Librarians' conference. And a letter, unmistakably from Estelle, the address hand-written in calligraphy script and familiar deep green ink. She briefly touched the letter to her lips, tempted to open it there and then. No, Jean, save it for tonight - electric-blanket, warm bed, glass of wine.

A swift flick through the rest revealed the usual offers to re-upholster, steam-clean, invest your savings/jeopardise your future. One at a time she binned them, tutting at the wastefulness. Careful, Jean. Still too young to be a grumpy old woman.

The last two envelopes were the most irksome, neither having the courtesy to address her by name. One seemed to think she was called 'discerning wine-bibber'; the other knew so little about her it was completely blank. She let gravity suck both of them into the bin, before drawing the blank one out again partly from curiosity and partly because the envelope had a silky feel to it - unusually expensive for a mail-shot?

She picked up an antique ivory paper-knife, a gift from Estelle, foolishly slid it into the envelope, and broke the seal.

Sergeant Ball closed his phone.

'Keith Mallan. Swears he's got the 'flu. Or hung-over, take your pick. So we're down to three shotguns tonight - two if Jeff Wynyard turns up late as usual. If he turns up at all.'

'Shotguns?' asked Batten. 'What do you need shotguns for? Don't tell me *hunting*'s involved? In an orchard? In the *dark*?'

Di Ball gave a mock sigh.

'Weren't listening, were you? Shotguns are part of the Wassail ceremony. You *do* remember the bit about banging a bucket with a hazel stick to frighten off the evil spirits? Say yes.'

'Er, ye-es...' *Evil spirits*? It's the twenty-first century, for Christ's sake. 'Yes, I *do* remember the hazel sticks.'

'Well, after the sticks it's the guns - fired into the branches.'

'To...?'

'To *finish* the job, of course - and spark the tree into life, bring on a new crop of apples. That's how my old dad explained it anyway.'

'And mine,' echoed Ball with a hint of sadness. His parents had died young, after their smallholding failed.

Batten diplomatically sipped his fortified cider. Police training and a university degree had somehow failed to cover the old pagan ritual of Wassailing, still practised in the Ball's ancient village of Stockton Marsh. Well, in the vast apple orchards surrounding it. In torchlight, on January 17th - 'old twelfth night' - when it was pitch-black and cold enough to freeze blood to a standstill. Thank god, Zig, there'll be a roaring fire in The Jug and Bottle afterwards, twenty warming steps downhill from your Sergeant's house.

It didn't matter to Batten why cider-soaked toast was placed in the oldest tree in the orchard, or why a well-oiled crowd of locals pranced round it, singing songs and banging sticks on buckets. Neither did he begrudge Sian Kemp her night of Wassail Queen glory. He could already imagine Erin's smiling joy as she watched her pretty daughter bless the trees and revive them with a slug of last year's cider poured round their roots. But firing *guns* at the bloody things?

'Presumably they fire blanks?'

'Oh yes, zor. And before you ask, they've all got shotgun licences - I checked.'

'Do you two *ever* leave the copshop behind?' asked Di Ball, shaking her head at the pair of them.

Well, I *try* to, Batten said to himself. Now. He didn't want to lose Erin Kemp, as he had lost others, to the pressures of police work. Balance. He was competing for a work/home balance. And hoping to win.

The ice-white envelope lay on Scilla Wynyard's kitchen table like a flat white stone. She had no way of knowing it was the second such delivery in Stockton Marsh that day. She picked it up, tapped it against her fingers. Silky, expensive, but no stamp, no address, no postmark. She'd found it on the prickly doormat with the rest of the mail when she came down for breakfast. Thank your lucky stars, Scilla, that Jeff drove off at sparrow-fart in his pick-up, to check on the lambs. If *he*'d opened it and read the few lines of anonymous bile...

The kitchen was chilly, something wrong with the Rayburn, but that wasn't why she shuddered. The letter's tone? Or the choice of words? It had triggered a thought, too, a memory. If she could only remember what it was.

Your deceitful head shall stoop, and your body too shall plummet down the winding staircase of death. Cold earth shall claim you.

Was it the Bible? It sounded like it. But where was she supposed to find a 'winding staircase of death' in their single-storey converted cowshed? She could hardly plummet down the two piddling steps that led to the front door! She searched the words again for anagrams and hidden clues - then cursed herself. Crosswords on the brain, Scilla. Obsessed with them, you. The letter she gripped in farmer's-wife fingers had delayed even a glance at today's *Guardian*, unopened, staring up at her from the scrubbed pine table, next to her untouched tea. She bought a different paper each day, to keep the crossword experience fresh. But this is *not* a crossword.

Beware, for the watcher's eye sees secrets. In the twilight, have I made my discovery.

Discovery? Discover what? If she had any secrets to discover they were so secret *she* didn't know what they were! *Stop it*, she told herself. This flippancy. *Stop.* This isn't funny. It's not a practical joke. It's...

Your eye shall be cast down, for darkness to devour.

Your eye? An obvious point clicked home. The letter was addressed to no-one. It didn't begin 'Dear Mrs Wynyard' or 'Hi Scilla'. And nothing on the envelope said it was intended for her. But if it was meant for *Jeff*, well, he didn't have any darkness that needed devouring. Did he?

And the fruits of your sin shall be denied you.

She scanned the worn worktops of the old kitchen, the unrepaired Rayburn, the cracks in the quarry-tiled floor. In the tiny garden, vague lumps of something green struggled to defy the frost. *The fruits of your sin*? I wish! When did sheep-farming become a road to riches? She flipped the letter over, but the reverse was blank. No demand for money, for repentance, for apology. No negotiation, no instructions. Vague, biblical statements, and nothing else. Have the Jehovah's Witnesses changed their approach? 'We don't ring doorbells anymore. We post anonymous threatening letters instead.'

Stop it! This isn't funny. Stop!

She flung the flimsy sheet of paper onto the scrubbed pine of the kitchen table. It shimmied past her stone-cold mug of tea, and floated over *The Guardian*. The damn thing's *alive*, Scilla! It came to rest on top of her phone.

Jeff's phone would be switched on, always was, out in the fields. If he hadn't gone too far there'd be a signal. Should she call, tell him about this...bile?

And ask him. Jeff? What is it you're not telling me?

Three

'Never bin a Jan'ry as cold as thisun,' growled Norm Hogg, hoiking his gun-bag onto his shoulder. He pushed into the long line of muffled-up Wassailers, nodding at the ones he knew. At least Joe Porrit was there with his shotgun, and Pete and Malcolm. And that clock-faced library woman, closing her mobile phone and staring back at him over her specs as if his book was overdue. He stamped heavy boots onto deepening frost. Cold enough in the lee of the church, but lined up at the orchard's edge, away from shelter? Brass monkeys!

'C'mon, Royce! Let's be *off*, 'fore we all freeze to death!'

Royce Beckett, the Master of Ceremonies, gave Norm a look. Predictable, old Norm. And correct. Royce Beckett couldn't remember it ever being this cold.

'We'll give Jeff Wynyard another minute,' Royce said. 'He's one of the shotguns.'

'Huh, when's *he* ever not late? An' I can *fart* louder'n his peashooter of a gun. Can't dawdle in this cold for just *'im*. We got kiddies here, freezin' to death. Let's be *off!*"

Sian Kemp resented Norm referring to her as a 'kiddie', though she was the youngest, amongst the forty pairs lined up in procession, stamping their feet as impatiently as Norm. Sian had thrown a fit when her mother insisted she wear thick woolly tights beneath her Wassail Queen outfit. What if they show up in the photos, on Instagram, on Facebook? The Woolly Wassailer, that's what the girls at school would call her. Or, worse still, the boys.

But mum had her way and Sian was grateful now, because it *was* cold, cold enough in the dark orchard to freeze brains, let alone feet. She smiled when Royce Beckett decided they'd waited too long for Jeff Wynyard and called for the torches to be lit. The flames flickered and caught, one torch lighting another till all of them flashed boldly at the surrounding dark, speckling every muffled Wassailer with shadowy light, and daubing colour onto cold cheeks and blue noses. The red and orange flares added not a degree of heat to the sub-zero temperature.

Sian *felt* warmer, though, now they were walking in procession down the frosted track, to the steady beat of sticks on buckets and drums. *Beat,* thrum, *beat,* thrum, *beat,* thrum - each vibration drumming through her young frame, as torches cast red shadows onto the leafless ranks of apple trees. She watched eerie shapes flow and dance along the black, bare branches as the rhythm of boots tramped beneath them, *beat,* thrum, *beat,* thrum. It seemed a long slog to the oldest tree in the orchard, but a walk seems further in the dark, she guessed, especially when you can't *see,* because you're flanked on all sides by lumpy muffled-up men. Shouldn't the Wassail Queen be on a tractor, or up on a horse, like Lady Godiva – or, better still, on a throne carried by slaves? Would she even be *visible* in the photographs?

On she tramped, fur cloak swishing to the thud of drums, flanked on either side by the two 'guns', Norm Hogg and Joe Porrit, with Royce Beckett in front and mum and Zig behind.

'Huh, colder than a witch's tit', grumbled Norm.

'He means colder than the ice in your lemonade,' Zig hurriedly explained.

Sian tutted. As if she didn't know what a tit was. Zig Batten. *Zig.* She still hadn't got used to his weird name.

'It's short for Zbigniev', he'd told her.

That's just as weird, she nearly said, but mum gave her a look. He was OK, though, *Zig,* for a policeman, a *northern* policeman - not that she was going to say. Keep him aiming to please, that was her instinct.

Wasn't mum's, though. Sian knew her mum backwards - or thought she did. Love. Mum was probably in love. And her green eyes were smiling, even in the cold. Smiling at *Zig.* Sian didn't mind. Better for everyone, mum's eyes smiling.

Jeff Wynyard was late setting off, as usual, and the roads tonight were too icy for speed. It'll make the return journey fun, won't it? Might need to cut back on the cider, Jeff, or leave the car at the pub. Chris Ball is a terror where drink-driving's concerned, and you don't want to cross the local plod. That's the trouble with villages. Everybody knows you.

Nobody around to know him right this minute, though. The rest of the Wassailers had already made their ceremonial way into the orchard by the time he slid his old red pick-up into a lay-by beside the church. His truck smelled of sheep, but then so did his clothes - and so did Jeff, most of the time. Sheep, rams or lambs surrounded him seven days a week and he'd yet to find a shower-gel or an aftershave that totally masked the stink. As Scilla kept reminding him.

He'd reminded *her* of it, though, when she had the gall to suggest he was having a secret affair. 'An affair? Who with? Some totty with no sense of smell?'

Scilla had done her usual - folded her arms and looked at anything other than him.

'You should have chucked that damn letter on the fire', he told her. 'Burnt its arse off!'

Or *you* should have, Jeff, when Scilla shoved it into your sheep-smelly hand. Secrets? Who *hasn't* got secrets? God save us from bloody busybodies!

He reached across the cab for his gun-bag and slid out the barely-used shotgun. The wooden stock was warm to his hand, the barrel cold. Just one creature it had killed, in all the years he'd owned it. Jeff had shot a dog, a dog savaging his sheep and immune to stones and curses. Three throat-torn lambs before his shaking fingers scrabbled in his pocket for a pair of cartridges and managed to load the gun. Good job it was a stray - if an owner had turned up he might have shot him as well. Scilla apart, sheep were his family.

As he climbed out of the truck his phone rang. He grabbed it and checked the screen. Huh. It kept ringing, there in his hand.

'Late enough already', he told it. 'After the Wassail's plenty soon for *you*' - and his dirt-grained finger jabbed down, returning him to silence.

Locking the pick-up, he shouldered the gun and set off. Tonight, the gun would fire only blanks, and he felt for them in the right-hand pocket of his Barbour. Live rounds were in the left. L for left, L for live. Granddad had taught him - and Scilla - to remember it that way. And blanks from the right-hand pocket were plenty loud enough to frighten evil spirits out of a frozen old apple tree.

'Frighten away letters from anonymous weirdoes, too', he told the orchard. 'And bloody secrets - and bloody *sheep*, tonight!'

If two barrels of a shotgun didn't do the trick, then three ciders in The Jug and Bottle surely would. And a couple more, just in case. He squinted at his watch. Late, again. A short-cut? Yes. He veered off, into the vast orchard. It was pitch-black and - true to form - he'd forgotten his torch. The distant sound of singing, faint flickers of burning brands and the whiteness of frost would be his guide.

He began to thread his way through the dark colonnade of trees.

Sian's tired feet were quickly forgotten once the flame-lit Wassailers halted at the oldest apple tree in the orchard - and it looked the part, a ramshackle contraption of struts and wires practically holding its branches and trunk together. Sian was happily coughing now, from the smoke that twined out and up from the torches, as they were hooked one by one onto a big semi-circle of stakes that ringed the ancient tree. They were hammered in earlier, when the ground was softer, mum said. It wasn't soft now, Sian thought. She could hear the scrunch of boots as the throng of Wassailers formed up against the half-halo of torches to complete the circle, as local tradition dictated. Sian knew all about circles and fire - they'd done Ritual at school, in Drama. With the vain pride of youth, the Wassail Queen stepped forward, to the centre of the flame-shadowed circle.

Scilla Wynyard wished they hadn't had another row. They'd been trying to ease back on the verbals. She would have handled it better if for once he'd got home before the food went cold. Late for everything, Jeff. Always.

'Well since *I* don't have any secrets, Jeff, this letter must be referring to *yours!*'

He had looked back at her strangely. Disappointment, was it? Dismay? Well, it was a *look*. A look she'd seen before.

'Does *she* have a name, this secret?'

Oh, what a thing to say, Scilla! We may be sheep-farmers but this isn't *Emmerdale.* Jeff just sulked, showered, grabbed his shotgun from the gun cupboard and drove off to the Wassail. When he goes silent, is it best to wait till his voice comes back? Last time, he'd stormed out of the house and driven to the pub with his blood on fire. Slept it off on the sofa at Malcolm Burley's house. Couldn't do much else, mind - Chris Ball nabbed his car keys. Last time, though, there were no *secrets*.

Through the half-frosted window, the spill of the streetlamp fell on her rusty old bucket of a van.

By the time the drums beat a loud tattoo, Sian's whole body was tingling - more so when Royce Beckett's hazel stick swung down and the drums abruptly ceased. In the flame-shadowy silence, a ring of smiling eyes turned towards the fur-cloaked Wassail Queen. Cameras flashed as she proudly raised an earthenware jug high into the air, pausing for still more photographs, then smoothly poured last year's cider around the trunk to bless the ancient tree. She heard the white frost crack and saw it melt and disappear where the warm cider fell.

Then more raucous singing, the tuneful and the tuneless in happy collision. Mum's soprano voice was crystal-clear - mum sang in a proper choral group - even against the deep bass of Royce Beckett. They didn't call him Royce the Voice for nothing. And Zig was singing too. She hadn't thought he would, didn't think Detective Inspectors sang. It's not macho, is it, singing? But he must have taken the trouble to learn the words because he was belting out the Wassail song with the best of them. He'd had a couple of ciders, she was sure of that.

'Old apple tree, we wassail thee,
And hoping thou wilt bear,
For the Lord doth know where we shall be
Till apples come another year.'

She heard the scrape of Pete Beecham's fiddle and an almost-in-tune guitar. Uncle Chris said Malcolm Burley's guitar-playing sounded better if you were a bit deaf - like Malcolm. Too much fortified cider had been drunk to make much difference.

'For to bear well, and to bear well
So merry let us be.

Let every man take off his hat,
And shout to the old apple tree!'

And shout they did! And not just the men. Every throat in the flame-flickering, frost-covered orchard opened and outpoured such a strident, ululating, ear-piercing scream that Sian felt sorry for any evil spirits that might be lurking in this or any other tree, in any dark orchard, *anywhere*. The fashion-defying mix of woolly hats, fur caps and thick mufflers could not dampen the sound.

'*Old apple tree, we wassail thee,*
And hoping thou wilt bear
Hatfuls, capfuls, three bushel bagfuls
And a little heap under the stairs!
Hip! Hip! Hooray!'

Topping their earlier cheers and yells, the crowd clattered sticks and glove-clad hands against saucepans and buckets and drums, noise blasting and blaring out into the trees and beyond, soaring upwards to the perfect blackness of the night sky. Sian was glad of her fur hood. Evil spirits didn't wear fur hoods or ear-defenders, more fool them.

Unseen, unheard, a nondescript van eased into a parking space in the narrow lane. Following the familiar old red pick-up was child's play. The driver's hands quietly locked the door, having also reached for a shotgun and checked for cartridges, in the left-hand pocket of a winter coat. Nondescript boots stepped soundlessly onto the frost-crushed footmarks of the Wassailers, and with the aid of a tiny pencil torch followed their track, adding nary a smudge to the impressions already made. Then the boots also detoured from the path and slid in silence past dark trees, stepping into the single set of footprints conveniently smudged into the frost by Jeff Wynyard himself.

Jeff could barely make out the circle of flaming brands that lit the Wassail when he heard the distant but unmistakable raised voice of Royce Beckett - '*Guns make ready!*'

Why was Jeff late for *everything*? He hurriedly loaded two cartridges into his shotgun, and clicked it shut. He wasn't stupid enough to sprint into the gloom carrying a loaded gun - blanks or no blanks - but he could at least add some noise to the proceedings, even if he wasn't actually beneath the ancient tree when he pulled the trigger. He could be *kind of* useful. He popped a plug into the ear next to the barrel, gripped the gun and raised it to his shoulder. Pointing it up at the bare branches of the nearest tree, he waited for Royce the Voice's signal to fire.

Unseen and unheard in the darkness behind him, silent hands gripped a different gun. The barrel pointed ahead, not up. And not at a tree.

Sian Kemp screamed, screamed with exhilaration as she was whirled around the old apple tree on the shoulders of the two men with guns. There should have been four, she knew, but two had not turned up. Joe Porrit and Norm Hogg, though, were plenty big enough to lift Sian high into the night air. They were two giant trees, arms raised like branches, their winter coats the colour of bark. Norm's deerstalker tickled her face as he and Joe spun her up and round through smoke, flame, shadow and frost, while the Wassailers sang and howled and racketed. When she was gently put back on the ground she was pleasantly dizzy, and the glint of shotguns flashed and fizzed across her eyes as two giant tree-men raised them to their shoulders and pointed them at the old apple tree.

'GUNS MAKE READY!' boomed Royce the Voice.

'READY AND WILLING!' replied Joe and Norm, louder still.

In the light of a flaming torch, Royce Beckett raised his hazel stick high into the air and began his incantation:

'Spirits true and good
Breathe life into the bud!
But evil spirits flee
From yonder apple tree!'

Was it the words or was it Royce's tone that gave Sian goose-pimples? It wasn't the cold. She'd already forgotten about that.

*'Into the dark
Upon my mark!
With powder and ball
Scatter them all!'*

The hazel stick swung down through flame and shadow and the guns flashed fire, blasting at the freezing air, shattering ears, orchard and sky with sound. *BOODOODOOM!* Instantly, a volley of screams and the clatter and clang of sticks on buckets and drums added to the cacophony. Royce Beckett's powerful voice rose again as the sound fell away.

*'Powder and shot
Shall scatter the lot.
Spirits, be gone!
Fire again!'*

On Royce's signal, more bright echoes burst from the guns - *BOODOOM!* To Sian, the second volley seemed almost as loud as the first and she was glad of her thick fur hood which muffled the noise. Looking round, she spotted a smiling Zig with his gloved hands over mum's ears. He probably hears gunfire all the time, she thought, in the police.

Jeff Wynyard was staring at his arms and legs. Why were they pointing in randomly different directions? And why was he on his back, a jagged dark contour in the white frost? He remembered firing - just the one barrel - and seeing the flare burst into the trees above his head. Then a kind of echo seemed to pierce him, shock him to the ground - the force powerful enough to spin his gun from his fingers and whirl it across the orchard like a plastic frisbee. In the deeper darkness, the frost beneath his back was warm, soft, wet. He heard - or did he feel? - footsteps move towards him, and then, ah yes, his shotgun being returned. He reached for it but his empty hand refused to move, and anyway that's not how to present a gun, its barrel pointed *at* you, barrel pointed at your *face* like that. Ridiculous.

In the distance, a mile, two miles away, three perhaps, he heard Royce Beckett's deep bass voice sing out once more.

*'Powder and shot
Shall scatter the lot –'*

Of course. That was why his gun was being returned - for the second shot. He could just make out the faint distant flicker of burning brands, higher in the night sky now, for some reason. But there *are* codes of practice. What imbecile waves a gun in someone's face, even a gun loaded with blanks? If you own a shotgun, you follow the code. Does this person know *nothing* about guns?

'*- Spirits, be gone!
Fire again!'*

And *how* did Jeff manage to fire? His fingers still refused to grasp the gun, and…no, he couldn't make out who was holding it, too dark…but the shotgun plain enough, six inches from his face.

And how did he see the flash, when his hand was a mile, two miles away from the trigger? Three miles, perhaps. Four…

And the boom, how did he hear the boom?

Four

Di Ball baulked at being called a feminist - she didn't want to be an *ist* of any kind - but as the hands of the church clock cranked towards eleven she was having decidedly feminist thoughts.

'*Oh yes*, we'll all meet at the lychgate in the morning, ten-thirty sharp.'

That's what they'd said. Well, *she* was here, frozen to the bone, but where were the three *men* who only last night had promised, promised to her face, to be here too, with their bin-liners and protective gloves - and their energy? Still sleeping off last night's Wassail cider, she'd bet cider on it. Cursing them under her breath, she did what she and her policeman husband did most of the time. Got on with it.

Chris had offered to help but he was on lates and she knew he needed to sleep. *So do it yourself, woman!* She strode resolutely through the lychgate and past the old village church towards the apple orchards, pulling on a pair of well-worn gardening gloves and hoping the low morning sun wouldn't reveal what she suspected last night's darkness had too comfortably concealed: a big mess. Four pairs of hands would have cleaned up the debris from the annual Wassail in a jiffy, but… Just do the best you can, Di, and give the three missing *men* a piece of your made-up mind, whenever they drag themselves into daylight.

Yanking a black bin-liner from her pocket, she stepped onto the narrow track snaking behind the church and clicked open the gate into the orchards, silhouetted in sunlight now. Last night's heavy frost was beginning to melt but it still cracked beneath her feet in places, and coated her boots as she trudged between the neat lines of trees and their long morning shadows. With scarred optimism, she approached the big semi-circle of stone-cold torches that had flared and smoked throughout last night's Wassail. She picked up cans and paper, empty bottles, spent shotgun cartridges, even a wayward scarf, stiff with rime, which she tied to an overhanging branch for its owner to reclaim.

Two bags she filled, before turning her attention to the curve of spent stakes that had given the Wassail such a shimmery atmosphere, despite the smoke that made the Wassail Queen cough and a few eyes run, her own included. She couldn't carry the stakes by herself but at least she could uproot them and stack them in a pile - a pile big enough to shame the hungover *men* who were supposed to be doing it.

By the time the hard ground surrendered its semi-circle of what looked to her like a skinny Stonehenge, Di Ball was sweating. The very last stake - always the way, Di - refused to yield, shaking its head and folding its arms and keeping its one peg-leg stubbornly cemented into the winter turf. She pulled and shook it, but it didn't budge. A male stake, clearly!

'You'll damn well move when I whack you with a fallen branch!' she told it.

And she went to find one, on the white-coated orchard floor.

Jean Phelps' phone sat on the hall table, uncomfortably close to the front-door, and its letterbox.

Not once in her long career had she cried off work. But work was impossible this morning. She stared at the plastic receiver she'd lied into.

'*That's right, at the Wassail. Caught a chill, I expect. What? Oh yes, frozen. Frozen, every one of us...*'

Frozen? She'd been hot. Hot with anger. No, not anger. *Rage*. And librarians are not given to rage. Her spectacles glared at the blank white envelope and its black bile of insinuation. Well, rage is what it deserves! With the tips of a thumb and finger, she marched it into the sitting room. The woodstove was doing its best, spluttering out smoke and faint wisps of red. Like the flaming torches, at the Wassail, last night. She offered the white paper to the red fire - a sacrifice. No, Jean, an exorcism.

But her thumb and finger refused to let it go.

Always finish what you start, Di, that's what dad had drilled into her. Mum too, in her softer way - an encouraging smile, a nod, a *good girl* afterwards. One stubborn, unbudging spike of wood - she almost left it poking out of the ground to shame the hopeless men who should be *here*, dealing with the damn thing, till she heard dad's voice in her head. Then mum's.

Mere twigs were all she seemed to find near the Wassail site, and her search for a branch hefty enough to loosen the stubborn stake drew her further away, deeper into the orchard. Last night she had tramped through these same trees in a noisy procession of drums and song, in the glow of torchlight. Today she was alone, in the silence of shadow. She remembered how as a child she played here, learning the seasons, watching bare trees leaf, seeing bud become blossom, watching the small apples form, grow, gain colour - and helping to gather the apples themselves at cider-pressing time.

She could never leave Stockton Marsh, she knew, though the calm productivity of its orchards sometimes disturbed her. The tower of the adjacent village church had become a kind of frontier. To the west of it, avenues of fruit trees filled the landscape. To the east, stone stumps dotted the graveyard. On one side stood tree after tree, strong and upright, waiting to bud, to blossom and fruit, and then the fruit gathered and transformed into golden liquor. On the other, clipped grass framed lines of granite headstones, mum's and dad's amongst them, each shielding a tinier grave.

Di's own daughter lay there, Gemma, a premature pip, whom she and Chris had laboured to nurture, only to fail. A tiny half-formed apple on a red umbilical branch, that's all they had made, living for a few bare minutes, on Christmas Day of all days, but not seeing in the New Year. And when the doctors had announced there could be no more apples, no more children... Last night, surrounded by Wassailers whining about the January cold, Di had kept her counsel. January would always be the coldest month for her.

'Why am I not blessed and revived?' she asked the orchard. *'I want to be a tree. A strong, branching tree. I want to bud, blossom, bear fruit.'*

But cannot.

Strangers sometimes lost their way in the orchard, so big was it, its tangle of branches looking the same in whichever direction one turned. Di stared at the blur of trunks and shadows, but saw a frosted graveyard and lines of stone tombs - before her vision cleared and the squat tombs grew into trees again.

'Wake up, Di', she told herself. 'You're no stranger. Tell your damn past to behave - it's hardly going to flounce away impatiently in a huff, is it? Where else can your past go, other than here, with you?'

She heard Dad's voice again - *always finish what you start, Di*. Then mum's.

Among the broken twigs and leaf-litter, she spotted a stout-looking branch. That'll shift *any* stake, she thought. When she drew closer, she saw it was not a branch at all. It was a shotgun, for some reason lying on the orchard floor, stock and barrel shockingly white with frost. She'd seen Norm Hogg and Jo Porrit replace their empty guns in gun bags and shoulder them back to the pub, too law-abiding and experienced to leave them in a parked car. They certainly wouldn't leave a gun out here on the grass, to rust and rot. So whose was this? She looked round the orchard, scanning left and right - for what, she had no idea - till the answer almost uprooted her.

All Di Ball could do was *see*. No other senses would function - swamped as they were by the eye-filling, sight-searing figure, smeared onto the white frost at her feet in liquid daubs of deep viscous black and red-brown. She tried to look past the red cleft jaw; could not. Tried to evade the erupted plum of mouth and lip, the blackened burst apology for a face; could not. Tried not to stare into the empty exploded eye, leering back at her, dragging her into its deep hypnotic blood-black cave. But could not draw her eyes away.

And then the anger came. A burning anger, at this waste. Absurd angry envy of this full-grown waste of a *being* - born, nurtured, clothed, and now discarded here, thrown away, flung down upon a frozen January bed of whitened, blackened leaves, while *she*, Di Ball...

She could not speak, could not scream, could not stand. If the solid trunk of an old apple tree had not prevented it, she would have collapsed onto the orchard floor, to join the shotgun. And *that*.

Five

It wasn't there, lying on the pillow next to her, Jeff's face, when she finally opened her eyes. It was nowhere to be seen. The clean pillow was uncreased, unused, and Jeff's watch wasn't on the bedside table.

Well, Scilla Wynyard knew it wouldn't be. She climbed into her dressing gown and stepped across the hall to the kitchen. It wasn't any warmer in there today than yesterday. No post, which was a blessing. No blank envelopes, Scilla, no threats - but the anonymous letter still there on the kitchen table where Jeff had thrown it, last night, before storming off to the Wassail.

'You should've chucked it on the fire.' he'd said. 'Burnt its arse off!'
She hadn't. The kettle hummed.
I wonder what kind of bed Jeff slept on last night, she asked herself.
'Perhaps I should phone Malcolm Burley, to check?'
No. Not yet.
She made tea. For one.

Neither Di Ball nor her winter boots were built for running, but running she was, past long lines of bare trees in the white orchard, down the frost-melting track and without reverence through the churchyard, running, stumbling, running over grave after grave - Di never did that, would *never* insult a grave - and then fumbling at the lychgate, fingers clumsy on the catch, and then through it to her own street and running up it, face whiter than the frost on her boots, speechless, and hardly noticing the hill, just running up it past The Jug and Bottle, running home to Chris and up the stairs, still with frost on her, and him sitting up in bed bemused and seconds later he was out of it and she was in, boots discarded - he put her straight into the warmth he'd leapt from, wrapped the duvet round her, clicked the electric blanket on, the kettle on, himself on. Work-mode now.

Chris Ball's training told him his wife was in deep shock, but training could not tell him the cause, and neither at first could she. Rita Brimsmore from The Jug and Bottle had seen Di run past like a ghost in a foot-race and, concerned, she rapped her knuckles on the Balls' wide-open door. Seconds later, she was making tea while Chris Ball dived into his clothes and tried to make sense of the few sounds his wife managed to utter.

When he retraced Di's route through lychgate and churchyard and through the frosted orchard to last night's Wassail tree he wondered why only a single dead torch remained sticking up from the frozen ground, like a warning finger. He tracked his wife's faint footprints through what little remained of the white rime, past discarded plastic bags, empty and full, to a double-barrelled shotgun shiny-white with frost on the orchard floor. An image of Jo Porrit and Norm Hogg flashed into his head, clean guns raised to their shoulders, firing high into the branches. The gun discarded on the white grass belonged to neither of them, he was sure of that.

The image crumbled when he looked beyond and saw the whitened, blackened dead carcass that had shocked the blood out of Di Ball. Had there been time for breakfast, the retch of it would be dripping from his chin right now, acid in his throat and a bitter taste fouling his tongue. What he stared at made him want to be home, to put his arms around his wife, to give her comfort, and have someone precious and dear put her arms around him, to give him comfort too.

Steeling himself to look again, with a Detective Sergeant's eye, he assessed the scene, estimating the angle and distance between the shotgun and the outstretched hand of the anonymous corpse. Its entire face had been blasted away and replaced by a mess of what looked like the cranberry sauce he'd spooned onto his plate at Christmas dinner - glutinous, lumpen, piled like a savage garnish into the dead cavity. Ball knew that if the distant gun was the weapon of death, the dead man could not have pulled the trigger. But if someone else did, or if another gun was used... Absurdly, he scanned the long shadows of trees for a lurking killer, protectively pulling his neck down into his coat collar, shivering from what he convinced himself was the cold.

Retracing his footsteps in the melting frost, he rang Parminster CID. After calling home to check on Di, he propped himself against a solid-looking apple tree and warmed his frozen fists in coat pockets. Even his big hands - four pounds of sausage, Batten called them - could do little more, till more like him arrived. If they'd eaten breakfast, he hoped they'd digested it.

Sergeant Ball got past the Parminster switchboard after the shifts changed, so it was a bleary-brained Inspector Batten who answered the phone. He'd worked with Ball for months now, socialised with him many a time - at last night's Wassail for one - and instantly recognised the terse tone in his Sergeant's half-frozen voice. Batten galvanised the team, dashed to his Ford Focus - the jangle of car-keys grating at his hangover - and Formula One'd all the way to Stockton Marsh, the ancient village he'd travelled *from*, less than twelve hours ago. He didn't relish what he'd find amidst the bare trees. If Ball, in his understated way, described a corpse as 'not pretty, zor', it would be nauseatingly foul to look at.

The few details Ball muttered reminded Batten he could well be a witness - though with nothing to report. What had he seen and heard last night?

Coils of smoke and shadows from flaming torches?

The loud clamour of drums and song?

Camera flashes when the Wassail Queen blessed the tree with the fruit of last year's crop?

And, yes, booming echoes as shotguns fired blanks - ridiculously loud - at evil spirits in an ancient apple-tree.

His hangover shrank as he gunned the car down skiddy back lanes. Alleluia, Zig, you've got a job that shrinks hangovers - the envy of your old school chums in Leeds, you are. Those poor hungover sods, slogging to the office, computer on, coffee on, printer on, then meetings, emails, marketing reports. Not like you - fresh air and country lanes. And suiting up, latex gloves, signing in, keep calm, lift the tape, duck beneath.

Oh, and looking. Assessing and looking. And looking again. And looking again.

Back in Leeds, over a pint or two, he couldn't abide it when those old school chums bitched on about '*my* bloody job'. Bloody job? I'll show you bloody. I'll show you *blood*. And the dead body that the blood's supposed to live in. And the consequence. And my bloody job doesn't jump back in the bloody filing cabinet at five-o-bloody-clock.

Skidding into the lay-by near the church, he parked behind an old red pick-up truck and hurriedly pulled on his wellies. In the graveyard, the headstones seemed to 'tut' as he thudded past.

A lot of strong cider went down last night, Zig. Let's hope it stays down, when you see what Sergeant Ball has seen.

PART TWO

ICE

Six

'*You've about eight inches missing, that's your problem!*'

'Eight inches? Eight inches of *what*?' Batten was shouting his questions into the loft, his neck at an awkward angle.

'*Lagging!*' his plumber shouted back. 'On your pipes. Well, *not* on 'em. 'S'what caused your burst!'

'Can you *fix* it?' Batten rubbed his stiff neck. Late for work - he was never late for work - and water pouring down the walls. A grubbied face appeared from the open hatch.

'Course I can fix it. I'm a plumber, dah-dah!'

And I'm a detective. Or supposed to be. He made the mistake of asking how much. You should be a plumber, Zig.

In the near-arctic air, the gritting lorry was nowhere to be seen and the frozen lane in front of his cottage guffawed at Batten's tiny scattering of salt and sand. The car slithered madly, cold sun reflecting from the white track, uncertain wheels crunching on cracked ice. He was down to his last few baskets of logs, too. Christ, Zig, it's colder here than *Yorkshire*!

When he finally skidded his size nines across the patchily-salted CID car park, it was Jeff Wynyard that greeted him. His face was hopelessly intact in the not-quite-smiling photograph that stared down from the centre of the murder board. Jeff was immune now to the black-iced roads and frozen pipes of a semi-glacial January. For a sheep-farmer who, the police discovered, worked sixty hours a week, he looked considerably fresher than the Parminster CID team slumped in a rag-bag of chairs around a meeting table covered with empty cups and full notebooks.

Batten apologised for his late arrival. They were too tired to care, and knew he put in more hours than they did. All were working flat out, foot-slogging along icy streets from one useless door-knock to the next, or driving on dangerous roads to less-than-helpful interviews with citizens reluctant to even open their doors, so cold was it. Worse, the responses so far were guesses at best, off-the-wall fantasy at worst.

'Something's frozen their memories,' DC Magnus said, blowing on her hands. 'Can't imagine what.'

DC 'Loft' Hick, the team's expert yawner, did what he was good at and triggered a chain reaction. Even Batten had to clamp his jaw shut out of stubborn professionalism.

'So, Hazel, how far d'you get with Mrs Wynyard this time?'

Batten had given the team's 'newbie', DC Hazel Timms, a fresh crack at the only real suspect to emerge - only because Scilla Wynyard fitted the standard statistical pattern: spouse, bedfellow, last-to-see-the-victim-alive. Or not.

'I wish I could say I'd taken her a bit further, sir, but…She's still in a daze. Pretends her mind's on sorting out the sheep farm but, plain as day, it's on *Mr* Wynyard, past, present and future. When I say 'future', I wasn't…'

'I know, Hazel, no problem. Carry on.'

'She knew where Jeff was going, sir, and she knew he drove, to the orchard. So, yes, it would have been easy for her to follow him and….'

The team completed her sentence with a hurried, collective nod.

'And I couldn't get her to suggest anybody - anyone else, I mean - who might have followed him to the Wassail. No names, no ideas, just a strange look on her face.'

Batten had seen the same look. But it could be Scilla's default position for all he knew. If only Ballie was here. They needed his local knowledge.

'I did take her through the anonymous letter again, sir, as you advised. Not easy. Tried to steer her back to before, but she can barely remember if she's changed her pants. If you see what I mean…'

Batten nodded. He hadn't yet fathomed Hazel Timms, but enigmas were nothing new. DC Eddie Hick had been around for months and the twitching, jerking, random pile of bones he used as a body could still bewilder friend and foe alike, particularly as the body was clothed in an array of arbitrary bits and pieces that could have been fished out of a skip. But give Hick a bacon sandwich and his mind lit up. Batten had still to find the elixir that might transform Hazel Timms. She was competent, attractive in a mousy sort of way, but a bit…distant? Was that the word?

'You're convinced it's a question of memory, then? She's not being evasive?'

'I don't know about 'convinced', sir, but if you pushed me I might lean towards her telling the truth. Maybe.'

Batten had already questioned the distraught Scilla Wynyard, his fingers trying not to tap-tap on the photocopied letter that lay on the desk between them. As anonymous letters go, he'd seen worse - though its malice was plain enough. So far, the police had as much idea as Scilla Wynyard about the letter's intended recipient. Jeff? Scilla? Both of them? And no hard evidence linking Jeff Wynyard's murder to the letter, whoever sent it. So far, they hadn't ruled out Scilla writing it herself.

'There's something *familiar* about the letter, or something *in* it', she kept telling them.

OK, can you remember what it is?

Her white fingers tightly twisted the corner of her fleece, as if trying to squeeze out an answer.

'No. Not yet.'

Instead, Batten had eased her towards the subject of guns. The fact that a second shotgun was locked away in the Wynyard's gun cupboard gave the investigation a brief lift, and interest fizzed when Scilla admitted it was hers. Jeff had bought the bloody thing, she said. It was the only time she swore.

'*What if I get crocked? And you're lumbered with the sheep?*'

She imitated the clipped firmness of his voice, calling him back to warm life from the frozen leaf-litter of the apple-orchard-floor, reinstating the obliterated flesh of his mouth, his lips, his tongue. Batten gave her time. DC Nina Magnus - sitting in - gave her a tissue.

'Jeff always took his gun, for frightening off stray dogs, foxes even,' she said. 'And sheep rustlers too, Inspector. Can you believe it, in this day and age? Having the gall to creep up at night and steal someone's livelihood?'

Batten believed it, from experience. Despite his northern urban background, much of his new role in Somerset was policing rural crime. Tractors and farm beasts were profitable pickings for the unscrupulous, and there were plenty of those. Nigh on a billion pounds a year, the cost to the nation. A city-boy like you is some use, then, Zig, out here in the sticks? Not much use to Jeff Wynyard, though, were you?

Scilla Wynyard gave further voice to her cancelled past.

'*Mine's too heavy for you. Thisun's lighter,*' she made Jeff say. Then, in her own unsteady voice, 'That's why he made me have the gun, you see.'

It's like being a surgeon, Zig, is police work. A scalpel with good intentions. Slicing into human flesh, right through to the bone. He continued to operate.

'So have you ever used it, the gun he bought you?'

She dipped her head, hardly moving.

'Jeff said I had to. Me, I couldn't hit a barn. '*It doesn't matter*, Jeff said. '*Use blanks, make a loud noise, that's the trick. Just make a noise.*' That's what he said I should do.'

Batten heard the echo as Norm Hogg and Joe Porrit fired Wassailing blanks at the old apple tree, to frighten off evil spirits. But not everyone fired blanks, that night. And the evil spirits didn't budge, Zig, did they?

'I tried. To say *no*, I mean. I said, Jeff, I don't want this shotgun. I don't like guns. Guns are dangerous.'

'Could she have pulled the trigger, do you think?'

Hazel Timms wanted to show her new Inspector the decisive streak she used to have, but fell back on reality. She simply wasn't sure about Scilla Wynyard. An intelligent woman, though perhaps not a contented one? Quirky? Was that the word? No law against being quirky. And no law against helping Scilla finish The Times crossword - as a sort of bonding exercise, Hazel told herself. In truth, it was because Hazel liked crosswords too. One of the clues was 'Joanna's pleasure, if curtailed by happy ending', three letters. Hazel saw Scilla's face twitch as she wrote 'Joy' in the blank space. That's no surprise, though? Is it? She didn't mention this to Inspector Batten.

'Maybe, sir. I couldn't go further, yet.'

Batten's view was much the same. That there was no trace of gunshot residue on Scilla Wynyard, on her clothing, or in her wardrobe, was a factor - though not a conclusive one. The shotgun Jeff Wynyard had bought her did turn out to be lighter. It was a 28-bore, smaller than the 20-bore found in the orchard, not far from the mutilated face of its owner. Nevertheless, 'Scilla Wynyard' was written in black letters on the murder board. The thick line from a marker pen was her only physical connection now to the neutral, almost smiling face of her once-husband.

Batten's troops knew the score. Hick would sometimes ape the terse accent of his northern boss, behind his back: '*If it's not ruled out, it's still ruled in. Lad.*' Sentiment doesn't come into it. Nor gender. A suspect says 'I couldn't hit a barn'? Keep your mind wide open. Scilla Wynyard knows how to fire a gun that's stored in a cupboard? Then she can shoot one that's squirreled away.

Or persuade a third party to do it for her.

'Let's turn to the murder weapon then. We know it didn't come from the Wynyard's gun-rack. So where *did* it come from? And where's the bloody thing now?'

As if in answer, the door opened. An entire team of eyes turned to stare, as the unusually reticent figure of Sergeant Ball paused for a moment, almost embarrassed to enter. When he did, it was in silence and with a face as cold as the ice he'd driven through to get here. His steady, ginger manner was nowhere to be seen.

'Ballie. You sure you want to be here?'

Ball was still on compassionate leave, caring for Di Ball. Her disturbed state, the doctors said, was acute stress disorder.

'Hardly surprising, is it?' he'd told them. 'She's a housewife, not a pathologist. She walked in on a corpse, in an orchard, with half its face blasted away!'

'Quite a trauma, yes, er, Sergeant. Quite a trauma.'

The specialist got up Ball's nose. He'd wanted shut of him.

'How soon will it go?' he'd asked. And how soon will *you* go?

'Mm, well, Mr Ball, not easy to say. Not unknown for these disturbed states to climb the ladder, as it were, into post-traumatic stress disorder. Too soon to tell.'

'Too *soon*?' Ball had a powerful voice when he needed it. '*You're* not living with it, are you? And she's not '*disturbed*'. She's somebody ELSE!'

She would recover, they coaxed, in time.

'*When?*' Ball asked. They were unable to say.

The police grapevine rapidly whispered, and a loyal Batten had failed to curb his reactions when a young Detective Constable, shipped in with the Murder Squad, too-loudly spouted a gobful of foul nonsense about the Mrs Ball he'd never met.

'Bit of a family Balls-up, booboom! They say she's gone nuts. Good job when *we* find a body *we* don't go nuts!'

In a blink, Batten rammed the loudmouth against the wall with the anger-fuelled strength of one arm, and thrust his moustache into the DC's shocked face. A chuckling confidante bled white and disappeared.

'Nuts? *NUTS*? How'd you like my knee in *YOUR* nuts? *EH?*'

The DC could not speak - or chose the belated option of keeping his ignorant trap shut.

'If you couldn't give a toss about your colleagues, then get off the bloody force! Or I'll *kick* you off!'

Without waiting for a response, Batten flung the big DC like a rag-doll down a corridor that was suddenly empty.

Ball looked round the meeting room, airless now, windows tightly-closed, radiators turned up high against the January cold. Locals in The Jug and Bottle could barely remember a colder start to a new year, but at least mulled cider was selling well. Ball had yet to sample any. He nodded at the room's occupants, awkwardly, unable to decide whether to speak, stand, sit.

'It happened in *my* village!' he wanted to say. 'It's *my* wife. How can I not be *involved*!'

Instead, he mumbled 'I should get up to speed, zor. Getting left behind, as things are.'

Batten knew the value of Ball's local connections, let alone the rest of his skills.

'If you're sure, Ballie?'

Sergeant Ball wasn't sure of anything, and looked it. Nina Magnus stuck a pin in the room's inflated elephant.

'We're all sorry to hear about Mrs Ball, Sarge. If there's anything we can do, any or all of us, you will ask?'

Ball gave a little nod. He wasn't even sure what *he* could do. Batten finished off the elephant.

'Take a break, everyone. Twenty minutes, tops, then back here.'

He led the slow-moving frame of Sergeant Ball into his cubby hole of an office. There was just about room for the two of them.

Batten learned that Di Ball's shaken-tree of a world had one saving grace - her sister, Belinda, who in Chris Ball's rich Somerset burr sounded more like 'Blender'. And Belinda/Blender was a nurse - part-time now, private contracts, but a skilled nurse nonetheless. On hearing of her sister's predicament she promptly arrived in Stockton Marsh, bringing with her a briskness and efficiency Chris Ball could only marvel at.

'She and I always looked out for each other, Chris, and she'll always be my little sister. You know what I do for a living, I'm a contract nurse. Well, Di's my contract now. Until whenever.'

Chris Ball tried to pretend he could look after Di by himself, then he tried to object, then he tried to pay. Without success. Instead, he was relieved of his spare keys and matron'd out of his own house by Nurse Formidable before the kettle had boiled.

'I'm a nurse, you're a cop. I'm useful *here*. You're useful *there*.'

And she pointed him up the road towards his colleagues at Parminster, where the murder that had shocked Di Ball into silence was screaming for closure.

'So, I need to catch up now, zor. I don't want to be a burden, but if you could fill in some of the gaps...'

A burden? Ball was a fine Sergeant, but hardly knew it. Squeezed into a tight chair in the tiny room, he looked like a burst sausage - and as uncharacteristically careworn and hunched as he was when Batten encountered him on day one of the murder investigation, moments after trudging through the disappearing frost of an apple-orchard, trying not to imagine what he'd find there. It was as good a place to start as any other.

Seven

Satisfied, a gloved hand carefully placed the sealed envelope on the scrubbed kitchen table. Letter number three. Odd numbers were discomfiting, but letter three would soon be gone.

It is not the letters, is it?

No.

It is what happens afterwards. Once the third is delivered, action will follow.

And after that?

The fourth. Naturally.

Four is a satisfying number. And fitting, as the final act.

Sharp eyes scanned the white surface for blemishes, for inadvertent markings, but found none. Inside the envelope, the cheap white paper, bought from a random superstore, was also unmarked except by hard black ink, without corrections. The typewriter was a dear friend, yet soon it would be smashed, without regret, into jagged shards of steel and iron. These, in turn, would be dispersed to random landfills, miles away.

Gloved fingers imagined the un-gloved hands of another, breaking the smooth white envelope's seal, removing the typed message with puzzlement, reading its pronouncements - its *warnings*. And surely reading it again?

Yes. Without doubt.

After that?

The dustbin, the fire, a locked drawer, the police. No consequence.

Time now for the third letter to be delivered, exactly as the others were. A skeleton-smile creased the hard edges of tight lips. Because of course it is not the letter.

It is what happens afterwards.

Eight

'I'll tell you what, Ballie, it's a long time since I've had to tape a crime scene myself, but when I got there you were useless - a bloody snowman when I rolled up.'

He was trying to soften his Sergeant's return to the grisly images that had shattered Di Ball.

'At least there were plenty of trees to wind the tape around. In Leeds it was lamp-posts and railings, mebbe a bollard or two.'

Ball nodded, unsmiling. Come on, Zig. He's a man. A professional. Stop patronising the poor sod.

'How much do you really remember, Chris? I mean, you *were* frozen. Do you remember me putting you in my car and switching the heater on?'

'I do, zor. Very much against procedure. I bet Forensics gave you a bollocking.'

Forensics wouldn't dare. They both knew that.

'Forensics were too busy. I've been to worse crime scenes, but only just.'

They relived the orchard-scene together, images in blood-black and frost-white drilling into parts of the brain where bad memories lurk and fester. The discarded shotgun that Di Ball had mistaken for a broken branch was bagged more in hope than expectation. Both men knew instantly they saw its position, too far from the body, the angle all wrong, that this was no suicide. And if the bagged shotgun turned out to be the murder weapon, well, did they ever get that lucky?

Both doubts were strengthened when the wellington boots of Doctor Benjamin Danvers finally tramped through leaf-litter and cold grass and the body was turned. Jeff Wynyard had a sickening wound in his back as well as his face - but the discarded gun still had an unfired cartridge in its second barrel.

Batten had mixed feelings about the nattily-dressed little apple of a medical man whose silk tie sported a tiny embroidered stethoscope. Doc Danvers notoriously relied on 'the appliance of science', as he lovingly put it, and habitually referred to deceased victims - male and female alike - as 'Mr Body'.

'As you have now noted, Inspector, Mr Body was shot twice - and no more than twice. From different distances and different trajectories, of course. Now, the facial injuries -'

Injuries? Every bloody feature's been blown away!

'- were inflicted at very close quarters - this close, I would suggest.' Danvers draped an open palm in front of Batten's face, so close he could have read his fortune, had he known how.

'The other shot was from thirty feet or so - I shall of course carry out detailed shot pattern analysis when Mr Body is transferred from these sylvan surroundings to my indoor Bodyshop and -'

Batten crowbarred a question. With Danvers, it was the only way.

'Which shot do you think killed him, Doc?'

'Ah now, who can say, for certain?'

Well, if *you* can't, what are you bloody *for?*

'Either would have, in all probability.'

Danvers' matter-of-factness gave Batten the creeps. The thought of Jeff Wynyard being alive, aware, when the second shot - point-blank - went into him... The Doc read his mind.

'He *probably* survived the first shot, temporarily, of course. If so, his vision may have been unclouded, night-time though it was.' He met Batten's eyebrows with an explanation. 'It's possible, Inspector, that he saw his killer.'

Well, he's not going to tell us who it was, Zig, is he? Inconsiderate of him, not to write the killer's name in blood, in the frost? Batten shivered at the image of Jeff Wynyard's frozen fingers and obliterated lips.

'If I may speculate?' Danvers had this strange way of cocking his head to one side when he asked a question.

Just nod, Zig.

'The shot to Mr Body's dorsal region is the first, and I make that claim with some certainty. As you will have observed, the wound is to the left, and the impact very likely spun Mr Body to his right before depositing him onto his back. The presence of leaf-litter on his rear, but not his front, would tend to confirm this speculation, yes?'

'You doing my job now, Doc?'

'Striving to assist, Inspector, striving to assist.'

Batten half-smiled. Sometimes a Danvers monologue did assist; sometimes not. Today, Danvers seemed in helpful mode.

'Without immediate medical aid - not normally available in a rural orchard on a pitch-black January night, Inspector - the blood loss alone would likely be fatal, not to speak of organ damage, shock, freezing temperatures - my drift is being caught, yes?'

Another wry nod.

'But, if surmise be allowed, Mr *Anti*-Body - presumably with a coup de grace in mind - then tippy-taps his toes – or indeed *hers* - towards the now prone and helpless Mr Body, and dispatches him with a further shot, at very close range, presumably from the second barrel.'

Unless there were two guns, in addition to Jeff's, and two shooters? Batten couldn't see why, but if it's not ruled out, it's still ruled in, whatever the Doc said. Or was still saying.

'And you yourself have seen the facial-feature-remodelling impact of the second shot, Inspector. Forensic Medicine meets Horror Movie? Dr Danvers meets Dr Frankenstein?'

Danvers' sense of humour was an acquired taste. Batten managed an unsmiling nod.

'What's come in since, zor? I haven't had time…you know, with Di being…'

Batten laid out relevant papers on the desk between them, picked out the ballistics report and pushed it towards his Sergeant, who studied it with an experienced eye, not needing the pencilled notes Batten had jotted in the margins. He dismissed preambles on observed velocity, pattern density, scatter and load, before homing in on what in more normal circumstances he would have called 'the giblets'.

'An *eight*-bore, zor? Not a twelve?'

A nod. 'An unusual beast', Doc Danvers had called the murder weapon. 'Overkill, Inspector, overkill - and both barrels of it.'

'I thought, that's a big gun, zor, you know, when I saw…'

Both men saw it again, the missing face of Jeff Wynyard.

'And tungsten shot, zor. Not lead.'

'Seems he wasn't taking any chances.'

'Or she, zor.'

Batten shrugged his acceptance, pleased to see signs of the working rhythm they enjoyed - in more normal circumstances.

'It's neither here nor there, Ballie. Could have used garden peas at that distance.'

Batten was struggling to comprehend how 'someone' – male, female or other - could stand over an injured man, point a shotgun at his face, and blithely obliterate its features by clicking a trigger. The act was beyond his moral compass, turned him cold. He draped a long arm over the struggling radiator, as Ball scanned more pages.

'That morning, zor, in the orchard, I knew it was Jeff. Pretty well.'

'Even without….?'

This time Ball nodded.

'Instinct, I suppose. We're all different shapes and sizes, zor, standing up or lying down. I mean, if you were lying on the floor here, with your face...hidden, I'd know it was you right away, wouldn't I?'

Batten looked down wryly at the restricted carpet. He'd have to ship out the two chairs they sat in if he wanted to lump his gangly frame onto this particular floor. And there was no leaf-litter, no grass, no frost. No blood. Ball followed his eyes.

'Not literally, zor. But you know what I mean?'

Batten knew.

'And even though Jeff was...the way he was, zor, I couldn't help thinking, well, he may have been late, but at least he turned up. Or tried to.'

'Seems he did more than that, Ballie. See?' Batten's finger coasted down the page to the next section of the report. Ball uttered a sad sigh when he read it.

'He fired off a round?'

'Well, a blank.' Batten jabbed at an underlined sentence. 'Spent cartridge, still in the gun, alongside a fresh blank.' He turned to the next page. 'A 20-bore, twenty-eight gram lead-shot - without the shot.'

'For the Wassail, zor, do you think? Or...?' Ball was belatedly wondering what Batten had already wondered. Did Jeff Wynyard fire at evil spirits in a bare tree, or try to defend himself against one evil spirit in particular. 'I could see Jeff doing that, zor. *I* would've.'

He saw where Ball was going. If you were close enough, even the discharge from a blank cartridge might damage an assailant... They'd checked A&E, local surgeries. Nothing. And the blood found at the scene was all Jeff Wynyard's.

'Blanks or not, you'd automatically protect yourself, you'd point your gun and pull the trigger, zor, wouldn't you?'

Batten couldn't say. The thought of even *pointing* a gun at a fellow human was disturbing enough. He had never fired a shotgun. Never wanted to before, and certainly not now. 'I imagine you might, yes. A natural reaction.'

Natural, Zig. Frost and thaw, orchards and apples. Life, and murder. Natural.

Leaving Ball to scan statements, Batten re-joined the rest of the team in the meeting room. He was surprised to see DC Hick slip across to his cubby-hole with a coffee for his Sergeant. At this rate, Zig, you'll be changing his nickname from 'Loft' - 'because he's full of crap, zor' - to Mother Theresa.

DC Nina Magnus was adding notes to the murder board. As Batten watched, she drew connecting lines between her jottings and three red dots on the enlarged map of Stockton Marsh.

'More from Forensics, sir.' She handed him a copy of the report.

'The gist?' Ball, he knew, would have asked for 'the giblets'.

'Mostly confirmation, sir. Fragments of the crimp and wadding from Mr Wynyard's cartridge were found here.' She tapped a finger at a dot on the map. 'Some in a tree, sir. In the upper branches, and no shot found, so...'

Batten nodded. Jeff had fired a blank at a tree, not an assailant. Well, Zig, he picked the wrong evil spirit to aim at. Magnus was pointing at two other dots on the map.

'A second wad and fragments of crimp here, sir.' She gave another tap, on the spot where Jeff Wynyard was shot first. 'A larger wad, they're saying. From an 8-bore. And more traces of crimp, a third lot, here. Second and third are from the same gun, as we thought.'

'From the murder weapon?' Batten trained his DCs not to leave information hanging in the air.

'That's right, sir, the murder weapon. And the third lot of crimp fragments...'

He let this hang. The whole team knew where the third lot was. He could forgive Magnus not wanting to say 'it fragmented into Jeff Wynyard's face, along with thirty grams of shot, which came out the other side, with half his brain'.

They both looked at the lines on the map. The position and angle of the two fatal shots confirmed the gross truth. Jeff Wynyard was shot first from behind, in the back, by an assailant who had deliberately stalked his victim. He, or she, must have followed Jeff when he strayed from the orchard's wide trackway. Why would a killer hide, half-frozen, amongst the dark trees, on the off-chance that Jeff might potter down a random short-cut towards a loaded 8-bore gun?

'Or it could it have been an arranged meeting, gone wrong, sir?' Magnus asked good questions. And she silently predicted Batten's reply.

'If it's not ruled out, it's still ruled in.'

Batten's private view was that no-one met, bumped into or chanced upon Jeff Wynyard, and 'happened' to blow his face and life away. Timing the shots to the sound of the Wassail guns was a well-prepared, deliberate act. A planned kill, malice aforethought, murder, pure and simple. Pure, Zig? *Pure?* Where the bloody hell did you get that from?

Despite the cold, he was hot now. Anger. Burning him.

There was a shuffling of feet as Ball entered. Instantly, the map became an eye-magnet. Jeff's body was clearly marked - and next to it, alas, the position of Di Ball, who'd found the corpse and suffered the consequence. Batten watched as Ball homed in. Sometimes the Inspector role was a struggle. Ask Ball about Di's health? Express sympathy? Keep calm and carry on? Ball's voice saved Batten's blushes, by choosing the latter, his eyes still fixed on his wife's name and on the arrow cementing it to the map.

'I was hoping there'd be something from the Wassailers, zor. Something useful.' He waved the large handful of witness statements he'd been leafing through. The team had been busy in his absence.

'So did we. Tracking them down in this weather wasn't a breeze, I can tell you. All bloody useless, including me - I was *there*.'

Ball and his wife were too. Batten chose not to say.

'It's because of the procession, Ballie. We were all paired up in a big line of two's. Even after a few ciders, you'd have to be blind not to notice someone slip away. There'd be a big gap, right next to you. And there wasn't.'

'There must be *something*, zor?'

How many times had Batten said the same - to his own DCs, to the plods doing fingertip searches, the door-to-door teams, the statement readers and background diggers, to Forensics. To himself. This wasn't the time to remind his Sergeant that the only 'somethings' they'd found had all been discovered by his Sergeant's wife: the litter she'd bagged up; a pile of stakes; a lost scarf she'd hung in a tree; a discarded shotgun. And of course...

'There isn't much. Everyone said the first volley was loud. We all assumed it was just echoes, didn't we? Echoing through the trees. One Wassailer - on the side nearest the crime scene - thought the first volley was louder than the second.' He didn't tell 'Uncle Chris' it was Sian Kemp - interviewed despite her mother's protestations. Sian had been tearfully insistent, her young ears keener than most, even beneath the fur of the Wassail Queen's cloak, a burst bubble now. 'Some of the others thought it *might* have been louder. Some said perhaps, some said maybe. They'd all supped cider, and it was pitch-black, so...'

Ball sighed at the ironies. He'd wanted four guns, and in the first volley he seemed to have got them. Then three in the second. And one of them a rogue gun, uninvited, evil.

'It's like that party game, 'Murder in the Dark.'' Hick's cack-handed quip failed to raise a Batten eyebrow. In the dark, Zig, is where we are.

'Jeff Wynyard drove to the Wassail, didn't he, zor?'

'He did. We found his pick-up in the lay-by behind the orchard. Must have been parked there all night. And, so far, nothing it in that might constitute evidence. They had a job starting it, by all accounts. Frozen engine.'

Ball was all-too-familiar with Jeff Wynyard's old pick-up, had helped mend it more than once. He'd told Jeff three times it needed a new starter motor, but Jeff didn't do anything quickly if he could avoid doing it at all. Late, Jeff's default position. A permanent one, now. This was not the time to say how well he knew the Wynyards, that he'd been at Primary school with Jeff and Scilla both - that he'd been the first boy to kiss Scilla, nine years old, though her sweetheart had always been Jeff. And that his had always been Di. He kept his counsel.

Batten too. They'd already tunnelled into Life with the Wynyards. They knew that Lonny Dalway delivered their milk, that their newspapers came from Stockton Marsh's Village Store. That Ball had been at school with Jeff and Scilla both, and was still good friends with the pair of them. Well, not with Jeff, now. And that Scilla Wynyard waited almost eighteen hours before bothering to report Jeff missing.

He'd stormed out of their house in sullen silence, she claimed, after a nasty row over an anonymous letter - a letter that Scilla might even have written herself. Batten was too clear-headed about procedure - when it suited him - to involve Ball in this yet. He kept the focus on Jeff's pick-up truck.

'We can only assume he was followed to the Wassail - no CCTV out there.' He tapped a long finger at the map. 'No tyre tracks either, by the time we arrived. Where's the bloody frost when you want it?'

'There were vague traces of footprints, zor, that morning. Well...Di's, at least.'

'Again, not when the SOCOs arrived, Ballie. Did you...?'

'I did what I told Forensics, zor. Kept my hands to myself. Retraced my steps. Tracked round the...victim. A few faint marks in the frost, what was left of it. Could have been anything or nothing.'

Ball shrugged. He'd been catapulted out of a warm bed, a disturbed Di on his mind. Didn't exactly turn up at the crime scene humping a murder kit.

'Can't stop frost forming, zor. Nor melting.'

Ball thought back to the Wassail. Flaming torches, and a few battery-fed ones too. The flash of guns, and of something else.

'Photographs, zor. Lots of photos, must have been?'

Batten flicked an arm at 'Loft' Hick.

'Hickie's on to it. Anything yet?'

Hick's head shook, possibly in response.

'We tracked down twenty nine cameras, Sarge, one kind or another, and I can tell you exactly how many photographs that comes to. Three hundred and bloody twelve - me and the techo's are half blind from staring 'em down. And that's not counting the ones of the Wassail Queen that ended up in *The Western Gazette*. There's a good one of you, Sarge' - he just managed to stop himself saying 'and your missus' - 'and about fifty of Sian Kemp. No-one took a snap of a murder though.'

'What about in the background? Or at the edges? There must be *something*?' Ball hadn't been there to supervise, his frustration bubbling over.

Hick considered dropping all three hundred and twelve on his Sergeant's desk.

'Sorry, Sarge. Too far away. Black trees. Lines of 'em. One black tree after another.'

Nine

Hardly a classic, despite its age. But the van was a good runner – and that was enough. The driver's seat felt spongy now, the radio was dead and the paintwork sported patches of rust. It went, though. Without sticking out like an elbow.

A well-thumbed bird book sat on the passenger seat. High-powered binoculars and tripod were securely locked away in the back. Careful, one must be careful with prized possessions, even out here in the sticks. The Common Crane was not unknown in Somerset at this time of year, and a glimpse would be a joy - difficult, but a joy. Stillness was the answer, and distance. And a bird-hide, also locked in the van.

A quiet, mechanical hum now, as the engine turned over, despite the cold.

The empty lane was icy, the gritted main road little better. Not a single pedestrian, and barely another car till the invisible van turned into the parking bay, dragging the first stirrings of a watery sunrise with it.

Lock the van. Carefully step through slush to the entrance. Load up the other van, and start the engine.

Batten ushered the team to the meeting table. The bacon sandwich effect was wearing off in the chilly room. Amid an embarrassed rustling of papers Ball sat down, thanking Eddie Hick for his gift of coffee with a twitch of his lips. It wasn't one of the bang-on skinny lattes that Hick regularly ferried from his favourite caff just off the High Street - the team had already drunk those. But it was a gesture, and Ball's wan smile acknowledged it. Since Di's illness - 'remember, it *is* an illness', the doctors said - he'd hardly smiled.

Hick's intervention kept the elephant out of the room when they resumed. Even so, Batten didn't feel ready to reprise the question he'd been asking when an awkward Sergeant Ball first put a tentative hand on the door-knob. Whatever the source of the gun that blew away Jeff Wynyard's face - and Di Ball's sanity - it could stay off the table just for an hour or two.

Instead, he turned to the question of alibis.

'How's the follow up on Keith Mallan, Nina?' Mallan was the other 'shotgun' who'd failed to turn up for the Wassail, because he was ill. Or said he was.

'Well, no less a character the second time, sir, Keith Mallan.'

Ordinarily, Ball would have added his smile to hers. He'd known Keith in childhood, and had 'dealt with' him a time or two since.

'And thank god for latex gloves', continued Nina. 'It was another of those where, you know, after, you need a scrub with neat bleach.'

Everyone nodded. Experience has its downside.

'You'd think he lived in Fort Knox. Same as the first time, a load of chatty palaver before he even lets us *in*, warrant and all. And I did all the chat. Him, words a fiver apiece.'

'Be useful to summarise both visits, I think.' Batten twitched an imperceptible eyebrow in Sergeant Ball's direction.

For Ball's benefit, Magnus reprised her initiation into Keith Mallan's 'home'. She'd assumed his sludge-green front door was painted in a deliberate shabby-chic attempt at streaks and gaps. When she finally made it into the 'sitting room' she realised 'chic' didn't get a look-in. Thank god he hasn't invited me to actually *sit*, she thought, staring at the brown patina liberally greased onto a sofa that might once have been beige. She counted a dozen empty bottles - beer, cider, wine - and could smell a dozen more. Or smell *something*. With professional restraint, she checked the locks on the gun cupboard, the bog-standard 12-bore shotgun, the licence. All the cartridges were lead shot or blanks - no tungsten steel in evidence. She knew any gunshot residue would probably have de-graded by now, but that was Forensics' problem, thank god. The thought of having to *touch* Keith Mallan, yuk. Magnus moved instead to his alibi for the night Jeff Wynyard was shot.

'*Here!*' Mallan said, thrusting a dirty piece of paper at her. It was a doctor's note. Glad of her gloves, she checked the heading, signature, date. Keith was unfit for work on the day in question, it said. He had 'something flu' - she couldn't read the doctor's writing.

'Right, so no work or Wassailing. What did you do instead, that night?'

'What d'you think? *Slept.* In a sick-bed.'

She tried not to imagine the sheets. 'And you were here all night, were you?'

'Where else would I be?'

The pub, the cider farm, the off-licence, the distillery...the orchard?

'Alone, were you?' The thought of anyone sharing a 'sick-bed' with Keith Mallan...

'Just me.' He folded his big arms. Prove otherwise, they said. Magnus made notes, in clean ink, on clean paper.

'An' I wan' that back.' He waved a filthy hand at the sick-note. 'Ad to *pay* for it! Ten bloody pound!'

Two bottles of plonk, she thought, casually wandering across the room towards the door she'd seen Keith slam shut as she came in.

'Where'd d'you think *you're* goin'.'

'I was hoping there was a loo,' she lied. Somewhere to throw up.

'Brok'n.'

She almost asked him: so what do *you* do, then, when you need to use the facilities? But didn't want to know. There were grounds for a search warrant, she was sure of that.

'He claimed he was in agony, sir,' Magnus said. 'For days. I checked at the Surgery and the sick-note's pukka - but it's the only one he's ever had.' She couldn't imagine Keith Mallan forking out 'ten pound' twice, on anything other than booze. 'So I'm wondering why he unclamped his wallet on this particular occasion, sir.'

Batten was wondering the same. 'Can we assume he was fit enough to pull the trigger of *someone's* shotgun, if he had a mind?'

'Don't see why not, sir. It was only a touch of man-flu.'

Several male eyebrows went up. Sod you, Magnus thought. Try period pain, sometime. She glanced across at Hazel Timms, hoping for a sisterly smile. Nothing.

'Any joy on the search?' The dawn raid had coincided with Batten's pipes bursting, and his frantic search not for clues but for a plumber.

Magnus reprised the follow-up visit to the Mallan 'home'. No rogue shotguns, no tungsten cartridges. No typewriter, no blank white envelopes, and no cheap white paper.

'White?' Hazel Timms had snapped. 'You expect to find anything *white*? In *here*?' She'd waved a latex glove at the grease-smeared 'sitting room'.

If you were black like me, Magnus thought, you'd feel hemmed in by white all the time. She settled for 'huh, you've only been here *once*.'

The kitchen that lay behind the firmly-closed door yielded nothing white - but a few traces of red. Spots of what might be blood were faintly visible on the grubby surface of an old pine table and a kitchen worktop, despite *someone*'s attempts to scrub them away. 'Forensics checked the u-bend, the drains, sir, all the usual. They swabbed half the house. Left it cleaner than they found it.'

If it *is* blood and it's human, Zig, who are we supposed to match it to? It could hardly be Jeff Wynyard's. No recent reports of missing persons, either. And no spare bodies in the mortuary, thank god. He raised a questioning eyebrow.

'Nothing from the Lab yet, sir, sorry. Dodgy or not, we can only wait.'

Batten inwardly groaned. Lab folk were 'the toxics', far as he was concerned. Like pulling teeth, waiting for them.

Sergeant Ball surprised everyone. By speaking.

'I can add a thing or two about Keith Mallan, zor. If you like.'

Batten opened his hands - 'the floor is yours'.

'We go back a-ways, me and Keith. He's a Stockton Marsh boy, as am I, though where the law's concerned we didn't catch the same bus. Even when he was a gamekeeper -'

'Was? He still is, isn't he?' Batten threw a questioning glance at DC Magnus, who threw it back.

'I said he *told* me he was, sir. It's being checked...' Along with a hundred other things.

'Oh it was true enough not too long ago, zor. Used to be one of the Wake Hall gamekeepers, did Keith.'

Ball paused, troubles from the less recent past briefly nudging aside his current distress. The giant Wake Hall Estate had swallowed up his mum and dad's smallholding, where he'd grown up free as air. His parents never recovered from the loss. While still a police trainee, not twenty years old, he'd buried the pair of them. Batten gave him time.

'He was prone to a bit of fiddling even then, zor, was Keith. In the end, it was a case of 'resigning by mutual agreement' - before the likes of me tapped him on the shoulder.' Batten and Ball shared a look. They knew from hard experience how things were done at Wake Hall.

'So what's he up to these days?' asked Batten. 'Apart from getting over a touch of flu?' Magnus noted Keith's malaise had been downgraded from '*man*-flu'.

'Oh, he's not fallen far from the tree, zor. He works in that big abattoir, over towards Chard. Always good with a carcass, was Keith. Be no surprise, to me at least, if those red stains in Keith's kitchen turn out to be deer. You know, venison. Never shy of a touch of poaching - even as a gamekeeper. If they're old bloodstains, my money's on that. He's not known for keeping a clean house, zor. Never did clean up after him.'

Magnus chipped in. 'They looked fresh to me, Sarge, the bloodstains. And the SOCOs agreed.'

'Well, could be he's unburdening the abattoir of a carcass or two? Doing a bit of home butchering, zor, selling the meat? Venison's worth plenty. And if he's nicking prime beef...?'

Batten prayed that's all it was. Keith Mallan as Sweeney Todd, cutting up a human body on his kitchen table? The image would have made him shiver, had DC Hick not chipped in - and without the usual twitchy preamble.

'Thing is, sir,' Hick consulted his notes, 'I've been doing the follow-up on Jeff Wynyard, right? And that abattoir, over Chard way, where Mallan works? Well, it's where Jeff Wynyard sends - sent - his sheep. You know, for butchering.' The click of ticking brains filled the meeting room. 'Just saying, sir.'

Batten stared at Eddie Hick, the only cop he'd ever met who could misspell words just by thinking them. But once in a while, 'Loft' stuck his thumb in a pie and pulled out a plum. *Just saying*? Hick's thumb had speared a fresh line of inquiry - which might warm up his frozen colleagues. Keith Mallan and Jeff Wynyard? The Wassail apart, did something undiscovered - or somebody - connect them? You don't blow away a face with a shotgun, Zig, because you've fallen out over a couple of dead sheep. So what more might it be? He set them to work, making a mental note to treat DC Hick to a bacon sandwich.

As the day grew older, though no less cold, Batten waved Ball towards his cupboard of an office. *There's something almost sheep-like about him today, Zig. Should he be here at all?*

'That was helpful, Ballie. We've missed your local knowledge.'

Ball had acquired Batten's silent nod.

'But it may be time you...' He nearly said 'went home', stopped himself. 'You know.'

Ball knew if he went 'home' there'd be Di's sister Belinda in one ear and Di in the other. Except Di wouldn't be in the other. She'd barely expressed ten indecipherable grunts at him in days, and not many more to Belinda. The Doctor got icy silence.

Staring at the claustrophobic walls of the cupboard-like office, Ball was shuttled back - against his will - to his Stockton Marsh cottage, to another cupboard, the kitchen cupboard he'd forgotten to repair. Last night, when Belinda was putting the dishes away, it snapped shut with a bang louder than a gunshot. Di screamed at the noise, turned ghost-white and collapsed into a trembling, sobbing lump on the kitchen floor. Ball tried to raise her up, tried to wipe tears and snot from her face but she pushed him away. *Pushed him away!* Never before, not once in their life together had she pushed him away. Belinda slowly calmed her, took her off to bed.

That used to be your role, Chris.

And, later, when *he* climbed into bed, it was the spare bed, and he was alone. Belinda was sleeping in their room. With Di. He lay awake for hours, till the cider he foolishly drank to dull his mind began to excite his bladder. He shuffled to the loo and back. Something unseen moved between his bare toes, a disturbing tickle, something with legs - *a spider*! None of his colleagues - not even Batten - knew of his fear of spiders. A muscled country cop, frightened of tiny spiders? Only Di knew, and she... He scraped his toes on the bedroom carpet, tried not to panic, switched on the bedside light, swished madly at his toes with a tissue.

It was not a spider. It was a piece of tickly fur, dislodged from the cloak of the Wassail Queen. He cursed his timidity. This was the room where Erin Kemp and Sian had adjusted the hem. Norm Hogg's gnarled reminder came back to him.

'Can't 'ave the Wassail Queen trippin' up on no cloak. Can't 'ave trippin'up at a Wassail. An' if someone was to *fall,* fall to the ground, an' be seen by the trees, well, that's bad luck for all the year. Laughed at, we'd be, by every evil spirit in the orchard! And come summer, where'd we be for apples? Eh?'

In his spider-panic, Ball's unaccustomed bedroom became a turmoil of trees, burning torches, smoke, noise, hazel sticks and Wassailers. And Jeff Wynyard too, a fallen man, there, on a carpet not of fur but of dead leaves, lying on his back on the frozen ground under black branches. Ball wanted to cross the landing to his own room, wrap his arms around Di, hold her, have her wrap warm arms around him, and tell him everything would be fine. If she could rediscover words, and if he could believe them.

He threw the piece of fur at the litter-bin. It floated derisively through the air and spidered onto the carpet. Struggling into his unfamiliar bed, he lay awake for a torture of time in the darkness. A dawn chorus of awakening birds sang him to sleep, as the cold sun rose.

Ball wasn't to know it, but Batten had been sleeping badly too. It never used to be the case when he stayed over at Erin's. Three or four times a night now, Erin was crawling from their bed to deal with Sian. Since the murder, Sian was a challenge.

'She doesn't sleep, Zig. She keeps getting up. I hear her switch on the lights - bedside *and* ceiling - hear her walking up and down, over and over, and then she's on her tablet, staring at the photos of the Wassail. Well, at those of the Queen, for all the use they are. She was so proud, front page in *The Western Gazette,* and then this happens. Damn photographs. Do you know, there's over fifty of the things?'

Batten could have told her there were three hundred and twelve, but there's a time and a place.

'And I do mean staring. She stares at each image, swipe, then another, swipe, swipe. Tears too, but silent. No other reaction - well, none I can see. But when I mention the Doctor she comes to life with a snarl. I shall have to get her to the Surgery - drag her, more like. Should I?'

How would you know, Zig? What deep knowledge of thirteen year old girls did you stash away in your half-empty relationship locker? Teenage angst - even angst triggered by factors he *did* understand - was beyond him. His gut reaction was to give Sian a hug, tell her that sadness passes, that it would all be fine. Unlike some of his police colleagues, he was open-minded about hugs. But it felt awkward, didn't seem 'right'. You've only to touch a youngster these days and you're an instant paedophile.

He and Erin were on a slow journey, rules unclear. Feelings for each other ran deep, yes, but experience didn't. Would Erin object if he wrapped a paternal arm round Sian's shoulder? Paternal, Zig? You're not her father. You're not anyone's father, and you never will be. So how to broach it? They talked in bed, but when it came to Sian, he wondered if even his finest words would be enough.

Head not quite bumping the office ceiling, Batten got to his feet.
'So, Ballie, perhaps you should go...?'
Ball shook his head.
'Plenty to do here, zor. Much to do.'
Batten nodded. He would stay as well, take his mind off Sian. And all Sian had done was *hear* about the body. If, like Di Ball, she'd seen it...
'Much to do, Ballie, yes.'
There's always work, Zig. He gave Ball a blokey tap on the arm. Common ground.

Detective Constable Eddie 'Loft' Hick watched as Nina Magnus and Hazel Timms topped and tailed their final tasks, ready for the end of shift. Nina Magnus he knew well, and liked, but he'd drawn no conclusions about Hazel Timms. Give her chance to get her feet under the table, boy, before you pass judgement. He gave a deep sigh. His follow-up into Jeff Wynyard's movements on Wassail night was a good hour behind schedule.

He switched on his laptop, watched it boot up. Why don't they get on, those two? A pair of females, amongst us blokes? You would've thought they'd be thick as thieves. Never one to spot the criminal nature of his own metaphors, Eddie Hick gave his shoulders a hopeful twitch as his screen lit up. He peered at the email he'd been waiting for. Yes! He was right. There *was* a witness! He grabbed a pencil to make a note, managed to snap the end off.

Nina Magnus still didn't know what to make of Hazel Timms. She's been here long enough now, girl, but we've never had a quiet drink, never had a heart-to-heart. Nina wasn't expecting Hazel to be a sister - for a start, Hazel was white - but, two female DCs, amongst all these blokes? They should be allies, yes?

She watched Hazel's back disappear towards the car park, as it did promptly at the end of every shift. Moonlighting, is she? Flogging sex toys and lingerie? Whiplash Timms, the DC with a sideline in naughty knickers?

Twice - Eddie Hick's birthday, and when Katie What's-her-name, the part-time Scene of Crime Officer left - Hazel had stayed for a bit of cake and a grudging giggle at the sexist jokes, but apart from that…Trouble with being a detective, Nina, is that when a question gets under your skin you can't help but scratch. Nina Magnus was a good detective. And as she reached for her bag and coat she was still scratching.

DC Hazel Timms might be the most recent addition to the Parminster CID unit but she was a good detective too - and plenty good enough to spot Nina's obsession with 'going for a drink' or 'having a coffee sometime.' Well, she didn't have 'sometime' to spare, so Nina would have to drink alone, or with her Mike Mike Mike, the other obsession that Hazel had swiftly detected. She started the engine, yawned, drove off, to begin another shift elsewhere.

Ten

It's like unravelling bowls of spaghetti, Zig, is trawling through phone records. To stop the numbers and codes merging into one, Batten slapped the transcript back on his desk and ran a straight edge down the page, just as he'd done as a child, learning to read. He wished Ball wasn't looking over his shoulder. At Primary school, that's what Mrs Chudleigh used to do.

'There, zor! Just as I said!'

Batten scanned the jumbled numbers, easing his ruler back up the page.

'No, no, zor. Down a bit...there!'

So far, almost every call made to Jeff Wynyard's mobile was to do with sheep. Sellers, buyers, vets, transporters, shearers. Is this modernity, Zig? We don't count sheep anymore. We nod off counting sheep-related phone numbers. Only when Scilla Wynyard's number appeared had he perked up - till Ball pointed out that all her calls came in at mealtimes, and they both knew why. Ball's excitement was caused by two other phone numbers entirely.

'And the other one's...there, zor! See, I told you! And just look at the date and time!'

Is Hickie putting something illegal in his Sergeant's coffee, Zig? Ball was sharp-eyed today, throwing himself into the welcome buffer of work.

'If you're right, Ballie, we might have got him.'

Batten stared at the evidence. In the week before his murder, Jeff Wynyard had taken not one call, not two, but *six*, from a phone registered to - Keith Mallan. And Jeff also took a call from a second phone, an old number whose source took a tad longer to unearth. This call came in barely ten minutes before a shotgun wiped out Jeff Wynyard's face. The string of numbers lay there, unravelled black spaghetti on a frost-white plate.

Batten wondered why Keith Mallan, too tight to fork out for a single bar of soap, would happily fork out for two phones and keep them both topped up. At least he didn't text, Zig. 'Meet me in orchard. If late, leave message. Need to blow your face off. Lol.'

'Was it for 'special calls', Ballie, his second phone?'

Ball hoped not. Keith Mallan was part of his childhood.

'We'll be a lot wiser, zor, when we've asked him.'

Once inside the dull green walls of Parminster Interview Room 1, rather than question Keith Mallan, Batten wanted to wash him. He stank. Of old sweat and unclean clothes, stale booze and ashtrays. And meat. Keith Mallan smelled of meat, that unpleasant scent of a butchers shop at closing time on a red-hot day. His scowl, though, was a response to the questions, not the smell.

'Already told you. An' I told whassername too, that black woman. I was asleep. In a sick-bed. Seen my Doctor's note, 'ent you? She tell you I 'ad to pay ten quid for that measly scrap o' paper?'

'And your fingers were so racked with pain they couldn't push a button on a mobile phone? Is that your story?' Bad smells and vinegar scowls were doing nothing for Batten's patience.

'S' neither here nor there. I told you, I called no-one. Got no-one *to* call!' Keith Mallan's scowl edged into self-pity. He'd already refused Batten's sarcastic offer of a phone-call, even tried to decline legal support. When a schoolboy solicitor turned up, Mallan's tone grew darker still. 'I'm on my ownsome', he kept saying. 'Not even a dog for company now. Got *no-one!*'

Batten silently hummed a soundtrack, Country and Western. Ball took a turn.

'Let's go back a week, Keith, yes? If you've 'got no-one', how come you kept phoning Jeff Wynyard? Doing a nice line in knocked-off booze, was he, on top of sheep-farming?'

Keith Mallan had watched a lot of TV. 'No Comment,' he said. The spotty solicitor merely shrugged.

Ball flopped a page of phone records onto the pitted surface of the interview table.

'Six,' he said. 'Six calls in a week.' His thick finger tapped on the transcript, six loud times. 'And all from your phone. Explain that, can you?'

Keith Mallan opened his mouth to try, then remembered 'No comment', so tried that instead.

Ball gave him time to sweat, tick-tocking his fingers on the steel table. If Mallan ever chose to play poker, he'd lose. His face twitched as he recalled his phone being removed from a grubby trouser pocket by the no-nonsense Parminster duty cop. Too much bad TV convinced him the fuzz need only press a button to gain instant access to his conversations. He tried to lick spit onto dry lips. He needed a drink. Not stewed tea, not water. A proper drink.

'It's something and it's nothing. I was after cheap meat, 's'all. Bit o' mutton. It's lamb they want, at the abattoir. Pay next to nowt for mutton. Don' tell me you've never 'eard Jeff moan 'bout the price of mutton in The Jug and Bottle?'

'Oh indeed, Keith, indeed. But that was kind of you, ringing him, six times, about mutton. Kind.'

'Was mutual. Scratch *his* back, scratch mine. Mutual. Or would've been.'

Batten cut in.

'Would've been? *You mean if you hadn't blown his face off?*'

Keith Mallan shot to his feet, till the four pounds of sausage that Ball used for hands shoved him back down again. If Mallan was only pretending to be angry, he was making a fist of it. The spotty solicitor took his chance, scraped his chair a foot further away from his client's body odour.

'*Blown his face off*? As if I'd do that to *Jeff*! To *anyone*!' He looked to Ball for support, but Ball's eyes studied the phone records as if they were next week's lottery results. 'How can you sit there and let this...this *incomer* speak to me like that? You never said that was why I was 'ere!'

'Why d'you think you *are* here then? *Eh?*' asked Batten, shovelling extra Yorkshire into the mix. This time, he didn't even get 'no comment'.

Ball flopped the transcript back on the table, gave a mock sigh and took his turn.

'Look, Keith, longer you keep swinging us a line about these phone calls, longer you'll be stuck here. So what's it to be?' In a stage whisper he added, 'My Inspector, he's mad keen to solve a murder. More than likely he's taking your silence as admission of guilt. Yes?'

It was Batten's turn to concentrate on the phone records. The white paper was becoming grubby. And so was he, from being in the same room as Keith. With a shuffling of chairs, Mallan conferred with his solicitor, Batten managing an arch smile as the young legal-eagle recoiled from the shock of Mallan's breath. A few stale whispers hissed between them. Batten overheard the word 'intent', but little else. This time it was the wonder-kid who spoke.

'My client wishes it to be known that he did call Mr Wynyard six times during the week before his death. But purely in an attempt to persuade Mr Wynyard to join him in a venture that may or may not have involved cut-price meat. As Mr Wynyard consistently declined to discuss this or any other venture, no crime was committed – certainly not *de jure*. I suggest, therefore, that you have no reason to hold my client and he should be released.'

Batten and Ball shared a wry look. Then Batten flicked the second transcript, for the second phone, onto the steel table.

'I don't think so,' said Batten. A long finger tapped at the underlined number, sharp eyes turning on Keith. 'You also phoned him from your 'special' phone, didn't you? This one here.' He flipped the second transcript at Mallan. 'About ten minutes before you shot him! Checking he was there, eh? There in the orchard? In the dark?'

A switch clicked in Keith Mallan's face. His vinegar scowl became a stark look of, what? Surprise? Then fear? Then panic? Batten thought Keith was pretending to be a lava-lamp till the facial tics and shades settled into a look that was the colour of pain.

'And Jeff trotted obediently along, didn't he? And you pretended to stroll along with him, two friendly shotguns on their way to the Wassail?' Batten leaned as close as he dare towards the odour of meat. '*And then you shot him in the face!*'

For a second time, Keith Mallan rose from his seat, so slowly and in such a mystified daze that Ball was too surprised to react. The two detectives watched a large tear run from Mallan's hardened eye and drizzle down his face, leaving a thin clean line in the dirt of his cheek. It dropped without comment onto the phone transcript, soaking into the thin paper like sad rain. A stained finger pointed down at the evidence.

'What's *she* doing phoning Jeff? She's phoned Jeff. *Jeff!* But she's never phoned *me?* Never phoned me, not ever once, not since the day she buggered off!'

Even Ball, who knew Keith Mallan, was frowning now. Batten lagged a country mile behind.

'That number, *there!*' Mallan's brown finger jabbed at the page. 'That's not my phone! That's *Meg*'s phone! I should know, I paid for it. Still do, just in case. In case she phones. But she's neither phoned me, nor answered, my Meg. Phoned *him,* but not *me.* Not a single word, not a one, all this time. *Meg.*'

More tears took on the hopeless task of cleansing Mallan's cheeks. Ball twitched so awkwardly he could have been DC Hick. Batten tapped his size nines on the vinyl floor. This time, Zig, Country and Western music's about right.

DC Eddie Hick knew better than to disturb Inspector Batten and 'Crystal' Ball in the middle of an interview. Instead, he scrawled one of his notes. Batten still had some of them, so curiously written and impossibly spelled they were collectible. This one was no exception.

New witness has come froward. Interviewed by phone. Saw two vans parked in lay-by, on night of Wassial. One red, presume Jeff Wynyard's. Other van not big, not small, a muddy brown colour, quote. No regitsranian number. No other info of significence. Night very dark, and witness late for apointmant. Will persue asap.

Satisfied with his handiwork, Eddie 'Loft' Hick anchored the note on Batten's desk under a brass fish paperweight, yawned, and managed to knock over the waste-bin as he headed for the car park.

By the time Keith Mallan explained himself, Batten's nostrils were sewers. Ball was coping better with Keith's carnal sweat than with the fuzzy edges of his own professional role - not least because he personally knew all three wives concerned. Di Ball and Scilla Wynyard were not the only significant wives in Stockton Marsh. Keith Mallan had one too.

'A wife? *Him?* Who'd marry *him?* Training to be a rat-catcher, was she, and Keith was homework?'

Ball's reply was an edgy shrug. Batten needed air, fresh air. And a pint of strong cider. And to believe in fairies.

Keith Mallan was not a sophisticated crook - barely a crook at all. Logging a few phantom sheep into the abattoir, writing Jeff Wynyard's name on the dockets, splitting the difference with Jeff - that was the extent of Mastermind's plan. And it remained a plan, because Jeff, it seemed, said a big firm *'No'*, six times over. Keith's other scam was siphoning off a few sides of venison from the abattoir to his kitchen-table, because he knew his way around a deer. After a bit of home butchering he sold the meat, cheap, no questions asked. His scam was obvious not just to the police, but to his employers too. Even if granted bail, Keith was out of a job.

Ball had gone quiet again. Di's on his mind, Zig, I'll bet.

'I've been thinking, zor. Keith's wife, Meg - still technically married, see - well, she was always hankering after a bit of glam.' Batten's eyebrows danced north. 'Yes, zor, hard to believe, I know. One of the reasons she left, the lack of glam.'

'Lack of glam? I can think of ten better reasons for her buggering off!' Batten had blown his nose till it bled but could still smell old meat. 'How'd he get her to say 'I do'? Air freshener? Bribed a hypnotist?'

'He was a good-looking lad ten year ago, zor. Still is, after a good wash...But no, it's this glam thing, see. Only glam he ever managed was a rust-bucket of an old MG Sports. Kept Meg happy for a fortnight, till the exhaust blew.'

Batten's eyebrows did the tango now.

'He's still got it, the MG. Two-seater. Only transport he *has* got. Offered me a lift once, but it's too small to shift the likes of me.'

Eyebrows screeched to a halt as Batten caught up. Hick's definitely put something in Ball's coffee, Zig. 'And the MG's too small to shift carcasses, that what you mean? You're wondering how Keith transported the spoils?'

'Well, zor, you don't shift sides of venison on a pushbike. Must weigh, what, seventy pounds apiece? He'd need a van, or something?'

'A van, yes.' Batten perked up. New lines of enquiry always perked him up. 'Or a pick-up, even? And some help?'

'Indeed, zor. To lug half a deer.'

'We're not looking for a vegetarian then?'

'Oh no, zor, it's a carnation we're after.' Batten let him get away with this one. 'And, zor, a carnation with an open mind when it comes to theft.'

'And maybe a shotgun?'

'Who knows, zor? Find the van though, pint of cider says you'll smell meat.'

The police declined to return Jeff's red pick-up truck just yet. Scilla Wynyard's protest siphoned off some of her anger, but that was the only outcome. How am I supposed to run a sheep farm, on my *own*, without a pick-up truck? The young female detective - needs to wash her hair, that one, and not even a smile this time - she said it's evidence, in a murder case. Gave Scilla a look: 'and neither have we finished with you, *madam.*' To think, I let her help me with my crossword, cooperating with the police in their enquiries.

Scilla Wynyard composed herself by telling a lie: you're not a suspect, Scilla. Just a sheep-farmer. Or learning how to be, fast. Because it's all yours now and it's all you've got.

She grabbed the keys to her rusty old van - ex-Post Office. Jeff had picked it up cheap and spray-painted over the red. Its colour now was anybody's guess, but it could manage a coil of wire, some bags of sheep-nuts from the depot and a motherless lamb. Will it start, this time? It did, but only after a cheque-book-worrying wheeze. Jeff never fixed anything if he could avoid it, and even when he did it was a bodge. Well, bodge-time is gone. *Scilla* time now.

Swinging the van across a half-gritted sheet of ice that used to be the A568, she crunched her tyres down frozen lanes towards the grazing land. The land Jeff said was theirs. Yesterday, she'd crunched her winter boots into the bank, and this morning, tail between her legs, into the solicitor's office. She'd never warmed to Mr Goode, or any man with an unnecessary 'e'. Jeff always dealt with Mr Goode. Jeff was in charge of rules and regs. Jeff was in charge of banks, paperwork, selling, and buying.

'Urr, well, Mr Wynyard may have told you that, but, urr, I'm afraid it's not the case.'

'Not the case? What are you talking about?'

'Well, the land is rented, you see. Urr, always has been.'

'*Rented*?'

'I can show you the agreement, if you so wish?'

Rented?

'No. No, thanks. Just tell me. Just tell me what I own, please, and what I don't.'

Mr Goode's white hands grabbed an imaginary melon, paused, and squashed it, hands coming together as if in regretful prayer, before sliding beneath his chin. 'Urr, well - all is subject to probate and its outcome, you understand?'

Scilla Wynyard nodded a 'hurry up'.

'So, urr, assuming no skeletons in cupboards, what you currently own is...your sheep - a vulnerably small flock, in the scheme of things - two used vehicles; a transporter; sundry sheep-pens...urr, and your house. But the fields, all the land, urr, is rented.'

'I'm sorry? How *can* it be? We *bought* the land. When Jeff's mother died. She left us the money.'

'She did. And as Mr Wynyard's - your - solicitor, urr, I duly dealt with the bequest.'

'*And*?'

'And, Mr Wynyard bought no land at all. He in fact used the bequest to repay significant debt. Had he not, you would no longer be living in your dwelling, since that was the surety. Against said debt.'

My *dwelling*? Pompous twat.

'But we didn't *have* debt. We didn't have much profit, but we didn't have debt! What are you t-'

'You have me at a disadvantage, Mrs Wynyard, since I naturally assumed *Mr* Wynyard had informed you of these financial obstacles? They were, well, urr, constant. The sheep farm was accumulating debt, I assure you. I have the documentation, if...'

She shook her head. It hurt. The sharp nails of a sick headache scraped the back of her eyes. The same shocked headache that drilled into her yesterday, when the bank said, 'why, Mrs Wynyard, there never *has* been a savings account in your name...'

You have a *dwelling*, Scilla, rejoice. You won't have to sleep on the street. Three rooms and a loo, a clump of daisies and a veg patch the size of a hearthrug. You have nothing in the bank to pay the rent due on the fields. You own a few assorted lumps of rusting metal, too few sheep, and a surfeit of anger. Secrets, Jeff?

Oh, Jeff. How did I come to this? I am a sheep-farmer's widow with no farm.

'Man-with-a Van', said the faded lettering on the side of the van. The driver, thinning hair sticking up like rough stubble, crunched down from fourth gear to third as he turned into Stockton Marsh. For some time now, he'd been talking to the van. Nearest thing to a friend.

'Only my old miser of a dad would buy a dirt-brown van like *you*. Dirt-brown and dirt-cheap. No-one else was mean enough.'

He couldn't remember how old the rust-bucket was. The clock said 180,000 miles, but it was lying.

'Man-with-a-Van, that's me. *Us*, I mean. It's what they call us, in Stockton Marsh. Want an odd job done? Try thingy, him with the van, old Tom Priddle's boy. What's-his-name.'

Driver and van chugged up an incline and turned into a bramble-shrouded parking space alongside a crumbling house, two-thirds-hidden by untrimmed evergreens and a mob of weeds. The damp front door still creaked, but why fix it, now? Mail sat on what used to be a doormat. Andrew Priddle almost laughed. Doormat? The thought of someone wiping their feet *here*? The only doormat in this place was *him*. He shook an elastic band from the mail, let it drop to the floor. The old man said waste-bins were a waste of money, wouldn't have them in the house. First letter in the pile invited him to join a wine club, huh, and be a wine-bibber.

'What's a wine-bibber when it's at home?' he asked the walls. 'Wine? Once a blue moon managed a *beer*, in The Jug and Bottle, whenever the old man coughed up a few grudging coins.' He screwed the wine-club advert into a ball. 'Even then, he asked for the change.'

Andrew Priddle had a mimic's skills, the skills of a silent listener. He practised, in the van. Rita Brimsmore, landlady of The Jug and Bottle, had no idea he could ape her posture and voice.

'How's poor old Taam? Getting about at all, no? Naat seen Taam in here since, goodness, don' know when...Pint, is it?'

Andrew Priddle's own angry voice returned. 'But she never says, *'Nice to see you, Andrew. How're you doing, Andrew? Coming to the quiz night, Andrew? Laats of prizes.'* Huh!'

Old Tom Priddle's boy. What's-his-name. To the entire village he was Man-with-a-Van or What's-his-name. If he was anything at all. He yelled his grievance at the filthy windows.

'Bloody village. Bloody Stockton Marsh. *'Oh yes, everyone knows everyone, in Stockton Marsh.'* Well you don't know *me!*'

He kicked the balled-up advert across the room.

'I'm *Andrew*. I'm called *Andrew*,' he yelled at the rotting door. 'And I'm 40 years old. 'Boy', my arse! Slave, skivvy, shit-sponge, that's me. Cleaning up after old Tom Priddle, soaking up curses in the old sod's rotting cottage, waiting for the old bastard to just bloody die.'

He flung down the rest of the mail. It slid barely an inch along the oil-cloth-covered kitchen table before it stuck, in accumulated grease.

'Well, he did die, right?' he told the table. "Took a trip down the stairs he was too mean to mend, sod him, and broke his miserly neck. Justice for Andrew Priddle. Three cheers!'

The old house was silent. The table, walls and door could not muster a single cheer between them. He turned to the window, staring through its grime at the smug roofs and chimney-pots of the village.

'It's just me now. Me alone. And I'll curse you, Stockton Marsh.'

Shaking an angry fist at the village, he grabbed at the mail, threw two bills aside. There was an advert, a handyman touting his services.

'Handyman? Demolition man, more like!'

He screwed the ad into a ball, flung it at the window. It stuck briefly, and slithered into the black sink. Next, a flyer, some music thing. An oratorio? What the hell's an oratorio? And who the hell's Michael Tippet? *A Child Of Our Time*? Laughter, desperate.

'A child? I've always been a child!' he coughed. 'And I've never been a child!' Coughs turned to sobs. 'But now, I'm a free Man!'

The empty walls spoke. *Free, Andrew, yes. But alone.*

A jackal laugh.

'Alone? Me? I'm with-a-*Van*!'

Crushing the flyer into a jagged lump, he flung it at the rotten door. It rattled the broken letter-box, and fell where he'd found it. The last item was a blank white envelope, addressed to no-one. His dirty fingers ripped the seal.

'There's nobody else here!' he yelled at the empty house. 'So it must be for me!'

Has he got spottier, the schoolboy lawyer, Batten wondered? He found himself staring at his blotchy cheeks, counting the zits, till legal-eagle-eyes glared back at him. It was still better than looking at Keith Mallan. Ball was plugging away, doing his best, but if Keith was mean with soap and water, he was a top-notch miser when it came to words.

'Van? Got no van. Y'already asked me!'

'I certainly did, Keith. A dozen times, was it?'

Mallan looked at the vinyl floor, looked at his hands, shrugged, fell silent. They knew he couldn't shift a carcass without a van. But if there was no van, he told himself, there was no theft, and he was innocent.

Batten's logic was more practised.

'Seems to me you're in a pickle, Mr Mallan. No?' He waved a freshly-copied manifest, received that morning from the abattoir where Mallan worked. Or used to. 'This is a list of carcasses that have defied veterinary science. They cantered out the back-door of your abattoir - even though they were all dead! Your managers, they're a funny lot. Seems they can count. Who'd have thought it?'

Keith looked at the floor, his hands, his lawyer; got no help from any of them.

'Three sides of venison and three sides of beef, says here. On three separate occasions, and all from your shift. So, what's that? Two nicked carcasses, three times over. Weighty, those lumps of meat. More than sixty pounds a pop, I'm told. Slip 'em in your pocket, did you? Smuggle 'em out? Or get the mice to do it?'

Mallan thought he'd better speak. 'Mice!' he spat.

'Yes, big human mice. Carcass-shifting, van-driving mice. *Shotgun-toting mice! Murdering mice!*' Batten slammed his hand onto the table for emphasis. He imagined the zits on the young lawyer's face exploding.

'I murdered *nobody!*' was all Keith could manage. Ball eased in, the soothing cop.

'We want to believe you, Keith. But poor Jeff Wynyard's lying on a slab with his face blown off. If you didn't shoot him, who did?'

A series of jerks and ticks signalled Keith Mallan's brain at work. He was stuck. Admit there was a van, get done for theft. Keep quiet, get done for murder! Well, he wasn't having any of that. He sneaked a glance at his lawyer. Should he let on, about what's-his-face, tell young chummy about the partner in crime? And is it *safe* to? What's-his-face, with that blank expression, he's just a driver, yes? Loopy, yes, but just a driver? Loopy...Loopy enough to shoot Jeff? In case Jeff decided to shop the pair of them? Loopy enough to load, aim? Fire?

More jerks and ticks, as Mallan saw the obvious danger. If I open my mouth, is what's-his-face loopy enough to shoot *me*? He sneaked a nervous glance at spotty-schoolboy, at Batten, at Ball, at the sickly green walls of the interview room. Not pretty in here, he thought. But safe.

'Oh for God's sake!' he blurted. 'It was just *meat!*'

Eleven

The fourth letter was removed with care from the old typewriter. There were no corrections. It was placed on the scrubbed kitchen table like a white tarot card. Once copied, it would be sent, very soon. The other three copies, three keepsakes, lay next to it. Soon, all four would be returned to the private place.

Gloved fingers eased aside the first. Successfully acted on, task completed, with satisfaction and in perfect safety. The police?

Hmph.

They took a day to *locate* the body, unhidden though it was. Perhaps they followed their noses, followed the smell of sheep. The first one stank of sheep. And is now a dead man stinking of sheep.

The second?

Female. Sent.

The third?

Male. Sent, this morning.

The fourth?

Very soon.

How shall they be defined, these…recipients? Objects of interest? Specimens?

No.

I am the watcher. They are my *observations.*

Unwavering eyes studied the remaining observations. What sequence of action?

Disciplined fingers drew the three letters, three white tarot cards, into a single pile.

Child's play.

One male successfully dispatched. A female observation next, therefore. And then the sequence repeated. Male, female. Male, female. Four.

The final *observation*, ah, a gift of winter, the chosen one. Chosen, transforming the watcher from one to *One*. An act of completion?

Yes.

The final act, her.

Twelve

Andrew Priddle poked a grimed finger under the letter's seal and ripped it open.

'It'll be an invitation to a cocktail party', he told the greasy kitchen table. 'Do pop round for drinkies, old boy.'

That new TV you've bought, with the big screen, you're watching it too much, Andrew, you should get out more. He laughed, cackled, at his own thoughts. *Get out more! Yes, in the van!* He did intend going out though.

'I have plans.' He'd heard them say it like that, on the telly.

The envelope was empty, but for a thin white sheet of paper.

'And I'm a good reader', he reminded the table. 'Keep that to yourself. Wouldn't want the village to find out.'

He quickly read the letter's few typed lines. The cheap white paper became a mirror, reflecting back the sudden whiteness of his face. He sat down, had to sit down, grabbing the greasy edge of the kitchen table for support, clinging on with his one free hand, white letter shaking in the other.

He forced himself to look again.

I am the watcher, the chosen one. Only the watcher may choose.

No creature shall be harmed, unless the watcher decrees.

The watcher has observed. You have killed a creature and I shall have my revenge.

Beware, for the watcher's wrath shall strike. The fruits of your sin shall be bitter on your lips and tongue.

Prepare yourself.

The white letter and the greasy table looked up at Andrew Priddle. They waited, expectantly.

He had nothing to say to either of them.

They did that, police stations. Loosened tongues. Keith Mallan was a word-miser at the best of times, but now they couldn't shut him up. No sooner get your nostrils used to the smell of him, Zig, and he makes your ears bleed. I love my job.

'Aarh, goes back centuries, it do, proper butchering. Carving up the carcass, sharing the cuts.'

Batten managed a look of boredom.

'What're you *talking* about? What goes back centuries?'

Crime does, Zig. They didn't invent it just for you.

'*Talking about*? I just *told* you what I'm talking about. *Butchering*. Proper butchering. Skilful, it is. Ancient.'

Batten wondered if a cold killer would idly use a word like 'butchering'? And in the presence of the police? Then he saw a faceless corpse, butchered on a carpet of blood-blackened frost.

'Middle Ages, goes right back. Used to do it after the hunt, butchering. Used to call it the 'unmaking of the deer'. Didn't know that, did you?'

Didn't *want* to know it, Keith. Batten let him rabbit on, from experience. Sometimes a juicy forgotten fragment popped out of the drivel. The drivel was the price you paid. Alas, when it came to venison, poaching, and 'unmaking a deer', Keith Mallan was drivel-master.

'Used to hunt the deer, the posh folk, and when they'd killed one, it was butchered, unmade, there and then. Still fresh, see? And everyone got a piece, for their trouble...O'course, the toffs got the best bits. Huh, no different today, is it?'

When did Keith Mallan become a food historian, Zig? Or a socialist?

'But they'd leave the pelvis behind. D'you know that? As an offering. To the crows. To the spirits of the woods.' Mallan paused, hoping for a sage nod from his inquisitor. 'Well, whatever. 'S all I was doing. Unmaking a deer.'

'Someone else's deer, Mr Mallan, as it happens. And more than one. I think we've established that.'

Batten flicked the statement that Keith was still laboriously checking. There wasn't much to check, so far. Tell him to shut up about deer, cough up about crime, and sign the bloody thing, Zig, so we can all go home. Unmaking a deer, indeed. Yes, and making the unmade slabs of venison magically make their way to anonymous freezers. After making sure folding money changed hands. Mallan's grubby fingers turned the statement over, suspicious eyes scanning, lips moving silently, word by word, checking he hadn't mentioned Mr Loopy-what's-his-name, in an unguarded moment.

Batten drifted off to Zigland... 'Unmaking'. Now that would be a skill the police could use. The power to unmake. Unmake the footsteps that tracked Jeff Wynyard through the frozen darkness of an apple orchard. Unmake the forces that twisted the mind that felt the hurt that caused the hate that loaded the gun that pointed the barrel that pulled the trigger that fired the shot that...

And unmake the gun itself?

Wake up, Zig. The police do not unmake; that's someone else's job. Prevent, avert, if you're lucky. Enforce, punish, if not. Rehabilitation, yes, after the fact, but that's for others too. And anyway, Jeff Wynyard was a person, not a deer. So which *someone* unmade him?

Keith Mallan's lips clamped to a halt. A dirty fist grabbed the pen, scraped something illegible into the statement. At last, Zig. Now you can bugger off, to tot up the unpaid overtime. Batten gave Mallan a 'not finished with you' look, and made a mental note to unmake the now-toxic pen by binning it. And use gloves, Zig. Crime-scene gloves.

The village of Ashtree was small, with a pub and little else. But there were views, of Ham Hill, of wide fields of fruit and ancient trees brimming with birdsong. Not tonight, though. It was pitch-black, freezing-cold and silent by the time he got home.

A bottle of Speyside sat on his coffee-table like a kitten waiting to be stroked. Booze is a woman substitute, Zig, admit it. Erin Kemp drank a glass of wine, once in a while, but never a golden Speyside whisky, never a heaven-in-a-glass. And she's not looking, Zig. So pour yourself a couple.

He settled for one, propped his socks on the sofa. From the stereo,

Tom Waits ground out *The Piano Has Been Drinking, Not Me*, as the woodstove guzzled the last few logs of apple-wood. It would soon be chilly in here, and time to warm up in bed. Alone. No Erin tonight. Theirs was still a weekend relationship. In any case, her soprano voice was rehearsing, with her choral group, for Michael Tippet's *A Child of Our Time*.

'It's an oratorio', she'd told him.

'What kind of pizza's an oratorio?' he'd asked.

Checking Sian wasn't in earshot, she'd whispered archly in his ear, 'the no-sex-for-sarky-sods kind, Inspector.' She called him 'Inspector', in bed, whenever he inspected. Well, not tonight. He inspected the Speyside. It would have to do.

Erin Kemp lived in South Petherton, five miles away. At first, staying at hers meant an overnight bag, checking the diary, checking if Sian was there. These days, he kept spare clothes in Erin's wardrobe. Hell's bells, Zig, there's even a drawer full of her lacy underwear in *your* bedroom, upstairs. If there's ever a raid, what will the police think?

He sipped whisky, recalling his very first visit to South Petherton, one sticky Saturday afternoon. Every shop was closed, the pretty hamstone village empty as a pocket. He half-expected to see tumbleweed roll down St James' Street, and a tweed-encased Miss Marple stroll up it.

'It's only like this on Saturday afternoons,' Erin said, apologising.

He was invited to 'tea'. There was no question of him staying over. 'Tea' was stiff, tight, until Sian, not yet thirteen, asked to see his warrant card. Erin gently told her off for being rude, but Batten flashed it anyway, let her open it, hold it, pretend to flash it herself.

'Do Detectives carry secret guns?' Sian's question drew a withering look from mum.

'We don't, no.' Not allowed. And I hate guns. We use charm instead, even those us from the North.

'Truncheons, then?'

And we've modernised, since truncheon days. 'I'll bring a baton, next time. If you like?'

Sian considered this. 'OK', she said.

Another sip of Speyside reminded him that after leaving Erin's place, he wandered in and out of empty South Petherton streets, an off-duty cop inspecting new environments, looking for clues. He found one, in The Brewer's Arms. Above the bar, a list of guest beers was neatly chalked up. Since two of the beers were from Yorkshire, he pleasantly inspected both. The restaurant even sold takeaway pizza. He wondered if they did an oratorio.

Tom Waits growled to a halt as the CD player clicked off. In the silence, Batten heard the soprano sounds of Erin Kemp, rehearsing *A Child Of Our Time*, miles away in South Petherton. Her pure voice seemed to filter through the hamstone walls of his Ashtree cottage, softening them. Which damn village are you living in, Zig, these days?

He shook himself, pressed the 'random' button on the remote. Sonny Terry and Brownie McGhee told him *Man Ain't Nothing But A Fool*, till his suspicion that the CD player was coupled to his phone proved correct. It rang.

'Sig? Sig? Sig, ah yes. You have thought?'

The unmistakeable Greek English of another Inspector - a Lieutenant in the Greek force - crackled down the phone. The two detectives had worked together last year in Greece, and a friendship was sparked.

'Makis. How are you?'

'How? How you think, Sig? I am as yesterday, when you ask me same question!'

'Just being polite, Makis.'

'Ah yes, polite. Being English-polite.'

'I don't know what else to be, Makis.'

He didn't, despite his name, despite his Polish- Russian-English parentage, despite being a Yorkshire city-boy transported to an unfamiliar rural Somerset. Lieutenant Makis Grigoris of the Greek International Cooperation Division cared for none of this. Batten was his friend, pure and simple. He had invited him - and Erin and Sian - to the Grigoris family home in Crete, for Easter. The Greek detective had countless cousins, and one was to be married. 'Easter, Sig, *and* a wedding! Many celebration! Best you not bring your liver, your kidneys, yes? Leave behind in England. More safe that way, endaxi?'

Last year, Batten had flown to Corfu, not for pleasure but to extradite a crooked lawyer with a warped liking for young girls. The girl involved, he remembered, was much the same age as Sian. Grigoris had been a giant, his humour and support getting Batten through the slow, hot days waiting for evidence to arrive. Greece had helped him too. No other country he'd visited had spoken to him so deeply. He loved the blue of its flag and its sky and sea, its wonderful scruffiness and long, clean vistas, and the crazy, lovely people. One of those crazy, lovely people was in his ear right now.

'So. You have thought?'

'Yes, Makis, I have thought. I thought it a very good idea.'

'You so English, Sig. Always answer like the English. Cannot you say Ne or Ohi?' He did a Greek version of Humphrey Bogart - 'Yes or no, kid? Too much to ask?'

'Sorry, Makis. That *was* a yes, a *ne*. I'd love to come.'

'Then, Sig, I tell you truth. I not bothered *you* come. Is your Erin I invite.' He mispronounced it 'earring'. 'More pretty than you, I am very certain!'

'Well, maybe Sian is the prettiest of the three of us, so...'

'Of course she come too. My daughters, they will play her. But your Erin, your Sian, they have said yes?'

'I haven't asked them, Makis. I was-'

'Sig, I very angry with you now. How many times I explain xenophilia?'

Greek hospitality to strangers needed no explanation. Batten knew the Grigoris home really was his home too. It was something he would never forget.

'Makis, I haven't asked them because I want it to be a surprise, that's all. Things are complicated here right now.' He had told Grigoris about the murder of Jeff Wynyard. But kept the detail to himself.

'Sig, you come or you not come? Ne, or Ohi? I have wine to make! And special raki!'

'Yes, Makis. *Ne*, I'm coming. We're all coming.'

Somehow.

As Batten's Ford crunched its way up the lane from his cottage to the main road, his regular postman, Ozzie, crunched his red van down it.

Normally, the two men stopped to say hello, but not this morning. Too bloody cold to roll the window down. Instead, Batten waved and carried on to Parminster. Postmen had slipped down his Christmas card list, of late. He was fed up of interviewing them. Anonymous letters, unguarded postbags, sorting office security, junk-mail procedures.

Surely you must have seen something? Nope.

Don't worry if it seems unimportant. It's still nope.

Could 'someone' slip a blank white envelope in with the mail, without you noticing?

Every reply was much the same.

'If I didn't notice, I wouldn't know, would I?'

Yes, but an anonymous letter?

'How am I supposed to know if a letter's anonymous?'

Well, blank mail then-

'Have you any idea how much blank mail we handle? Have you?'

Er...

'Charities. Wine clubs. Spring bulbs. Broadband. Timeshares. Stair-lifts, walk-in bathtubs - even incontinence pants!'

But some of it-

'It's not *addressed* to anyone. Isn't that what 'blank' means? We just shove it through the letterbox. Everybody gets it. They don't *want* it, but they get it anyway!'

In his rear mirror, he watched Ozzie climb from his bright red van, packages and letters in hand, and pick his careful way past frozen potholes to the few cottages fronting the lane. At least his size nines missed the black ice that nearly upended you, Zig. What goodies is he dropping on your doormat today? Please, Ozzie, no incontinence pants for me. And when I get to work, nothing that might make me wish I owned a pair.

At Parminster, the coffee was scalding but the building was cold. Batten stifled a yawn and took a sip. Eddie Hick had double-checked, but his witness could do no better than *a muddy-coloured van, parked in the lay-by, near the church, around eight. Is that all? Nothing else? I was late. It was dark. I came forward, didn't I? You should be thanking me!*

He set the team to work, brass neck at the ready. Track down a muddy-coloured or just plain muddy van of nondescript size, indeterminate age and nil registration. If you'd be so kind. He felt the daggers, soon as his back was turned.

In Batten's cupboard-office, Ball chewed a bacon sandwich with little enthusiasm, while defending Keith Mallan with plenty. Does your Sergeant's local knowledge come with downsides, Zig? This loyalty to Stockton Marsh - the Wynyards and the Mallans in particular – is there a price tag?

'And he's never before let us down at the Wassail, zor, despite moaning about the cost of cartridges.'

Batten woke up.

'How come he's still got a shotgun licence?' Beginning to wish *nobody* had, Zig.

'He'll not have it long, zor. What with the drinking and all.'

'Likes his drink, eh?'

'No more than me and you, zor - till Meg left him. Filled the gap, I suppose.'

Batten scanned his notes. 'Last year?'

'Well, she disappeared last year, zor. Come as no surprise if she'd upped sticks before that. Quite a looker, Meg, and plenty of rumours in the village - you know, fancy man on the side? No obvious candidates, though.'

Batten thought of one obvious candidate, too dead to ask. He peered through the glass partition at the photograph of Jeff Wynyard, on the murder board. A mugshot of Keith Mallan - cleaner than the real life version - was pinned beneath. Both men were handsome, in a rustic sort of way.

'Disappeared? She's not under Keith's patio, is she?'

'Doubt it, zor. He doesn't want shut of her. He wants her back.'

'Has he tried deodorant? Scowl-removing cream?' Erin Kemp's green-eyed smile as he touched the perfumed softness of her bathed skin flashed into Batten's head. Mind on the job please, Zig.

'I'll try sorting him, zor. You know, clean yourself up, Keith. Perhaps see if I can talk to Meg, if we ever track her down?'

They'd rung the second number countless times - 'my Meg's phone'. Not switched on. No answer. No voicemail. And no trace of Meg.

'Within professional bounds, I trust, Ballie?'

'Oh, I wouldn't waste my time, zor, if Keith was a hopeless case. But there's dodgy, and there's bad. And I don't see Keith as bad.'

Not convinced, Batten's eyebrows said. He sipped his coffee. It was as cold as the room.

Ozzie the postman pushed a plumber's bill and a handful of bumph through Batten's letterbox. Looked a bit glum today, did that tall copper, and not even a 'good morning'. Pressure of work. Just like you, Ozzie, so get a move on. Dropping more mail into the thatched cottage next door he turned towards the van, lifting his foot over a frozen pothole with practised ease. Both eyes and his other foot, though, failed to spot the same treacherous slew of black ice that had almost upended Batten. Ozzie slid, skidded, flew up and landed down, all in a breath.

The lane was empty. Everyone's at work, Ozzie, and so should you be. He tried to get up. Oof! His ribs groaned, his right hand growled. With the left, he fumbled for his mobile phone.

Thirteen

Thank god for work, Batten thought. Mid-morning, he'd nipped out, driven over to Sergeant Ball's house with a bunch of flowers and big jar of apple chutney, naively hoping he could chivvy Di Ball back to happiness. She barely recognised him. If she smiled at all, it was when he blinked. Di's sister-cum-nurse, Belinda, spoke all the words that were spoken, made the tea, served the biscuits, and did her best to cut through the thick glacier wrapped around Di Ball. Slumped in an armchair, Di stared at the flowers, threw a vacant glance at the chutney, shook her head at the tea. She shook her head at Batten too.

'It *will* pass,' Belinda said as she saw him out.

'How long...?'

Belinda shook her head, an older version of Di.

'I wish I could tell you. Tell *Chris*. God help me, I wish I could tell my sister. But she's getting the care, and with the right treatment...Soon? Six months? That's how it is right now.'

He noticed the tired redness in her eyes. Di's nightmares had yet to depart. Chris Ball had mumbled that sleep was proving a problem for the three of them. He'd meant a problem for Di. Chris and Belinda were merely collateral damage. Batten corrected himself. They were *all* collateral damage, him included.

Batten had seen and felt the fallout from murder. Murder doesn't stop because the victim stops. It keeps tunnelling.

For the first time, and to his deep shame, he gladly walked away from the Balls' warm cottage in Stockton Marsh. A place of sanity, a safe haven? It used to be. Batten tried to imagine what his Sergeant must feel like, leaving work, daily, and driving 'home'.

PC Jon Lee still harboured dreams of working permanently in CID. He nearly made it last year, or so he thought, and when he bumped into Inspector Batten again he assumed his boat had docked. But Batten said hardly a word. Must be having an off-day, Jon. With regret, he watched

Batten's stooped shoulders grow smaller. On your way, Jon, get on with it, Jon. He was chuffed to be 'assisting the Murder Squad', even if he wasn't doing it too well.

Door to door follow-up was mostly routine, but every now and then you sniffed out a bit of missed info with brownie points written all over it. Or, conversely, you came across a highly-trained awkward sod, like this one, who answered the door dressed in grimy overalls immune to soap. Lee vaguely remembered the man's name, from the last time he'd assisted CID, though it still sounded like the owner had just invented it.

'You wan' know *what*?' asked Norm Hogg. 'Wan' know if I lost anything, at the Wassail? Nearly lost my toes! All ten of 'em. Frozen, I was! We all was!'

Lee persevered. 'I mean, sir, did you lose an object of any kind?'

'An object? What's an object when it's at 'ome?'

'Well, sir, a possession of some sort? You know, you arrived at the Wassail with it, but left without it?'

Norm Hogg couldn't decide whether to ask the audience or phone a friend. He gawped at PC Lee - who gawped back. At the briefing, Lee was specifically told not to mention the scarf that Di Ball had found when cleaning up litter from the Wassail site. 'Your job's to elicit information *from* a witness, not *give* it - remember that.' Elicit. He liked 'elicit'. He tried eliciting.

'An item of clothing perhaps, sir? Something easily lost, in the darkness?'

'You don' mean my underpants, then?' Norm Hogg coughed a sound like laughter from between brown teeth. 'Be only too 'appy to lose my underpants, even in all that frost! Some choice totty at that Wassail, aarh.'

'Not an undergarment, sir. Something -'

'An *over*garment? That what you mean?'

'In a manner of speaking, sir. Something you could lose, but without noticing you'd lost it? At the time? In the dark?' Lee realised he was sounding like a riddle. 'Something striped?'

'Striped? Socks?'

'Not socks, sir, no. Something...' Lee vaguely waved his hands in the general direction of his neck. Like playing charades, this, with Lucy, at home.

'I din' lose no tie. Don' wear ties, striped nor any other.'

'Not ties, sir.' His hands waved again.

'Scarves? Striped scarves? 'S'at what you mean?'

'Well, that depends.'

'Depen's on what?'

'On whether you happened to lose a striped scarf, sir. At the Wassail.'

'Nope. Don' possess no striped scarf - and not because I lost it neither!' More laughter spluttered out, as Norm Hogg pointed his grubby overalls indoors. A disappointed PC Lee pocketed his notebook and turned to go.

'She 'ad one, though, as I recall.'

'She?' Lee un-pocketed his notebook.

'Librarian. Whassername, she was in the pair front of me, in the procession. Striped scarf, aarh.'

'Brown, was it, sir?' Lee knew it wasn't.

'Brown? If it's brown, how's it goin' be striped? No, green and blue. Long thing, slung over 'er shoulder. 'S why I saw it.'

'This Librarian, did you see her remove the scarf? Did she do anything with it?'

'Do anything? What, a striptease, full monty? *Do* anything! It was freezing, already told you.'

Lee ignored the sarcasm, wondering why a phantom librarian should remove her warm scarf in all that frost.

'Well, did you see her leave the Wassail? Wander off somewhere?'

'Saw nothing. How could I? Too busy, I'm one of the shotguns - an' only two on us bothered to turn up! Too bloody busy to notice women stripping off and disappearing. Too bloody frozen, too! Mention that, did I?'

Would she ever again enjoy the unmistakeable clack of a letterbox? And the satisfying dumph as cards and packets hit the mat? The noises were gunshots now.

The mail was worse. Bills which Jeff had always 'dealt with' were stacking themselves into a tower on the kitchen table. Secrets, Jeff, secrets. She rescued a cardboard box from the re-cycling, flung the bills into it. Maintain some order, Scilla, maintain control. How will you live, otherwise?

She'd cancelled the milk, the farming magazines. God knows, cancelled the newspapers too, and now not even a daily crossword to take her mind off... Rummaging, she found a half-completed book of cryptics from *The Guardian*. It lulled her in the vague direction of sleep. The sheets and pillowcases were clean - ironed, for once. She'd rammed the heavy iron down on the creases, steam hissing out like spite. The bed still smelled of Jeff.

Her dreams asked her, *Scilla, how will you live?*
I shall live on air.
You can't do that.
No?
No. Only on money.
Money?
Yes.
Money, then.
How, then?
She had no answer.

Jean Phelps put down the phone but it didn't change her mood. The sense of disturbance refused to go away. A scarf. They wanted her to reclaim a lost scarf. 'If you'll be so kind, Ms Phelps?' He sounded thirteen, the policeman - but he wouldn't say who had handed it in. Has my sanity been handed in too? Perhaps I could reclaim *that*, while I'm there? She vaguely remembered wrapping a big striped scarf round her neck before setting out for the Wassail, but had no memory of returning without it, despite the cold.

Because she hadn't been cold at all. A burning rage travelled with her, in procession through the lines of frosted trees. Its heat remained, despite the whiteness of the orchard floor. Even the deafening shotguns, blaring above the frost, could not pierce the strength of her anger.

No-one knew. The other Wassailers saw only a librarian's tranquillity. Her bespectacled smile, carefully fixed to her face like the hands of a clock, ticked out the steady sound of false calm. But inside...She had needed to cool down, unwinding the cloying coil of wool. It must have slipped from her neck in the clamour of noise and darkness.

All the Wassailers were questioned about poor Jeff Wynyard, but the black female detective made no mention of a lost scarf. Jean's instinct was to say she didn't want it back, the scarf. It was probably filthy anyway. They insisted she collect it.

Oh dear, a police station? Could she deal with a police station?

Could she deal with the police?

Di's sister, Belinda, phoned out of the blue, and a minute later Ball's pained face dashed to the car park, dashed 'home' - with his Inspector's blessing. Without warning, Di's nightmares had become day-mares too - loud day-mares, disturbed, a jumble of flashbacks and screams. Sounds, mostly, but some almost-words, some noises that might almost be words. Till today, Di had stopped bothering with words. It could be a development, Belinda said. Chris Ball, not a religious man, prayed she was right, and drove away.

Batten sat back down in his cubby-hole office, glad that Parminster CID was momentarily a ghost town, Ball gone and the whole team out, sliding down icy streets on cross-checking duties. He rarely had the luxury of quiet time to reflect. His deepest thinking happened at home, with his socks up on the sofa, a CD playing in the background and a golden glass of Speyside in his hand. Stretching out long legs as far as the desk would allow, he picked up his pen, scratching more notes onto a list that was getting longer.

Murder weapon? Where is it? Shotgun licence?

Muddy-brown van? Who/who has access?

The Wynyards? Strength of relationship? Enemies?

Keith Mallan? The truth? Meg Mallan? Where is she?

Anonymous letter? Connected to murder? Typewriter? Source of paper and envelope?

He sighed at the lack of answers, especially beneath the two most significant headings on his pad - *Suspects*, and *Motive*. Come on, Zig, get stuck in. He began to delve.

Till the phone murdered the silence.

'Can someone get-'

All the someone's are out, Zig. Get it yourself. It was the front desk.

'Who?...Can't she come back later?...Well, who's the appointment with?'

Oh. Sergeant Ball. Blast.

'Put her in Room 2.'

Room 1 still smelled of meat, far as Batten was concerned.

This time his long frame was jammed against the cold legs of a steel table.

'Any reason why you didn't reclaim it?'

'I don't even recall losing it, Inspector. And it's merely a scarf, after all.'

Was this the time for Jean Phelps to tell the police she had been deeply distracted? By matters of greater significance? Should she tell him the scarf went unnoticed because of the burning anger which had consumed her? Was, in fact, still consuming her?

I am a librarian, she wanted to say. As a profession, we do not countenance anger. Anger is loud. We prescribe books for it, carefully. We promote the value of reading. Anger exacerbates; reading alleviates. Books are an antidote.

But for Jean Phelps, the antidote had failed. A livid anger suffused her; a boiling anger at the assault on her way of life. Violent anger. She had no experience of such an emotion, did not know what to do with it. But something must be done...

Expecting to see Sergeant Ball, her near neighbour in Stockton Marsh, she had been surprised and a little perturbed when the tall Inspector Batten sat down at the hard steel table. She fell back on small talk, to settle herself.

'We rather missed you in the village pantomime this year, Inspector.'

Batten had reluctantly played a tree - a very cider-tipsy tree - in the Stockton Marsh 'panto' on Christmas night last year. Never again. Sergeant Ball, who always took a central role, got the bum's rush when he tried to sign Batten up for a repeat arboreal performance.

'Not even if you pull out my fingernails, Ballie, my teeth, and any other bits I'm attached to. The answer's *No!*'

This year, Batten successfully played a contented audience member, laughing at the improvised plot, the rustic jokes, cross-dressing and raucous Somerset banter that masqueraded as a pantomime. Erin and

Sian hooted at 'Uncle Chris' and his yokel version of Bill the Barman.

'I seem to recall hitting you on the head with my sign, Inspector, last year. By mistake, I hasten to add.'

Jean Phelps being a librarian, her annual pantomime role involved wielding a 'Shhh!' sign at choice moments in the 'plot'. Yes, he recalled her stage-whispered 'typecast again!' And the painful bump on his head. But it wasn't bit-part reminiscences that brought her to the Parminster CID office, where she sat demurely in a plastic chair, as if reluctantly collecting a fine on an overdue book. And Batten had work to do.

'I did intend to speak to Chris - to Sergeant Ball, I mean...'

Batten nodded his understanding. Jean Phelps lived ten doors uphill from the Balls' cottage.

'...but, with Di being poorly, and, as I understand it, Sergeant Ball being called away...'

Jean Phelps paused. Obvious reasons, yes, for speaking to Inspector Batten instead. But not the real reasons. Would it be better to reclaim her stupid scarf, and just go home? *Home?* Home is what's at stake, Jean. She drew on her inner strength, and pitched in.

'Forgive my presumption, Inspector, but my sense is that you are a professional, a discreet professional - though we have met but three or four times, at the panto and in The Jug and Bottle.'

'And at Sergeant Ball's house, Ms Phelps. Di's birthday, last year?'

'Of course, yes. Poor dear Di. Is there any...?'

Batten shook his head. Whatever state Di was in, it was up to his Sergeant to choose who knew.

'Well, we shall live in hope - and a thousand other clichés. And please, do call me Jean.'

He gave her an encouraging smile. When it mattered, he could clothe himself in a policeman's patience, and his instincts about Jean Phelps were positive, so far. She seemed cultured, warm, not a time-waster - and he didn't have time to waste. He briskly summarised: lost your scarf at the Wassail - Di Ball found it the following day - didn't know you'd lost it so didn't reclaim - been interviewed about Jeff Wynyard - saw nothing suspicious - you've nothing to add. He was about to push back his chair.

'Well, there is in fact something, Inspector. Something else.'

Sod's law, Zig. Just when the office is quiet.

She reached into her bag. Careful tips of fingers drew out a blank white envelope. Touching barely a corner of it, she laid it with distaste on the steel table.

'This dropped through my letterbox, Inspector. The day of the Wassail. With the rest of the post. I'm the sole person to touch it - apart from the postman, of course. And whoever wrote it.'

Batten's impatience hit the 'off' switch. The police had said not a word about the Wynyard letter, neither to press, media nor public, and Scilla Wynyard had been firmly warned to keep her mouth clamped shut.

'I came very close to burning it, Inspector. But our demons must be confronted, no?'

He stared at it, a second blank white envelope. Your plod feet are tingling, Zig, eh? Keeping his face impassive, he reached into a drawer for a pair of latex gloves and gently eased a single sheet of thin paper from the white envelope.

Jean Phelps touched her fingers to his hand, delaying his reading.

'I know Chris Ball would have sympathy for my predicament, Inspector, because - though local - he is, like you, a broad-minded man of understanding. I am hoping that because you are *not* local you will agree to employ a necessary discretion? I love my village, you see. And I would like to continue living here in the way I choose - happily, but privately - without censure from those less broad-minded than you.'

Her long, concerned stare and the pressure of her fingers on his hand were rewarded with a nod, his softer nod this time. Her fingers returned to her lap, his eyes to the letter.

Snake in nature's grass! What shall be your reward, you who live a foul, corrupting lie?

Dispassionately, Batten took the letter's aggression in his stride. It was typed in the old-fashioned way, precisely punctuated and with not a single correction. Even through latex gloves, the thick silky feel of the envelope was at odds with this cheap paper.

Pain awaits you, you who hide behind books, and she who hides behind blood.
What revenge, for your dalliance in sin?
Blood drawn from your own warped veins shall inscribe your name in the Book of Justice, for the world to see.
And she who lies with you in the sinful bed of abomination, her deep green blood shall be the deadly ink that carves her name there too.

Batten looked up at Jean Phelps. Did an air of guilt suddenly waft across her face? Or was he unwittingly persuaded to paint it there by the letter's crass insinuations and by his own unconscious conformity? All he knew for sure was that the letter's tone had climbed from aggression to threat. He had no idea why deep green blood should get a mention.

Beware, for the watcher's eye has seen. The foul fruits of your perversion shall be hard sharp stones on the path to your banishment.

No demands for money, repentance, or apology, Batten noted. And no signature. Just like the Wynyard letter. He looked up to ask his questions but Jean Phelps' eyes had become tiny rivers, seeping down her lips and cheeks, dripping from her chin into the dead space between face and floor. To him, the letter was nasty. To her? He couldn't begin to imagine. He gave her a moment.

'Ms Phelps, given your understandable wish for discretion, can I assume there's been no previous…gossip? No leakage, no revelations -?'

'No sign in my cottage window saying 'Dangerous dyke lives here', in big pink Gay Pride letters, Inspector?'

Batten did his best to smile.

'No, Inspector. No revelations at all. In my village, I am a professional person, a librarian. I sit on the Parish Council, I appear in the annual panto, I attend quiz nights in The Jug and Bottle. I enjoy plays, recitals, coffee mornings. Predictable, safe, and happy - by and large.'

'By and large?'

'Need I spell it out? I have sexual urges that are 'orientated differently from the norm' - as my Counsellor at university once put it, mealy-mouthed witch. But I satisfy these urges only *outside* the village. In the metropolis, on foreign holidays and suchlike - and, believe me, with absolute discretion.'

Batten scanned the letter once more. Absolute discretion or not, it made references that smacked not of guesswork but hard knowledge. And the final paragraph was familiar. *Beware, for the watcher's eye has seen.* Wasn't there an identical phrase in the Wynyard letter? He would check. Jean Phelps, tear-free now, had done checking of her own.

'My partner is called Estelle, Inspector. I doubt you need know her full identity at this juncture. She too is a professional - a London-based haematologist, with the NHS.' In case Batten didn't know, she added, 'blood, Inspector. Estelle works with blood, as the letter vividly reminds us.'

'I've not come across *green* blood before, Ms Phelps.'

'It's Jean, please. And that is my greater concern. You see, in an attempt to remain private and discreet, Estelle and I avoid modern digital forms of communication, avoid them like the proverbial plague. Can you imagine us popping our secrets onto the various organs of social media? *Twitface*, is Estelle's collective name for them all. 'Twatface' I'm afraid, when she chooses to be impolite. She and I would be gobbled up, wouldn't we, Inspector? Trolled into oblivion.'

He could imagine. Whatever else Jean Phelps had, she had wisdom.

'No, Inspector, no *Twitface* for us. We rely on good old-fashioned hand-written letters. Things of joy to write, seal, send - and receive.'

'But someone's been reading them? Other than you?'

'It must be so. By interception, or by invasion. Nothing else makes sense. But if by invasion, there is not the slightest sign of illegal entry into my cottage -'

'Ah, but -'

'No, Inspector. No 'buts'. I value my security and have locks to prove it. And by profession, I habituate to tidiness, to extreme order. Friends remind me that even the contents of my fridge are shelved according to the Dewey Decimal system. If something in my house was out of place by even a millimetre...'

Batten lifted his fingers and palms towards her in a gesture of temporary acceptance. He would check, regardless.

'So, Inspector, I can only conclude that *interception* has taken place. How else would Mr Mrs or Ms Anonymous know that dear Estelle works with blood? That she writes to me using green ink? That she and I are what we are?'

He nodded as she talked, while ordering his own thoughts tidily. Jean Phelps' concerns were individual, personal. His were multiple, professional. He would send Hazel Timms and Eddie Hick to the local sorting office, again - to question the staff there, again. A discreet examination of Jean's cottage would be arranged, despite her certainties. Then Nina Magnus would delve with sensitivity into the wider world of Jean Phelps herself. A personal intrusion, yes, but a necessary one.

As soon as Jean Phelps left, he would compare the Wynyard letter with the one he held in his hand. Why should two very different women receive foul letters - seemingly from the same person? He parked the implausible thought that either Jean or Scilla wrote both. All the same, easy enough to drop an unsigned envelope through your own letterbox, claim it arrived in the post, put the police off the scent?

'Jean, do you always open your letters the same way?' The top of the anonymous envelope was sliced, not torn.

'I do, Inspector. I use an antique paper-knife. And - before you ask - no, I do not examine the seal beforehand, to see if it has been interfered with. Why would I?'

No reason at all. Till now.

'You say that this…this *bile* could easily have ended up in the bin, unread?'

She nodded, sadly. Batten wondered if other anonymous letters - sent to her house, or to those of others - might also have ended up in bins, pending a trip to the recycling centre where they belonged. But why go to the trouble of writing such bile, if the bile might be discarded unopened? It made no sense. Unless you posted it to yourself, of course.

Fourteen

Nina Magnus failed to notice the nondescript van, with its dirty brown paintwork, as it pulled up two cars behind her at the traffic lights. Her current focus was on the pale-blue Renault, ticking over, four cars in front. When the lights changed she would continue to follow, keeping her distance but deftly staying in touch. Training, that was the key. She'd been attentive, she'd practised - proud of it. You're a natural, her police driving instructor had said.

Hazel Timms pulled away from the lights, steering the pale-blue Renault through traffic past shops and pubs and into Parminster's suburban housing zone. She veered left and left again, dog-tired after another long shift, completely oblivious to the compact Toyota four cars behind. It turned left too, then left again.

Magnus was careful to park several doors beyond the modest semi as the Renault pulled in. Shielded by tinted glass, she used her wing mirror to clock the house. A small conservatory ran along one side, overlooking a garden that clearly lacked a gardener. The grass was trimmed, but that was all. Untidy privet dangled over the low front fence and rampant stalks of clematis montana pulled at the branches of an old conifer tree. It looks half-dead, that tree, thought Magnus. Like it could fall on the house, crush it, at any moment.

And just what are you doing here, Nina? Nosy old busybody now, are you, girl? Well, I gave her every chance, didn't I? How many times can you invite someone for coffee? How many times can you hear 'No thanks, Nina,' or 'I'm busy', before... Before what, girl? Bloody detective. You should lock your curiosity in a desk drawer, and drive away, free. Get out in the air. Walk. Somerset's a walker's paradise, for heaven's sake. Be curious about that instead.

Huh, you try walking through frost and ice, in a winter like this one. Put your foot down a rabbit hole, disappear down a badger sett. Right now, you can't tell where the bank ends and the river begins. Might as well be here, satisfying my...

Movement at the side of the house. Hazel Timms, still wearing the clothes she drove home in, wrinkled her nose as she hauled two big bags of rubbish to the dustbin and threw them in. Or is it a chopped-up body, Nina? Maybe it was chopped up on the sheets that Hazel now pegged on a rickety whirligig dryer? They might have been white, once upon a time... As Magnus watched, Hazel ran two slow hands through hair that needed attention, spine arching into a yawn, arms stretching into the air and sighing back down again. Magnus picked up her long-lens camera. You're not going to snap her as well, Nina? That's out of order, girl! Shut up. I need the lens, to see if I'm right.

She was. The long yawn had become a stream of tears, mega-tears, flowing down both cheeks like melt-water. Magnus watched them glisten. At least you had the decency, girl, not to click the shutter. Come on, drive off now. You're an intrusion. You shouldn't be here.

As she fiddled with the camera case, her distant colleague wiped away tears with a used tissue and went back inside. A chastened Magnus slapped her own face. Seen enough, girl? Feel better? Feel superior, mm? She put her hand on the ignition key, stopped. Hazel Timms was emerging again, not with rubbish bags this time, not to hang out old sheets to dry. She was pushing a wheelchair, and it wasn't empty.

Magnus couldn't tell how old the man was, muffled up beneath a blanket. Shamefully, she raised the long lens, aimed it. Wisps of yellowing grey hair. A vacant face, the colour of the sheets hanging glumly on the rusting dryer. But a family resemblance, surely? Hazel's dad? About the right age, perhaps? Oh, Nina, behave. He could be sixty, yes, but he could just as well be ninety. We look for alertness, don't we, as a clue to age? And there's none. She put down the lens. Shame bottomed out yet, Nina? Need a touch more peep-show before you toddle off?

Before she could, Hazel had parked the wheelchair on the trimmed lawn and gone inside. Seconds later she was helping a frail woman in a thick coat through the conservatory's open door and into a garden seat next to the wheelchair. Now *that*'s family resemblance, Nina. The woman's cheekbones were pure Timms. Eyes too, though these were active - and lips, moving, talking. For a rebellious moment, the detective in Magnus wanted to move closer, eavesdrop, hear the words. Wanted to know.

Then Hazel Timms was patting the woman gently on the shoulder, smiling at her. A bony, aged arm moved towards the wheelchair and gently held the man's hand. There was not the slightest reaction. The other hand stretched slowly upwards and touched Hazel Timms on the cheek. Both women's eyes were glistening now.

Nina Magnus drove away, to stop her own eyes joining in.

His oak desk and in-tray felt like a front door with a letterbox nailed on. The two anonymous letters were heavy in his hands. He re-read the Wynyard letter. Sent to Jeff, not Scilla, so the current theory had it, if only because it arrived the same day Jeff was tracked, shot, and shot again. As to what the letter meant, Batten was as puzzled as the rest. What's to be deduced about the writer, from these few nasty lines? Bugger all, Zig.

OK, what did the writer mean by *the winding staircase of death*? No sign of a staircase in the Wynyard's single-storey home, or anywhere near it, so was this meant to be metaphorical? No bloody idea, Zig.

And *the watcher's eye sees secrets*?

'Jeff's only secret was the huge pile of bills he left behind!' That had been Scilla's reaction.

But if she knew nothing about the bills, Zig, what else didn't she know?

'And I'll tell you another thing, Inspector. Any *'fruits of your sin'* are pure fantasy. I'm struggling to live', she said, immediately regretting her choice of words.

Batten turned to the Jean Phelps letter. Here, at least, some kind of mind was fathomable - a nasty homophobic busybody mind. A *someone* who intercepts private letters written in a distinctive green ink, and threatens to spill green blood. They had grilled countless postmen and postwomen. More were lined up for a squeeze through the wringer. Batten was sick of the sight of Royal Mail uniforms.

Having two letters to compare should have helped. Should have. Same language, and same writer, 'very probably'. Same typewriter, probably a Remington. Batten knew the probable model number - and how many thousands were probably still out there. Apart from that... He shuddered at the irony: what the police need is a third letter. A larger sample, more data, a more definite inference.

The heavy letters felt slimy too. Thugs and sharks he could deal with. In criminal terms, they were almost honest. But anonymous threats, from cowards who remain hidden, never showing themselves... *I'm a detective, Zig, and on a good day I'm a good one. But I'm not bloody clairvoyant.*

The letters stared up at him, two frost-white eyes. *Who wrote them, Zig? What had Hickie said?*

'Can't have been Keith Mallan, sir. They're not grubby enough.'

Batten looked at his watch, and groaned. Keith Mallan was next.

'You did *what?*'

They didn't believe Keith. Who would? But he stuck to his story, once they'd dragged it out of him.

'Already told you. I used 'Man-with-a-Van'. From Stockton Marsh. Young thingy, what's-his-name, with the brown van. Cheap as chips. Aarh, an' thick as a brick with it.'

'Too thick to ask embarrassing questions? *Eh?*' Batten and Mallan would never get on. Both men knew it. *The rogue part of Batten wanted to drag Mallan out of his cold steel chair and wash his mouth with soap - wash the rest of him too, Zig, while you're at it. He should have let Ball ask the questions, but was having quiet doubts about his Sergeant's neutrality. There's a downside to everything, Zig.*

'Too thick to ask *any* questions, young thingy. Only question he did ask, we's unloading a side of venison from his van, an' he says, 'it's meat, is it?' Didn't even know what venison was, didn't know it was deer. Never seen a mobile phone, neither, so he says. Have to leave a message, on an old answering machine from World War Two. Cuh, another planet, him.'

'But you persuaded him to drive down to Earth and shift the meat you nicked?'

'Persuade? He'd roll in snow for a twenny pound note. I just joked him along, told him I was bringing work home, from the abattoir, bit of overtime. 'Just like me', he says. '*What?*' says I. He gives me a look, as if *I'm* the stupid one, and says 'the van'. 'Always brings the van home, don' I?' Joking, was he? Don' think so. Loopy as a coil of wire, that boy.'

Mallan decided not to mention his deeper fear about loopy Old Tom Priddle's son.

Without Ball's local knowledge, Batten would have struggled to unearth the real name of 'Man-with-a-Van'. Mallan swore he didn't know it.

'Always called him the Priddle boy - old Tom Priddle as was, I mean. 'Old Tom's boy'. Always called him that.'

Andrew Priddle was no longer a boy, according to Ball.

'Forty if he's a day, zor. Old Tom treated Andrew like a child and I suppose he stayed that way. Social Services took him into care a time or two, in the early days. Andrew, yes, that's his name. I confess I struggled to recall it, and I live barely a mile down the road. He's one of those people who make up the background. I see him in the old van, once a blue moon, but that's about it. After his legs packed up, I never saw Old Tom at all, and then he passed away, a little while back. The house - if you can call it that - it's up to its neck in muck and brambles. Even the trick-or-treaters give it a wide berth. You'll have trouble finding the front door, zor.'

And so it proved. DC Hick struggled his way round the back while Batten hammered on a roughly-painted rotten strip of wood with a letterbox hacked into it.

'Anything?'

'No sign, sir.' Hick winced as he pulled a giant thorn out of his thumb. 'It's a mess. Had to risk life and limb just for a peek through the back windows. There's fifty years of rats and rubbish round there. And flesh-eating brambles. But nobody human.'

Batten cursed as his foot went into a pothole full of cracked ice, thawed just enough for tyre tracks to leave an imprint. Tyre tracks suggesting a wheelbase wide enough for a medium-size van. A brown van. But no sign of it.

And no sign of the silent figure who, unbeknown to Batten, had stood on this very spot at midnight when the ice was still hard as rock, also seeking Andrew Priddle. And also disappointed not to find him home.

'Bugger', spat Batten.' We'll have to come back.' He shook freezing-cold water off his boots; kicked at the ice, for good measure.

Hick's good hand went to close the rickety gate. A thorn got him.

The day after the old man croaked, Andrew Priddle decided to sell up and disappear. Some 'developer', or whatever they're called, would snap his hand off. Bulldoze the stinking cottage, hack out the brambles, build expensive houses on the land. Too soon, though. Too suspicious, upping sticks right away.

Instead, he pretended to live in 'the family home', while renting a little brick cottage, hidden away in the Blackdown Hills, miles from Stockton Marsh. If anyone asked, he'd say he slept in the van. He had the means now, the patience.

'Learnt plenty of patience, didn't I?' he told the steering wheel. It nodded patiently back.

'Work all day, and fetch and carry half the night too, cleaning up the old bastard's stink. I'll give you patience!'

But patience went out the door when the letter dropped through it.

In the twilight the watcher has seen. You have killed a creature and I shall have my revenge.

Well, he wasn't inclined to wait around for that.

The fruits of your sin shall be bitter on your lips and tongue...

No. Not if Andrew Priddle could help it. He gazed through the windscreen at the neat cloak of trees lining the road, and gazed beyond them, back in time, to the graveyard trees at the old man's funeral.

'Funeral? Huh, me and a priest.' *Ten bloody minutes of nothin', for his fat fee,* that's what the old man would have said.

Afterwards, at 'home' he'd gone through the old man's things, hidden away under piles of brown tabloids, medicines past their sell-by, porn magazines. All clouded with cobwebs and dark dust.

Keep yer nose out of my stuff, you bugger. If he had a pound for every time the old man waved his stick and said that... An old school satchel, a manky toilet bag that had never held a bar of soap, a biscuit tin marked 'photographs' - never seen a photo though, not even in black and white, no snaps of a father and his son. No snaps for sure of a mother.

'Wouldn't be surprised if he's buried her in that brambled slagheap of a garden!' he told the biscuit tin.

Even the filthy bedside cabinet was locked, and the old bugger's hidden the key. Yanking it, all he did was disturb more layers of dust. He sneezed the worst of it out of his nose and mouth, tasting the dry, past-laden foulness of the house, tasting his own foulness too, like an injection, sharp, angry. As the anger rose in his throat he cursed the lock on the cabinet door, rattled it, shook it till the anger swelled and exploded and he kicked at it, smashed it, sliced its top off like an egg, enjoyed the crack as the entire cabinet burst apart, the shudder as it shattered and splintered, the brute freedom as his foot burst through the rotten wood.

He felt the vibrations through the sole of his boot, up his shin, thigh, groin, stomach, and into his chest where a heart was supposed to beat. And for the first time ever, he *felt* his heart, felt the thud of it, throbbing, yelling, screaming in his 40 year old chest.

'*Life!*' screamed Andrew Priddle at the empty house. '*I have life!*'

He had to pull the brown van off the road, hands shaking on the gear stick, slippery with sweat. He dropped his head onto the steering wheel, banging his brow against it in anger and grief, anger and grief, anger and grief. When he lifted his head to the rear-view mirror, a small smile of memory crept across his face.

Because his life had begun again, at that moment, when he booted the shards apart and felt the shock - as dusty wads of banknotes fell out, thumping to the floor. The shock fizzed through him as more wads spilled from the school satchel, the biscuit tin, the filthy toilet bag. He grabbed at them, one by one, piling them onto the old man's empty dirty bed, breath bursting from his lungs and anger anger anger erupting from his bitter mouth, shaking the dust and dried cobwebs from the grimed ceiling onto the thinning hair of his gullible head.

Poor? They were beyond poor. Unrepaired gutters, a roof that doubled as a sieve, blackened floors, a loud, empty fridge, the house so cold in winter that, even before sunset, ice would form like stone on the dank dirty water in the sink.

But the miserly old bastard was a giant lie. Banknotes - too many to count - salted away, hidden, in the fetid bedroom the old man never left. Mum's money, was it? That would explain a lot. 'Certainly didn't rob a bank, did you?' he asked the empty bed. 'Would have had to move your lazy arse to do *that*!'

And for what? Not to benefit Andrew Priddle, not put aside for his education, no, nor for his holidays, nor to buy him a new suit or a fancy pair of shoes for a once-a-blue-moon night on the town.

Winter rain spattered the windscreen like tears. He shook the memories away, released the handbrake.

'Greed, that's for what,' he told the wipers. 'Greed. For…possessing. For *spite*.'

The driver's seat was lumpy and uneven. He could afford better, but he mustn't show his hand. 'Those banknotes are real, and no-one knows I've got them.'

Someone does, Andrew. Someone who shoves nasty little letters through your door.

'That money's mine,' he told the windscreen.

'And I'm bloody well keeping it.'

Fifteen

Alone, Batten woke early, as he often did on his day-off. His winter boots were still drying out from yesterday. The woodstore was empty and the woodstove cold, and his Ashtree cottage radiators were sending out more groans than heat. Your first chore, Zig, once you've called the plumber again, is arranging a fresh supply of logs. Perhaps a muddy brown van will roll up with them?

Day-off or not, he had already jotted more questions in his notebook. *Vans*, the first heading said, and beneath it was scrawled *Brown? Or just mud?* The search wasn't helped by winter roads full of brown slush and salty grit that stuck to cars like...mud.

Next was *Who?* Scilla Wynyard had a van, and it could be mistaken for brown, yes. Or for mud. It could be mistaken for a lot of colours. It had reminded Batten of the sepia-tinted photos in his Aunt Daze's album in Leeds. Andrew Priddle's van was dirty brown, too, but with *Man-with-a-Van* stencilled on its sides. The lettering was faded, according to Ball, and might not show up in the dark. Jean Phelps had a beige car, not a van. Keith Mallan swore he only had an old MG Sports, bright red. It made no difference what Meg Mallan drove, because they couldn't find Meg Mallan. Batten was beginning to think she was buried under Keith's floorboards. With his unused stash of soap.

Or was there another van entirely, belonging to Mr Letter-Writer? Last night, driving home to Ashtree, Batten began to see muddy-coloured vans at every junction, vans that could have been any colour at all in the dark, covered as they were in the dirt of a messy winter. He picked up a pen to scrawl, *is the witness reliable?* but the pen wouldn't work. He flung it at the kitchen bin; missed.

At least the cooker did work and the battered Italian coffee-maker was bubbling away. Almost as loudly as the phone.

'*Gone*? Gone where?'

As soon as Batten opened his mouth he knew it was a stupid question.

'We don't *KNOW*, zor!' Ball's raised voice made the phone tremble.

'One minute she's there, next minute...Belinda's still out looking. I'm just back. No sign of her. And the last thing we want is a hue and cry. Di's in a bad enough way as it is. Villages, zor. And villagers. Everybody knowing your business.'

'But they're your friends, Ballie. They'd help you in a blink, every single one of-'

'They would, zor, I don't doubt. But we're...private people, me and Di, when all's said and done. They know us, true enough. But the...understanding of us, zor. That's different.'

Silence. Batten's eyes wandered to the unfilled mug on his worktop, his nose to the rich aroma of fresh coffee being brewed.

'I would never ask you, zor, if it wasn't...'

Batten's day-off, an expectant coffee mug staring up at him.

'I'm at wit's end, zor, I don't mind admitting. Di, she could be freezing to death out there. She could be...' He wouldn't allow himself to say 'damaging herself.' Batten heard his voice crack. 'And I know you understand us, zor. You know us, both. Know us on the inside, I mean.' He could say no more.

Batten saw the vacant eyes of a silent Di Ball, slumped in a chair, shaking her head at him. Did he know Di Ball 'on the inside'? It didn't matter. He turned off the stove, reached for his car keys.

'Where have you looked?'

'Where haven't we, zor?' Ball was frozen. If he stands still any longer, Zig, the local kids'll be round, with a carrot, two pebbles and a scarf. The whitened glacier-garden of Ball's Stockton Marsh home could have been Antarctica. Batten's Ford had only just made it up the frozen hill. He didn't relish the skiddy journey back down.

'Belinda's trying the woods, over yonder.' He waved a glove past the house. 'I've been everywhere and back again, on the quiet. You know, pretending to go for a stroll, keeping the lid on.'

'The orchard?' Batten knew it was an obvious suggestion, but his frozen brain could think of nothing else. Frozen, Zig? It's more than that.

'I went in the orchard, zor, but...well, you know the size of it. First place I tried to look.'

Ball was white, from something other than cold.

'We'll both look again. Yes?'

Batten set off, pretending to be calm and decisive, wanting to get Ball moving before he turned to ice. His Sergeant followed, in bemusement rather than hope.

They made their way into the vast space, through a canopy of spidery winter trees, covering as much ground as they could together, but twenty yards apart, searching behind fallen stumps, scanning left and right, calling out as they trudged through. For Batten, it was a walk through a frozen dream. Ball looked like a man who felt nothing at all. In the distance Batten could make out the lines of Police tape flickering in the chill breeze, corralling the crime-scene.

There was no trace of Di.

Batten was absurdly glad not to find her here, in this place of pain and death. Even in thick socks and winter boots, his feet were two cold stones. He wished his memory was a cold stone too.

The brrrr of Ball's mobile shattered the white dreamscape. Batten expected shards of ice to shoot down from the bare branches like winter knives. Ball stared at the phone in his hand, unable to answer. Brrr. Brrr. Brrr. Brrr. Batten grabbed it. It was Belinda.

'Come on,' he told Ball. 'This way.'

The two men heard Di before they saw her. The click-pause-click of the churchyard gate as it opened and closed behind them punctuated the wildness of her screams. They're loud enough to wake the dead, Batten thought, regretting his crassness when he spotted Di in the graveyard. She was kneeling before a tiny headstone. He knew instantly whose it was. Belinda was struggling to stop Di clawing at the hard ground with ice-white fingers, one hand already tinged with blood where nails and flesh had hit frozen earth. Di's strength was beyond Belinda. The two men tried to raise Di to her feet, gently at first, but then more firmly, almost roughly when she fought to stay, her arms and hands flailing at the grave with the heightened strength of the disturbed.

'I WANT!' she screamed. 'I WANT!'

Howls flooded from her chest in a rush of sobs, giving way to a thin keening as she was eased away. Ball was as shocked by Di using actual *words* as he was by the situation.

'I WANT...I *want*...I want...' Then the words dried up and Di Ball returned to the dark cocoon she'd briefly left.

A child, Batten thought. She's like a child. His eyes fell on the gravestone and read the name, 'Gemma Ball', carved smoothly into white marble. He cursed himself, took off his coat, draped it around Di's shoulders as Belinda dashed to fetch the car.

Ball mimed a 'gently does it' at Belinda. Let's retain our privacy, our dignity, his hands said. He gently wrapped a handkerchief round his wife's bleeding fingers, drawing them beneath his coat, to donate what little warmth remained amid the graveyard 's ice.

When Belinda returned, Batten recovered his coat and wavered by the car, no longer certain what to do. Should he offer to help at 'home'? He laid gentle enquiring fingers on Ball's big hand. The stocky Sergeant, preoccupied now, paused, an embarrassed look on his face. Too far, all this, too soon? His Inspector's help to search was one thing. He could lie to himself it was all part of the job. The police did that, didn't they - looked for...missing persons? But when it came to Batten witnessing the fresh chaos of his once-sane home? That was another thing entirely. Too far, yes, too soon. He touched his boss-friend on the arm.

'I thank you, zor, from my heart. You know I do. But better if it's just Belinda and me, to... You understand?' He almost said, 'Di knows us'. With a final reassuring tap, he climbed into the car, half in reluctance, half in relief.

It's morse code, is it, Zig, with you and him? Tap-tap- tappety, on a hand, an arm? Stopped using words, have you? Batten watched the car trundle towards a private chaos, towards a silent lost world. Yes, Zig, morse code. Better than words, sometimes.

Andrew Priddle drove longer distances now, staying away from Stockton Marsh as much as he liked. Not that the village noticed.

'Huh,' he told the gear-stick, 'they're the reason for it.'

The scruffier the van became, the less the village employed him. No more collections from the depot, from the feed-supplier, no more helping with the Christmas post. 'We have our own transport, thank you very much,' the school said.

Man-with-a-Van did rubbish removal, cheap deliveries for e-Bay, anything he could get, just to pretend he needed the cash. It suited him, spending time away.

'Not as dumb as I look,' he told the indicators.

Andrew Priddle turned the dirty brown van off the main road and into the Blackdown Hills. Minutes later, he turned off roads altogether, shuffling along a dirt track to his brick cottage with its double-length garage. A nondescript old hatchback, bought with cash and no questions, was already parked at the far end. He locked the van and the garage's entry door, and slid a key into the heavy Chubb on the exit door. After still more locks, he was in the cottage – a short-term holiday let, cash deposit, all-inclusive rate and none of the bills in his name.

'Thick, am I?' he asked the missing village.

Warm air from the pre-set radiators greeted him. The furniture was sparse - but it was clean, and his to enjoy.

'No bloody 'watcher' can watch me here,' he told the bathroom, its blind tightly closed.

Hot water. He luxuriated in the shower till clean spray washed bad memories down the plughole. *Come out of there, you bugger! Draining the tank again! Think I'm made of money?*

'Sod off, old man,' Andrew Priddle sang to the water gurgling in the drain. He laughed along with it. 'You're dead.'

The mirror in his bedroom was clean. He combed his hair, what little there was, splashed on the after-shave he'd bought. 'Twenty quid!' he told the mirror. He'd had to drag the notes from an unaccustomed wallet. 'My food for a week, twenty quid', he told the wall. 'When the old man was alive.'

He'd paid even more for the polite suit, shirt and tie. For the first time in his 40 year old life, he enjoyed dressing, enjoyed the warmth of the room, the feeling of clean cloth against clean skin. And a reflection in the mirror that didn't stare back at him and snarl.

The next house rental would be the last, and a long way from prying eyes. Two hundred miles and more this time, this final time. Suffolk, on the coast. Because somewhere inside him was a memory - young, he must have been very young - a faint, thin memory of having been there. With mum, was it? He told himself it was mum.

And because it was a world away from Stockton Marsh, a new world, safe, anonymous. With a new suitcase full of old banknotes to spend on nobody but him.

'But before I disappear,' he said to his house-keys, 'we'll teach that village a lesson or two.'

A new Andrew Priddle rolled the hatchback out of the garage, double-locked the exit door, and drove away.

As Ball's car crunched into Stockton Marsh, Batten strode single-mindedly back through the churchyard, to the grave of Gemma Ball. He stood in silence for a moment, reading the inscription. His nose began to run. Fumbling out a hankie, he blew, wiped. It's the cold, Zig. Sure, Zig, lie to yourself.

All the surrounding graves told the age of their incumbents. Not this one.

Loved while she briefly lived.

And then, below:

And always.

The ground beneath the headstone was now a random patchwork of scraped earth, disturbed borders and the broken stems of a miniature rose. He could read Di Ball's desire and pain in the claw-marks made by her hands, where they had scarred the brown soil and scratched at the patchy winter grass. He could feel the power that drove her fingers into the frozen ground. In her desperation, she had dug impossibly deep into the ice-hard grave.

Behind the church, he found an old spade and broom, and did what little he could, filling and smoothing the holes, sweeping pebbles back into place, conscious he was only tidying a surface and powerless to deal with what lay beneath. But neither could he walk away and do nothing. That's the trouble with you, Zig.

As he returned the spade and broom, his eye fell on the latched gate leading to the vast apple-orchard of Stockton Marsh, the gate he and his Sergeant had rushed through towards the heart-hurting screams of Di Ball. He'd walked through that same gate twice before: in procession, to a cider-fed, torch-lit Wassail; and in dread, towards Jeff Wynyard's corpse. It was his habit to revisit crime scenes, alone, hoping for fresh thoughts, a shuffling of evidence, a new perspective. You don't *have* to, Zig. Look at the photographs instead, the diagrams, the videos. They're graphic enough, for Christ's sake. And you're only here by chance this time, on your day-off. His feet edged away from the scene; his mind towards it.

Pulling his coat more tightly around him, he unlatched the gate. You've got to stop doing this, Zig. Doing what, Zig? This hanging about, where dead bodies are.

Once more, he processed through the colonnade of trees. The point where Jeff Wynyard stepped from the well-worn track onto a less-travelled short cut was still marked by Police tape. He stood for a moment, wondering. Did Jeff simply react to being late? Did somebody beckon him, persuade him to deviate? Did he follow someone, someone with a torch perhaps - someone as yet unknown? Was the favoured theory true - that Jeff himself was deliberately tracked through the darkness, in a planned attack? Or was it all pure whim, chance, unexplainable?

Trudging on, he talked himself through the scene.

'Jeff's late, he hurries along the track, shotgun in hand. He hears singing, hears the incantation, hears Royce the Voice' - the police had tested this was possible over the distance involved. 'He knows he'll never make it to the Wassail; too far.'

Batten looked towards the site, towards the oldest tree in the orchard, but even in daylight he could not pick it out, could barely see the nearest strips of 'Police Line - Do Not Cross' tape, still sealing off a wide area, still flapping round the trunks of a dozen young trees.

'He loads his gun - blanks, we know - waits for Royce's command, and fires a round up into...this tree.'

Crimp and wad fragments from a 20-bore were found near the marked tree. Batten brushed his hand against its trunk. He raised a mimed shotgun to his shoulder, clicked a trigger, heard the silent boom. And recoiled from the imagined shock of an 8-bore cartridge blasting him in the back. Batten had spoken to Jeff Wynyard three or four times at most, in The Jug and Bottle. But he was with him now, here, in frost and ice.

'He's hit on the left side, and the force pushes him to his right.' Batten twisted his body. 'It's a big gun, spins him onto his back.' He turned some more. 'His own shotgun flies from his hand and ends up…there.' Forensics had marked the spot, dispassionately, several feet away. 'If Doc Danvers is correct, Jeff's vision could be unclouded at this point. So he may have seen his assailant - recognised him? Or her? Or was it too dark?'

With a faint sense of queasiness, Batten took a short step to where Jeff Wynyard's body was found. By Di Ball first, with repercussions. By her husband. By Batten. An absurd thought broke in: 'thank god I was third in line.'

He steeled himself to look at the spot, becoming Jeff once more, feeling footsteps move towards him, sensing a gun, sensing malice.

'Jeff must have watched, as the murder weapon moved closer and closer to his face? Waited, helpless - the killer a foot away - for Royce Beckett to call for the second shot? And as soon as Royce did…'

Batten tried to imagine a mind that could point a gun at a human face and callously wait for the 'correct' moment to fire. He tried to imagine a clear motive, too, since none had emerged. But stepping into the shoes of this particular killer was beyond him. Zig-the-cop was frustrated. Zig-the-human relieved.

Blood-black stains were still faintly visible on the frozen grass. Well, visible to him. A professional need to finish the task pushed his feet towards the Wassail site and the oldest tree in the orchard, where he, Erin, and Sian the Wassail Queen had sung and screamed at imagined evil spirits, in complete ignorance of the real ones. His stone-cold feet refused to go. Feet, Zig? Your *feet* are making the decisions now?

Instead, with a silent nod of respect to Jeff Wynyard, he headed back to the church. Go home, Zig. Warm your house. Drink hot coffee. Two graves in one day is more than enough.

Sixteen

As soon as it opened, Sergeant Ball set off to the pharmacy to collect Di's pills.

'These should alleviate,' the doctor said. 'Until...'

Driving out of Stockton Marsh, shoulders down, he began to wish the pills were for him. Mood-lifters, sleep-givers. Hope-makers. At the right-turn, a dirty-brown van chugged past in the opposite direction, coming in from the A303. Ball did a double-take, pulled over at the next lay-by and grabbed his phone.

Andrew Priddle kept his eyes on the road, as ever. The old brown van was all his now. He was careful not to break it. Even had he spotted Sergeant Ball, he would have kept driving. That's what a Man-with-a-Van does, he delivers, goes 'vanning'. And this and that. He had no idea the plod were itching for a chinwag. Make a change if someone was.

It's a temporary problem. That's what Jean Phelps told herself as she pulled back bolts and unlocked locks. *I used to click a single deadbolt and go happily to bed.* Now, she hardly slept, awake half the night fearing an intruder, the other half dreading the arrival of more white bile through her letterbox.

In the cold air, her breath became a frosty punctuation mark of sighs. She locked all she had just unlocked, pulling and shaking the big front-door for safety's sake. She would be glad to get in the car, lock it from the inside, switch on the heater and Radio 4. And drive to work, safe and secure, colleagues all around her, hot tea and a crossword at lunchtime. With a practised effort that was wearing thin, Jean Phelps eased a calm librarian's mask over her fears.

It stayed there for five seconds.

That was how long it took to turn left, walk to the car-port and reach into her bag for her keys.

It didn't matter which postman delivered the mail. Batten knew the sound of the letterbox would never be the same, not till the hidden letter-writer was unearthed. He picked up the pile of bumph. Junk, mostly, and thankfully no blank white envelopes. There was a card from Aunt Daze, his mother in all but name. Apart from a Christmas visit, he'd hardly been up to Leeds this winter - dodgy roads, soaring rural crime and a murder were fair excuses. Erin Kemp was the real reason. He'd ring Daze, tonight, crime permitting. She understood.

He peered through the curtains at the receding postman's back. He was new, this one, filling in for Ozzie, away soaking up the winter sun in Tenerife, or so Batten imagined. Watch out for the ice on those potholes, he told the nameless man. And watch them yourself, Zig. Because your day-off was yesterday and it's time to go to work.

Andrew Priddle was ambivalent about the police car pulling him over. It was still morning, so he was happy to have a chat. Might not get one all day. But what exactly did they want to chat about, these two uniforms?

The thick-set one got out of the passenger seat and took a long look at the brown van. Nothing wrong with it mechanically, if that's what you're worried about, mate. Just had an MOT. You pretended to sigh at the cost of parts, didn't you, Andrew? You agreed to repairs, and paid in used notes. Got plenty, now. So switch off the engine, give him your idiot smile, and speak when you're spoken to.

'Money helps you relax,' he told the hand-brake. 'Shall me and you have a chinwag with Mr Plod?'

Andrew Priddle assumed his What's-his-name face, and rolled down the window.

When the call came in at Parminster, Nina Magnus sensed trouble. Batten knew Jean Phelps, and Ball knew her better. Jean was a friend of Di Ball's too. The protection of the law is for everyone, regardless, she reminded herself, and Jean had received neither more nor less protection than the current norm, economically-restrained though it was. Police security checks, redundant advice about door and window locks, drive-by patrols, a helpline.

Well, Nina, none of it bloody worked, did it? She reached for her coat and keys.

The two detectives, one stocky, one tall, asked different questions from the two Mr Plods who pulled him over. And they spent a lot longer doing it. Before, he would have worried about losing money, about losing a customer, about a whack from the old man's stick. *Pulled over? By the police? You reckless bugger!*

'I've got all day,' Andrew Priddle silently told the interview room walls. 'I don't need the work anymore.'

Most of their questions seemed to be about meat. They said his van still smelled of it.

'Don't have much of a sense of smell, me, these days.' Because I adapted, didn't I? Living in that stinking house, living with the old sod's' stink. 'Couldn't tell you what the van smells of, if I'm honest.'

'Well, Mr Priddle, it smells of meat, believe me. Venison, perhaps?'

He liked the tall one, liked the 'Mr Priddle'. Dignified.

'Venison, right. That's what Keith said. I didn't know it was meat. Never had venison.'

'But you admit using your van to transport carcasses from the abattoir, to Keith Mallan's house?' Batten didn't know what to make of Andrew Priddle.

'It was one of my jobs. I'm Man-with-a-Van. Keith wanted them moved, so I did.'

'Didn't mention they were stolen, I don't suppose?'

'Keith said it was like homework. Taking work home. He's got this really big freezer, Keith. I helped him take the venison stuff to his house. From the van.'

Batten pointed an eyebrow at his Sergeant. But Ball couldn't think of a question that hadn't been asked three times already. Own a shotgun, do you, Andrew? *No, Mr Ball, I've got a van.* Ball gave a faint shake of the head, and they took a break. Andrew Priddle didn't mind. They gave him tea, in a paper cup, like on the telly.

'Well, I've had more stimulating interviews,' Batten said.

'I did warn you, zor.'

'Is he safe to be left on his own, this bloke? He's like a grown man, in nappies.'

'Old Tom wasn't made for nurture, zor. After Sophie up and went, young Andrew got raised same way as the dog. Whole house stank like a dog-kennel.'

But Andrew Priddle doesn't stink, Zig. He may dress badly, but he's clean. And a faint whiff of after-shave? Ball had noticed too.

'I expect it was a blessing, zor, when old Tom popped his clogs, crippled and all. A blessing for both of them. Only himself to look after now, young Andrew, him and that rotting pile. Expect he has more time to wash, zor.'

Batten had only seen the outside of the Priddle house - if you could call it that. Try to wash the windows, they'd collapse. Perhaps Andrew Priddle's punishment, for whatever petty crime he might have committed, is having to live there? Batten stroked his moustache, with thumb and finger.

'Right. So what do we do now, Ballie? With Andrew What's-his-name?'

Two hours later, old Tom Priddle's boy had been cautioned, though he still seemed unsure why, and released. Batten and Ball were not there to wave him off. They were at Jean Phelps' house. Nina Magnus was already at the scene when they arrived.

'The drive-by car saw nothing, sir. Can't blame them. Only so many patrols they can do in a 24 hour day.'

Batten nodded. Budgets. Efficiency. Logistics. Try telling the general public, just after crime's kicked them in the crutch.

'Neighbours?'

'Usual story, sir. Tall hedges. Doors and windows firmly closed against the cold. And, well, you know the place. Conservation village.'

He nodded again. No in-fill here. No selling off your garden to build three expensive bungalows. Jean Phelps lived a good fifty yards from her next door neighbour, and liked it that way. Or used to.

Sergeant Ball returned, shaking his head.

'Nothing, zor. From the woods there's a well-used dog-walker's track that leads up to Jean's.'

'Not even a footprint?'

'Oh, plenty, zor. A clog-dancing team's held their AGM there. Even if we had a shoe...' He shrugged. 'Sod's law, plenty of tree-cover by the house, and all evergreens. And the street lamps click off at midnight. Energy saving, zor.'

Batten pulled a face. Upsides and downsides.

'Let's take another look at the damage.'

The three of them trudged back across the garden to the car port. Yesterday, Jean Phelps had a small three-door Ford, in a sort of creamy-beige. A librarian car, Zig? Today, she had a creamy-beige car with green paint splattered over its roof and daubed across the bonnet and wings. Green paint had dribbled down the wheel arches. Had the weather been less cold, it would have made it into the hub-caps too. The windscreen was clear, except for three letters, each a foot high, each a different bright colour. Batten read the code: a Gay Pride rainbow.

'L.I.E.', the letters said. The 'L' was a deep pink, a feminine shade. Here, it stuck out like a jackboot.

'Vandals are getting more colourful by the day, zor.' Despite his troubles, Ball was striving to reclaim his old, dry self, but his bruised empathy was still off-key. 'Or it could be that Turner Prize thing, I suppose.' Seeing Batten's look of disapproval, he changed tack. 'And no sightings of a person covered in green paint and prejudice, zor.'

Batten didn't expect anything else. No prints on the letters, and, once trailered away by Forensics for testing, he was certain there'd be no rogue prints on the car either. Whoever did this was well prepared and canny - walked where the dog-walkers go, left no distinctive tracks, used the darkness. They'd dig out the source of the paint, all four shades of it, but good luck with that too.

Hazel Timms, Zig, she's done a stint with the Antiques Squad. Why don't you get her to interpret the bloody brush strokes, so she can tell you what you already know? That the police are searching for an anonymous homophobe with invisible rainbow fingers?

Jean Phelps, sedated in a warm bed, was only too aware what the colours meant - an anonymous threat made real. The green blood of Estelle's letters, bleeding from a private vein, trickling into the pink trough of public rumour. Was this the 'path to your banishment' that the letter had threatened? Even in her dazed state, the anger and *rage* were still there. She could imagine the questions in the village shop, the pub, the street.

Who'd want to do that?
And why those colours?
Well...
What? Oh, I see...

Outside in the frozen air, Batten closed his eyes, but the rainbow scars remained. Failed her, Zig. Next time, fail better. Or better still, succeed.

Seventeen

Another day. Where do they go, Zig? Though struggling with two sleazy letters and their consequences, Batten still managed to wave at Ozzie the postman as he drove past. He was surprised when Ozzie didn't wave back, till his wing-mirror reminded him it wasn't Ozzie. Wake up, Zig. Ozzie's on holiday. Sun, sand and sorting in Tenerife. Ozzie's stand-in today was thinner, and more serious-looking. Batten didn't feel moved to wind down the window and chew the fat with this one, muffled up against the cold - and against other people, by the look of him. He tried to remember where he'd seen him before. Delivering mail to Erin's, at South Petherton? Or have you interviewed him, Zig, god help you, him and every other bloody postman who's been within a sniff of Jean Phelps and the Wynyards? Who cares? If he pops a fat cheque through the letterbox, you'll hug him like a brother.

Batten's Ford Focus crunched up the lane, to Parminster. The Royal Mail van crunched down it, and the thin postman got out. He put a handful of mixed bumph through Batten's letterbox, but no fat cheque. He could almost tell now, just by handling the mail, what was inside each envelope. It was a question of experience.

Not his usual walk, this one. He'd already finished his regular route. But whatever the route, being a postman was a comfort, a deflection. Park the van, shoulder the bag, walk the walk. Straight lines of streets and gates and garden paths, straight lines of front doors, each with a shiny letterbox, waiting to be fed, mouth gaping open like a chick.

The bag was a fair lump, small parcels, the weight. He knew what was in each item. CD's, paperbacks - easy guesses; contact lenses too, because of the packaging; letters for reading, bumph for the bin. He didn't miss much.

Walk the walk now, watch for ice, dogs, potholes. Straight lines of streets and gates and garden paths. A shiny, comforting letterbox at the end. A lot like Santa Claus, a postman.

'Anything from that other phone, Hazel?'

Which other phone? Be specific! Dad used to say things like that, to Mum. Now Dad only speaks to strangers. And you and Mum are the strangers, Hazel.

'You mean Keith Mallan's phone, sir?'

'I mean *Meg* Mallan's phone - or the one Keith's supposed to have given her. So he tells us.' Batten didn't believe a word Keith Mallan said. And if we ever unearth *Meg* Mallan, Zig, plug her into a bloody lie detector.

'Still not switched on, sir. No recent record either. Last record was a top-up, about 4 months ago, in...' She rummaged through her busy desk for the transcript as Batten waited. And he did that thing with his eyebrows, Hazel. Again.

Nina Magnus saw it too. You'll get used to it, Hazel, her smile said. Wait till those northern vowels tear you off a strip, girl. You'll wish it was only eyebrows. Timms failed to return the smile, but this time Magnus understood. Batten once said, 'Nina, I wish I had your patience.' *I* wish *you* had, she'd wanted to reply. But he was right. She was good at patience. She could tolerate. You learn to tolerate, being black. Perhaps Hazel would learn too, perhaps not.

'Ottery St Mary, sir. It's in-'

'Devon, yes.' You might be northern, Zig, but you went to school, eh? Birthplace of Samuel Taylor Coleridge. And William Makepeace Thackeray's stamping ground. Is there a brewery there, where Otter Ales come from?

Timms ignored his interruption. 'And that's the last record of a plastic card being used, sir.'

This time Batten and Timms nodded in unison. Meg Mallan - or whoever had the phone - was living in the cash-economy. Which could mean a lot of things.

'OK. Keep an eye on the phone, then.'

Timms considered teaching her own eyebrows to do semaphore. So they could say, 'did you think I wasn't going to? *Sir.*'

Batten had spotted Nina Magnus's wry smile.

'Any luck?' he asked her, to get her mind back on the job. You bloody hypocrite, Zig.

If Magnus didn't know her Inspector better, she'd have suspected a wind-up when he put her on sourcing the white paper and envelopes that dropped anonymously through Jean and Scilla's doors. She hadn't been the first ethnic trainee to be sent to the coffee machine for 'a black coffee with some white milk in it,' and she wouldn't be the last. Batten was above that, thank god.

'Waiting for Forensics, sir. They're working on the watermark. On the envelopes.'

Batten pulled a face, nodded, and clomped to his office. He was ambivalent about the backroom johnnies he called 'the scientists' when feeling benign, and 'the toxics' when not.

Magnus smiled at Timms as they watched his back recede. No smile in return, just a pale, almost stark-white face. Right now, Magnus had gone off white. Roads, pavements, windscreens – all plastered with frost and ice, day in, day out. And does Batten know how many types and grades of white paper there are? How many suppliers, how many stockists? Hell's teeth, how many *shades* of white?

Well, he probably does, so get on with it, Nina. It's the grind of the DC's life. Could be worse. She glanced over at Timms, at a twitching Hickie and the rest of them, bent over desks, checking the past and present of Jean Phelps and the Wynyards; tracking down muddy-brown vans; searching through green paint suppliers; trying to pull missing Meg Mallan out of a hat.

Through the glass partition of his cubby-hole, Batten watched them work. He'd been a DC, not so long ago, hadn't forgotten. His first boss, in Leeds, was D.I Farrar, with gnarled northern vowels hewn out of coal.

'Welcome to CID,' he'd said. 'You do know what CID stands for, don't you?'

Batten did, told him.

'Nay', said Farrar. 'C stands for Conscientious. D stands for Dogged and Determined. And don't you forget it.'

'What's the 'I' stand for, then?' Batten had cheekily asked. You could be cheeky with Farrar. He had a sense of humour. Not like some of them.

'Snarky sod. 'I' stands for *Information*, and until you've dug it up, checked it, and checked it again, you don't know if it's any bloody use at all. And it mostly never *is*. So crack on!'

He'd cracked on, as his DCs were doing now, next door. The CID office at Parminster was a tight, busy place at the best of times, but felt blister-packed around him today. The walls were closer, his desk fuller. He swept aside an avalanche of tasks and reports, each queuing up for one more tumble down the mountain. Only when he could see his desk, could he see his way.

Then the blister-pack burst open and Erin Kemp's green eyes crossed the room and glided towards the tiny glass partition. Her eyes always made him glow, two green thoughts beaming from a face whose skin had a natural deep gold sheen. This was only her second visit to his 'work' world. The first was when she discreetly dropped off his house keys, absent-mindedly left on her bedside table one morning when their minds were on more sensual matters.

As she drew closer, he saw two green eyes set in a face of ice. And what were they saying? Horror? Catastrophe? Ever since the Wassail, they'd been having problems with Sian. School bullies had promoted her from Wassail Queen to Wicked Queen, as if a thirteen year old could cast spells powerful enough to entice evil spirits into an orchard, or conjure murder at a Wassail. Sian's withdrawal and insomnia were growing daily worse.

The bass drum of realisation boomed in Batten's chest. Something has happened to Sian, the core, the non-negotiable centre of Erin's world. He froze on his side of the doorway; she, a ghost, on the other. He wanted to speak non-work words, give her warmth, reassure - but his team was all-of-a-bustle at computer screens, gutting files, dragging answers from invisible souls at the ends of phones. All of them looked up, suddenly silent, as Erin Kemp burst in.

Before Batten could move or speak, her frozen face was through the door. With barely the tips of a thumb and finger, she reached into her bag and drew out a blank white envelope. It hissed like acid on the newly-cleared surface of his desk.

PART THREE

A Veil of Snow

Eighteen

Batten could have been planted in his cottage garden, he was so still. All that moved was steam from the mug of coffee clamped in his gloved hand. He leaned his long frame against the porch, gazing in awe past fields of cows and leafless rows of soft fruit, past a valley of ancient trees towards the long bulk of Ham Hill. In the strange blue light of early morning, the old Iron Age fort was no longer a take-it-for-granted slab of brown hamstone and trees. The hill's War Memorial, a stone beacon rising up at the eastern end as if to guide the sunrise, was exactly where it had been yesterday. But that was all.

Ham Hill was white. Not the patchy, see-through white of recent frost, but a cloaking white of deep, fresh snow. The ancient trees were hung with white, the fields clothed in white. Winter-empty rows of soft fruit were now winter-full, a glare of snow-fruits hanging from the branches, crisp and fresh. Had he been closer, his gloved hand could have reached out and picked one.

Against their backdrop of white, the near-ground cows became a jigsaw, only the black of their black-and-white hides visible in the deep snow that covered yesterday's meagre grass. A collective lowing - calling for cattle-food, he guessed - made the whiteness shimmer with sound and the steam of breath. Nearer still, his shoes were almost covered.

He was struggling with the unfortunate beauty of snow. Because you're a miserable git, Zig? No, Zig, because work must be done. Frost and ice are bad enough. Frozen roads are one thing, but roads closed altogether...

Snow. Blocking the roads, swamping the crime scene, covering winter boots in a cold whiteness - whiter than the tent that had covered Jeff Wynyard, what was left of him.

Whitened trees and the morning chill flashed him back to the orchard. He was gazing at the white tent, the white crime-scene suits, loops of white Police tape flapping in a wind sharper than switchblades. Gazing at black blood staining white frost. Dyeing it.

Snow dulls sound, he knew, but the remembered *click-click-click* of police camera-shutters pierced him as sharply as on the day itself. Death must be recorded, Zig. A bizarre image of Sian Kemp formed in his head. She was all smiles in her Wassail Queen cloak, one foot on Jeff Wynyard's blasted body in trophy-hunter-style, selfie-stick and camera-phone in her hand, grinning inanely for Instagram and Facebook. He blinked, and the landscape became a single sheet of paper in a white anonymous envelope. Black letters oozed foul words into the ice-white blanket of snow.

Wake up, Zig, for Christ's sake. Shake yourself. There's work to do. Finish your coffee, man.

He lifted the mug to his lips. Cold.

Erin Kemp was wearing her thickest coat, but it made no difference. She rubbed what felt like dirt from the bathed skin on the back of her hand. Today, her green eyes almost matched the glum green walls of the Parminster interview room. It was clean enough, yet dirt and dismay seemed to fill it. Was it in the air? Or in her?

A heartbeat ago, she was singing joyful Wassail songs in a torch-lit orchard, watching her own smiling daughter parade in a Wassail Queen cloak of fur. Now, Sian's smiles had frozen. Erin's too. A heartbeat ago, she was sitting snuggled up to Zig, close, on her soft sofa at home.

Detective Inspector Batten of Somerset CID sat opposite now, in a hard steel chair, his hands on a hard steel table. And it was a faintly embarrassed Detective Constable Hazel Timms that sat next to him, pen and notebook poised.

'Why has this happened to *us*?' Erin wanted to ask. If she could see inside the mind of Zig Batten, she would read the same question, and many others. Who has done this? And why pick on Erin and Sian? And why now?

'How many more times? I don't encourage poisoned vipers to send threatening letters that make my skin crawl! What kind of man would write this? I have no idea. And I certainly don't know *why*, for heaven's sake!'

Or what kind of *woman*, Batten wondered - to himself? Erin was unhappy that he was the investigating officer. Awkward, yes. He remembered Ball saying 'it happened in my village. It's *my* wife. How can I not be involved?' Well, some of the cap fits, Zig.

'At work then? Are you positive there's no-one there who….?'

Erin was business manager of a local cider farm. It was where they first met.

'You've seen them all!' She hesitated, not knowing whether to call him Zig or Inspector. 'And I don't share my private life with them.' The female detective just sat there like a lump. 'They're either wet-behind-the-ears, or way beyond. In any case I'm in my office. I'm not exactly on *display*.'

'What's-his-name, from the shop?'

'Colin? *Colin*? Oh, now you're being ridiculous.'

No, I'm being thorough. And refusing to accept assumptions. It's what I do when *I'm* at work.

'You did say he was a bit doe-eyed? If I recall?'

Erin Kemp's green eyes stared at the cold steel table, at the windowless walls. At least she couldn't see the snow, in here. She gave Batten a look. *If I recall?* She liked Zig deeply - oh, loved him, be honest - but did she like his tone, right now? It's just police procedure, she tried to tell herself. The CID imperative. A consequence of the need for police at all.

'Well, he followed me round like a puppy at first, but he was just nervous, till he got to know how things worked.'

If it's not ruled out, Zig, it's still ruled in. 'And now?'

Now? As if she knew! *Is* Colin different? *Everything* is different. Colin had grown into his job, learned the cider business well enough. But that doe-eyed way of looking at her? Did he still stare a moment or two longer than…? Oh, ridiculous. He looks at everyone that way. Surely? And he's only met Sian twice, three times at most. Her shoulders sank. Misery is heavy. The heaviness of doubt pulled her head further down. All for a few short words, she told herself, in foul black ink on flimsy white paper.

Batten watched Erin Kemp as she slumped, became small; watched her dulled green eyes flick round the room, unfocused, unsure. They fell on him, but he looked away. My god, he thought, what will happen to her when I ask tough questions about Sian? What will happen to *us*?

'It's enemies on street corners now,' she mumbled. 'Colin; the distillery men; the cleaner. Every salesman, customer, passer-by. Lonny Dalway - you know, who delivers our milk - all he did was wish me 'good morning' yesterday and I started to wonder... And when I go home, I stand in the drive and check for footprints in the snow. Why can't I be somewhere *else*, where it's all normal again?'

He couldn't tell her of the surprise 'somewhere else' visit he was planning. To the snowless warmth of Crete. He, Erin and Sian would spend Easter at the family home of his good friend Lieutenant Grigoris of the Greek International Cooperation Division.

Now though, he could neither spoil the surprise nor guarantee it. Unless a breakthrough came, it would not be international cooperation that Erin and Sian Kemp experienced. They would be staying in Somerset, under the watchful and protective eyes of only the English police.

And you, Zig, you're one of them.

He postponed the issue of Sian. Best to patiently wait for the evidence, he lied to himself. Even so, Erin Kemp left in tears. Hazel Timms' presence in the room kept Batten in check. Back in his cubby-hole office, he re-read the anonymous bile that Erin had dropped on his desk - days ago now. He re-lived her shaken words.

Found it on the doormat - with the mail - opened it - not thinking - threw it in my bag as if it was hot - managed to make it to the loo - Sian was beside herself - I shocked her, I'm afraid, my behaviour - cleaned myself up, told a white lie, got her to school - I didn't know where else to come, Zig, but here.

At the time, Sergeant Ball had been sympathetic, despite troubles of his own. And clinical.

'I can't imagine Mrs Kemp picking that up, zor, opening it. Sweet Jesus, reading the bloody thing.'

No, Ballie. You can't. And stop calling her 'Mrs Kemp'. When did you become all formal? Steady, Zig. You know when.

'Same typewriter, zor?'

A Batten nod.

'Same person who wrote it?'

A half nod. The expert view was 'very probable'. Let's hope it's not a whole gang of threatening bastards out there.

'Any result on fingerprints, zor?'

Result? A shrug. Evasive.

'Ongoing,' he said. Fingerprints. Where fingerprints were concerned, there might be complications. Delicate complications.

Ball misread his reaction. 'I do know it's personal for you, zor. But I'm just trying to do my job. This letter's not like the others. Is it?'

'Well…'

'I mean, same person or not, zor, it…it homes in.'

It did. It 'homed' in. Here, in his hand.

I am the watcher, the chosen one.

The watcher has chosen a Queen.

The Queen needs neither mother nor man.
The mother's voice is sweet but the tune is false. And false too, the man who lies with her in a bed of sin. Death shall remove them.

My Queen shall have no body but the watcher's body, no heart but the watcher's heart. For the watcher and the Queen shall be One.

Make ready.

Batten dropped the letter on the desk, half-expecting it to eat into the varnish and burn through the wood. Little wonder it made Erin's skin crawl. He needed to wash his hands, scrub the skin away, bleach the flesh.

He glanced at his scrawled notes.

'*Make ready*' - for what? He'd already put his pen through '*some kind of unwanted union between the 'Queen' and 'the chosen one?*' 'English-polite', that's what Grigoris would have called it. He scrawled tougher words. *Kidnap? Rape? Murder? All three?*

The next note said, '*the Queen needs neither mother nor man… Death shall remove them - how? When?*' He scrubbed fresh ink through this.

'English-polite', Zig, while someone deranged is threatening to *kill*, to kill Erin, to kill you, just because you happen to be in the way? Be angry, Zig. It's allowed.

He threw the notes aside. He had spent only one night with Erin since the letter arrived. A broken night. He'd grown almost used to Sian not sleeping. Now it was Erin too. She cared little enough about the threat to her own person, but the vicious letter wasn't aimed at her. The insidious threat to Sian was hacking at Erin's world.

If you were her, Zig, you'd surround your Wassail Queen daughter in cotton-wool and chain-mail, and pull up the drawbridge. Because police protection has limits. Safeguarding a 'potential victim', from an 'unidentified threat', by an 'unnamed perpetrator'? Well, good luck with that.

And the threat to you, Zig, if you're the 'man' in question? Well, yesterday I was. And by the skin of my teeth I am today.

But tomorrow, if my hunch proves true, who knows?

Being alone yourself, you began to watch others who were also alone. Didn't you?

Yes. The woman with the green ink. The scruffy man.

You watched the scruffy man who drove the brown van, always by himself, coming, going. Watched from the bird-hide, up in the copse. Barely see into the filthy windows through binoculars, but there was a place where a broken gutter threw rainwater at the glass and cleaned it and you could watch, right down into the house. The scruffy man was sometimes not alone. There was an old man there, on sticks or a frame thing. He waved his arms around a lot, one at a time, waved his sticks, that is. And the scruffy man, the younger one, had to help him up and down the stairs, and the old man seemed angry, hit him with the sticks, often.

And early, a Thursday was it?

Yes.

A Thursday morning, all the way up the steps the old man comes, with the younger man, and one of the sticks whacks down hard on the scruffy man's back and he swings his arm at the old man and down he tumbles, down, sticks and all, down the whole staircase. And the younger man just stands, at the top.

How long, before the van drives off? A minute? Two?

Yes.

Does he go for the doctor or an ambulance?

No. He does not.

No-one came. The van stayed away all day. Bad behaviour. It was getting late when it returned, the van. And Doctor Pym from the Levels drove up and then a police car and Mr Bacon, from the undertakers.

You kept watching, after, because now the younger man was always on his own. You saw him, didn't you, with the banknotes?

Yes.

Watched him count them, one by one. And into a suitcase, and into the van. Where did he take it, do you know?

Not yet.

Andy Connor was a Forensics whizz-kid. Child's play to him, testing the letter and its envelope, doing the necessary. Normally, he would have popped the results back in the grinder and sent them over to Parminster, but... He'd had a social drink with Batten, a time or two, and they got on. He drove over himself, despite the frozen roads, and was sipping a welcome hot coffee for his troubles.

'I wish I was a plumber, Zig. There's sod-all coming out of this radiator.'

Batten's office had been an iceberg for days. At least it made him work faster.

'Andy, you didn't drive all the way over here to keep warm.'

Both men smiled. They were past the small-talk stage.

'Keep forgetting you're from Yorkshire, Zig. I'll come out with it. Fingerprints.' He dropped a report on the desk, gave it a thoughtful tap. 'Got any idea how many grubby fingers handle a single piece of mail on its way from them to you?'

'I could answer quiz questions on it, Andy.'

'Right. Well, smudges on top of smudges. And the few we can identify are all predictable. There's only four postmen work that route - same four we printed for the first letter, and the second.'

'Scilla Wynyard and Jean Phelps. I'd not forgotten.' A half-smile kept the comment friendly. Too much to do. Social niceties can wait. 'Third letter?'

'Yes, Zig. Bloody nasty little thing. Obviously there's Erin's prints. Mrs Kemp's, I mean. They're in there.' He tapped the report. Erin Kemp had been a reluctant subject. 'Won't do your job for you, Zig, but a double Scotch says you'll eliminate all five. The four posties do the sifting and sorting - whether it's paid post or blank bumph. They share the villages, vans mostly, some walking, so they either plonked their mitts on Exhibit A when it came in, or when it went out - through Mrs Kemp's letterbox with the rest of the bumph.' Andy juggled his niceties. 'And of course, Mrs K's not wearing gloves when she picks it up off the mat, and opens it, and...'

Batten reverted to a nod, the 'hurry up' one.

'Still working on the envelope, but there's no saliva. Clever sod used the self-sealing kind. And good luck with tracking the paper - cheap crap again, hardly exotic. A few tiny traces of fibre - turns out it's leather. Quality pigskin, but something and nothing, unless we find the glove itself...'

'Why've you come all this way to spout the obvious, Andy?'

'I'm getting there, Zig. It's 'cos your office is so bloody cold.' Both men knew that wasn't the reason. 'Why I came is, well, why I came *myself*, is there's another set of prints - envelope and letter both - but no match in any database, so...'

'So we're back where we started?'

'I don't think we are, Zig.' Andy Connor's social niceties were struggling now. 'You see, the rogue set...well, from the size of the prints, it's a kiddie.'

Cold or not, Batten's brain still worked. Andy Connor watched it. He didn't need to spell things out.

What else could Batten do? Instead of hauling Erin and Sian down to the copshop, he brought a fingerprint kit to the house - not quite procedure, but safe enough. Hazel Timms was there, for protocol. And because she was new, and didn't know him.

He let Timms lead. Presence of the parent, full consent, a signature, and, yes, later, of course, if you wish, you can watch the prints being destroyed. He didn't correct her, didn't say they're only destroyed once the subject is eliminated.

And Sian wasn't, yet. Some way to go before she became an 'elim'. All he managed was, 'don't worry, Sian, it's only ink. It'll come off your pretty little fingers with one good wash.'

She had delicate hands, like her mum. Batten could have told them it was ink-free, on a scanner, down at the station. But why dig more holes for yourself?

For Sian, the process was at least a novelty. Erin stared coldly at the white card and the black smears of ink. She didn't know who to be angry with. Last night it was Sian.

'YOU DID *WHAT?*'

Sian kept shaking her head, tears splashing onto Batten's arm as he sat opposite.

'You went into my *BAG*? And removed that...that...How *dare* you, Sian? After all we've said about trust, about...boundaries? And, my god, you *read* it! READ IT! I'm so *angry* with you! I...I don't know what to say!'

Stop saying it then, Batten thought. He took his own advice, kept quiet. Sian was crying loudly now. Because of the dressing-down, Zig? Or the threats in the letter? She half-sobbed, half-screamed, flinging her arms around her mother so tightly that Batten saw Erin wince.

You know which it is, Zig.

Hazel Timms' strangely vacant face projected a semblance of calm as she explained to mother and daughter - because that's what they had now become - the process of formal questioning that would take place. It was how the law worked. It was about fairness, about evidence and outcomes. There were safeguards, of course. She listed them.

Sian's tears stopped, and she nodded in grudging agreement. Not Erin. She could find nothing positive to agree with. Despite her wrath she was a mother first of all. Her wrath had only roared at Sian because it could not roar at the real cause - anonymous, cowardly, concealed. Erin Kemp is livid, Zig, but not with you.

Yet.

He did not correct Hazel's summary. He told neither Erin nor Sian that 'formal questioning' means a systematic trawl through all possibilities. Until evidence rules them out, they continue to be ruled in. Batten knew from hard experience that bizarre acts and motives were not restricted to adults. Did Sian handle the letter out of curiosity and concern, because she witnessed her mother's shock and tears? Or had she already handled it? Because, in some disturbed attempt to reinstate the glory of the Wassail Queen, she wrote it?

Zig was one hundred percent certain she hadn't. The words, the tone, were older than thirteen, the circumstances wrong. But Detective Inspector Batten had no such luxury.

Neither man looked forward to telling Erin Kemp.

Nineteen

The Parminster team didn't need to be asked. They may have been detectives by trade, but they were human by species. They redoubled their efforts, as a matter of course.

It was not a matter of course for Sergeant Ball. The consequence of murder had not receded at home, and though Di Ball was making tiny improvements it was hardly happy families. Now, his turmoil was re-doubled. More threats, against another family, against two more women close to him - one still a child, much the same age that Gemma would have been...

And against Zig Batten, too. Uncle Chris pulled the mask of a smile across his face and did his best to keep it there, but it slipped without warning and it slipped often. Chris Ball had begun to wring his hands. He never used to. It was an invisible neck he was wringing.

The smile snapped and anger burst through when Hickie whinged once too often about 'bloody-muddy-brown vans!'

'*GET ON WITH IT!*' Ball roared. The office went quiet. Batten shuffled the pieces, sent Ball to interview more postmen. The rest got on with it, not least a chastened Hick.

'Sir? I've got - Sir!'

DC Hick had two voices: his bacon sandwich voice - words softened by chewy sounds - or his office voice, which came out in bursts whenever his febrile body came to rest. Batten realised he'd never heard Hick speak in a non-work setting. You'd hardly invite him round, would you? He'd either crush food into the carpets or smash the furniture. He's only just safe here, at Parminster, and we're the *police*.

'Sir, I need - you need to-'

'Patience, Hickie, it's not time for your bacon sandwich.' Or your tranquilliser.

'*Sir!*' Hick's arms were doing semaphore. His right arm paused long enough to grab a pencil and jab at a much-doodled piece of paper on his desk.

Batten had slowly warmed to Hick - slowly because Hick's intelligence was cunningly hidden in a body that was part-windmill, part wrecking-ball. Batten strolled over.

'Well?'

The pencil became a pump, sucking up Hick's voice and squirting it at Batten.

'That woman, sir, librarian-'

'Jean Phelps?'

'Her, sir, Phelps. She's got her own car.' Batten knew Jean's car was still with Forensics, but where Hick was concerned he'd learned to wait five seconds before he rolled his eyes. 'Some crappy Ford.' Batten had a Ford, too. It made no difference to Hick.

'And that narrows things down, does it?'

'No, sir. Yes. What I mean is - her own car, yes - but insured to drive another one - and it's a van.'

Batten changed gear.

'What kind of van?' And if it's brown, Zig...?

'Dunno, sir. Yet. Just putting the registration in.' He jabbed a pencil at the PC screen, snapped the point off. From a safe distance, Batten looked over Hick's shoulder as the screen ticked and flashed.

'Oh. Shit. Sorry, sir.' Hick's balloon farted in silence as it flew through the air, flopping on the desk, next to the broken pencil.

Jean Phelps did have access to a van. It was a mobile library, bright blue. And far too supersized to fit in the narrow parking bay near the Wassail site, without blocking the entire road.

'Hickie?'

'Sir?'

'Keep looking.'

Hours later, it was not Hick but Magnus who called Batten over.

'Might have got something, sir,' she said, hedging her bets.

'Is it contagious?' He was trying to lighten things up, and doing a useless job of it.

'Might be *significant*, sir. Look for yourself.'

Magnus pushed her notes towards Batten. Neat handwriting, perfectly spaced, no doodles. Not like your scrawl, Zig. He read the neat script.

'Had chance to double-check?'

'Just about to, sir.' She pointed at the phone extension and he picked it up, listened in.

'...You're absolutely sure of this? I mean, is there any chance that...?'

The voice on the other end belonged to the Stock Control Manager at *Superstore UK*. He took his job very seriously.

'I *began* my career selling stationery, Constable. And twenty years on, of all our products, I know it inside out.'

'Well, can I check the dates again?' Magnus recited a bit of the calendar, and got a 'definitely, yes'. Batten's toes were tingling. 'And no other stores stocked that particular envelope. You're sure? I can't emphasise how important this is.'

'Constable, I'm at least as good at my job as you are at yours.' The Stock Control Manager let his comment hang in the air, for effect. 'You're surely familiar with the notion of a 'bin-end' - the left-overs of a batch of wine, sold off cheap in a wine store or an off-licence? A remainder? A remnant? Yes?'

Magnus would have pulled a face at the phone, but Batten was there.

'Well, similar things happen in the world of stationery. We accumulate odd batches, despite my stock control system being *extremely* precise.'

Batten pulled a face at the phone.

'The envelopes in question were all that remained, of saleable quality, that is, from a discontinued batch that suffered considerable water damage.'

'Ended up with the wrong kind of water-mark? Yes?'

The Stock Control Manager was immune to humour.

'As I have said, all that remained was a mere six boxes, 20 packs to a box, 12 to a pack. Doubtless, Constable, you can manage the simple calculation without my assistance? Yes? For the sake of efficiency, we shipped the whole consignment to one store, the nearest. Clear now?'

'Oh, absolutely. Yes.'

This time, they both pulled a face at the phone.

'When high quality goods are offered at such bargain prices, the shelves rapidly empty, and we re-stock with new lines. When the stock is gone, our computer system instantly and accurately informs us. And I have now informed *you*. Twice. Goodbye.'

Batten grinned as Magnus stuck her tongue at the phone. High spirits had gone AWOL lately, in the CID office. He called Hick, Timms and the others over.

'Summarise, would you please, Nina?'

She did. The three envelopes enclosing three sheets of cheap paper were top-grade, and all from the same batch.

'Andy Connor in Forensics put them through the VSC - Video Spectral Comparator, something I've yet to set eyes on.'

'We had one, when I was with the Antiques Squad,' Hazel Timms offered. 'For checking forged documents and such. Crown Prosecution Service likes them. The results stand up in court, I mean.'

Magnus gave a surprised nod. She didn't know Timms had been with Antiques. Because she knew next to nothing about Timms. She ploughed on.

'Upshot is, Andy identified the watermark - it's unique to that product – and I tracked down the supplier'. She wanted to say *eventually*, but didn't expect Batten's new good humour to stretch that far. 'The envelopes all came from a small batch, left-overs, from a flood in the warehouse. *And*, they only went on the shelves two days before the Wynyards and Jean Phelps received their letters. According to the stock control computer, they were all sold within three days.'

'So we have a three day window to investigate', added Batten. 'Two, most likely, since the letters were received on the morning of the Wassail. Narrows it down, for a change.'

'Narrows it down to where, though, sir?'

My, my, Hazel, Magnus wanted to say. You've even begun to ask questions now.

'We got lucky, Hazel, for once. Reassure them, Nina.'

She did. 'One store. Just one.'

The sound of positive thinking ticked through the room. CCTV. Till-receipts. Witnesses. Mug-shots. IDs. Traffic cameras. Chains of evidence. Hick twitched out the obvious question.

'Local?'

That was where their luck fell away. Magnus broke the news.

'Afraid not. Gloucester. Eighty miles.'

The high spirits dipped. Gloucester was out-of-area, and eighty miles away. In the snow.

'Get on with it,' Batten said.

The Parminster team got on with it faster than a greyhound with diarrhoea, but the results were just as messy. On the days in question, CCTV at the Gloucester branch of Superstore UK was a no-no. *'Technical issues'*.

'Huh, heard that before,' mumbled Hick.

'Bit of luck one day, kick up the arse the next,' Batten told the team. 'Get used to it. Let's summarise what we do have. Nina?'

Magnus ran her pen down the list.

'I'd like to think we've moved on, sir, but...' God, Nina, you're beginning to sound like Hazel Timms. 'On the basis of transport, opportunity and time, there's still Scilla Wynyard with an ex-GPO van that could pass for brown. Andrew Priddle we know about. Meg Mallan we don't know about. Keith Mallan - no sign of anything other than his old MG, and that's red. And I do mean red. After that, it's Mystery Man. Or Woman. If we had even a partial registration number...'

'If we had some bacon, we could have bacon and eggs', said Batten, 'if we had some eggs.'

They'd heard it before, mostly at times like this.

'Let's get Scilla Wynyard and Andrew Priddle checked out again. Anything else?'

Eddie Hick wasn't sure he should mention Jean Phelps at all, given his previous misplaced excitement over her brown van - which turned out to be a bright blue mobile library the size of a house. And neither was he sure what colour *ockry* was. He'd learnt to trust Batten though, so bit the bullet.

'Sir?'

An eyebrow - *this better be relevant*. 'Yes, Hickie?'

'Sir, she's got another one, sir.'

Her Majesty's got another corgi, Zig, and she's personally informed Eddie Hick? Batten waited his customary five seconds.

'Jean Phelps, sir. Another van. Well, access to.'

Batten saw a giant canary yellow Winnebago with bicycles strapped to the back and a satellite dish on the roof. 'And?'

'Library Service van, sir. From a car pool. A van pool, I mean. Little Vauxhall van. For delivering sets of books, pamphlets, quality control visits. Such like. So they said.' Batten's silence made Hick even more uncertain. 'She does drive it, sir. Just this minute got a mileage chit. Did over 200 miles, that week. 200 miles? There and back to Gloucester, and a bit left over?'

'Tell us the van's brown, Hickie, and the bacon sarnies are on me.'

'Well, that's just it, sir.'

'*Just it?*'

'It's just that I don't know what colour it *is*, sir. It says *ockry*, but I've never heard of it.'

Batten was on his feet now, alert. He squinted at the black squiggle that Hick passed off as writing.

'That's *ochre*, Hickie. Ochre.'

'Ochre, sir? What colour's that?'

'Ochre, Detective Constable Hick, is bloody-muddy-brown.'

Twenty

The four letters, four copies, four keepsakes, were removed from the private place and set down on the scrubbed surface of the kitchen table. Comforting, the letters. Careful hands smoothed creases from each letter, arranging them in a crisp, straight line.

Straight lines, like the lines of beds in the dormitories, four lines of four beds in each room. Too young, weren't you?

Yes.

Couldn't say 'dormitory', didn't know what it meant in any case. Didn't know it was just a roomful of beds. And queuing for meals, in silence, in straight lines, they insisted on that, the nuns, and woe betide you if you didn't. Nightly-cleaned shoes that didn't quite fit, a ruler on your knuckles if you got your seven times table wrong, and mass three times a week. Sunday, Tuesday, Thursday. But growing to like it, the rhythm, the discipline. The comfort of the known. Keeping a careful eye, learning to be straight, to be tidy. Staring through the window, whenever you could, hoping for a glimpse of the sea.

Queenie, too, had neither mother nor man. You replaced them, didn't you?

Yes.

Queenie was small and sad and wore a white frock. You looked after her, saved a space in the breakfast queue, whispered the answers in class. You missed her, at night, in your dormitory, but beamed when she appeared next day, for watered-down milk and old cornflakes. Queenie was like you. She wanted to visit the sea.

Bullies came and bullies went, at the home. The bigger girls bullied Queenie, but you were tall for your age and stopped them. You protected her, your friend, your only friend.

Once a month, the nuns and staff took everyone into town. Queenie saw the happy children with mothers and men, together, in the shops, the park, the cinema queue. Once a month was not enough for Queenie.

We all went to the funeral, despite the snow. Even the younger ones had to. As punishment?

Perhaps.

Queenie climbed up the chapel's stone staircase, all the way to the top, hoping for a glimpse of the sea. It was too far away. She threw herself off the roof. The little white coffin was lowered into the brown earth and the straps withdrawn, like snakes.

The old nun, the one from the book-room, who wouldn't let you have the book on birds because you spilled gravy on the book before, the nun with the stick, she threw a handful of soil onto the coffin. It made a noise like plates breaking in the breakfast hall, but nobody cheered; a noise like rats, laughing. She should not have done that, should she?

No.

It was bad behaviour. Everyone trooped back to the home, in pairs, in a long straight line, but you looked back all the way, watching for Queenie, stumbled twice and got a slap for it, but watched all the same. Could you see her?

No.

The dormitory was cold that night. It was always cold. All the buildings were.

Keep watching? Carefully?

Yes.

One day you'll see Queenie again.

Sian was artificially asleep. For how long, who could say? The prescribed pills were mild, barely effective, but Erin would not allow a stronger dose.

'A coward threatens her, and then her mother drugs her? I don't think so, Zig.'

Sian had been interviewed with as little formality as the law allowed. Nina Magnus and Hazel Timms saw to that, delved carefully, found nothing untoward.

'It's so she can be eliminated, that's all,' Batten told Erin.

The look of horror she gave in response taught him to choose his words more carefully. You're drained, Zig, running on caffeine.

He had driven mother and daughter home, tucked his car out of sight round the back and locked them in it till he'd checked each room in Erin's house, working systematically from back door to front. Then the icy garden, log-store, garage, shed. Now, stretched out on Erin's sofa, Batten was so tired he could have yawned for England. He rarely stayed over at Erin's midweek.

So, why tonight, Zig? Bed-sharer, or police protection? I'm trying hard to do both, Zig.

'Do you remember the first time you invited me round here, for dinner?'

Of course she did. Despite the rubble of her current life, the memory was still treasured. They sat over there, just the two of them, at the dining table overlooking the garden where outdoor lanterns dappled white light onto the blossom trees. Sian was at Granny Kemp's. And the woodstove was lit, not because it was cold, but for mood. The cashmere top, chestnut-brown, and a pricey pair of 'not your daughter's' jeans. Candles on the table, and the emerald earrings, the ones that only came out of the box for special occasions. She'd bought ceps and chanterelles, made a wonderful mushroom risotto.

'And I gulped down every last mouthful, didn't I, even though I can't stand the smell, taste or texture of mushrooms?'

A half-smile now. It was some time before he'd confessed his hatred of the damn things, and she was mortified, as if she'd tried to poison him.

'You ate the lot' she said.

'I ate them for you. It was you I was looking at, not a plate of bloody mushrooms. I felt...you know.'

So did she. Before.

'I'd never been good at trust. It's because I'm around criminals and crime, I suppose. You dig up a lot of deceit. But I felt it, trust.'

She'd worried about him being in CID. High divorce rate. Once was enough for her.

'And I hoped you felt it too. I think you did.'

Yes, I did, she admitted, silently. But that was before this fear, for my child, and looking over my shoulder, and locking doors I've never locked, and hearing sudden noises in a night that was never as dark as this...

He took her hand. She didn't push him away.

'Every threat's an earthquake, Erin, I do know that. I'm feeling the bruises too.'

She cocked an eyebrow at him. Oh, really, Zig? Got a threatened child, have you, on sleeping pills, locked in a cupboard? He re-grouped.

'Not everything gets swept away. You know, cling to the rubble? Trust each other?'

Her throat was sand. 'I do trust you, Zig.'

He gave her cold fingers a premature squeeze.

'But I don't want to be rubble, Zig. I want to be complete. And I'm not sure if you can guarantee that.'

All Margaret Mallan could see through the dark window was darkness. At least the pub had been quiet tonight and she'd got off early. Sometimes her arm ached, ached like a heart, from pulling pints. If she had lost her love of Cornwall in daytime, she'd gained a dread of it at night.

Right now, she didn't even like her name. Not the first part, and the second part least of all. Everyone called her Meg - she insisted on it - but she couldn't do much about the 'Mallan'.

'Don't be daft', her inner voice said, 'course you can! You can speak to a solicitor. About divorce. A solicitor with a big sharp legal cleaver, to chop your marriage lines in two!'

But she hadn't. Nor had she spoken to Keith. Wanted to, but...

She carried her mug of tea from the cold kitchen to the cold sitting room, sat down by the measly fire. It was a short journey. The rented flat was barely big enough for a gnat. Let alone two.

When there *were* two. She stared at the empty chair opposite. He didn't last long, did he? Mathew. First he dragged her to Devon, then told her he 'fancied Cornwall'. Owed someone cash in Devon, more like. Cornwall was empty enough when Mathew was here, but now, huh.

Are people like their names? *Matt*, she'd called him. Table-Matt? Door-Matt? Huh, Matt Emulsion - beige, cut-price, thin, despite his looks. Should have called him *Mutt*. Mutt and Meg. Two gnats in a rented cage, kitchen the size of a toilet seat - and the bathroom no bigger. Not that Mutt spent time in either.

And never in her life did she want to see a rabbit again. Certainly not cook it, chew it, pick the shot and bones out. Rabbit. Matt's contribution to 'the household'. Rabbit-rabbit. Shoot a bagful and cart them home for *her* to deal with, when what she craved was soft hands and softer sheets. *Mutt.* Happier with a live round than a live woman. Grubby himself, but the shotgun cleaner than snow.

Keith was just as grubby but at least he could cook. And proper red meat.

Meat. *Mutt.*

Meat...Keith.

For the umpteenth time, she looked at that bloody phone of his, wondering whether to switch it on.

'You twerp, Meg,' she said, to the dying fire. 'What have you gone and done?'

Composed. People said how composed Erin was. '*Used* to be,' Erin Kemp sighed to herself. The two of them ate a silent meal, the only words spoken by Zig. 'Was it OK?' He'd cooked. Pasta. He'd be classed as a fair cook - if food had any relevance right now.

Afterwards, they tried to talk - she about her feelings, he about solutions. Cut back the trees by the front door, reduce dark areas where *someone* could lurk, he said. Her lost composure showed itself.

'Perhaps we could chop the blossom trees down too, raze the garden to the ground? No, no, keep the garden just as it is and I'll make myself invisible instead! Would that 'solution' be acceptable to you?'

She didn't raise her voice, rarely did - wouldn't, with Sian in the house. Policy, or gritted teeth?

'Look, I'm only advising a sort of 'heads below the parapet'. I'm not suggesting you-'

'You're not suggesting I disappear, then? Move to Siberia?'

No need, Zig. Siberia's moved *here*, outside and in.

'Erin, look, it's temporary. It's a case of changing a habit or two.'

'A habit? A *habit*? Oh now I understand, Zig. Become a nun! Hide in a nunnery! That's the obvious 'solution'! I'm sure they'd take Sian too, as a *novice*. Well maybe we will! And on our own!'

Erin Kemp stormed from her chair and gale-forced into the bedroom. Batten heard the door ram shut behind her. He could hear sobbing on the other side. She'd never slammed a door in all the time they'd been together – Erin Kemp did not slam doors. He didn't know whether to go and comfort her or wait for the storm to pass. He chose the latter. Best for her, he lied.

Upstairs, Sian Kemp barely heard the slamming door. She was staring at the Facebook photos, swipe, then another, swipe, hardly seeing them. Empty frames, and inside each one was a fur-clad Wassail Queen who used to look like her. Lost, now.

The sense of loss grew inside her like cancer-cells. Losing mum, that was the cancer now. There are three ways to lose mum, she told herself. You can lose her to Zig, but was there something to be gained from that? That wasn't what frightened her. You can lose mum because a faceless person - not even Sian's imagination could see a face in the words she'd read - because a faceless person wants to…

She refused to say 'kill' mum, but minds are not lips, are they? You can't zip it shut, your mind. Somewhere in her head the word formed and the word grew, and 'Kill' it said. Kill. Kill. And mum gone, and Sian alone, at thirteen, entirely alone, in a blink.

But loss cursed her more savagely still. Instead of losing mum, she knew now that the Wassail Queen could be lost *from* her. *No body shall you have*, the letter said. *No heart*. She'd read it, ink blacker than night on paper like ice.

And now she would give every non-living thing she possessed to un-read it, to return to a time when she'd never held it in her hands. She wanted to un-hold the thin white paper. She wanted never to have lifted her eyes to it, never to have understood those words.

Batten slumped onto Erin's sofa. Sian was either asleep upstairs, or awake and staring at lost glory on Facebook. He looked with regret at the silent music system. He was still in some ways a stranger here. It was not his home. The room's silence set his brain to work.

No, Erin wasn't going to disappear. Nor is she invisible, Zig. Mr Bile - or Ms - can plainly see her, can plainly see Sian. This 'watcher' can see them in dozens of public places, in the street, at school, at work, driving in cars, locking and unlocking doors. *The Western Gazette* had printed a double-page feature on the Wassail, spotlighting the pretty, fur-cloaked Queen in photographs small and large, an ogler's paradise. There were too many places where unknown eyes could watch, and prepare. But the police watching out for Sian and Erin - as best they could - had seen nobody but Erin and Sian.

Erin is not invisible, Zig, no. But, a single door-slamming incident apart, neither is she loud. *The mother's voice is sweet but the tune is false,* the letter said. Well, where might Erin's sweet voice have been heard? He knew where he planned to look, first thing tomorrow.

Now though, he needed sleep. The area car was on alert, and his own car parked round the back. Two pints of strong cider, though, were inside. There'd be no driving 'home' to Ashtree. He listened at Erin's door. A very faint sobbing. He stared at the sofa. Not quite long enough for his long legs to sleep on, but...

Oh, shake yourself, Zig. Sleep's a reward. Go and earn it, with better-chosen words.

He double-checked all the locks, left the hall and back door lights on, put a soft hand to the bedroom door.

Meg Mallan didn't want to go to bed, but couldn't think of anything else to do. She hated sleeping alone. Keith's mobile was still gathering dust on the cheap coffee-table as she dragged herself past it on her short journey to the bedroom. When did they last speak? A year? Must be. She still knew his number, backwards. Used to ring it sometimes when he was on nights and she was in bed. Alone.

Oh, Meg, shake the dust off! She grabbed the phone and switched it on. With eyes half-closed, and hand and hope shaking, she punched at the keys till she heard ringing in the world she left behind twelve months ago.

For a moment she imagined it was Jeff Wynyard who answered, till reality bit her heels. Thank god she hadn't got through to Jeff that night when... Mind you, if she had, she might not be here now, like this.

It was not Jeff's voice. It was a woman.

'Mrs Mallan? Hello? Is that you, Mrs Mallan?'

Mrs Mallan? Yes, Meg, that's you. It's still your name. Speak, then, you dummy.

'Keith?' Is that you, Keith?'

Strange. A female voice? Never expected Keith to be with... She tried to blurt out an apology, through lips of dry clay.

'I must have - I must have dialled - mistake – I'm- '

'Mrs Mallan? Please stay on the line. This is Detective Constable Timms, from Parminster CID.

I do appreciate you ringing.'

Ringing? I didn't ring. Well, I rang *Keith*. But he has a woman.

'Keith...?'

'No, Mrs Mallan. My name's Hazel Timms, from Parminster CID.'

Hazel. He has a new woman. Called Hazel.

'We'd be very grateful for a few minutes of your time, Mrs Mallan. To clear things up?

Would that be OK?'

Well, at least he's found someone polite.

'No, there's no need. I get it. Be in the way, wouldn't I?'

Hazel Timms wanted to thrust her hand down the phone and give Meg Mallan a shake. But no sense rocking a boat you've gone deaf and blind failing to locate.

'You wouldn't be in the way at all, Mrs Mallan. This is Parminster CID. We'd very much appreciate a word or two?'

'A word or two?'

'Yes. About Keith.'

Twenty one

Mr Sleep must have slept elsewhere. Batten and Erin woke up late, unrested, tense. Sian had slept even less but the doctor's stunningly original advice was to 'keep calm and carry on', for now. That meant a silent breakfast and a slow ritual that Batten hoped was not standard fare in teenagers preparing for school. Grunts and dark looks figured strongly.

Batten hated being late, hated lateness in others. But despite lacking the patience to bide and abide, he resisted telling Sian to shift her snail's arse. Erin had no such qualms.

'*Now*, please, Sian. It's me or the Headteacher. Choose.'

Sian chose, hoisting her schoolbag as if it was a dead cat. Grabbing her own bag, Erin flung open the front door - before jagging her whole body back into the hall, shocked, stark-white. Sian's hands clamped onto her mother's arm, and Batten could feel her shaking as he squeezed past. In the doorway, the flatly staring face of the postman peered back at them. His hand was invisible, hidden in his postbag.

It's only the postman, Batten wanted to say as he pushed himself forward, Erin and Sian cowering behind. Postmen are like doctors. And policemen. House-to-house calls are part of our job. This postman was of the same mind.

'I didn't mean to shock you,' he said. 'We've all been told, at the Depot, about...you know.' He waved an apologetic free hand in the vague direction of Erin and Sian.

Batten nodded. He'd already spent an eternity questioning postmen at the Depot. This morning, bleary-brained and unrested, he couldn't even recall if this postman was one of them.

'Not that us being told is much help, of course.' A thin smile shrugged out. Batten felt Erin freeze as the postman's hand came out of his bag. 'It's just mail,' he said, pushing a peace offering of packages towards them. 'Books, I suppose. Too big for the letterbox.'

'Thanks.' Batten was unable to stop himself scanning for blank envelopes. He knew what the books were. A biography of Michael Tippet, and a performance history of *A Child Of Our Time,* ordered online and eagerly awaited. Erin showed not the slightest interest now. Batten put them on the hall table. 'Yes, difficult,' he said.

The postman nodded and turned to go. After a step or two, he turned back.

'There's not one of us, at the Depot, who wants it to be this way.' He was addressing Erin and Sian now, over Batten's shoulder. 'Staring at every piece of blank bumph. Wondering if, you know, when we push it through the letterbox...'

Erin tried to nod, to accept the apology.

'It's taking us twice as long. And then there's all this.' He waved at the icy driveway, a ski-slope.

'No problem,' Batten said. 'We understand', as the postman skidded towards his van.

Neither Erin and Sian's faces, nor their trembling frames, looked like they understood.

After briefing the two uniforms in the area car, Batten followed Erin as she dropped Sian at school then drove herself to work. He did not continue on to Parminster; instead he drove back to South Petherton.

He hadn't told Erin where his first call of the day would be, nor with whom. She would have been livid at the further intrusion into her personal life. *West Country Choral* was Erin's escape, her new private world, her chance to freely use her soprano voice, instead of listening to the voices of others. The much-awaited performance of *A Child Of Our Time* was barely a month away, and she had missed the last two rehearsals, through 'illness'. However much she disliked white lies, they were mounting up. Yours too, Zig. She thinks you're questioning postmen. Again.

'Hear your own version - your own voice, not someone else's.' That's what *West Country Choral's* leader said, time and again. It was advice Erin Kemp embraced. In normal times.

Would anything be normal again? Not even the roads were normal today on the short drive from South Petherton to the Burrow Hill Cider

Company, where she worked. A police car blocked both sides of the narrow road. She was ambivalent, now, about police cars. A uniformed constable trudged along the lines of finger-tapping drivers, repeating his mantra - *black ice - van in the ditch - ambulance is on its way.* She left the engine ticking over, the heater full on.

Perhaps it's a brown van, in the ditch? She wasn't supposed to know the police were looking for muddy-brown vans, but Zig's phone rings wherever he is, and how can you not overhear?

The thought of listening and the tension of waiting got the better of her. Against her chorus leader's advice, she fed the CD into the car stereo. Missed rehearsals were her excuse. The Sir James Pritchard recording, one of the best, quickly drowned out the tick-tick of the cold engine. Soon, she would sing soprano in *A Child Of Our Time.* Before, she'd sung within the safety and support of a large chorus. This would be her first solo. Just now, 'solo' felt more like 'alone'.

'You have a fine voice', the leader kept telling her. 'The rest is confidence, nothing more.'

Confidence. A fickle friend. Comes and goes like snow.

The strings gave way to voices, filling the small car. *The world turns on its dark side - it is winter,* they sang.

Erin Kemp fast-forwarded to the first soprano solo in Part One. A professional voice, well-rehearsed orchestra and a fine chorus washed over her, there, in the cold queue of cars, in the ice and frost.

How can I cherish my man? sang the soprano. *How can I cherish my man in such days?*

The still, sad beauty of the music entered her, moved her, drawing tears from her green eyes. They trickled over high cheekbones and dropped unhindered onto the steering wheel.

Erin Kemp knew the libretto backwards. She tried to sing, tried to align her own voice with the crystal-clear voice flowing from the CD player. It was the solo she would soon perform, to a public audience.

How can I cherish my man in such days? Or become a mother in a world of destruction?

She tried again, tried to squeeze words from a dry throat past cold lips, as the soprano voice soared. *How can I comfort them, when I am dead?*

Words refused to form on her tongue. She pressed the fast forward button, grimacing at the irony of the phrase, till the music rose, solo merging with chorus, emerging and merging once again. *Steal away*, the voices sang. *Steal away...*

Chorus, soprano and strings fused and swelled, the car filling with spiritual sound, trembling, swaying with it. Erin Kemp could not tell where her tears of appreciation ended and her tears of dismay began.

Till all was drowned out by sirens as the ambulance came.

Dennis Quirke, *West Country Choral's* membership secretary, was aptly named, and got up Batten's nose in seconds.

'Strange? Anybody strange? Well, Inspector, *some* would say we're all strange here.' Mr Quirke waved his sinuous arm beyond his office window at South Petherton and gave a smug chuckle, dark eyes crinkling through large round spectacles. Jesus, Zig, he looks like Harry Potter, forty years on.

'I mean, that's villages for you, Inspector. Well, villag*ers*. Traditionally, we've always been...unique. No?'

Batten didn't have time for banter, and Dennis Quirke was bantering backwards.

'Mr Quirke, please. If nobody strange, then what about *strangers*? New faces, unusual types, maybe folk you wouldn't expect to buy tickets for classical stuff?'

Mr Quirke bridled at 'stuff'. '*Recitals*, Inspector. Oratorios. Choral works. Occasionally a little light opera. We do not offer 'stuff' - neither to 'strangers', nor to our highly-valued mailing list.'

Batten raised his hands, palms-up, in silent surrender. It kept them away from Dennis Quirke's throat.

'Let's turn to that mailing list, then, sir. Any recent members stick out?'

'Stick out? Stick out, Inspector? Mrs Sore Thumb, perhaps? First name 'Like-A'? Mrs-Like-A-Sore Thumb, who loves to hear '*stuff*?'

Dennis Quirke was prickly at the best of times. You're turning him into a bloody hedgehog, Zig. Throttle back a bit.

'Is it a case of sending an email, making a phone call, to get on the mailing list?'

At the mention of 'mailing list', Quirke perked up. Mailing lists were works of art; beauteous; almost able to sing.

'*Ordinary* members join via such methods, Inspector. But the more discerning take up our platinum option - an option that few other choral societies provide. We do think of ourselves as special, you see.'

You'd never have guessed, Zig, eh, if Harry Potter hadn't told you?

'For a miniscule additional fee, new members may sit-in on a small parcel of rehearsals – it is instructive for them to meet us, as well as hear us, in a new dimension? Meet us as people, not merely as voices, no? And of course we may recruit new voices this way. Have you a voice?' he asked, without conviction.

If you'd heard me at the Wassail, after a cider or two... Batten shook his head, while eyeing a copy of the mailing list that sat on Quirke's desk like a smug white flatfish.

Quirke stroked it. 'Alphabetical order, of course. But in my mechanical brain' - he pointed an upturned palm and five long fingers at ten pounds of computer on his desk – 'dates of enrolment are efficiently recorded and stored. Useful, I would suppose?'

About time something was, Zig.

'If you so desire, Inspector, I can summon up Excel and magically re-order the list so the more recent enrolments are first. Would that serve?'

Batten nodded, waiting for Quirke to wave a conductor's baton and shout 'Spelleamus!' Instead, ten long fingers flexed like a masseur's, and the PC hummed. Neatly tabulated lists of names began to peer from the screen. A touch smugly, Batten thought.

'Recent these names may be, Inspector, but strangers they are not. I know all of them in some capacity. I pride myself on my customer relations.' He tapped at the keys and the list re-ordered itself. 'Voila! Inspector. Every recent enrolment, for your delectation! Platinum members first!'

He chuckled at his handiwork. Batten wished he would sit down, let him look over his shoulder at the screen, but Mr Quirke was an ex-performer who had forgotten to retire. He recited each name, not quite to music.

'Alison Warr, she is my most recent 'stranger', indeed completely new, an incomer' - he gave Batten a look. 'Alison aspires to opening a bookshop - and we wish her well on her possibly mountainous journey. Hard to believe, Inspector, but we have empty shops in South Petherton now. It's a *scandal.*'

What's he expect you to do about it, Zig? Make shopping-related arrests?

'Alison, yes, she joined on the third of last month...' Dennis Quirke broke off, feeling Batten's hot breath on his neck. 'Well, you're clearly quite able to read the date for yourself.'

I can read all of it myself! Just shut your trap, and print me a copy! Quirke reminded Batten of Chaucer's Man of Law, who 'seemed busier than he was.' Batten was just *busy*.

'Wendy Meredith, from the Co-op, she joined next, as you can see...then one-two-three-four new members from Over Stratton - a village no longer culturally-benighted, I'm pleased to say. I'll just scroll down to the next page...'

While scrolling, Dennis Quirke repositioned himself over the screen so only he could read it. Batten's fingers flexed, strangulation mode.

'...Mrs Pomeroy, wife of the new churchwarden – tut-tut, no first name, but I know for a fact she's a Rosalind. Bear with, while I amend...'

He tapped at the keys once more. Batten dreamed an axe, whistling down, blood and fingers splattering the floor.

'Then there is Michael, Michael Stove, from the Parish Council...Terence, our postman...Alan, Alan Bacon - an undertaker, but the *liveliest* man...Valerie from the garden centre - she is a genius with a hanging basket. Her petunia arrangements enliven my cottage every year...'

Your cottage could use a hanging basket, Zig. With Dennis Quirke's severed head poking out of it. He butted in.

'This lot are all recent platinum members, you say?'

Quirke grimaced at 'this lot', but managed a curt nod.

'So they all have access to rehearsals - they can sit-in and listen?' To *A Child Of Our Time*, for example.

'As I have said, for a nominal extra fee, we-'

'Scroll back a bit, then...There, stop. This...Terence, your postman.'

'Terence...Veech, yes, our very own postman, for the most part.'
'Right. Print his address for me, would you? *Please?*'

Terence Veech was still at work when Batten parked outside his hamstone house, even though it took him an age to find. Veech lived on the distant fringe of Stockton Marsh, up a steep lane and in stark isolation. The nearest house was - no, Zig, there *isn't* a nearest house. And if Veech didn't live alone, whoever he lived with was far away.

Batten peeked in through the windows. Tidy. Not a cushion out of place on the white sofa. No obvious dirt anywhere. He thought of Andrew Priddle's house, and Keith Mallan's. He couldn't see them being pals of Mr Veech. Neither could he see an old Remington typewriter, sitting conveniently on an antique desk, next to a handy supply of cheap paper and ice-white envelopes. The garage was locked, and windowless. If a brown van lurked there, it was for another day.

The high gate into the garden was also locked. Batten walked back into the lane, hopped over a low wall into the field adjacent to the house, and climbed up into the fork of a dead tree. His own garden at Ashtree was coming along, slowly, but this garden was miles ahead. Lush lawns in straight lines, their edges smooth and clipped; a wildlife pond that looked to be nearly finished; bird tables and nesting boxes galore, and crisply-planted rectangular borders with 'bird-and-butterfly-friendly' written all over them. Whatever Mr Veech was, he was also a countryman. Envious, aren't you, city-boy?

Suspicious, too. The tingle of toes when a coincidence pops up had not gone away. What will you find, Zig, when you track down Mr Veech's transport? And where was he, on the day *someone* bought a dozen ice-white envelopes?

Twenty two

The pure white virtue of preparation allows for options to be reviewed. You remember reading Von Clausewitz?
 Yes. *'No plan survives first contact with the enemy.'*
 Yours has not.
 Tuesdays. The tall policeman never stayed at the Queen's house on Tuesdays, never lay in his bed of sin on Tuesday night, nor slithered out of it for work on Wednesday. Carefully watched, carefully planned. The policeman's car was never there. And the house is on its own, shielded from the road by thick trees and a swathe of honeysuckle.
 That morning was perfect, the snow gone, and no more forecast for days. No footprints. You came prepared?
 Yes.
 For the final act.
 Reverse the van into the drive.
 Open the rear doors, ready.
 Pepper spray concealed in the postbag, next to the stun-gun.
 Pretend to be checking, till their door opens.
 Turn. Ah, good morning. Registered letter. Must be signed for, I'm afraid.
 Pen's not working. It's the cold, well no surprise there - and throw in a disarming laugh.
 Do you have a pen handy, at all?
 And then she turns, the mother, to find one, and the pepper spray hits them.
 Follow up with the stun-gun, and they're down.
 Mother into the van. Discardable.
 Quietly close the doors.
 Be at One with the Queen.

But the tall policeman was there. The enemy's frame blocked the way, killing the plan.

Three bodies?
Three.
Too many, all at once?
Yes.
Better to deal with the policeman, first?
Correct.
Shotgun?
Yes.
The shotgun, then. Safely-hidden?
Of course.
And I know where.

Zig Batten sighed out more breath than his body was supposed to hold. When you're planning to turn up the heat on one suspect, the last thing you want to turn up is a *different* one. He glared at Meg Mallan's image on the video screen. She couldn't see how sharp his eyebrows had become. After being tracked down and shepherded across Cornwall and Devon, she'd arrived in Somerset in a justifiable daze.

Now, the daze was gone and she was cannily saying nothing that could be construed as an answer. Nothing useful about Keith Mallan, and even more nothing about Jeff. Or maybe you've been asking the wrong questions? Hazel Timms had fared no better. You should have let Ball do the interview, Zig, despite his partiality. He jerked his head at Timms and they stepped through the interview room door, to begin again.

Every question about shotguns drew a vacant stare. *Christ, Zig, she's taken lessons from Andrew Priddle!*

'Well, Keith's got one. Apart from that...'

'Did he ever teach *you*? To shoot, I mean?'

'Keith?'

No! Buffalo Bloody Bill!

'Hmph. Get too close to Keith's gun cupboard, load of lip in your face.'

'Liked his gun, did he?'

Did he? You're such a slow learner, Meg. Keith liked *you*, was that it? Keeping you safe, away from the guns, and nothing else?

'No more than...some,' she said. Slow learner or not, she knew enough to keep her trap shut about Matt's shotgun. Matt, her ex...

Batten waited in vain for the 'some' to be defined. Timms tapped her pen, for something to do.

Funny word, Meg, 'ex'. What do you call someone, before they become an ex? Oh, even you know the answer to that, Meg. It must be a *why*, mustn't it? *Why* then? Why *Matt*? Just to give Keith a kick, was it, give him a nudge? Well, you messed that up, didn't you, Meg? Ended up with a handsome lump of nothing, beige as his name. Pale beige. Apart from his gun. Just for rabbits, he said. A freezer full of rabbit, only useful thing he left behind. Well, sod him. It wasn't rabbit she wanted now. It was proper red meat.

Batten rubbed his moustache, and turned to the phone transcript on the desk between them, the same transcript that Keith Mallan's tears had stained, dirty marks fading now. A long finger tick-tocked on the underlined call, the date and time barely ten minutes before...It got on her nerves.

'OK, I phoned him, phoned Jeff. That night. Didn't know it was the Wassail.'

Is Keith still contagious, Zig? He's contaminated Meg with miser-word-itis. And buggering off wasn't a cure. She's still got it.

'And?'

'Oh, well. I've always liked Jeff, you see.'

'See? No, I don't see. See what?' All Batten could see was a woman in a cheap dress a size too big. Or she's lost a pound or two? If she filled it, the dress, she'd fill it well. A few crow's feet, lines in her lips. But attractive. Rustic. He pushed the thought away.

'*Why?* Why did you ring him?'

Meg Mallan gave Batten a knowing look. Men. Eyes like hands, running them up and down, all over you. It gave her a feeling of power. She didn't like the feeling anymore.

'Well. I thought Jeff might...I thought Jeff might help. You know?'

No, I don't bloody know!

'Fancied him, did you? Fancied his *body*?' Timms dropped her pen. Batten was tired, cutting verbal corners, slicing them off.

Meg Mallan ignored the brusqueness. Used to Keith's, wasn't she? She pondered. Poor Jeff. *Did* she fancy him?

'I suppose', she shrugged. 'In a way.'

Batten yawned. Stop asking her what she means, Zig. Try silence. It's bloody working for *her*.

Meg Mallan yawned too. Tired of Batten, of this tired interview room, tired of that mousy-looking female detective who said nothing, just sat. With her dirty hair. Meg noticed dirty hair. Even when you're skint, you can have clean hair. She stared at...she'd forgotten her name. Thames, was it? Go home and wash your hair, Ms Thames. You've *got* a home, I suppose? Inspector Angry, I suppose he's got one too - guard-dogs and a barbed wire fence. And where's *your* home, Meg? Back in Cornwall? She ran a hand through her hair. Clean, yes. Not for long, though, if she stayed in this windowless room. And which bright spark chose that shade of green? It's like sick.

'Good-looking man, was Jeff. Once he brushed up. Despite the sheep.'

Batten wondered if Meg would ever discover the art of the complex sentence. Or the sheer joy of two simple thoughts being logically connected. He raised both eyebrows, to galvanise her.

'I thought Jeff might help. Might have a word with Keith.'

'With Keith? *Why*?' Meg Mallan seemed an unlikely silent partner in a sheep scam out of *Wallace and Gromit*.

'Why? To put a word in. About *me*. Sort of...negotiate.'

'*Negotiate*?'

'Be a middle-man.'

'A middle-man? What, to twist Keith's arm, cut you in on the deal?'

'Deal? What deal?'

Is this woman stupid, Zig? Or just smarter than you?

'The stolen venison deal? The stolen beef?'

Meg Mallan gave Batten her own version of eyebrows.

'Venison? What do you mean?'

'Why don't you tell me what *you* mean? Mrs Mallan?'

Mrs Mallan? That's you, Meg. You're still the Mrs Mallan he's talking about.

'When I say 'negotiate', I mean like a...you know, to mend fences, between me and Keith. Smooth things over. So Keith and me could...you know.'

Neither Batten's eyebrows nor the rest of him could cope. Hazel Timms dropped her pencil for the second time. *Jeff Wynyard*? As a marriage guidance counsellor? Not the kind of moonlighting you had him down for, Zig. And what might *Scilla* Wynyard have to say?

'Funny choice for a go-between, Jeff Wynyard?'

Meg Mallan smiled. Nice pair of cheek bones, Zig.

'Went to the pub together, Keith and Jeff. Three pints of cider and they're brothers in arms. All the same...a good-looking man.'

'*Man*? Which one?'

Meg Mallan had forgotten Timms and Batten were there.

'Looked a lot like Jeff, did Keith. My Keith.'

Sergeant Ball dreaded more questions about Keith Mallan. It reminded him of being asked what you were like at school, as if you ever knew. It's other people you notice, at school, and Keith was one of them. And Scilla. And Jeff. And, of course, poor Di.

What was worse, Batten always seemed to wait till the two of them were drinking 'casual' cups of coffee in his tight little cubby-hole of an office, where it was too small to hide.

'Didn't you say he'd done a bit of poaching, Ballie?'

'Much knowledge and little proof, zor, where Keith's concerned.'

Nothing's bloody changed, then, Zig, has it, where Keith's concerned? Batten's toes began tingling as soon as he asked Meg Mallan about Keith and his guns, and the tingle wouldn't go away.

'Use a 12-bore, did he? For the poaching?'

Ball spotted his Inspector's angle, straight off.

'Well, he didn't use an 8-bore, zor, if that's what you're thinking. Too heavy, too loud. More likely a .410. Lighter. A poacher's gun.'

'Foldable?'

'Indeed, zor. Hide it under your coat, but still down game with it.'

Batten pondered. They'd found a licensed 12-bore in Mallan's house, but nothing else. Keith was in enough trouble as it was. If they found an unlicensed poacher's gun too? Or an 8-bore...

'Who are Mallan's cronies?'

'Apart from Jeff, you mean?'

Batten managed a sad nod. 'Bothers-in-arms', Meg Mallan had called the pair of them.

'Who else might be 'minding' a gun for him, then?'

'We've done the rounds, zor, not that it took long. Keith's less popular than he was. Put it this way, he drinks at home nowadays, instead of in The Jug and Bottle.' Ever since Jeff was killed, Ball could have added. 'No sign of a rogue gun, though.'

Batten knew he was clutching at straws. But he didn't like the smell of Keith Mallan.

'If he gave Meg a phone before she buggered off, could he have given her anything else?' Apart from fleas and a bottle of eau-de-carcass.

'Can't see him getting any further with Meg than with Jeff, zor. Can you?'

Can you, Zig? Yes, Zig, I bloody-well can. The day I accept a confession at face value, I'll transfer from CID to the priesthood. He finished his coffee. Squashing the thought of Keith Mallan into his empty cardboard cup, he flung both of them at the re-cycle bin.

'Keep 'em looking, Ballie, for that 8-bore beast. And any other guns they might find.'

Twenty three

The final act drawing closer, blood beating faster and memory growing strong. No, not strong - it had always been strong - but...clear?
Yes.
A clear picture: straight lines of children, in tight pairs, and Queenie one of them, nuns at front and back shepherding them all through the gates of the home. Woe betide any child that broke step or edged too near the roadway on the march into town for the monthly visit, this time to the museum where the stuffed birds were. The girls wore hooded brown gabardine capes, the boys flannelette blazers whose cuffs wore through.

Queenie shone out against the trees as we trudged past, against the iron railings and the dull shop fronts. She glowed like moonlight against the dark wooden frames of the glass display cases. Finer than all the displays, was Queenie. When she paused to peer in that half-sad way at stuffed owls and peregrines, she could have been a bird herself.

Queenie. Like a small pretty bird in her brown hood and white dress, her eyes dreaming of the sea. She had neither mother nor man, but you are both mother and man to her?
I am, yes.
Is the picture clear enough now?
Clear.
The woman and the police detective are obstructions. To be removed?
Yes. To be discarded.
Then my new Queen will be clothed in a brown hood and a fine white dress.
But remove the policeman first?
Indeed.

Batten pulled his Ford Focus into the lean-to garage and switched off the engine. The automatic lighting was working - he'd carefully checked it yesterday – and he gave the garage an all-round look before getting out of the car. Nobody.

He was equally careful when he came round the side of his house to the front porch. The climbers by the door had been trimmed back, hard. Erin still refused to do the same at her house in South Petherton. Defiance is admirable, Zig, but dangerous.

Nothing to be seen in the front or back gardens because it was dark, cold, late. The field next to the house was a closed black curtain. Once inside, he dropped the deadbolt, checked upstairs and down. He was staying in, at Ashtree, tonight.

He shoved a lump of yesterday's cottage pie in the microwave, ate it standing up while *A Child Of Our Time* boomed from the stereo. He still hadn't read the CD notes, hardly listened to the words. The mixed tones of the orchestra were dark enough for a dark winter night.

When the soprano solo began he switched it off. The voice wasn't Erin's - yet in a way it was. Erin was in the room, in the walls, but questioning now. Doubting. He scrabbled in the CD rack for something else.

Tom Waits growled out song after song, till the CD told Batten the only kind of love is stone blind love. He grabbed the remote and switched off altogether. Early night, Zig? You could use one.

He turned off the lights and got as far as the bedroom when the phone rang.

Hidden by a tall hedge, the figure in dark clothing gazed across the empty field, till the downstairs windows darkened in Batten's house. When a light came on upstairs, the figure calmly eased forwards, leaving only faint smudges, not footprints at all, in the hard mud. Boots wrapped in cloth saw to that. The loaded shotgun felt neither heavy nor light, and the glass cutters almost weightless.

The cutters would not be needed in any case. Batten's home, his habits, had been carefully observed - doors locked but the bedroom sash-window always open at night, winter or not, always a gap as wide as a hand, for fresh air. And there it was, the noise of the window-catch, and the unmistakeable scrape of the sash. An extending ladder, feet also muffled, dangled on a shoulder strap. And a torch no thicker than the shotgun barrel. Wait, for sleep. Climb. Torch and shotgun on the window ledge and poking through. The beam clicking on, the first barrel firing into the bed. He was used to the recoil, now. Check by torchlight, and then the second barrel, for certainty. Back across the black fields as sleepy neighbours swear they've heard a car backfire.

Wait, patiently now, in silence. For the light to be extinguished.

It was Grigoris, again, phoning from Greece. Swamped by work, Batten had forgotten to phone him back. He lay on the bed, yawning, guilty.

'Sig, how can you be police and not have diary? Tell me how is so? All the calendars of England, they all are destroyed, yes?'

'Apologies, Makis. It's difficult, just now.'

Batten had not shared the problem of Erin and Sian with Grigoris, friend or not. The Greek Lieutenant knew nothing of the threats made to the three of them. While a trip to a warm Crete at Easter was a joyful thought, a thought it remained, right now.

'At first you say you come, ne? And then, Sig, you say you will say me *when*? And so I wait, but then you say no thing! I think is broke, your phone, yes? Is broke one-way? Only way it work is I call from Greece!'

He would have to tell Grigoris the truth. Rude, unfair, not to. He began to find the right words.

Below Batten's window, muffled ladder ready on the hard ground, the dark figure heard voices within. A man's voice, deep, which he recognised. But was there a second voice? Too quiet. A quiet woman's voice, perhaps? No second car outside, but... Voices, still. Wait. Listen. Be sure.

The sounds continued.
Two people?
Yes.
One barrel each?
No.
Too little certainty?
Yes.
Abort?
Indeed.

The pure white virtue of preparation is a worthy rule.
Obey it.
Withdraw?
Yes. Another day will come.

Batten put down the phone. Grigoris was sympathetic, but persuasive too. Crete at Easter would be a relief from their pain, would be a joy, he said. Batten succumbed, the moment Grigoris, in his bizarre Greek-English accent, began to *sing* to him.

'Forget your trobbles, come on, get heppy,
I'm gonna tock all your cares a-why!'

Climbing into bed, Batten recalled his response.

'I surrender, Makis! If you stop your bloody awful singing, I promise we'll come!'

Grigoris laughed as only he could, and ended the call. Snuggling into the duvet, Batten was almost asleep when the last line of the song came to him.

'Sing Alleluia, come on, get happy,
Get ready for the judgement day.'

Twenty four

'Me, I always carry a pack of tissues', Nina Magnus told Hazel Timms. Batten had teamed up the two of them, and they'd been at it for hours. Magnus wasn't too sure about the *team*. 'Always useful, tissues, if a victim blubs.' Or a suspect.

'We should carry lie detectors,' said Timms. 'Twice as useful.'

Sitting in Scilla Wynyard's freezing kitchen, Hazel wished she was carrying a blanket. Magnus was feeling the chill too, not least from Scilla Wynyard.

'Well, can you recall your whereabouts *one* day before the Wassail, then?'

Scilla Wynyard just stared back at Magnus, frozen. For variety, she stared at Timms, whenever Hazel took a turn. She hadn't offered them tea. Looking after the pennies now.

'Whatever I told you before. Nothing's changed.' For Scilla, nothing had. And everything.

'You said you drove to the village shop, first thing?' Magnus knew the answer. They had witnesses. But none for the afternoon.

'If I did, I did. I don't even know what happened yesterday, let alone...'

Timms took over.

'Is it a good runner, your little van? I mean, this weather?' Timms glanced through the window at an ex-GPO van parked outside. It looked like camouflage, hints of red pushing through the blotchy brown dullness of an amateur re-spray.

'It goes. Best it can.'

It goes. Time goes. Jeff goes. She wished these two would go. Rita Brimsmore, from The Jug and Bottle, was saving the pub newspapers for her. A day old, but at least there were crosswords. Yesterday's *Times* sat on the kitchen table, waiting. Huh, yesterday's times. She sometimes went to a cafe, sat for an age with a cheap cuppa and the crossword, watching other people's lives tick by. Here, in her converted cowshed, she could only watch her own.

'Vans can overheat, on longer journeys, can't they? Even in the frost?'

'Wouldn't know.'

'But you must have to get about a bit, what with the sheep, and all?'

Get about? Yes, to the bank, solicitor. Undertaker.

'I'd forgotten about the sheep.' Because she was angry with the sheep. Furious. And how can you be furious with sheep? Scilla Wynyard stood up. 'I have to do the sheep,' she said.

Magnus flashed Timms a look. Have we finished here? Timms shrugged back. What was there to finish?

'You didn't need your tissues', Timms said, in the car.

'No,' said Magnus. 'We didn't.'

The typewriter?

Gone.

Smashed into metal shards and jagged pieces, dumped in random bins and landfill, many miles from here. White paper?

Burnt.

The envelopes?

Incinerated too.

Gloved hands caressed four letters, copies, four keepsakes, smoothing them into a neat, straight line on the kitchen table. Four photographs of the Queen, snipped from *The Western Gazette*, were added to the line. For incineration too?

No! To be kept safe, in the private place.

For revisiting. All have merit. All satisfy.

Today, the hands selected letter number two. An enjoyable result, despite the extra journeys to acquire and dispose of the paint. She brought it on herself, that library-woman. Green ink, humph. You noticed the green ink on the letter straight away, did you not?

Yes.

Then another, and then one every week. Sometimes two, three, more. Foolish, not to read what it said, the green letter?

Indeed.

And full of such disgust. A woman with a woman. When the older children at the home made foul jokes about the nuns, you did not believe them?

Not then, no.

The clock-faced woman with the spectacles, the book-woman, you observed her, in Taunton, at the library, pretending to talk to men? Pretending not to be a nun. But the green letters - ?

Yes. They proved it.

Just as the older children said. The library-woman was a foul lie. Her letter, it was child's play to write.

Erin Kemp left work early, truthfully pleading a headache. To help clear it, she donned warm clothes and spruced up the garden, re-filling bird-feeders and sweeping debris from the fringes of the lawn. Yesterday, she had disturbed an over-wintering hedgehog while tidying up the borders. Sian had helped her carefully re-cover it with small branches and twigs, a timely lesson in the care of living things.

Erin liked that Zig was a gardener too. His own garden at Ashtree was slowly coming along - as was Zig himself. None of her previous relationships were bad men, but she could find no core to any of them. Zig was stronger. Not without his drawbacks, but at least the kind of man who safety-checks the tightrope before you walk across.

Today, she wasn't even sure if it mattered.

'Perhaps this is how you are, Erin?' she said to herself. 'Perhaps you'll always be a doubter, always feel you 'don't deserve?'

She scraped a broom over black mould forming on the far edge of the patio where the sun barely shone. One thing was clear: she didn't deserve the black mould forming on her life right now. Invisible threats; disrupted relationships; a traumatized child.

As the broom rasped at the mould, she understood how people lost faith in the rational, how if the New Testament of forgiveness weakens, the Old Testament of vengeance rises up. If the law is no protection, then let's sweep away the foulness without it. But how can you sweep away what cannot be seen? Where was the neck she burned to wring? And anyway, when a mere child is threatened, hasn't the law already failed?

'You've safety-checked the tightrope, Zig', she said to thin air. 'But we've still to walk across.'

Despite the cold, she felt the heat of rage, rage at faceless threats, but also at herself for being…what? Cursed? She remembered the Wassail, the yelling and drumming and incantations, the shotguns booming into the trees to frighten off evil.

'It hasn't gone, Erin,' she told herself, as she dumped the mould-stained broom back in the shed.

Today, if the faceless coward who sent that page of bile to her door was unearthed, like the hedgehog in its nest - what would she do? She knew the answer. To protect Sian, if the moment ever came, she would thrust her garden fork into the coward's heart - oh, yes, the heart, if there *was* one - yank it out and stab again and again and again for as long as it took.

Jean Phelps and Chris Ball had been in the same pub quiz team for as long as they could remember. Before, she would have been pleased to see him, even on police business. Now, with the village rumour machine chugging noisily away, she was not so sure. The tall Inspector would have been preferable. He didn't know her.

'Is Di a little better, perhaps?' she asked. She poured herself her best Columbian coffee. Sergeant Ball shook his head, at the question and at the coffee. Last time he sat here, she poured him cider, he recalled. He looked through the window at the frost, wanting to be somewhere else.

'Oh. You know,' he said, feeling her eyes peering over her spectacles at him. 'Er, it's the days before the Wassail I need to focus on', he added, unsure now whether to call her Jean or Ms Phelps. He settled for neither. 'The two days before, as it happens.'

'They were weekdays, Chris. I went to work, as usual. As I said before.'

'You'll have driven there, presumably?'

'Yes, of course.' Today, her sick-leave now over, she'd driven to and from work in a hire car. Not in a little Ford with green paint splashed over it, and a rainbow-coloured 'LIE' daubed on the windscreen.

'But once there, you used a Library Services van, is that right?'

'Well, that week I did. I was shuttling sets of books to and fro, while also doing my proper job.'

'Your proper job?'

'You know what I do, Chris. I'm a Senior Librarian. I show others how it's done, and check that they're doing it well. And more often than not they're volunteers, in these times of library closures and redundancies.'

'It's a brown van, is that right?'

'Brown? Yes, I suppose it is.' Not green. Not rainbow-painted.

'You did a fair few miles, that week, then, in the van?'

Jean Phelps pointed her spectacles at Chris Ball. Why are you here?

'I don't see the relevance', she said.

'Oh, loose ends being tied, that's all. If you knew how many bits of string we have to check...'

So, I'm one of your bits of string now, am I? Jean Phelps hardly knew what she was anymore.

'Two hundred miles, was it, that week?'

'If you say so. I'm a librarian, not an odometer. Why is this important?'

'Well it probably isn't, but we have to check. Would you have gone north at all? Gloucester way?'

'Gloucester? I work for Somerset. What business would I have in Gloucester?'

What indeed. 'So you didn't?'

'My work diary will tell you exactly where I went, and at what time, and very probably who I met, trained, quality controlled or passed the time of day with. I presume you wish to see it?'

She could feel her anger returning, and this was Chris Ball, who she'd known for twenty years.

If she didn't like the import of *his* questions, how much rage would she feel when she ventured out into the village?

Twenty five

Hazel Timms drove into the Parminster CID car park after a long and late yesterday and an early start today. She could have done without another sunrise visit to the Royal Mail Depot. Whipping the car door closed, she might have kicked it too, had she not noticed Batten watching her. He'd just stepped out of his.

'You alright, Hazel?'

Am I alright? Oh, fine and dandy. Sir. Up all night with Dad, trying to convince him Mum wasn't an intruder, then up a good deal longer putting ice on Mum's swollen cheek where he'd slapped her. 'He was just defending himself, Hazel, from a stranger in his house.' 'But we live here, Mum. We're not strangers.' You sure, Hazel?

'Oh, you know, sir. Postmen.'

He'd sent Timms to check on Terence Veech.

'Any luck?'

He's like a younger version of Dad, is Batten. Without the Alzheimer's. And does he expect me to report back in a car park, surrounded by ice? She pulled her coat tighter, as a hint, and because it's *bloody freezing*.

'Well, let's get a coffee, shall we, first of all?' he said.

She dipped inside, without reply. What's he want, a medal for chivalry?

She sat down in Batten's office. If you swung a cat in here, you'd hit the walls. And knees two feet apart was...She hoped he hadn't noticed her hair needed attention. If ever she found the *time*.

'White? You sure?'

Sure? Ooh, no, I'm just a silly girl, so distracted by fluffy kittens and embroidery that I forgot to check the registration and the colour code. Which is in fact *glacier-white!*

'It's definitely white, sir. A small van, old, yes, but white and nothing else. And no sign of a re-spray from or to.' She added, 'from or to brown,

I mean', in case his caffeine hadn't kicked in. She refused to add, *I did a careful drive-by to double-check. White van parked by the front door. Garage open and empty. No other transport anywhere in evidence.* Presumably Batten trusted her to have managed that?

'Blast'. He'd wanted Veech's vehicle to be brown. 'No other transport, though?'

'Apart from a Royal Mail van, pillar box red, with logos and lettering? No, sir.'

She's a bit cutty this morning, Zig. Wrong side of the bed. He was disappointed with the information, not with her.

'Serves me right, I'd convinced myself he was our brown-van-man, Mr Veech.'

Hazel Timms swallowed. *You won't like the rest of it, then.*

'There's a bit more, sir.' God, Hazel, he did that thing with his eyebrows again. I wish he wouldn't do that. 'The three days in question, when the envelopes were on sale...'

'Yes?'

'Terence Veech was officially off sick, sir. And some days either side. I got a copy of the doctor's note from the Depot Supervisor.'

'Well, if he was off sick he was free to get himself to Gloucester, what's the problem?'

'The problem is, sir, the Superstore's one of those big out of town places, out in the sticks. No public transport, just a massive car park, and-'

'So? He drove a *white* van there to buy his envelopes, not a brown one.'

'He didn't, sir. He couldn't.' She produced the doctor's note from her folder. 'Unfit to drive,' it said. 'Badly sprained wrist, bruised ribs and elbows, and a twisted ankle. A bad fall, on the ice. He didn't drive up and down the M5 in that state, sir.'

It crumbled away, Batten's image of Terence Veech, anonymous letter in one hand and a weighty 8-bore shotgun in the un-sprained other.

'The Supervisor said he limped into the depot with the doctor's note, in an arm brace and a big sling, looking like death.' She didn't give Batten the Supervisor's actual words – *this 'effin ice, it's knocking 'em down like ninepins! I swear the buggers are taking it in turns!* 'When I say 'limped', sir, I mean limped in, in a taxi.'

Batten's coffee tasted of brown mud. Bloody muddy brown mud. He got to his feet. Hazel Timms did the same, awkwardly, in the cramped space. He opened the door to let her out.

'Cross-check it all, yes?'

She nodded and left. *Does he think I wasn't going to?*

He might not be the fastest learner, but having been speared twice by giant thorns at Andrew Priddle's rat-trap of a house, DC Eddie Hick made sure there'd be no third time. Thick leather gloves, to keep his hands safe from thorns *and* from the cold.

He rattled his gloves against the rotten door. Echoes, but nothing human.

'And make sure you take a proper look round the back.'

That's what Batten had said. Hick was prepared for this too, and dragged a long stout stick from his Jeep. With no search warrant, he could do little more than flick back a few waves from the sea of brambles, poke aside an out-of-control buddleia and skirt round the beds of nettles. A black dust sat on the weeds like glum soot, flying into the air and onto his coat as he reached the back door and rapped with the stick. Only echoes, again.

'Does this bugger Priddle *live* here?' he asked himself. 'Or on the bloody Moon?'

A peer through the grimed back windows revealed an empty cell of a kitchen - well, it had a sink and something black that might have been a cooker - but no sign of life.

'Come on, Eddie. You've gone above and beyond, for the Northern Fork' - his private name for Batten. 'Crystal' Ball was the Spoon. On bad days, the pair morphed into the Fork'n Spoon.

Clutching his stout branch, DC Hick turned towards his Jeep, till his foot crunched through something chalky and brittle. He peered down, then closer. Yuk. It was a rat's skull. Used to find them in dad's old barn when he played there as a kid. He scuffed at the surrounding weeds with his stick. More rat skulls appeared, bony bodies too, all spread around a broken drain by the filthy back door. To his relief, the drain was too iced-up to stink.

His gut told him to get back in the Jeep and into a hot skinny latte, but Batten was always banging on about the D in CID standing for Dogged and Determined. He sighed, scuffed aside more rubbish and knelt down for a closer look.

The bodies, he saw, were riddled by shotgun pellets. Lead pellets lay scattered on the ground and pellet holes peppered the skulls. The dead rats had been there for some time, picked clean, bleached and frosted now. He took several photos with his camera phone, cleared the distaste from his throat by gobbing on the buddleia, and made it to his Jeep unpierced by thorns.

'How come you're full of pellets?' he asked the rat skulls. 'Andrew Priddle swears he doesn't own a gun.'

Pleased with himself, he headed back to Parminster, failing to spot the figure carefully concealed in a copse three hundred yards away, and watching through strong binoculars.

And also searching for Andrew Priddle.

Chris 'Crystal' Ball needed neither second sight nor years of training to detect the silence as he clicked open the door to the village shop. Three of them, suddenly peering at recipe suggestions on the backs of packets as if the elixir of life was written there. He bought bread, milk, *The Western Gazette*. Isn't there enough gossip in the newspaper? Do you need me and my sick wife too? *It's an ILLNESS!* If Di had a cold, or something you could stick a plaster on, you'd ask about her health, wouldn't you? Nobody did.

Nobody had asked after Scilla Wynyard either, yesterday, when she met the same chilled silence, though softened by a false smile or two. A moment before, it had been: *They say she's selling up...Nothing to sell, I heard...She'll have to move away...Well, is that a loss?*

It had been worse for Jean Phelps, when she called in to buy a bottle of the wine she needed more and more. Not even false smiles for her, and a colder silence. Refusing to succumb, she'd turned to stare at the three gossips, stoutly defending the village against invasions of empathy.

'I'd always wondered what it would be like', Jean said, 'returning a library book with fifty years of fines to pay.'

Like Scilla and Jean, Chris Ball paid his fine, and left.

Four letters, four copies, four keepsakes, were removed once more from the private place, unfolded and set down on the scrubbed kitchen table, one by one. The satisfaction of holding them was incomplete today.

The first - the sheep man - got what he deserved: vengeance.

The second received a firm corrective lesson.

The third?

Humph.

That man must be hiding, perhaps beneath the weeds and brambles of that sewer he lives in. If in fact he lives there at all?

Has the bird flown? A thin smile leaked out at the metaphor. If he has, some indication will need to be sent to the police?

Yes.

Number three shall not enjoy the fruits of sin.

Gloved hands found renewed satisfaction in smoothing the creases from the fourth and final letter. The tall policeman had been fortunate, but there was virtue in preparation. He would soon be removed.

And after that?

After that, completion.

Twenty six

When was the last time he'd held a bottle of bleach in his hand? Keith Mallan couldn't remember. He could barely remember how the vacuum cleaner worked. Or the washing machine. He'd spent an age with his hands in dust and bleach and soap, and the noise of the steam-iron and the vacuum and the spin-dryer yakking away at him.

Meg had finally agreed to come round, tonight. To their house.

'*Your* house, Keith', she'd reminded him. She wouldn't be a pushover, whatever her desires. Talk at his place first, then hers next time. And I mean *talk*. Softly-softly, wait and see.

With unrealistic optimism, Keith put badly-ironed cleanish sheets on the double bed. When he opened the wardrobe, the stench of sweaty trainers hit even *his* nose. He shifted them to the boot room, with the other bad smells.

'Don't let her go in there, Keith. She'll walk straight out again.'

No time to clean it, what with everything else. Mind you, given what was hidden there, best if she did walk straight out again?

He focused on the other rooms - kitchen and lounge, downstairs loo. And the bedroom, just in case. All the empties were in the re-cycling, hidden round the back of the house, and he'd scrubbed away the venison stains from the worktop.

He washed his hands with distaste, for the umpteenth time, and switched on the oven. The smell of roast beef would soon blot out the smell from the boot-room. And impress Meg, he hoped.

'You might have lost a few hairs, Keith,' he told himself. 'But you still know how to cook.'

And how to use a gun. He removed pellets and bones from the rabbit he'd shot. Rabbit terrine starter, with some of that left-over quince jelly. She loved rabbit, did Meg.

Why on his midweek day-off was he feeling…off? Midweek was a strange land, the land of work. But here he was, at home, trying *not* to. Balance,

Zig, remember? Erin often reminded him. Sometimes she nibbled his ear, as punctuation. Not lately, though.

Batten tried hard, ticking away the morning on domestic tasks - the pile of washing; cleaning out the woodstove; changing the sheets. And ironing, which he hated. He hated central heating too but was glad of it now - glad too that the plumber had worked his magic. The windows would have ice on the inside if the boiler hadn't been repaired.

He gave the warm sofa a stare, the rack of CDs a glance. No. Sofas and music are rewards for the evening. Midweek daylight was for outdoors, for fishing. But with the lakes frozen solid...

Instead, he pulled on thick socks and walking boots and a padded waterproof, but not for his accustomed cross-country hike. The famous Somerset mud was now a treachery of polished glass, a man-trap of rabbit runs and badger holes cunningly concealed beneath snow and ice. Difficult to solve a murder at the best of times, Zig, but with a broken leg? He compromised.

Struggling along the skiddy surface of the lane outside, he reached the main road. The gritted tarmac was hardening, but it was safer than walking on the pavement which shone like glassy rock. And roadways are even safer when nary a car rolls down them. The cars are all queuing up outside bodyshops, Zig, waiting to be repaired.

The reward for a long trudge up the lane was usually a long view from the top, but not today. The whiteness had turned into the glum colour he remembered from his time in urban Leeds, when the snow, soot and diesel-dirt mixed themselves into dull shades of grey, and a cold hazy sadness clothed the sky. Ham Hill could barely be seen in the distance. It looked like a long decaying body on a mortuary slab.

Snap out of it, Zig.

Lines from a Loudon Wainwright song crept into his head, as his feet stuttered through frost and salt. Something about taking your dog for a walk, in the snow and ice, and the dog doing what dogs do - but you won't smell it till April or May? He began humming the tune as his feet skidded on brown slush. April or May? Three months of winter yet, the weatherman said.

At least it felt more like Spring by the glowing fireplace in The Five Bells. Today, he could happily forget that the log grate had long gone and a gas-driven version warmed his hands. Three frozen pensioners sat in the dining room, stoking their cold bodies with hot lasagne. Apart from that, the pub was empty, except for a single customer sitting at the bar, wiping the shine of cider from cold lips. Batten didn't recognize him.

'Afternoon, Zig. Day off?'

Batten looked again. Without his red van and uniform, Ozzie the postman was incognito, commonplace, though his voice should have given him away. His Royal Mail van hopped daily to the half-dozen houses down Batten's lane, but if Ozzie was a nickname, and if Ozzie had a surname, neither Batten nor his neighbours knew it - nor anything else about him.

'Ozzie? Thought you were in Tenerife?'

'Huh, I wish.'

'First time I've seen you here, of a lunchtime. Day off too?'

Ozzie said nothing, but waved his non-drinking arm in Batten's direction. It was heavily strapped, elbow to wrist, and purple-blue bruising had crept past the bandage and across his hand.

'Ouch,' said Batten.

'That's what I said, right after falling on my behind. Post Office should give us ice-skates. Or one of those helicopters from Yeovil.'

'Looks painful.'

'Huh. You should see my ribs. Even hurts to drink!'

To prove it, he winced his way through the remains of his pint. *Well, Zig, he delivers mail on the dot, so his sense of timing's no surprise.*

'Another one?'

'Why not, Zig? Better than talking to the walls.'

Batten sat at the bar, ordering cider for two and liver and bacon for himself. He hadn't imagined Ozzie living alone. *And you're another one in no rush to talk to the walls, Zig.*

'When will you be able to…' Batten mimed driving. Easier than miming shoving bumph through a letterbox.

'Another week. They've signed me off till then, anyways. But you know what? Rather be at work. I like the rhythm of it. It's predictable. What's to do, this weather, if you're off sick? Everything's either frozen or shut. And even when it's open…'

Ozzie waved an undamaged arm at the near-empty pub. The muzak had switched itself off. Three pensioners digested their pasta in silence. With no words left to share, they twitched redundant lips at the free magazines, to ward off emptiness.

Batten drifted too, to Philip-Larkin-land. What was that poem about empty nights being followed by the antidote of working days? He couldn't remember. Ozzie snapped him out of it, draining his pint and nodding at the clock above the bar.

'My shout next time, Zig. Appointment with the doc.'

This time, he waggled his bandaged arm, and left. As Batten watched him pilot his bruised ribs through the pub doors, Philip-Larkin-land returned. What *was* that poem? Something about postmen going from house to house, like doctors? Was that it?

Alone now at the bar, he stared at the onion-coated liver on his plate, shovelled in a forkful. Aunt Daze would call it winter food. As he chewed, it was work and postmen and doctors that stayed in his thoughts. And postmen on the sick list, with plenty of midweek leisure on their hands.

Twenty seven

Another bad night. Hazel Timms couldn't get Dad to bed, and Dad got abusive and yelled at her. *If you don't leave now I'm calling the police!* I *am* the police, Dad. Or supposed to be. I'm your daughter too, remember?

Batten had no idea these thoughts were tightening Hazel's face when he strolled across to her desk, but it gave him pause. Was he piling her with work, without realizing it? Because she's new, unproven? A dusting of guilt settled onto his shoulders like snow, but he asked his question anyway.

Hazel Timms wished Batten wouldn't stand over her like that, when she was at her desk. He was tall enough already. And was he implying she was a *snail*?

'Yes, sir, of course I did. It's *ongoing*.' She'd heard Batten use the same words, and if it's good enough for the goose...

'So, Hazel...how soon do you think you'll...?'

Get round to it? Is that what he means? When will I 'get round to it'? When I've had a bikini wax and done my nails? She ran a tired hand through drab hair. Damn him, how much unpaid overtime does he expect me to do, checking every blessed postman who's ever stepped within a sniff of Stockton Marsh? The Depot Supervisor was roundly fed up of her. Geoffrey Gentle! What a name for a grumpy lump like him.

'Don't try telling me you know how busy we are, Constable! It's not roads and paths out there, it's an effin' bobsleigh-run! But if we're five minutes late with the mail? I don't know what's worse, all this talk of new-fangled drones delivering the stuff, and putting honest postmen out of work - or snow and ice laying the buggers off even faster! I've got more effin' staff off sick than I've got delivering!'

Hazel Timms had taken a deep breath, and persevered with Geoffrey Gentle. She did the same now, with Batten.

'I've cross-checked every postman - and woman - who's officially or unofficially been within a country mile of the Wynyard's delivery route, and Jean Phelps' route, and...'

She almost blurted out 'Mrs Kemp's route', but had enough self-control left in her locker to put the brakes on. One of Batten's eyebrows twitched, that was all.

'Upshot is, sir, every one's a blank so far.'

'But you're sure they're not –'

'I don't take their word for it, sir.' *I might be female, but I'm not brainless!* She took a breath, glanced through the window. The view was ice. Batten leaned on Hazel Timms' desk, hoping the grip of his hands on solid wood might help him think deep thoughts about postmen. Timms edged her drab hair further away from him.

'The only ones left are those who were off-sick during the Wassail week, and they're next, sir. And when I say I've got a list of them here, I do mean 'here'.'

She flicked a hand at a desk papered with files, transcripts, post-its, report sheets and note-books, all demanding attention. Data danced a jig of derision on the PC screen. At least the phone wasn't ringing. Yet. She pulled the list of 'off-sick' postmen from the chaos and waved it at Batten. Like a white flag, Hazel?

'There are three postmen on it - slipped on the ice, all of them. And the cross-checking's in the diary.' *When I've finished the other nine jobs you've given me!*

Batten cast his mind back to his own days as a Detective Constable, swamped by 'conflicting priorities', learning fast that murders are murder to manage. Was he wasting his time - and Hazel's - on postmen? And were the rest of the team wasting theirs on newspaper boys, on private delivery firms, on any Tom, Dick or Jane with any reason at all to drop a letter through a seemingly random door?

He saw Ozzie the off-sick postman in The Five Bells, holding a pint of midweek cider in his undamaged hand; saw Terence Veech holding a sick-note in his. Hazel Timms voice broke through.

'So, yes, I do have the sick-list. And, yes, the cross-checking interviews are scheduled. And, before you ask, sir, yes, Terence Veech is top of the list. Sir.'

Batten diverted some of his own tasks to Eddie 'Loft' Hick, reminding him not to file them in his loft, with the other crap. Then he lifted

Terence Veech from Hazel Timm's desk and put him on his own - or in his car, at least. He drove to The New Levels Surgery, wondering which bright spark came up with a name like that.

'Have you got an appointment? We're very busy if you haven't got an appointment. Have you?'

Batten stared back at the acid glare of the 'receptionist' whose name badge said she was a Joy. His dislike of any jobsworth was ingrained, but he had a special hatred for those who couldn't even muster a smile. Joy seemed not to care that folk turning up at a doctor's surgery are already feeling like shit. For a full five seconds, he showed 'Joy' what an unsmiling face might look like in a mirror.

'I *said*, we're extremely busy' - she gestured at the ice outside - 'you *must* have an appointment. *Have* you?'

He flipped an unsmiling warrant card under her nostrils. And he wasn't bloody well going to explain himself to the cow. He could do stand-offs. Had the certificate. The silent impasse grew louder, till Joy crumbled, throttled her phone and breathed Snow Queen icicles down it.

Doctor Pym wasn't much better, his smile so deadly Batten silently renamed him Doctor Grim. Terence Veech, the postman in question, was one of Pym's patients. His medical records were up on the screen, but Batten wasn't getting a look at them - no chance.

'Ye-es, fell down while bird-watching', Pym said, checking his PC. 'I remember distinctly - unusual story, his. But true. He's a twitcher, and it turns out he has his very own bird-hide - portable of course - and he plonked it too near the edge of a dry stream, poor man. *It* fell, and he of course with it, down a bank and onto gravel and rocks. Technical term is 'arse over tip'?' Dr Pym gave another false smile. Batten failed to return it, by policy. The Doctor took further refuge in the PC screen.

'Upshot was, he broke two ribs. And severe bruising. Painful.'

'Presumably you signed him off work? Gave him a sick-note?'

Pym corrected him. 'A *Doctor*'s note, Inspector. That's the term we use, for accuracy.'

Batten gave Pym an Inspector's note: two sharp eyebrows.

'It will of course have been recorded…'

Keys tapped. Batten imagined the data was already there on the screen, and the tapping was entirely about control. He tapped his own loud finger on the desk.

'Let me see...anti-tetanus jab...painkillers...ah yes, *and* a Doctor's note. For seven days.'

Pym's eyes danced from the screen to the wall-clock. Batten showily looked at his watch.

'He *was* in a state, Inspector. Had it been me, I would have signed *myself* off. I did not do so out of sympathy -'

You can believe that, Zig, eh?

'- nor because he happens to deliver our mail. Our very own postman, Mr Veech. That's why we know him. Certainly not because he's a regular patient – only two appointments since he registered.' He scanned the on-screen records again. 'Yes, two, in four years - we like that. Patients who appear when actually ill. Do you know the collective noun for 'patients'? Well, I shouldn't say it, because I do still think of medicine as a vocation, but *my* version, invented of course, is a Glut. A Glut of Patients. Because that's what we have.'

He flicked another sly glance at the clock.

'Right, so the second appointment would have been recent, then. A bad fall, on the ice?'

'Recent? Not at all. Over two years ago. And it was certainly not a fall on the ice, Inspector. It was in the middle of July. A touch of plantar fasciitis.'

'A touch of what?'

Doctor Pym gave Batten a 'got-you' look.

'Why, Inspector, I thought you would have heard of it. Rather painful inflammation of overworked tissue, mostly affecting the heel? Commonly known as Policeman's Foot?'

Batten ignored the jibe. July?

'*July*? That can't be right.'

Doctor Pym resented the suggestion.

'Not right? Of course it is. I would have the NHS, the BMA and the Government down on me like an avalanche if it was not - and deservedly so.'

'Are you sure there's not a more recent visit? Could he have seen a colleague? A locum? A nurse?'

Doctor Pym was not amused.

'Even if he had - and he *did not* - it would be recorded. He would not have made it past Reception.'

Yes, Zig. Joy would have chopped his bloody legs off, instantly curing his plantar fasciitis. Batten wondered if Pym was right. He produced a copy of Veech's sick-note and flipped it across the desk.

'How do you explain this, then?' he asked.

Special Doctor Grim specs peered at it.

'Mm', he said. 'Yes, the date is recent, and it looks a little like my signature. But, thankfully, it isn't.'

'Why so sure?' As far as Batten was concerned, the squiggle could have been written by a chimpanzee.

'Why, Inspector? Several reasons.'

He began to enumerate them on his fingers. Batten stopped himself wondering where the fingers might recently have been.

'One: forgery is an issue, so we are ultra-careful. Two: the date fails to correspond to our - extremely accurate - treatment records. Three, and most significantly: the code number on the note - bottom left, there, in a smaller font - fails to correspond to the batch number on any 'sick-notes' we have ever issued. If Mr Veech requested - and was granted - a *Doctor*'s note, it did not come from this doctor - *moi* - nor did it come from any other doctor or locum at this practice, because, Inspector, *this* note is not coded to this practice. Full-stop.'

'Coded? When you say 'coded'…?'

'Inspector. Our Doctor's notes are pre-printed. On a pad. Ours still have an integral carbon copy, though digitization will doubtless consign such things to the museum. More significantly, the notes have a code number which is part of a batch. When we start a new pad, the batch numbers are logged into the system. Rather like the numbers on the replacement cheque-book your bank sends you, yes?'

Batten's plod-feet tingled.

'This note' - Pym waved it with disdain - 'did not. originate. from here.' He looked squarely at the wall-clock now.

Batten was thinking of the implications. And wishing Terence Veech was in custody. Suspicion rumbled, like a stomach that's been empty for days.

'What happens when you run out? Of sick-notes?' He said 'sick-notes' deliberately.

'We do not 'run out', Inspector. *We* have a stock-control system which, when our supply is low, triggers an order to our official supplier, using our specific security password. Each pad has batch numbers, in a sequence. Which we carefully *log,* the moment it arrives.'

Pym's patience had expired. Batten's too.

'Arrives? How?'

Doctor Grim's eyeballs scoured the ceiling.

'Arrives? In the *post.* How else would it arrive?'

Twenty eight

Minutes after pulling into a parking space near the two-thirds-empty cafe, a silent driver's hands swapped the cold steering wheel for a warm cup. The newspaper was for staring at today, and the quiet of the cafe was a healing balm, drawing out wounds, floating them away on the steam of tea.

The peace snapped and crumbled like a biscuit as two men in Royal Mail uniforms flung the door open, dragging in frozen air and guffawing louder than the Laughing Policeman. And did they have to sit so close, jabbering away in the booth right behind, one *snorting* tea down his throat, the other punctuating his slurps with a phlegmy smoker's cough? Sorting offices must be noisy places. Raise your voice to be heard? Or because you like the sound of it?

'You been interviewed yet?' asked tea-snorter.

'Interviewed? Haven't even applied.'

'Not for a job, you wanker. By the police.'

'Why, what have I done?'

'I dunno. What *have* you done?'

'I've done nothing. I just go to work. What are them things called?'

'*What?*'

'Those oblong paper things?'

They both said it at the same time.

'*Letters!*'

The first postman snorted a cackle, the second a mucous-riddled cough. All but one customer looked round, annoyed, but the cafe owner knew his Royal Mail regulars, and how much they spent.

'What about you, then? Interviewed *you*, have they?' asked cough-factory.

'Nope. I'm innocent.'

'Innocent, you? Cuh.'

'Innocent - because I don't deliver where the plod are looking.'

'Oh yeh, where's that?'

'Stockton Marsh, Einstein. I thought everybody knew. Is gossip *banned* at your depot?'

'I don't listen to gossip.'

'You won't wanna hear mine then.'

'Won't I?'

'Nope.' Tea snorted down a throat. Then, thank god, a moment's silence.

'Aw, you git,' coughed the second postman. 'Try me.'

Two sets of elbows moved closer in conspiracy.

'Well, there's four of 'em deliver up there-'

'Up where?'

'You deaf? Stockton Marsh!'

'Ah, right.'

'And, they've all been interviewed, about anonymous letters, and more than once, I can tell you. But who was specially taken off his shift for the fuzz to interview again? Do you wanna know?'

'No.' A laughing cough. 'Course I bloody do!'

'Well. It's Veechy. *The Birdman.*'

'I don't know any birdman. You don't mean that actress, do you?'

Tea-snorter gave his oppo a look of total bemusement. '*What*? What bloody actress?'

'Ingrid. *Ingrid Birdman!*' Cackling hacks spluttered out across the cafe. A man at the table in front plonked a desperate hand over his cup, to protect the contents.

'You pillock. I'm talking about Veech. Or *Terence*, as he insists on being called. I call him Tel, on purpose, but my lot call him *The Birdman* - because he *is*. He's a twitcher. Not a single joke in his repertoire, but he knows the name of every bloody bird that flies in of a winter and flies out again in spring. Tried to get me to join the RSPB. *Me!*'

'RSPB? What's that?'

'Royal Society for the Prevention of Birds, you thick git. Do y' know, Veechy's got his own bird-hide?'

'What, where he hides birds? I had one, but the wife found out.' Cough. Cackle.

'*Pratt.* Anyway, word is, the plod are onto something with old Veech.

179

That they think he's *the one*. No surprise, way he looks at you.'

'What, is he bit, you know?'

'That's just it. He's not a bit anything.'

'Ah, been neutered, has he?'

'Cuh, nothing to neuter. Already missing.' A draining slurp. 'You seen the time?'

'Nope. Haven't looked.'

Tea-snorter rolled his eyes and waved a stainless steel diver's watch at smoker's cough.

'Well, look then! We're overdue.'

Two loud, refreshed postmen coughed and snorted from the cafe, bustling past the much-relieved incumbents. They failed to notice a silent tea-drinker, pretending to do the crossword while recording every snorted cough of information about Mr Veech, who warranted the very close attention of the police. *Terence* Veech, the postman who maybe slips anonymous letters through the door, with the rest of the mail. Terence Veech, the strange Birdman with his own bird hide, who watches birds.

And perhaps people, too.

Twenty nine

Ball put the phone down and gave his Inspector a thumbs up. Through the glass panel of his office, Batten's reply was a satisfied nod. He got to his feet. All the ducks in a row now.

'Hazel?'

He's done it again. Just appeared at my desk, from nowhere. Already late, she was just about to reach for her bag and coat.

'Sir?'

'Any chance you can do another hour? Two, tops? That list of postmen? Need to cross-check the elims, for first thing tomorrow. Can't afford clutter when we bring Veech in.'

Hazel Timms dropped her hand back on the desk she thought she'd done with for today. Who could she call? Who was left? She'd used up every ounce of neighbourly goodwill. You're in the red, now, Hazel. Curse of the only child. You're 'it'.

'Um...' She would have to tell him. *Sorry, sir, dependent parents at what passes for home, cancel the unpaid overtime please.* And cancel CID, Hazel. This isn't Inspector Batten of The Welfare Trust. And bloody Nina Magnus is just sitting there, earwigging, having a gawp. 'Um, well, sir...'

'I'm at a loose end, sir,' Magnus said. 'I can stay on, if you like?'

Batten looked at Timms. That peculiar blank expression he'd almost grown used to. He looked at Magnus, smiling, nodding. He shrugged, gave the file to Magnus. As long as it gets done.

'Fine. You know what to do, Nina. Leave it on my desk.'

And he was gone. Timms stood up, grabbed her coat, bag, keys. She gave Magnus a look, curious, uncertain. She'd grown used to being 'it'. She didn't think there was any other way.

'Um, thanks', she said, her pale face colouring. 'Sorry. Um. Look, I need to go.'

Nina Magnus understood. She watched Hazel Timms dash for the car park, for another hard shift at 'home'.

Checking Batten wasn't in earshot, Magnus phoned Mike, apologized. Got him to cancel their table at The Raj Tandoori.

It was Jeff's idea, to put the Twitter account on her phone.
'You get instant news, if thieves hit a sheep farm. You know, nearby. Warns you - to keep a look-out on your own flock.'
And for safety's sake, you always took your shotgun, Jeff, didn't you? Scilla Wynyard unlocked the gun cupboard and removed hers. Twitter had spoken. Thieves in the vicinity. She stuffed blank rounds in her right-hand pocket, live rounds in the left. Jeff's dad had taught her: L for left. L for live.
She checked Twitter once more, and noticed the Avon and Somerset Police logo. Huh, seen it plenty of times, just lately. Even the cops tweet now.
If you have information regarding anonymous letters delivered to domestic properties in South Somerset, please come forward...
She read the tweet again. Letters? Plural? How many? Till the rumours about poor Jean Phelps seeped out, you thought you were the sole cursed recipient, Scilla, didn't you? Yes, and I can still recite every foul word of the letter that came through *my* door! Against her will, phrases re-formed across regretful eyes.
The 'you' in the letter was Jeff, the police thought. Scilla hoped they were right, but felt doubly cursed for thinking it.
Your body too shall plummet down the winding staircase of death.
Was this supposed to be some cruel jibe at Jeff by an unknown foe? Some vicious reference to Jeff's body falling to the ground?
And the cold earth shall claim you.
Well, it had. The funeral was days ago. She buried Jeff in Stockton Marsh churchyard, not far from where he was shot. Scilla Wynyard stared at the walls of her converted cowshed. Cold and cramped for two. But now, for *one*? An echo. A desert. Her eye fell on the cardboard box where she also buried the unpaid bills.
And the fruits of your sin shall be denied you.
Not tonight, they won't. The police had returned Jeff's red pick-up truck, and it sat outside. Scilla Wynyard pocketed Jeff's car-keys, and grabbed the gun he'd taught her how to shoot.

Andrew Priddle had no idea Somerset Police used Twitter, but then he wouldn't know Twitter from a side of venison.

If you have information regarding anonymous letters delivered to domestic properties in South Somerset, please come forward...

He was old-world, pre-digital. He read the same message in black ink on white paper, on a fresh flyer pinned to the Police section of the Parish Council Notice Board. He read it again, squinting through the glass as the light faded. When circumstances demanded, he dropped in to Stockton Marsh, in the invisible old car he'd bought now, not the van. Once he'd done what needed doing, he dropped invisibly out again. He looked over his shoulder, both ways. He was alone in the deserted street. It was too bloody cold to be outdoors.

Should've stayed in the Blackdown Hills, Andrew. Watch the new large-screen telly, feet up on the clean sofa, a care-free boiler pumping out heat. He read the flyer for a third time. The words hadn't changed. Anonymous letters. And the police seeking information...

His thick coat could not prevent an icicle forming at the base of his skull, the cold of it chilling his neck, his spine. Chilling his fingers, that only this morning had eased more banknotes from his ample supply. Locked away, Andrew. Safe.

Unless someone other than you knows where? Cold seeped from fingers to arms and chest, to the pit of his stomach. It chilled him all the way down to his toes, planted on the icy, hated pavement of Stockton Marsh, where yet more frost was forming.

It was almost dark. Time.

Go home, Zig. Dawn raid tomorrow, so an early night won't go amiss. He sensed twitching shadows outside his office door, and knew immediately who it was.

'What the matter, Hickie? Has the Government banned bacon sandwiches?'

Hick hoped not; he could use one right now.

'No, sir. It's guns, sir.'

''What, they've banned *guns*?' Batten wished they would. He'd spent half the afternoon discussing the odds of Terence Veech having an 8-bore shotgun cocked and ready in his hallway.

'Andrew Priddle's gun, sir. 'S'what I mean.'

'Andrew Priddle hasn't got a gun, Hickie. You checked, remember?'

'Then's then, sir. Now's now.'

Batten was too tired for a philosophical debate on the nature of time. He was late already. He wanted to be home, but Hick twitched more violently still, magma rumbling up from legs to chest, ready to erupt through a fissure in the top of his head.

'Spit it out, Hickie. Out with it.'

'I've done a bad thing, sir. I went back.'

'In time?'

'*No*, sir. Back to his house, Andrew Priddle's. But he wasn't in. Again. But it's the rat skulls, sir.'

Eddie 'Loft' Hick had the knack of retaining a logical train of thought in his own mind, while destroying all sense of one in the person he was talking to. Magnus once described him as a multiple-choice question on legs - each leg heading in a different direction. Batten had learned to wait five seconds.

'I've got one here, sir.' Hick waved an evidence bag.

'Does that contain what I think it does?'

'Yes, sir. Evidence.'

'No, Hickie, I mean-'

'Rat-skull evidence, sir. Shall I let you see?'

Batten fell back on Hick's favoured method of communication - silence and a jerky wave of his hands - and Hick opened the bag. True to his word, he drew from it the white bleached skull of what city-boy Batten could only assume was a rat. He peered at it, as Hick's report on his last visit to the Priddle residence came vaguely back to him. He'd skim-read it, that day, along with thirty other documents.

'It's these things here, sir. The holes.' Hick's fingernail tapped at half a dozen small round holes in the back of the skull. 'I give the skull to Andy Connor in Forensics, and he said they were likely what I thought. And I picked up a few of these and handed them over.' He pulled a small see-through evidence bag from the pocket of his Oxfam jacket and held it up. Shotgun pellets.

'Tell me it's an 8-bore and they're tungsten-steel.'

'Can't, sir. Andy says it's lead, and from the pattern and weight, it'll be a .410. Near as dammit.'

Guns were not Batten's specialism, but he knew what a .410 was.

'A poacher's gun?'

'Round here they call them that, sir. Popgun, against an 8-bore. But they kill stuff.' He waved the rat-skull-evidence.

Batten was a confusion of guns. An 8-bore killed Jeff Wynyard. Jeff himself owned a 20, Scilla a 28. Keith Mallan had a 12-bore, or used to.

Zig, how many bloody bores does it take to make a shotgun?

A .410 was smaller. But it could kill more than rats. Get close enough and it comfortably downs a man.

A poacher's gun? Keith Mallan was a poacher. And someone had riddled a pack of rats with .410 pellets at Andrew Priddle's house. And Andrew Priddle had shifted stolen venison for Keith. And Keith knew Jeff. And Scilla. And Meg Mallan knew Jeff and Scilla too...Batten looked out of the window. It was pitch black outside, and he had to be up at 5am. He shook himself.

'We'll deal with this after the raid on Veech's place. Better write it up, Hickie, all of it.' *And use a spell-checker.*

Hick screwed his face into an embarrassed ball. 'Er, well, sir...'

Batten's penny dropped.

'This bad thing you've done, Hickie? Would it have anything to do with search warrants?'

'No, sir. It wouldn't. Well. Yes, sort of. I mean, I didn't have one.'

'You didn't have one when you helped yourself to this rat-skull? And the pellets?'

'Sir'. Hick hung his head. Batten saw a jerky schoolboy wearing a dunce's hat, and standing in a corner.

'Anybody see you?'

Batten wasn't above 'discovering' - during a legitimate search - the very thing he'd found during a rogue one.

'Not a soul, sir. Quiet as a grave.'

Hick was wrong about that.

Chris Ball was already fed up by the time he got home, so was less than pleased when the phone rang as soon as he stepped through the door. That's the trouble with being a cop. Everyone in the village thinks your house is the police station.

'Well if it's been put out, it's out, isn't it? So what's the problem?'

Joe Porrit was walking his dog when he saw it, a fire, in the cricket pavilion. He doused it in no time, with his foot and a fire blanket.

'I thought you'd want to go through it. You know, for clues?'

What I want is a pint of cider. Not to gaze at a piddling pile of embers in the cricket pavilion. Chris Ball was a rugby man, at the best of times. One of the things he shared with Batten was a disdain for cricket. When Batten/Ball first appeared on the duty roster, they'd both taken a fair bit of stick.

'Clues? What, the vandals wrote their name in the smoke, did they?'

'*No.* You know, trace evidence, DNA. Isn't that what you do, these days?'

Ball let out his heaviest sigh. They all watch too much TV, these days.

'I'll send uniform over, Joe. Just make sure the fire's out, and call the fire brigade if you think they're needed. OK? I've only just walked *in*.'

Joe Porrit closed his mobile and harrumphed. Not himself, Chris Ball, these days.

Thirty

Not even a dog-tired Batten was daft enough to shout '*Police!*' and blithely rap his knuckles on the door of a man who might be waving an unlicensed 8-bore shotgun.

Well, Zig, that's exactly what you did last time. Yes, Zig, but he wasn't there, was he? Huh, lucky for you. And your plod feet were only *tingling* then. They're thumping up and down like pistons now. Threatening letters, interception of mail - twice, at least - theft and fraud, for starters. Plenty of grounds for the search warrant sticking out of Ball's back pocket. But next to nothing on the biog sheet sticking out of Batten's. Terence Veech's history was a Children's Home, an independent living centre and the Royal Mail. Apart from his RSPB membership, his name barely appeared on a document. Perhaps he's from Mars, Zig?

Batten sat in his car, parked well down the lane from Terence Veech's lonely house. He hated early morning raids - not because of the early, he could do early - but because the results were often useless. That's not what's on your mind today, Zig, is it? No, Zig. It's once we're inside and the search begins. It's what we might find.

What if a Remington typewriter turns up, Zig? White envelopes with a unique watermark? An unlicensed shotgun? And if Veech turns out to be the sod who's threatened Erin and Sian...

The heater was full on so he and Ball didn't freeze. He envied the body armour, bulletproof vests and helmets of the armed police who were clambering - surprisingly silent and agile - from an unmarked van the size of a tank. They looked warmer than he felt. The official 'visit' to Terence Veech's house was fronted by a team of firearms officers, and a team leader who'd already told Batten and Ball in no uncertain terms that 'I call the shots, right?'

Unfortunate use of words, Zig, but your track record is no better so don't gloat, eh? He quietly closed the car doors and he and the search staff followed the armed team as they dispersed around the house. Batten was happy to stay well in the background, crossing all his body parts as guns and helmets shuffled into position.

'ARMED POLICE!'

Loud shouts burst through the early morning stillness, gloved fists hammering on the heavy front door. Silence. Repeat. Silence. With a splintering thud the door was rammed open, smashing against the wall, bouncing off and smashing again. Batten looked at his Sergeant. Both men briefly closed their eyes in appeal. Please, god, no gunfire today.

Helmets and body armour disappeared into the house in a flurry of yells. Then the silence returned. Moments later, the team leader poked his helmet round the broken door, beckoned to Batten. He and Ball followed him in. And gunfire was there none.

DC Eddie Hick was relieved he didn't have to get up at 5am, but was still miffed not to be part of the team giving Terence Veech the once-over. He sat down at his Parminster desk and did what Batten had told him: wrote up his visits to Andrew Priddle's house and his 'chance' discovery of a rat skull peppered with shotgun pellets. After a nudge from Batten, he'd re-written history. This time, he managed to 'observe' a rat-skull sticking out from under a patch of weeds on the public right of way *outside* the Priddle home. Lies and white lies, Eddie.

He did his cross-checking too. Despite his twitchy exterior, he was good at CID - Conscientious, Informed, Dogged and Determined. An hour and a bacon sandwich later, he'd wormed his way through old records of a Somerset weapons amnesty, because the name 'Priddle' popped up there. The uniform who'd signed the chit was PC Jess Foreman. He was one of the 'cider fuzz', as Eddie called rural beat coppers. Hick knew him from previous cases. He picked up the phone.

'Tom Priddle? Now how could I forget old Tom Priddle, Eddie? Meanest old sod this side o' Taunton - and there's plenny to choose from. One o' the smelliest, too.'

Hick could imagine. He'd been to the house.

'Tom didn't zackly *hand in* a gun, if I'm honest. But keep that to yourself - don' want folk thinking I bend the rules.'

Perish the thought, Eddie.

'No, let's just say I did a bit of...persuasion, if you get my drift?'

Hick did. Cider fuzz or not, Jess Foreman was six foot two in all directions.

'See, old Tom had a gun, an' he had ammo, and there were reports of him taking pot-shots at anything that moved - from out his bedroom winder. He couldn't get about, with his legs an' all, but he still had his own way of doing things. No licence for doing it, mind.'

A chuckle began in Foreman's boots and six foot later vibrated the phone.

'I did suggest an option - entirely of his own free will, o' course. Suggested he *choose* to hand it in, the gun. *Voluntarily*. Before I handed *him* in with it! We filled half a room, with that weapons amnesty. Lugers from World War Two, Brownings, a couple of sawn-offs -'

'Destroyed, was it, Jess? The gun?'

'Oh, all of 'em were, Eddie. Steel girder in an office block by now.' Another deep chuckle rumbled out.

'What was it then? Just for the record? Wasn't an 8-bore, I bet?'

'Hoo-oo, old Tom could barely *lift* an 8-bore. An' it'd blow him out the winder soon as he pulled the trigger. No, it was a folder, you've seen 'em. Little poacher's gun. Y'know, a .410.'

Foreman gave a last rumbling laugh as Hick cursed. He scrawled a misspelt note to leave on Batten's desk.

'And I'll tell you what, Eddie. Good job for old Tom we did melt it down. Bloody lethal, it was. Lucky it din' blow the miserly old bugger's face off!'

Though much warmer inside Veech's house than in the frosted lane, Batten and Ball wished they were still outside.

They'd arrived too late, all of them, for the gunfire.

From the doorway of the white sitting room they stared at Terence Veech, spread-eagled on the sofa, arms frozen in place like a mannequin's. They were assuming it was Veech. Half his face was missing. A heavy shotgun lay on the floor at his feet, and a bright-red cartridge had fallen down and perched itself like a red tassel on top of his dislodged carpet slipper.

It wasn't the only thing that was red.

Red-black blood shocked the white upholstery. Shades of splashed thick red were glued into the white sofa and spattered on the white wall behind. Batten could smell the smoky bitterness of gunpowder in the pristine room. It wasn't pristine now. It looked like Jackson Pollock had dropped in, to do a mural.

Batten was quietly relieved when Andy Connor and the Scene of Crime staff took over. His turn would come, soon enough. He and Ball stepped outside, where the cold was welcome.

'The sod's topped himself?'

'Looks like it, zor.'

'Did he get wind we were coming?'

Ball blew out his breath. *How*?

'I'm pissed off,' Batten said. 'Dreamed of getting my hands round the bastard's neck.' *Won't want to touch it now, Zig, will you?*

Ball nodded. Di's sister, Belinda, had pointed out he was wringing his hands lately, for some reason. Now he knew why.

Despite the cold Batten was blazing hot. He walked down the lane, to cool his thoughts. It didn't work. When he trudged back, Doctor Benjamin Danvers was getting out of his car. Don't worry, Zig, the doc's bound to cheer you up.

'Ah, Inspector,' Danvers said, as he pulled on crime-scene clothing. 'Chilly weather for death, mm? When my time comes, I would hope to shuffle off the mortal coil in more tropical climes. A sandy beach, a cocktail in hand, perhaps? Expansive view of the azure sea and the vast awaiting sky, no?'

If he doesn't get on with it, his dispatch'll come a lot sooner, Zig. Danvers took the silent hint.

'Rrready to pronounce', he said. 'Now, where would Mr Body be?'

Batten pointed, and Danvers waddled off. Ball shook his head; Batten rolled his eyes. It was just an act, they knew. Last year, at one especially disturbing crime-scene, both men had watched quiet tears drip down the Doctor's cheek.

Who'll shed a tear for Terence Veech, Zig?

Who?

Andy Connor called a reluctant Batten back in.

'Can't be definite yet, Zig, but there'll be plenty.'

Batten winced at the crime-scene. Plenty enough all ready. Doc Danvers was still doing to Mr Body what the State paid him to.

'The Doc and me seem to be of the same mind, Zig.' Connor lowered his voice. 'Makes a change, eh? Death occurred last night, around eleven, he says, give or take. Single shot- '

'Wouldn't need two, Andy, from an 8-bore bloody shotgun.'

'True enough, Zig. If he'd managed to load it.'

Batten's eyebrows went into overdrive. Andy Connor saved him the trouble of translating them into words.

'The red cartridge on the floor - tungsten steel shot, by the way - it hasn't been fired. And both barrels are empty. Clean as a new pin, but empty. He'd been cleaning it. Fresh oil and all the kit and caboodle laid out on the kitchen table. He'd put newspaper down. Very clean, the house.'

Was clean, Zig. He could already see black swirls of fingerprint powder on a dozen white surfaces. Not to mention the blood.

'What do you mean 'if he'd managed to load it?"

'Half-empty box of cartridges on a side-table by the sofa. Other half in a cartridge bag. Looks like he was stocking up. For some mischief or other?'

Batten thought of Erin. Of Sian.

'Must have been trying to load the gun when he was shot, Zig. But he never even got the breach open.'

'Not a suicide? You *sure*?'

Andy Connor gave Batten one of *his* eyebrows. Don't push it, mate.

'Not unless right after he killed himself, he managed to nip out and hide the gun that killed him. Then nip back in, and arrange himself over there, like that.' Andy waved a latex hand in the general direction of the mannequin on the spattered sofa.

'Well who-?'

'That's your job, Zig. Probably not Jehovah's Witnesses, though, or the pizza delivery man. So far, no sign of fingerprints that don't belong to the victim. Doesn't seem like a house that's had visitors.'

It's had *one*, at least, Zig. But *who*? Batten shook himself awake, trudging after Andy Connor into the gleaming kitchen. Carefully-overlapped sheets of newspaper protected the kitchen table, where a gun-cleaning kit was laid out, each part a perfect hand-span from its neighbour, and all the parts in a neat straight line.

'The killer got in here, Zig.' Connor pointed to the kitchen door, and to a paved path which led to the garage. 'And out, presumably. It was still open this morning, by all accounts, when Jesse James and his gunslingers came round the back.' Like Batten, Andy Connor had mixed feelings about guns, even in the hands of trained cops.

'No sign of forced entry, 'cos it wasn't needed. He she or it either had a key, or, most likely, the door wasn't locked. Found a set of house keys on the body.'

Batten wondered if the man who occupied this isolated house had become forgetful? Or arrogant? Or something.

'Trace evidence? Say yes, Andy.'

Connor hedged his bets.

'A house this clean, if we find anything at all there's a fair chance it's been walked in from outside. But you know the score, Zig. So far, only a faint suggestion of a footprint, over there, heading in.' He jabbed a finger at a marker on the floor, by the back entrance. 'Something and nothing, not even enough to say man woman or child.' Connor paused. There were sensitivities where a 'child' was concerned, and he'd kicked them with a size ten foot. 'It's a smudge at best, but, well...you can see my thinking.'

Yes, Batten could. He saw a killer entering through the kitchen door, having ghosted along the path at the rear of the garage. A killer who must have been watching the house, who saw and heard Terence Veech follow the same path from garage to kitchen, and fail to lock the door. Veech was a tall man, like Batten, but hardly a scarecrow. Yet he needed to load a gun to defend himself.

Batten saw Veech's killer throw open the kitchen door, gun in hand. Saw Veech's shock. Were words exchanged? About what? He saw Veech raise his futile 8-bore shotgun, maybe even pull the trigger, saw his realisation, saw his desperate dash towards the box of cartridges. An empty gun against a loaded one. Pursued, he got as far as the white sofa. No longer white.

'What was Veech doing in the garage, Andy?'

'Interesting question, Zig. Come and look.'

More often than not, Norm Hogg and his smelly black mongrel tottered down the road for a mid-morning snifter in The Jug and Bottle. He walked himself and the dog past its open door today.

'We's not welcome', he told the dog. 'Been warned off, we have', he said, as if it was the dog's fault.

Last night, the cider was dryer and stronger than ever, and Norm had glugged more than was good for him. It loosened a tongue that never needed lubrication, but got plenty regardless.

'All this bad luck, it began at thar Wassail', he told anyone who would listen. 'Wrong shotguns, wrong places. Supposed to drive evil spirits away, not invite 'em in. Shedding blood all over an orchard floor! Only one thing 'appens when you do that. In they come, every evil spirit in South Somerset! We conjured 'em *up*! Brought 'em down on our heads! And have they gone?'

His companions looked over their shoulders, worried now.

'*No*! They have *not*!'

Rita Brimsmore, The Jug and Bottle's no-nonsense owner, gave Norm a beady eyeball, which he ignored.

'An' it's all Chris Ball's fault, there's the truth. Should never 'ave let Jeff Wynyard be a shotgun in the first place, with that farty little pea-shooter of his - and when's Jeff never late? Four proper guns, that's the lore, not two and a pair of unwanteds. Never rid an orchard of evil by goin' 'bout it cack-brained and skew-whiff!'

Rita Brimsmore's other eye flashed. Norm Hogg lowered his voice, but carried on.

'I mean, evil has its ways, don' it? You'll see, in the Spring, when the blossom dies and the bees don't come and poisoned apples kill every tree in the orchard.'

Norm's companions considered a world without apples, a ciderless world.

'An' you can see how evil sends revenge, eh? You can see how it sorted Chris Ball?'

His companions couldn't, even with cider for help.

'By sending down madness! *That's how*. It's filled Di Ball's head with a bucketful of madness! Poured it into 'er. That's what evil's done. And Chris Ball's half-crazy himself from having to deal with it!'

Norm leaned closer still to his cider-drinking confidantes, even as Rita Brimsmore pretended to wipe the clean corner of the bar where they perched.

'An' I'll tell you a secret - I *saw* her, Di Ball, not long back, wandering in the graveyard like a ghost. And not even wearin' a coat! In this weather! Dragged she was, by evil, to where the dead are. Death and evil, pullin' her. Ravin' like a madwoman, she was. An' her eyes were mad too, whiter than the frost, I saw 'em! Oh yes, she's not right in her mind - and it's evil that's done it!'

Norm would have punctuated his announcement with a glug of cider, but he'd already glugged it. He shuffled closer to the pumps and waggled the empty glass at Rita Brimsmore. She crooked a landlady finger at him and drew him to the far end of the bar.

'Norm', she said. 'I've gaat a message for you.'

'A message? For *me*? What message?'

'It's a message fraam them evil spirits o' yours.'

'It's *what*?'

'You're banned, they said, the evil spirits. Don't try drinking here again, they said, naat till you've washed your mouth out. You'll naat be served.'

Norm Hogg garnered a few choice words for Rita, a mere woman. But two dark gimlet eyes discouraged him.

'If there's no warmth in your heart, Norm, for folk in pain, then I feel saary for you.'

Norm's hand still gripped his glass. His empty glass. He began to protest.

'You can't-'

'Norm', said Rita. 'One more word and the only cider you'll ever drink here is the cider you'll drown in. Now *go!*'

Norm Hogg slid from his bar-stool with a final look of defiance. Well, he said to himself, you was right, Norm. He shuffled away, slamming the pub door behind him. You was right, about evil spirits.

They're still here!

The garage where Terence Veech kept his van was as pristine as the house used to be. Batten counted four numbered markers, planted next to each seat of evidence.

'We've got a devious sod here, Zig.' Connor pointed at a thick wooden block lying on the workbench. It looked like a railway sleeper. 'One of the slabs that cover the inspection pit, there.'

Batten saw five more sleeper-size blocks, set into a recess in the garage floor. The pit looked unused, as bleached and clean as the rest of the place. There was a gap over the pit where a sixth block had been removed.

'Take a close look at number six, if you'd be so kind.'

Batten did. It was hollow, lined with some kind of oiled cloth, and strengthened with rods. A tight-fitting lid was fashioned from the same wood. Inside, he saw two compartments, one long and round, the other chunkier.

'The barrel and the stock?'

Connor nodded. 'Bloody clever place to hide a gun.'

'Well done for spotting it, Andy.'

'Not sure we would've, if the cunning sod hadn't been inconvenienced. Which isn't to say my boys and girls are half-blind.'

He pointed at the second marker, which sat next to a heavy club-hammer.

'The head's been cleaned and re-oiled, Zig. Do you know, every tool in here has. Not a single spot of rust or a blemish to be found. Except by us, of course.'

He gave a smug laugh and pointed to the handle.

'Metal dust. Faint, but useful, forensically-speaking. 'Specially when our hawk-eyed genius over there spots a tiny bit of metal jammed behind that work-bench.'

An embarrassed but pleased Forensics officer smiled back at Connor, and carried on scratching names and dates on evidence bags. Batten peered down at the third marker.

'Take my word for it, Zig. It's the letter 'x'. Snapped off an old-fashioned typewriter. And when I get it to the lab, a pint of cider says it'll be a Remington. Another pint says the metal dust'll be from a Remington too. No sign of the rest of it, but interesting, all the same?'

'Indeed it is, Andy.'

Batten weighed up the connections.

A concealed 8-bore shotgun which clearly belonged to Veech - despite the lack of a licence?

A typewriter clubbed into dust - apart from one metal 'x'?

A postman - *ex*-postman, Zig - who types anonymous letters and has no trouble whatsoever delivering them?

Did the corpse next door belong to the man who blew away Jeff Wynyard's face with a shotgun?

'The 8-bore, Andy? Murder weapon, from the orchard?'

Connor shrugged. 'Slow down, Zig. Gimme chance to test it. But given you don't believe in coincidence...'

'Suspicious of 'em, Andy. I'll go that far.'

'Either way, you'll not see many 8-bores nowadays. Collector's piece. Or a knock-off that got under the wire.'

Batten would bet cider on it, even against Andy Connor, who could down the stuff faster than Chris Ball and Norm Hogg put together. But what of the other recipients of Mr Veech's typing skills?

'Any green paint here, Andy?'

'Now, we did look, Zig, as close as ever. But if it was Veech who decorated Ms Phelps' car, I doubt he stirred his pots of rainbow in here, before or after. We'll test all the brushes, blahdiblah. *Could* be him, and maybe he cleaned up elsewhere? Or...'

Damn, Zig. Loose ends. He hated loose ends. Did Veech have an accomplice, to splatter green paint on an inoffensive car? Or is someone else writing letters too? Someone also keen on vendetta? Batten rammed his hands into cold pockets. If it's not ruled out, Zig, it's still ruled in.

'You haven't asked me about his white van, Zig. Not losing your touch, are you?'

Batten hadn't missed the van. How could he? It was old but spotless, and glaring at him. He didn't tell Andy Connor the correct name was *glacier*-white. Arctic weather outside, Zig, and next door a stone-cold corpse laid out on a snow-white sofa. Will winter never end?

The back doors of the van were open, and more numbered markers had been placed inside. Batten saw a tripod, a large pair of binoculars, the kind that bird-watchers use, and two rolls of some sort of loose, drab cloth. He pointed at them.

'What are these, Andy? Don't tell me Veech was into knitting?'

'We gave these a good delve, Zig, in case he was hiding something - and in a manner of speaking he was.'

Connor tapped a gloved finger on the smaller of the two rolls.

'That's a bird-hide, Zig. You know, what twitchers use, so the birds don't spot 'em while they're spotting the birds. It's basically a camouflaged tent. You sit in it, and there's a hole for your camera and binocs.'

A recurring phrase in the anonymous letters leapt at Batten. *I am the watcher...* He pointed at the larger roll.

'What's this then? An over-sized marquee for watching *albatross*?'

'Now, now, Zig. Sit tight, you'll enjoy this. We've fine-tooth-combed it for trace, so I think we can safely do a demo.'

He beckoned to two Scene of Crime staff and did a little mime with his hands. Batten watched the stage magician's act. The thin camouflage cloth was unrolled and he saw gaps in it where apertures had been cut out. His penny dropped, once more, as the SOCOs draped the netting over the glacier-white van, sliding the apertures over windows and windscreen, lights and grill. But not, he noticed, over the number plates. Simple hooks, ties and sticky pads held the skimpy netting flush and firm in place. The glacier-white van disappeared. Batten stared at the new one.

It was bloody-muddy-brown.

Ball could only manage a shrug when Batten showed him Veech's transformed van. He was too tired for excitement. Crime scenes eat time, and this one had swallowed all of his. He could barely remember getting up this morning. It had been pitch dark and cold. The light had gone now and it was pitch dark and cold again.

All the same, he was quietly relieved about the van, for the sake of Scilla Wynyard and Jean Phelps, whose access to brown vans now seemed less relevant. He said none of this to Batten, because he knew what the answer would be. Hick's parody of Batten's northern twang was still fresh: *if it's not ruled out, it's still ruled in.*

'So we've got a murder, zor? Not a suicide? And not with an 8-bore after all?'

'Looks that way, Ballie.'

Both men sighed. Three steps forward, two steps back. Someone's permanently arrested an armed killer – before the police could. All we need do now is catch the someone. And get a rogue gun off the streets, before 'someone' uses it again...

'Andy Connor's hedging his bets as usual, but he says from the shot pattern and the pellet size he's guessing a much lighter weapon.'

They were thinking the same thoughts now, if from different angles. Batten was assessing likely suspects. Ball was thinking how little physical strength one needs to shoot a smaller gun.

'Didn't suggest it was a .410, zor, did he? You know, a poacher's gun?'

'And he didn't suggest it wasn't. Sergeant. He says he'll tell us soon, whenever the doc finishes picking pellets out of Veech's skull.'

Batten never understood why someone would make a career of that. '*And what do you do, old boy?*' *Me? I work with the dead for a living.*

Huh, you should talk, Zig.

'So we'll be sending invites to an interview party, zor, over at Parminster?'

'*I* will, Ballie. You'll be getting off home early.'

Ball's protestations hit a cloth ear.

'Veech's house has a lot of rooms. You'll be leading the deep search, soon as we have daylight. Every nook and cranny, mind, every floorboard. Paper and envelopes, top of your list. Make'em look at everything.'

Because you have to find out *why*, Zig, don't you?

'For all we know, he might still have an un-posted pile of nasty mail, ready to go. Veech might be dead, but plenty of other folk need closure.'

He stopped himself saying *and they mostly live in your village.*

'And while you're there, unearth a neon sign with the killer's name etched on it, eh?'

Ball humphed. In your dreams.

'Now go get some sleep. I want you all bushy-tailed and hawk-eyed at sparrow fart. Clear?'

Ball raised his hands in submission, and Batten watched his broad back grow smaller. Di Ball needed her husband home, he told himself, though whether true or false he had no idea. His other reason for sending his Sergeant off was less transparent. He wanted to have a crack at Keith Mallan, without Keith's old school chum in the room.

Thirty one

Chris 'Crystal' Ball's homecoming was a mixed affair. Slogging back to Stockton Marsh after an early start and a late finish, he'd barely stepped through the door when Di tried to throw him out again.

'*No guns!*' she hissed, '*No guns!*' Was it gunpowder she could smell on her husband's clothing?' Or did heightened senses help her guess where he'd been? She trembled and shook and hissed. '*No Guns!*'

Ball bit his tongue, once more. At least her lips had formed a pair of sounds that were almost words. With Belinda's help he calmed Di down. They compromised. A shower, a change of clothes, clean hair. A pill for Di, a cider for him. Why not try it the other way round, Chris?

But it was only Di's lips that tried to hiss 'No Guns.' In her mind, she was saying 'No Death.' The words swirled around like black rainclouds in her skull, acid showers of thought spinning and spinning as they had done for days, for days, for days - no death no death no death no death no death no death no... Senses and memories, biting her into confusion. The smell of guns, from the Wassail was it? And Chris, yes, the smell of guns on him, how dare he turn up here like that? There was an orchard, wasn't there, and a dead man? And Chris must have had a gun and shot Gemma, in the orchard, buried her, and they made Di go to the grave but it was too cold and much too small and they - too young, so young - they couldn't carve her age into the stone. She'd killed Gemma, must have, must have shot her. *No!* Chris did that, yes, with his gun? No, no, he didn't have a gun, never had a gun, nor she, never would, no. NO! *NO GUNS!*

Did she say that aloud, or in her head? Belinda's looking at me, staring. Chris staring too. He's washed his hair. When did he do that? There's dust on the carpet, gunpowder, is it? Clean the carpet, Di, wash it, scrub it. *Stop looking at me!*

But they looked, and they listened.

'No death. Please. We must have no death.'

That's what Di said, what she said out loud.

'No death. Please.' She said it again, the spinning swirling no-death mantra in her skull finding its long lost way into her throat. The words joined up, leaking out past her un-blackened, un-destroyed lips and teeth and tongue.

And she was heard.

Batten hadn't gone home at all. Too much to do. Murder galvanises everyone. Except the victim, Zig. The interview rooms were full - but not of witnesses. None of those. A distinct shortage of those.

He put down the phone. Andy Connor had confirmed their suspicions. The gun was 'almost certainly' a .410. A poacher's gun, which could be folded, and easily concealed beneath a coat.

Batten stepped back into the room where Keith Mallan sat on a steel chair at a steel table. Keith's sort-of-wife, Meg, was in the interview room next door. Scilla Wynyard and Jean Phelps didn't know it yet, but they would shortly experience the rat-a-tat of police knuckles. Andrew Priddle would have been high the list, if only because Batten had yet to work out what he was *for*. But 'young what's-his-name' and his muddy-brown van were in Wonderland, or Narnia, or maybe Mordor. His rotting house was pitch-black, and empty as a grave. They had no grounds for a search, in any case.

'O' course I knows what a poacher's gun looks like! I used to be a gamekeeper, din' I?'

Keith Mallan was as unhelpful as before, but at least he smells better, Zig. Meg's influence? Or fresh clothes, bleach, a long shower and a scrubbing brush - to get rid of gunshot residue?

'Yes, Keith, you did. You're not one anymore though.'

Mallan managed a sigh. He used to be a lot of things. Gamekeeper. Poacher. Abattoir man. Used to be a husband, too. He wondered where Meg was, wondered what she was doing, right now.

'No', he said. 'Not anymore. I'm not anything, now. Nothing.'

Batten cut across, before the Country and Western music swelled.

'So where is it? Your poacher's gun? Rented out, is it, to poachers?'

'Told you. Don' 'ave one.'

He hoped it was still where he'd hidden it. Fifteen year old poacher, cuh. Made a noise like a herd of deer, trying to creep through the undergrowth.

Got him by the neck, gut-punched him till he puked, teach him a lesson. Kicked the kid's arse and confiscated his gun, a little .410. And the cartridge bag, too. Come and reclaim them, anytime. And meet the Magistrate while you're at it. Never saw the little twerp again. And it was handy, that folding gun.

The twitching face of Keith Mallan reminded Batten of Eddie Hick. He changed direction.

'Last night, Mr Mallan? Just confirm your whereabouts, will you? Or did you bring a sick-note?'

'Sick-note!' spat Mallan. 'Told you. Was with Meg.'

'Oh yes, so you said. Spring-cleaning, the pair of you?'

'Talking. Told you. We was talking.'

'And what time would that have been?' At Keith's miserly rate, a short conversation could last till Doomsday.

'She's in a Bed and Breakfast place, over Lopen way.'

Batten knew. They'd collected her, dragged her to the station in a huff.

'Midnight, suppose. 'S'when she kicked me out.'

'Kicked you out? Awww. No nocturnal nookie, eh, Keith?'

Batten removed an image of a ripe Meg Mallan from his overactive mind. Soon be seeing her flesh in the flesh, Zig. And it'll be instructive, hearing what *she* says. He glanced at his notes.

'Seven till midnight, you said. And just talking. Long time that, even for you.'

'I took her to The Sailors. She's gonna be barmaid there, starts next week.'

Not if she's in custody, Keith. The Sailors' Rest had confirmed the arrival of Meg and Keith around seven or so, because they knew Meg from before. Pub restaurant till ten, then out the pair of them went.

'Between ten and midnight you were at the B&B, that right?'

'Told you.'

'And are you going to tell me 'no witnesses', too?'

'Witnesses? Was trying to have a private talk. Too many folk wagging their ears in The Sailors.'

Mallan looked at the tape machine, turning. Too many wagging ears in here, as well. He wondered what Meg would say, whenever the police talked to *her*.

Yet another list. Murder spawns many a list, eh, Zig? *Lists.* Erin always wrote one, for the supermarket. At Ashtree, when his fridge was empty, he just clocked the kinds of things he needed and went to the shop. He hated lists. The list on his cubby-hole desk had some awkward names on it.

Scrawled across the top of the page was *Who knows how to shoot a gun?* He ran his finger down the candidates.

Scilla Wynyard? Yes.

Jean Phelps? Says she doesn't.

Andrew Priddle? Old Tom had a .410, and used it, so Andrew might know how.

Keith Mallan? Knows guns backwards. Especially the poacher's version.

Meg Mallan? Says she doesn't.

Nina Magnus had reported Meg Mallan's sworn dislike of guns. But Meg was less definite about when Keith left her temporary bed and breakfast joint.

'Could have been midnight,' she told Magnus. 'We were talking. Not watching a clock.'

'He left without you, presumably?'

'Keith?'

'Oh, there was someone else, was there?'

'Someone else? No. Me and Keith.'

'Talking?'

'*Talking.*'

'Till midnight?'

'Thereabouts. *I said.*'

'And when he left, you stayed?'

'Course. Where else would I go?'

Where? Keith's place? *Veech*'s place? Where indeed?

Batten didn't know either. Not yet.

But he did know there were two other names, at the bottom of his list. General suspects only, nothing specific about them, as far as guns went. But procedure is procedure. This time he'd avoid saying 'it's just for elimination purposes.' He'd fall back on 'technicalities', and other weasel words.

Batten's maxim, *if it's not ruled out it's still ruled in*, was bound to bite him in the bum someday. How best to 'eliminate' Erin and Sian Kemp? How best to deal with the tricky issue of their whereabouts around the time Terence Veech was shot? They had motive, they had opportunity; he doubted they had method and means - but he had no freedom to make assumptions.

Should he send Timms and Hickie? You'll get it in the neck, Zig, if you do, for not sending yourself. Get it in the neck now. Get it over with.

Dog-tired, he did, with Magnus present 'for procedure'. Sian gave him a hard look. Erin's green eyes grew smaller, darker, every time *routine* and *formal* rolled out.

Just as well he needed sleep. He'd be sleeping alone again, at Ashtree, tonight.

Erin Kemp's waning enthusiasm for rehearsing *A Child Of Our Time* was not boosted by Zig's arrival. As soon as she saw DC Magnus standing next to him in the doorway, she knew this was an official visit, nothing else. The visit made it harder still to get Sian into homework mode. Perhaps Granny Kemp would fare better, god help her.

To Erin, the rehearsal was a shambles. She barely hit a note all evening, spent more time apologising than singing in key. She knew every member of the chorus because the chorus was where she began. What would they be thinking? *We* could do better than you, if *we* got a chance to go solo?

Michael, the leader, simply did what they were here to do: he rehearsed. He was consistent, supportive, clear. Erin Kemp used to be all of those things. *The cold deepens*, sang the chorus, and she did her best to sing with them.

After a break, they tried *I would know my shadow and my light*, and she dug in, to prevent tears forming behind her eyes - but not because of the music. Doubt, Erin, doubt. Admit it. You're brimful of the stuff. Too much trouble for Zig now, mm? Or is he too much trouble for you? The conductor's baton flicked towards her, drawing her into the voices. Chorus or solo, Erin? Which do you really want to be?

Why can't I be both? asked a voice in her head.

You can, said another.
But how? asked the first.
It's a question of shadow and light, was the reply.
I only want the light, said the first.
Alas. One doesn't come without the other.
Michael raised his baton.
Deep River, the chorus sang.

It was pitch black and silent, but at least she had yesterday's crossword. It smiled up at her from the kitchen table. A glass of Jeff's cheap whisky smiled up at her too, but she could only scowl back. Scilla Wynyard grabbed the glass, threw the contents down the sink. The few sips she'd swallowed did nothing for her palette and even less for her mind.

She escaped into the crossword. One across was easy, a warm-up exercise. *Skint first, there's the point, and now smashed too [6].* Skint...broke? The point? Of the compass? N for north? Her black pen scrawled 'Broken' into the white space. The whisky bottle was still there, staring.

Two across distracted her. *Only a saint can climb a dizzy height like this - or a guitarist [8, 2, 6].* An anagram perhaps? Saint is St. And with 'height like this', that's 16 letters, the total in the answer. *Dizzy* means jumbled up, no? She jumbled up the letters, looking for the name of a guitarist. The 2 could be *of*? No. No *f*. Could it be *de*? Manitas de Plata, the flamenco man? No, Scilla. Wrong letters. Doesn't fit. Maybe not an anagram?

Stuck. The whisky bottle stared. She grabbed it, shoved it back in the cupboard where it belonged. There's drinking, Scilla, and there's thinking. Which are you going to do?

Her gaze returned to two across.

She clicked her pen, like a trigger.

Homework. Sian Kemp usually sped through it. The praise, for doing it well, and being told she was 'making excellent progress'. Huh, not tonight. She was stuck, and mum was out rehearsing. She asked Gran, and they looked at the page together. Gran's eyeballs grew and grew.

'It's algebra, Gran.'

It's double-dutch, Gran's eyeballs said.

Well, Sian, chuck it. Dump it. Tell the teacher you've gone off algebra. And school. And bullies. And postmen. And letters. And the police. And *Zig*. She shoved the homework back in her bag.

She wasn't supposed to know he was planning to arrest a postman. Sometimes him and mum behave as if young = deaf, squared. And then he turns up here again with a load of pants about 'whereabouts' and 'technicalities'.

'You'll be safe, now,' he told the pair of them.

Refused to say why, though, didn't he? Mum went to rehearsal in a sulk.

Well if mum can have a sulk...The words of the letter she shouldn't have read came back to her, made her shiver.

Safe. You'll be safe now, that's what Zig said.

She opened her school-bag. Pulled out her double-dutch algebra homework.

Best to walk away from a crossword, when you're stuck, and walk back later with a clearer head. Scilla Wynyard put out the re-cycling. There wasn't much. Not now. It didn't take her long to trudge across the kitchen to the back door, where the bins were, and to trudge back. Yesterday the little house was an echo. Today it's a postage stamp.

Stop it, Scilla. This thoughtless use of words. House. Postage stamp...Letter. Just do your damn crossword, can't you? Go on, attack it!

Two across stared cryptically up at her from the kitchen table. *Only a saint can climb a dizzy height like this - or a guitarist'* [8, 2, 6]. Not an anagram, then. A pun? A play on words? What do guitarists climb? A scale, a musical scale? And saints? Something to do with plainsong? Saints climbing up plainsong? No, damn it, Scilla, no.

She was tempted to open the cupboard where the whisky bottle sulked, but sometimes answers just arrived, on unseen wings of intuition. She loaded her pen, fired *Stairway to Heaven* at the blank squares. Yes, a saint could climb one of those. And wasn't it a big hit? For Led Zeppelin? Some monster guitar solo? She imagined skilled fingers climbing the fretboard, could almost hear the tune in her head.

You're supposed to be curbing this thoughtless use of words, Scilla. *Stairway to Heaven.* Stairway. Staircase. *The winding staircase of death,* in that damn letter.

Three short paces across her single-storey kitchen, that's all it took. She flung open the whisky cupboard. Drinking now.

She was thinking, too. About the letter. And making herself remember.

Thirty two

The search was taking an age. Terence Veech's belongings were cluttered all over the house - no, hardly cluttered. They were meticulously organised and categorised, arranged, shelved, boxed. Obsessively so - and so many of them. It felt to Hazel Timms like she'd been here since Christmas!

She wished Christmas hadn't popped into her head. Best forgotten. Mum had bought Dad a bottle of his favourite wine, a vintage Bordeaux, but as soon as it was open, on Christmas morning, he accused Mum - and then *you*, Hazel - of plotting to poison him.

It got worse. Mum was in tears and Dad lost his temper, lashed out at Mum again. You had to do it, didn't you, Hazel? Had to use restraint techniques, on your own father, there, on the Wilton carpet, till he calmed down. Had to apply your police training, on Christmas Day, in your own front room. The turkey never made it to the oven. And peace on earth to all men.

Time to decide, Hazel? How much longer can you be a cop all day and then work another shift at night? Or, worse, the other way round. And, sod's law, a murder case. Pressure from above, from below, from everywhere, your time belonging to anybody but you. Personal life? Out the door, away on the wind.

She flexed her latex gloves, covering a yawn with one hand while opening yet another box with the other. A box belonging to a man she'd questioned, face to face, and who seemed neither more nor less suspicious than anyone else on her list.

Batten's concise, northern voice broke in. She hadn't seen him arrive. An instruction, but he chose to couch it more politely as a question. Not always the case, in the Force, she'd found.

'Hazel, when you finish here, can you do that little box room at the end of the corridor? Yes?'

Brisk, he was, not brusque. She'd wanted to throttle him, a time or two. His fault, or hers?

'Sir.'

Terence Veech had rooms enough for a family.

And each room full of more impersonal *stuff*. No-one had yet unearthed a photograph, a memento, a child's drawing. There were none of those worthless bits of tat kept only for their memories. Mum and dad still had some of the naive little paintings she'd done at school, age six - not that they could remember where they were. Hazel Timms tried to imagine a person with no certificates, no pictures of a prize-giving or a school play, nothing at all smiling up from the mantelpiece or the windowsill. The anonymous Mr Veech had no future, and no past. Not the slightest hint of a friend, a sibling or a parent.

'Even you have parents, Hazel, on a good day', she told herself.

Her gloved fingers rippled through a collection of unframed prints. She assumed he had intended to frame them, because most of the wall-space in the spare room was already covered in prints and original paintings - her time with the Antiques Squad told her so - antiquarian maps, samplers, pencil sketches. Terence Veech's personal past may not have been on display, but art history was. He was a collector.

She glanced across the hallway to the adjacent room. When Sergeant Ball set them to work - it felt like a week ago - he awarded himself the short straw and was kneeling on the carpet of what looked like a small library. He was sighing his way through shelf after shelf of book after book, a thousand of them perhaps. Hazel Timms liked books, but a thousand? Gulp.

Ball caught her eye, flicked his eyebrows north in frustration.

'Expect I'll be brainier when I'm done,' he said, with a chuckle.

That he still managed to chuckle at all, given the burden of his wife? Was he a little...lighter today? Or just lighter than you, Hazel?

When Chris Ball left the house that morning it was still dark. But, for the first time in weeks, it was not a lonely exit. Belinda was sleeping, but Di Ball was awake. She said very little when he left, but what she said came out as words.

'Careful. Yes?' And she took his hand.

'Careful,' he nodded. He smiled back at her as the cold engine warmed.

Don't worry his mind said. No guns today. That was yesterday.

Hazel Timms knew she was damn lucky to be working with people like Sergeant Ball, lucky to have fallen in with a good team. Because that's what you did. You fell in. Whether you drowned or swam was pot-luck, to a large degree. Even 'Loft' Hick was OK, once his body came to rest.

She ought to give more back. Would it hurt to 'have a coffee sometime' with Nina Magnus? She'd had more conversations with the folk from the Murder Squad, and they were only passing through.

'Anything?'

She hadn't noticed Batten glide up to her. He managed his team, she'd give him that.

'Lots, sir. But not in the way you mean.'

'I thought with your background' - he meant the Antiques Squad - 'you might spot something or other. Not that *I* have, mind.' Batten was searching Veech's bedroom, and drawing the same blanks.

'It's as if he's collecting history, sir. Art, books' - she waved a hand across the hall - 'to fill his own vacuum. That's what it looks like to me.'

Batten was thinking much the same. Tongue in cheek, he'd imagined a postman collecting stamps, but no stamp albums were in evidence. Veech's bedroom revealed walls hung with seascapes, strictly organised by School. His own sketchy memory spotted Newlyn, Penzance, Staithes. Perhaps Veech dreamed of the sea. He'd get Hazel to take a closer look.

'Any patterns?'

'There's no one thing that's gob-smackingly valuable, sir. But overall value? Well, I'd happily own it, if you see what I mean. Only obvious gap is abstract art. There's none at all. If it's not representational, he doesn't collect it. Literal-minded, maybe?'

Batten allowed himself a sigh. *Something*-minded. 'Crack on, then.' He was gone as quickly as he arrived.

Hazel Timms echoed the sigh, and moved on to the large collection of framed samplers adorning the box room walls.

Andrew Priddle paid cash for the two cheap hold-alls, smiling at the irony as he did so. The glum shop assistant thought he was smiling at her, a cold day somehow warming up.

'Paid cash for a stash for my cash', he chuckled to his wallet.

He'd made a decision, about the money. He would split it into three, hide it in three separate places now, only known to him. A suitcase and two hold-alls.

'And this time', he promised them, 'there'll be no-one to watch us.'

It was signed, the agreement to sell the old man's house. He didn't want to see the bulldozers blow the walls down and trundle their tracks over forty years of filthy weeds, dank stone and bad memories. Once the legitimate money came through he could stop pretending, and behave like a man with cash of his own. A free man.

The journey to Suffolk and back took longer than expected, but he'd made the arrangements. Soon, he would be living on the Suffolk coast, with his own private view of a sea he'd dreamed of.

And many a bloody mile from Stockton Marsh.

'A few quid hanging on these walls too, eh?'

Hazel Timms could only guess. Good quality antique samplers, not too faded, could fetch hundreds. Veech had, what, over two dozen? And not a turkey amongst them.

'Just these walls alone, sir, there's maybe four or five grand. But if that's what you spend your money on...'

She knew what she spent *her* money on. Medicines, repairs, transport, cleaning. Three people, two pensions, one wage. And Terence Veech hung five grand on a wall for nobody but him to see.

'Anything else in here?'

'Still looking, sir. Place is chock-a-block.'

Batten nodded. He'd found a further wall of seascapes, and Ball was still checking book after book. Batten had flicked through one - *How To Build A Wildlife Pond*. In his own garden at Ashtree he was thinking of starting what Veech had almost finished: a nature-friendly pond, with a solar-powered pump and natural filters. His project would be on a much smaller scale than Veech's. Smaller garden, and less time on your multipurpose hands, eh, Zig? He noted the title and author. When he bought his own book, it bloody-well wouldn't be this one.

Snap out of it, Zig. He stepped out into the hallway.

'Sir?'

'Yes, Hazel?' He turned back, to see Timms picking through a sort of padded craft-box, with compartments for scissors and thread.

'You need to see this, sir.'

Batten knelt down as she lifted something from the box. Carefully, he laid a large evidence bag on the carpet, and Timms unfolded a piece of cloth.

It was an oblong of honeycombed material, a sampler in the making. When he'd spotted the bird-hide in the back of Veech's van, he'd jokingly asked Andy Connor 'does Veech do knitting?' No, Zig. He does embroidery.

He and Timms stared at Veech's handiwork. The sampler was in four neat horizontal sections, one above the other. The first said *Letter One*. Next to it, a skilled hand had depicted a line of sheep, in white wool, and below, lying down, a shepherd. Not lying down, Zig. Dead. A lot of red wool was in evidence.

Letter Two had a beige car, crazily picked out with added green, the green threads flowing into a stripe of rainbow. The word *Lie* was added, neatly, in pink wool, as punctuation.

'Ballie! Get in here and have a look at this!'

A curious Sergeant Ball stepped over and knelt down. Batten heard his knee click, an old rugby injury.

'*Four* letters, zor?'

Batten nodded, a gloved finger tapping on the dead shepherd in Letter One, before pointing at *Letter Three*. It took up more of the cloth, because it showed a descending staircase, neatly picked out in black. Red wool stained every step.

Ball's eyes flicked between One and Three, but it was *Letter* Four that his boss now struggled with. Framed in gold thread was a swathe of blue he guessed was an unfinished sea. *My Queen*, it said, above a precisely embroidered image - a child, Batten assumed. The facial features were incomplete, but Batten guessed what they would look like, had Veech lived to finish them. He'd finished the dress, though - a white dress - and an unmistakeable brown cloak and hood, picked out in fur. Wassail Queen fur. The final decoration was a single word: *One.*

Batten clambered to his feet. Veech's bathroom was as bleach-clean as the rest of the house. He threw up, in the ice-white toilet bowl.

Timms pretended not to notice Batten's white-faced return from the bathroom. A concerned Chris Ball rose from the carpet, clicking his rugby knee back into the 'walk' position.

'I can finish up here, zor. Be surprised if there's any more to find.'

He waited for his boss to say *if it's not ruled out, it's still ruled in.* Bash him over the head if he does, Chris, with a framed sampler - there's two dozen of the buggers. One of them a sickener.

But Batten had had enough. Weariness, he told himself. Sure, Zig. And nothing to do with what you found.

'No, Ballie. We'll *all* finish up. Soon be dark. Seal the doors and get uniform onto it.

We can resume tomorrow, when we've had some sleep.'

And when you, Zig, have got your thoughts straightened out. Right?

Leaving Ball to top and tail, Batten drove home to Ashtree, still sick to his stomach.

The morning's post lay on the doormat, a savage reminder. He swept it up, flung it onto the old blanket box he used as a coffee table. He'd given it a polish, and the mail promptly slid off the shiny surface and dropped back on the floor. Cursing, he bent down again.

Anonymous white letters peered up at him. They had fallen on their blank side.

'Sadistic sod, aren't you, Mr Gravity?'

The whiteness continued to stare, and he imagined a pair of hands sliding foul letters into ice-white envelopes, ready for delivery. Before the obvious struck him.

He poured himself a large glass of Speyside and flopped down on the sofa, conflicting thoughts whirling through his mind, fighting for supremacy.

The winner was not anonymous letters. It was a more formidable question: how will you break the news to Erin Kemp? And, lord knows, how will you tell Sian that though she's safe now, there's even worse to come? What can you say to them about Terence Veech and the images in his sampler? Flip open your wafer-thin Police Thesaurus, will you, and conjure up soothing words?

Don't tell them, Zig, only when you have to. It'll be months before it's settled. Or just keep your mouth shut altogether? Sure, Zig, and then burn all the evidence and every newspaper, and smash all the television sets and the radios and the phones and laptops and tablets, and kill all their neighbours and all their friends - so Erin and Sian never have to see or read or hear every sick detail that will be exhumed forensically and recorded professionally, throughout the grim proceedings of the Coroner's Court? And while you're at it, promise Sian Kemp you'll rip out the tongues of every bully at her school, so they can't remind her either. You pratt.

He poured himself a second glass of Speyside. Bit early, Zig, even for you?

Piss off, Zig.

While Batten was pouring whisky into a taut glass over at Ashtree, Ball was ushering his tired team out of Terence Veech's half-searched house and into assorted vans and cars.

'Get off home. I'll wait for uniform. Had an early night last night, didn't I?'

No-one disagreed, relieved as they were to see some lightness return to their Sergeant. Lately, you had to fill out a risk assessment just to talk to him. Predictably, Timms was first away.

'Doesn't hang about, our Hazel, does she?' twitched Eddie Hick.

'Well, lucky Loft, you've only just signed *in*, so you should talk.'

Magnus jangled her keys and slammed the door of her Toyota. Hick watched the car crunch down the frozen hill, wondering why Magnus had suddenly begun to like Hazel Timms.

'There's no understanding women, Eddie. Don't even try.'

He got into his Jeep, drove off.

Ball watched the cars teeter down the icy slope away from Veech's empty house, and pulled his mobile from his pocket. But he didn't call uniform. Neither did he seal the door. Not yet. Instead, he phoned Di, to say he might be late home.

Then he took a powerful torch from his own car, and went back inside.

Thirty three

Ball was a puzzle. Glum, understandably, with Di on his plate. And at breaking point, that day in the graveyard. Then lighter, yesterday, for twenty four hours. This morning, slumped at his monster Parminster desk, his face was dark again. A different darkness, which Batten couldn't fathom. Just get on with it, Zig.

The morning briefing was what it says on the tin. Brief. They all knew about the sampler, knew it was in the safe hands of Andy Connor and his merry men. Batten shuddered at the thought of Connor's forensic trawl revealing some further message. Wasn't there enough already?

He didn't want to go back to Terence Veech's house. How could a place so meticulously clean make you feel as if you'd swum in a sewer? Ball's only contribution was to agree that, yes, it's probably a waste of time.

They went anyway.

Batten did his best to lighten his own mood as he and Ball began their deep search of Veech's kitchen, whirls of zinc powder still staining its whiteness. Once in a while, flicking round the hundred waste-of-space channels on his TV set, Batten had come across old re-runs of *Whose House Is This?* Invariably he switched off, bunged on a CD, or picked up a book.

Now though, searching the dead man's home, it was 'whose house is this?' that popped into his head, even as his gloved hands picked through spick and span kitchenware, arranged in strict categories - colour, size, purpose - a heavy old dog-bowl the only jarring note. Pristine cupboards held dried pulses, quinoa, jars of herbs, pine-nuts, packs of wholemeal linguine, lined up in rows, stacked to attention.

'*Who lives in a house like this?*' asked Lavinia. Or it might have been Cressida, or Letitia, or some other over-smiling wannabee-presenter with a made-up name.

'Postman Pat,' he replied, silently. 'And it's not his house anymore. He's left it to the State.'

They hadn't found a will, or even the vaguest indication of next of kin, and Batten didn't expect they would. This Postman Pat didn't even have a cat. Batten had met a thankfully small number of killers, some of them from happy families - at least on the surface. But it was the puzzling loners that disturbed him most, the ones with nobody to speak for them, visit them in prison. Or bury them. They had cars, goods and chattels - and homes. And not a soul to leave them to.

Batten thought of his own home, a hamstone cottage smelling of fresh coffee and apple-wood. He saw its hand-made bookshelves and CD racks, the oak and pine furniture he'd brought back to life with his own sweat; saw his lanky frame ducking automatically under its low beams. He saw its garden, with long views across orchards and fields of soft fruit towards a Turneresque sunrise over Ham Hill. 'Who lives in a house like *that*, Lavinia?'

Who indeed, Zig? Till recent 'tensions' intervened, he'd spent more weekends at Erin's than at home. When he was at home, he missed her. And when at hers, he missed home. Two ends of the same thread, but he didn't know how to tie them. Or if. After the Coroner's Court has finished with Erin and Sian, Zig, you'll be lucky to have an 'if' at all.

'Find anything, zor?'

Ball had learned to spot Batten's occasional drifts into Zigland. And a good thing too, Zig. Better for your productivity.

'Pasta. He has plenty of wholemeal pasta. Well, he had.' Batten tossed a packet of linguine into the spotless cupboard, as Ball's back hurriedly turned to obscure his current search area, the shelf of whole-food cookbooks standing to attention on the worktop.

'What you got, Ballie?'

Ball knew what he'd got. He was just shocked to find it here.

'Oh. Well, this, zor. Alas.' Ball reluctantly handed over a well-thumbed Bible. It had been stacked amongst the cookbooks. He'd unearthed a Bible yesterday in Veech's library, and quietly dealt with it, assuming it to be the only one. Hick's parody of Batten now kicked Ball up his own backside - *if it's not ruled out, it's still ruled in.*

Batten thumbed through the Bible. 'You trying to convert me, Ballie? Today's reading is from...?'

Ball's serious face clicked Batten into professional mode. He turned to the place where a thick leather bookmark poked out. *The Book of Revelation*. Ball pointed to a passage with several words underlined in pencil. The words were not random. Ball could be sharp-eyed, on a good day. When Batten connected the string of phrases, he wished it was a bad day.

Well - now - it was.

Forcing himself to double-check, he again scanned the words that had wiped the ginger colour from his Sergeant's face. The bits and pieces of biblical prose made vague sense enough on their own, but when they were strung together...

Batten read the first extract.

Verse 20 ...*that woman Jezebel...to commit fornication.*

He tried not to think of Erin reading it too, but he knew at some point she must.

'Bloody hell.'

'Bloody hell indeed, zor.'

The extracts that followed were worse. But the final verse was the sickener. Batten could not bear to read it twice.

'Bloody...*HELL!*'

In Batten's head, Letitia was chirping again.

'So let's sum up the evidence', she said. 'The clinical cupboards; the precise paintings and alphabetically-ordered bookshelves; the absence of family photographs and mementos; the non-existent will; the cruel images in an unfinished sampler. And now, a King James' Bible, with nauseating extracts from *The Book of Revelation*...'

He finished the sound-bite for her.

'What bastard lives - *lived* - in a house like this?'

PART FOUR

Equinox

Thirty four

Spring forward. Fall back.

Batten remembered it that way, and pottered round his Ashtree cottage putting every clock forward by an hour. No snow to brighten the dark night outside, but ice remained, an unwelcome guest. With Somerset still frozen, the idea of Spring seemed absurd. At least there would be more light. God knows, we could use more light.

He flopped onto the sofa and adjusted his wrist watch. Time forward, Time back, with a mere spin of a finger and thumb. Why can't a murder case be moved forward or back like that? He was reminded of Keith Mallan babbling on about the unmaking of a deer. If only the cops could *make* and *unmake*? Without having to wait for Suns and Moons to decide the frontiers?

Tough, Zig. Your job is to police the frontiers, not re-set them. Terence Veech tried. And if an unknown killer hadn't blown his face away, he might still be trying. Batten shuddered at Veech's definition of 'success'; at what his new frontiers might feel like.

Pack it in, Zig. There are roughly zones between right and wrong, and you're a border guard.

He crossed to the shelves of CDs, deliberately racked haphazardly, so he could close his eyes and choose one at random. His habit was to then ask, 'Is this what I need right now?' The answer was often 'no'. He thought of the clinically-arranged shelves in Veech's house. Shelves with a strict 'yes' stamped into every one.

A 'yes' of his own guided Batten's hand. The ice outside was thick and hard and he'd cranked up the woodstove to compensate. Wearied by winter, he needed true Spring, needed Summer. He drew out an old favourite: Delius. With a small whisky in hand, he settled his feet on the sofa as *The Walk to the Paradise Garden* washed over him, notes floating down like blossom.

By the time the real summer came along, the search for Veech's killer - if unproductive - would edge towards the 'Cold Case' file. His first boss, Inspector Farrar, had warned him: *learn to live with them, Zig, cold cases.*

Have you learned, Zig? No, Zig, I bloody haven't. Cold cases often contained what Farrar called '*an 'inge*' - a moment, a turning or tipping point when a kind word, a bit of guidance, might have cooled the hot blood of escalation. Batten felt for the perpetrator who woke up innocent on Monday morning and went to bed a killer on Monday night - maybe with no plan or intent - and lived with the invisible mark of Cain forever. While waiting for an Inspector to call.

Then another voice in his head whispered, *Tell that to the victims, Zig. And those left behind.* He thought of Veech - both killer and victim. Was a warm word missed, in his case? Terence Veech, who left nobody behind at all?

'If the CID had a magic wand, Zig, what would you do with it?' best friend Ged once asked him.

Use it for 'unmaking'? For going back or forward in time, injecting a bit of help, a kind word? Steer Mr or Ms Red Mist back to calmer waters, to a place of moral horror at what they *almost* did? Or whisk the more malicious perps out of their hiding places in Radstock, Romford, Redcar, Rye, and drag them back to due legal process?

'There's the other way, too, Zig, isn't there?' old pal Ged had asked. 'And no magic wand required.'

He meant the fantasy way, which pops up when a smug crook with a pricey lawyer evades social justice.

'The kick in the crutch way', Ged called it. 'You want to, I want to! Sometimes, Zig, even the Judge wants to!'

Ged was a Chief Inspector in Leeds. They'd done their initial training together.

'We've both had crooks thumb their noses at a twenty year sentence, eh, Zig? Crooks covered in more guilt than the walls in a Chinese restaurant! We should be *required by law* to kick the buggers in the crutch. A personal reminder - 'your file's still open, mush!''

Even as the music seeped into him, Batten's ambivalent foot twitched at the thought of a sharp kick up the middle of Terence Veech. But you'd never *do* it, Zig? Would you? He heard a more serious Ged.

'You've still got a moral compass, Zig. Try to remember which pocket you put it in.'

The music ended and he clicked 'repeat'. As the sounds re-played, he wondered where his moral compass came from. Not from Eastern Europe. His father was a half Polish, half Russian, half-drunk trawler skipper, drowned at sea when Zig was less than two years old. His English mother and her new husband lasted barely a few months more, the M1 rather than the North Sea their nemesis. His real parent in all but name was his mother's sister, Aunt Daisy - Daze, he called her - and she had moral compass enough for a tribe. The only time he'd thought of leaving the police was when all he seemed to do was turf low-life off the streets so that high-life could look down their posh noses in more safety.

Aunt Daze's steely Yorkshire vowels asked him, 'Don't the likes o' me deserve safe streets too, Zig?'

He sipped his whisky, closing tired eyes as the music soothed, till his drift towards sleep was jarred by the ringing phone. It'll be Lieutenant Makis Grigoris again, Zig, and he'll ask, *'Why you not say me when your flight she land in Crete, Sig? Your phone, she is broke?'*

Not sure there'll *be* a flight, Makis, he might have to say. If Erin Kemp stays lukewarm.

It wasn't Lieutenant Grigoris. It was Sergeant Ball.

He was still having his dark moments, but Chris Ball could see daylight now. And the daylight shone on the debts he must repay. Jean Phelps was one of them. Ball agreed with Batten. They had failed her. And having failed her, they then had to delve once more into her whereabouts, when Veech's body was found. She'd been at a Librarian's Conference in Warwick. With sixty other librarians, each as precise as Jean.

'It's normally me and Di and Jean, zor, at the pub quiz. We've been a quiz team for years. They call us *The Fines*.'

'The *what*?'

'*The Fines*, zor. Speeding fines and library fines. You see?'

Batten saw. But he'd poured a whisky, and didn't feel like driving over to Stockton Marsh for The Jug and Bottle's monthly pub quiz.

'Di is improving, zor, and I say that with a joy I never thought to feel again. But she's not ready for the pub yet. You understand? Jean, though, I've told her - let's get you back on the ladder, soon as you're able. Least we can do. There's only three or four in the village, zor, who are a bit, you know. And if there's me and you, kind of bolstering Jean between us?'

Batten reached for his coat and keys. Erin was at last-minute rehearsals for her Michael Tippet oratorio. This time, Zig, you won't have to slog through a pitch-black orchard. Or a graveyard covered in frost.

Scilla Wynyard almost remembered what she'd forgotten, but just as it was about to break the surface, it sank again. Instead she tidied her converted cowshed. It didn't take long to wipe the kitchen table and shuffle old newspapers into a pile. Most of them were open at the beloved crossword page. She scanned each one, just in case. No. She'd completed every clue.

'And I bet they're all correct, Scilla.'

Yes, Scilla, if you had anything to bet with.

All the newspapers were old. One crossword caught her eye - her contorted margin doodles suggesting a slow search for the answers. Ah, Stairway to Heaven, it was that one. Tougher than some. She put the kettle on.

As it heated up, so did Scilla. Yet another night, alone, in the tired kitchen. Another slow night, and no-one to blame it on. Well, let's blame it on the police! The hurt of their questions had not gone away. Insinuations, raised eyebrows, guns, vans. Secrets. And now, it was *please confirm your whereabouts on the night of such and such.* Someone else had been killed. A postman. Well, not soon enough!

'My 'whereabouts'?' she'd said. '*Here*! In the cowshed!' With *me*. With the *cow*!

They didn't tell her, at first, it was a shooting. But that's as far as their decency went. Searched her gun cupboard again, didn't they, soon enough. Then all the palaver about gunshot residue. Yes, Scilla, blame it on the police!

Steam wreathed up from the kettle. It's climbing the stairway to heaven, Scilla. She stared through the coil of steam at her reflection in the kitchen window. A pale ghost stared back. Stairway to *Heaven*? Stairway to death, more like. She and Jeff in a four room shack, two piddling steps to the front door - no bloody sign of a staircase to heaven!

The crossword flopped into the bin, but she continued to stare at it. Sometimes answers just arrive, Scilla, on unseen wings of intuition, don't they? As the kettle sang, old Tom Priddle flew out of it, borne on wreaths of steam. Broke his neck falling down the stairs in that rotten house of his, yes? Well, Scilla, that's a 'staircase of death'? Right?

From her fleece pocket she fumbled her copy of the letter that had slimed through her door all those weeks ago. January 17th.

'Not a date I'll ever forget, is it?'

The winding staircase of death...? It had always felt wrong, that letter, and she was ashamed for gracing it with any logic at all.

The Priddle house was much higher up the lane, thankfully, and far enough away for smells not to filter down on the wind. When was the last time she saw old Tom? Two years ago, was it? Saw the boy, Andrew, a while back. Still a lost soul, that one. Bit like you Scilla. You've got your cowshed, he's got four rotting walls and a roof like a colander.

How many times had she searched a crossword clue for a complex answer when a simple one was staring her in the mouth? Of course. The letter in her hand wasn't meant for *her*. Or for Jeff. *The fruits of your sin?* Fruits? Benefits? Money? There were none. There never had been.

But Andrew had smartened himself up, when you saw him drive by? New haircut, was that it?

'Something new about him anyway.'

Something. And then something more.

Thirty five

Stockton Marsh's church tower was floodlit, a beacon, still guarding the entrance to the orchard where…

From her sitting room window, Di Ball gazed out at the honey-coloured hamstone. She gazed at the church clock. A minute or two to eight, it said. She'd gazed endlessly at that clock and all the different times it told, these last few weeks. And at images within, too, still vivid. She could accept them now, accept a dead Jeff Wynyard, speechless in the frost - and accept she was not the cause. Di Ball could bear it. She could speak.

But not in The Jug and Bottle, not yet. Too soon to be quizzed. When Jean and Zig dropped round though, she at least had a smile for them.

'More likely to win, without me,' she said.

Only six words. But all of them hers, from her own lips.

The sitting-room clock chimed eight times. The quiz began at eight, and part of her missed it. Distracted by the clock she almost failed to see - surely not - Scilla Wynyard? It was, it was Scilla, striding past her window, with a… *WITH A SHOTGUN?* Yes, yes, gripped tightly in her hands. Di shuffled to the window, craned her neck and saw Scilla's back moving fast, striding fast, shoulders tight, striding towards the pub, towards Chris and Jean and Zig, *The Fines* team.

This isn't a nightmare, Di. You saw it, saw *her*. Saw her yesterday, too. First time you step out your front door and she's there in the street, still in a rage at Chris. Just for doing his job?

'*All my life I've lived here - just like you, Di! And what do I get from your husband - who's still alive, not like mine? Nasty questions, insinuations! Where was I when? Have I got a shotgun? Where do I go in my van? Do I have secrets? As if I'm a vengeful bloody floozy with no morals!*'

Di Ball's world shifted. Back to guns and killing and the waste of life. The past tried to shift her further back, to the waste of another life, a child's life, barely that, a half-formed, dying apple in Stockton Marsh's churchyard.

But the past had lost its power. Tiny words and a growing voice told her so. *Then* was then, it said. Now is now. And she knew what 'now' was. *Now* was Scilla Wynyard, *with a SHOTGUN*, striding up the hill towards The Jug and Bottle where Zig and Jean were. And Chris.

She struggled to find a coat, drag it over her shoulders, struggled to slot heavy feet into unaccustomed shoes and unlatch the door, the door that felt like the latch on the churchyard gate. She'd fumbled at the latch, clicked it, on the day she found… How many weeks ago was that?

Tonight, now, she stepped out into darkness, street lamps and telegraph poles like tall trees with shadowed branches. She almost turned back, to the known, the safe, but Chris was down there, twenty halting steps downhill in The Jug and Bottle, and she feared what she would find as she dragged her heavy legs one step further, one step more and another, and fumbling with the big oak door, reliving once again her fingers on the latch, on the gate to the churchyard, that day, and pulling open the door. And entering.

Batten sipped his pint of cider slowly, mindful of the breathalyser. It was good to have seen - and heard - Di Ball's improvement, but he didn't fancy the spare room at the Balls' house tonight. Jean Phelps was on her second large glass of red wine, and he couldn't blame her. She sat between the two detectives as if they were bodyguards. Well, Zig, we are. There were one or two looks. Ball whispered that Norm Hogg, crumpled against the bar at its farthest end, had only just been allowed back in.

'Give Rita credit, zor. A landlady with a heart. Not like some.'

Ball gave Norm a grudging nod. I've not forgotten, Norm, the nod said.

'*Everybody READY?*' sang the unmistakeable voice of Royce Beckett, and Batten tried to get in the mood. He wondered if Jean Phelps had.

Question Number ONE!

Royce the Voice peered over his specs at question number one, opening his mouth to speak at exactly the moment the pub door banged open and every quiz player in the room turned to look.

Andrew Priddle stood on the threshold.

Not his kind of thing, a pub quiz?

Man-with-a-Van?

Young thicko?

Can't recall the last time What's-his-name came in here for a drink. Can you?

He stumbled to the centre of the room. Batten paused, mid-sip. You send out the bloodhounds, Zig, without result, and the bugger turns up in the local pub, with not so much as a by-your-leave. And Scilla Wynyard, too? Don't tell me she and Andrew have formed a quiz team? *The Loners?* And why's she jabbing Andrew Priddle in the back, with a big stick?

Batten slowly settled his glass on the copper-topped table. It's not a stick, Zig. It's a shotgun. And it's jammed in Andrew Priddle's spine. You've seen it before, the gun. It's the 28-bore that Jeff gave Scilla. Didn't she swear she couldn't hit a barn with it? If she pulls the trigger in here, and the cartridges are live, she'll not need to aim. It'll pepper everyone in the room. You, Jean Phelps and Chris Ball included. Even Norm Hogg had put his half-full glass on the bar, and was staring, eyes like moons.

Batten stood up to move in front of Jean as Royce the Voice, mid-question, sank down in his seat. Chris Ball stood up too, the shock of guns reclaiming his face, frosting his ginger cheeks with the memory of other frozen faces, Jeff's and Di's. All gun-shocked, now.

A *gun*! Invading *my* pub, *my* village, with my *house* not twenty yards up the road. *I'm not bloody having it!* He moved towards Scilla Wynyard, just as Batten did the same.

The gun swung sharply towards them, in strong and steady hands. Scilla Wynyard's gaze was intense, her meaning clear - *SIT DOWN!* They remained standing, a protective barrier, Jean Phelps behind them. In the warm pub, Batten's feet were stone.

Scilla Wynyard's gun jerked back towards Andrew Priddle.

'YOU!' she yelled. The gun nudged him forward. 'It was for *you*, wasn't it? My letter? It wasn't supposed to come to me. It was for *you!*'

Man-with-a-Van stood in the centre of the room, shaking, his empty expression full - full of fear, full of other people's eyes.

'See, Andrew', he told his shaking hands, 'every eye in the pub is on you now. The spotlight's not shining on What's-his-name. Nor Man-with-a-Van. It's shining on Andrew.'

His hands were too disturbed to reply. He spoke silently to the room of eyes instead.

'You'll know it's Andrew, won't you, next time? Andrew Priddle. You'll know that's my name, won't you, next time you see me?'

The shotgun nudged him harder in the spine. *Speak*, she was telling him.

'I am speaking!' he yelled. But no sound came out. He tried to shout, 'She's gone mad. *She's gone crazy!*' His voice absconded.

Batten focused on the gun, speaking to Ball, also without words. Is it loaded? Can we take the risk, in here? No. Follow your training. And bloody-well hope for the best.

Andrew Priddle focused on his new shoes.

'I only came back to pick up the post', he told the shoes. 'Things to be signed, for the house-sale. Had another haircut today. She must've seen me, driving up the lane in the old car. Gel. The barber put gel on it, didn't ask him to. He spiked it up a bit with the hair-dryer thing.'

His new shoes stayed silent.

'I was checking on it, the haircut, in the rear-view mirror. She raps on the driver's window. With a shotgun...*'Out!'* she says. One word, that's all. Shotgun in my ribs all the way down the lane, not a soul in sight, no-one to ask. For help. And she shifts me all the way through the village, up the main drag, from one streetlamp to another. Is it loaded? Is it? Do I take a chance? Or bluff it out? It's only What's-his-name, old Tom Priddle's boy, he wouldn't harm a fly. He hasn't got the marbles.'

He raised his head at the room full of eyes.

'Then she marches me in here. You'll save me, won't you? I'm Andrew. Andrew Priddle. Old Tom's boy.'

None of the eyes said a word.

'It's not their turn to speak, Andrew. That's how it works, in turns. *Her* turn now, because her gun just jabbed you in the spine again.'

'It was your staircase, wasn't it?' Scilla Wynyard hissed at him. 'Your staircase of death, in the letter. Wasn't ours - we practically live in a bungalow!'

We? For a brief moment in Scilla's mind, Jeff was alive again. Till the shotgun in her hands reminded her.

'Old Tom Priddle, he fell down a staircase, didn't he? Or maybe you helped him? Gave him a nudge, did you? And get seen doing it? You didn't see me, when you were struggling through that filthy garden of yours with that big boxed TV. What was it, a 40 incher? *Rewards of your sin*? Is that what it was?'

Batten's eyes flicked between the gun, Scilla's trigger finger, and Andrew Priddle's face. You can hardly blame him for showing fear, Zig. But his reactions? Staircase, rewards…? Did he look as if a pair of pennies dropped? Andrew Priddle's face, it's redder than Mars. *Say* something, Zig.

Chris Ball beat him to it.

'Scilla. If all this is true, let's get to the bottom of it. Do our job.' He indicated Batten, who wished he hadn't.

'Chris is right, Scilla. Why don't you let us have a word or two with Andrew, eh?'

'A word or two? Just like the pair of you had a word or two with *me*? Afterwards, after your 'word', you and your female henchmen, I felt like a scarlet woman. We can do without a word or two from you!'

Batten made the slightest movement towards her, his hand gently raised in supplication but she snapped the barrel at him again.

'*STAY!*' It was what she said to the dog, walking her, like when she saw young Priddle hump the big, brand-new TV into that foul pile of a house he lived in. Barely seen him unpack a loaf of bread or a bottle of milk into the damn place before, let alone a flat screen television.

Batten moved again.

'*It's loaded* - in case you think it's not!'

He moved back.

'I loaded it myself, both barrels, just like Jeff showed me. Live rounds, too, from the left hand pocket. L for left. L for live. *Live*.'

There were tears in her eyes now. She's at danger point, Zig, emotion dulling her judgement. Talk her down, before the trigger's pulled, or the gun goes off in her hands. Do *something*, before she kicks the last dregs of reason into a ditch, and splatters someone. Batten checked who else was in range. Apart from him.

Andrew Priddle was very much in range, the shotgun jammed in his spine, except when it waved at those two detectives. Gun. He wished he'd never seen or gripped that other gun, Keith Mallan's gun. Bloody peashooter of a .410. He jabbered silently to his hands, his shoes, to the eyes in the room.

'After we moved the carcasses, in the van, Keith takes the back door key from under a plant-pot hidden in the woodpile, I saw him. Saw him nudge the little shotgun with his foot, pushing it further behind the big freezer, hiding it, before we put in the venison. I went back. Wish I didn't go back.'

Well you did! said his shoes.

'Keith's never home, these days. I just gets the key, borrows the gun. Still got some .410 cartridges left over, from when the police took dad's away. Voluntarily, that's what the big policeman said.'

Andrew Priddle's hands found their voice. *I must have held it, then, Keith's gun?* Yes, it wasn't your fault, Andrew. It was your shoes that went there, to Keith's. It was your hands that held the gun, loaded it.

'It was *you*', he told the shoes and hands. 'You got in the old car and turned the key and changed the gears and followed him, that postman, to his house. And you went back again, didn't you? Hands on Keith's gun this time. You put it in the car, the gun, and drove up there again, to where he lives. And you walked to his door, shoes, didn't you? And you went inside.'

He castigated his shoes.

'It was *you* who barged your feet through his kitchen door, not me. *You shouldn't have done that!*'

The shoes just stood there, sullen. Andrew Priddle ran out of objects to blame, but the memories kept coming. They jabbered on.

'That tall postman's face, when he sees the .410 pointing at his head and me staring up at him. Huh, eyes like two hard nails, that night. I showed him. Not too popular at your depot, are you, *Terence*? Overheard your chums, in that cafe, didn't it? I've seen you, delivering, to the village shop. 'Got a nice big cheque for me, Terence, today?' Don't smile back much, though, do you? And you're not smiling now, *Terence*, eh, at my .410 pointing at your face? I warned him off. Nudged the bastard with the barrel, just like Scilla Wynyard's nudging me.'

Then he wasn't in The Jug and Bottle anymore, but in the postman's house, clean, neat, not like Priddle Castle, and the postman had an enormous gun and he pointed it and pulled the trigger and the pee made Andrew's trousers wet, and he waited for the bang, waited for the pain, and to fall and die. But the gun clicked then clicked again, nothing more, and the postman ran from the kitchen and across the hall to a white sofa.

'And I run after him, yes. *I've been looking for you!* he's shouting. He grabs a cartridge, has it in his hand, a bright red cartridge for the empty giant gun, and NO, I shouts back, *NO!* I waves the gun, just to stop him, just to shut him up and the .410 jumps and there's a smell of powder and a flash, an echo, and his face is missing and the wall turns red.'

Andrew Priddle screwed his face shut at the memory and flew back from the postman's house to The Jug and Bottle, speaking to the eyes in front of him - she's crazy this woman, gone crazy with grief, she's mad with loss, I know about such things!

'*Someone get this gun off her!*' his own eyes yelled. But no words came out.

The pub had never been so silent, so still, and the sound of the opening door was the loudest crack, the most baleful squeal Chris Ball had ever heard. As Scilla Wynyard turned at the sound, Ball foolishly began to move, hoping to swipe the gun upwards and away - till he found himself staring at the ashen face of his own wife, standing in the doorway, his old Barbour thrown across her shoulders, and two wrong shoes worn absurdly on the wrong feet. He saw the gun twitch away from the door back into the room and then as swiftly arc back to point squarely at Di Ball.

Please god, no. No more. That was all he could think.

'Scilla.'

Di's small, lost voice, barely a whisper, finding itself, and an unsteady hand slowly pointing at Scilla Wynyard's hands and what they held.

'Scilla. No guns. No more guns.'

Scilla Wynyard looked at the long steel wand gripped in her fists, as if someone else had put it there. Di Ball moved in front of Andrew Priddle, raising her other hand to Scilla Wynyard.

'How many more, Scilla?' was all she said.

The women looked at each other, two reflections in two mirrors. We know about loss, said their eyes. Our two worlds, they're full of it. Di Ball's eyes added a question: why risk more?

'Enough of guns, Scilla. Give it to me now.'

And to Chris Ball's amazement and to his fear, she thrust out a hand, palm up, towards Scilla Wynyard. In the silence, the snouts of the twin barrels were a pair of animal eyes, glaring at all who looked at them, turning them to stone. The gun seemed to grow, expand, swell, filling the whole bar, growing so huge that Chris Ball thought it could only explode, peppering them all, turning them all to pulp, blowing away their teeth and lips and tongues.

But the gun slowly shrank back to normal size, the barrel faltering, dipping, till it pointed not at Di but at the pub's patterned carpet. Scilla's tight fingers slowly unravelled, sliding from the trigger to the stock, then falling to her side, empty.

Chris Ball leapt forward to catch the gun before it hit the floor - an unintended shot might still kill - and held it at arm's length in one hand while reaching for his wife with the other. Norm Hogg unfroze himself from his seat at the bar, and quietly took the gun, turning it away, ejecting both cartridges. Then his shaking hands lifted his half-full glass and drained it.

The snap of the breech seemed to puncture the silence of The Jug and Bottle and it was not lead-pellets but a shrill babble of yells that peppered the walls and ceiling. In the commotion, Andrew Priddle eased quietly towards the still-open door. Batten tracked him all the way, kicking the door shut with a loud size nine, and nudging a white-faced Andrew Priddle back into the room.

But with a peremptory hand this time, not a shotgun.

Thirty six

Why, Zig, can't they be as lively as this when we chase sheep-stealers and tractor thieves? Why do shotguns perk them up so bloody much?

Batten looked across the office at his busy team. If he yelled *'unpaid overtime'*, would they down tools and go home? Scilla Wynyard hadn't gone home. She was in a holding cell. She may not have shot anyone, but *assault* was written at the top of Batten's notebook, and would likely end up on a charge sheet, just for starters. He had a babble of pub-quiz contestants for witnesses. Another more ambivalent witness, Sergeant Ball, was at home looking after Di.

'Shaken, zor, but no longer stirred', he'd said, down the phone.

'Take as long as the pair of you need', Batten had replied. Because you can do without Ball's ambivalence right now, Zig. Scilla Wynyard can resent *your* questions all she likes. You weren't at school with her.

More difficult to deal with was Andrew Priddle. Batten had scooted him over to Parminster on the reasonable assumption that a police doctor needed to look him over.

'You've had quite a shock, Andrew.'

So have you, Zig. And thank the lord for *A Child Of Our Time*. At least Erin was away rehearsing. She could just as easily have been at the pub quiz in The Jug and Bottle. Could she, Zig? Erin is edging towards the fringes of your life, these last few weeks. Imagine her face if Royce Beckett's first question had been, 'why are *shotguns* measured in 'bores'?'

It was Hick's first question that snapped Batten out of it.

'Sir? What we gonna hold him on, this Priddle bloke?'

What indeed, Zig? Not on the grief-ridden accusations in Scilla Wynyard's ramblings, that's for sure.

'Nothing, Hickie. Yet. If the doc says he's not 'at risk', he'll be a witness. You can help him with his statement. 'Please assist us in our enquiries', and similar smarm. He'll like that, will Andrew. Then we'll see what snippets pop out.'

'Can't let the bugger go, sir. Spent my best years looking for him.'

'Have faith, Hickie.'
You too, Zig.

Andrew Priddle spoke silently to objects around him. He chattered to the universe of things. Things that started out as strangers quickly became his friends, like the tape machine in the interview room, the scratched metal table and the bolts that locked it firmly to the floor. The floor was sort-of lino, like in dad's house. But cleaner.

The tall policeman will want to talk to *me*, he told the floor, because I was there, in the middle of the pub, in the spotlight. 'Mr Priddle'. All the policemen called me that, and the doctor too. And now, they call me *Andrew*. Andrew Priddle. *Me*.

They can think I'm stupid if they like. Gunshot residue? I know about that, from the big TV, and I know what 'trace' is. And, sorry to mention it, Keith, but that .410 of yours, it's at the bottom of Quarry Lake - deepest in South Somerset, so the man on the telly said. And my clothes, from that night, all burnt and the ash raked through. Can afford new clothes, can't I, any time?

Andrew remembered standing under the shower in the rented house tucked away in the Blackdown Hills, and letting the water cleanse him. No old miser battered on the door with an angry stick. Andrew stood in the shower for days, months, for forty years. It was a long christening, the first he'd had as far as he knew. You don't even know that about yourself, do you Andrew? Don't even know if you've been christened or not? He stood there, till the tank ran dry and the cold water reminded him where he was. And the reason.

He heard movement outside the door. Interview Room One, it said, on a little plastic sign. *I'm* Number One, he told the metal table. Andrew Priddle. Number One.

He glued on his Man-with-a-Van face, his What's-his-name voice, and picked out a few odd words from the script he'd been rehearsing.

Hick and Batten were well-trained, but there were sensitivities. In the duty doctor's opinion, Priddle was only just this side of 'at risk'. *So go careful, Inspector, mm?*

Once the witness statement was topped and tailed, the two cops watched Andrew's snail eyes scan the pages in halting harmony with his lips, before a loopy signature coiled itself onto the white paper, and the pen was politely returned.

'It must bank up a bit, Andrew? The mail?'

That almost bovine expression, Zig, there it goes again. Is he putting it on, or what?

'On your doormat? The mail? With you being away so much?'

'Away in the van? Is that what you mean, Mr Batten?'

'Yes, Andrew'. And other things.'

'I sleep in it. The van. When I'm away. Cheaper.'

'What, this weather, sir?'

Andrew liked the other one too, the one with the twitch. Liked that he called him 'sir'.

'Used to the cold, me.'

Hick and Batten could imagine. The Priddle residence looked freezing from the outside. The problem was how - legally - to get *in*side.

'But when you come back, from being away, there'll be all those letters to deal with. I get mostly bills.' Batten added an encouraging smile.

'I don't get many bills. Don't buy much.'

'Mrs Wynyard -' was that a little shudder from Andrew, Zig? No surprise, she shoved a loaded shotgun in his ribs. 'Mrs Wynyard even got an anonymous letter through her door. You know, a sort of threatening letter. Do you remember, in the pub, she said her letter should have been sent to you?'

'To me? Why?'

Because you pushed Old Tom down the winding staircase of death? If you had the wit? Batten wished he knew, one way or the other. Hick took a turn.

'No letters like that came through your door, then, sir?'

Hick was rewarded with a shudder too. This time without the mention of Scilla Wynyard. Andrew Priddle's face clouded over after that, and ten more questions drew ten bovine replies.

'I'll tell you what, Andrew. I think it's time we all had a cuppa, eh?'

Andrew Priddle smiled at Batten. It was a curious smile, as if his teeth were still learning how, as if the curl of his lips was held in place by gelled spikes of hair like question marks.

Batten rummaged three blank white envelopes from his drawer and stepped across to DC Hick's empty desk - empty because the cleaners had been in. Hick watched Batten deal the envelopes onto the polished surface. His eyes twitched up at his Inspector, and down at the white blanks again.

'St Valentine's Day, sir? You shouldn't have.' Hick lacked the dry levity of Sergeant Ball.

'Let's imagine these are Veech's anonymous letters, right?'

Hick twitched a 'so what'.

'Which one's Jeff Wynyard's?'

'They're all blank, sir. Can't tell.'

'Fair enough. Which is Jean Phelps' then?'

'I said, sir. Can't tell.'

'Well, if *you* can't tell, Hickie, what if...?'

Hick's hands jerked from his desk to crack his knuckles, loud as a gunshot. He swore it helped him think. The noise went right through Batten, came out the other side.

'You can't mean what you mean, sir? Never. Our Mr Veech? His house, it's like...it's like a robot lives there. You're not suggesting...what, he got 'em mixed up? *Veech*?'

Batten's face was suggesting precisely that.

'Look what it explains, Hickie. No *winding staircase of death* at the Wynyard's place. But there's one at the Priddle's. What if Scilla Wynyard was right?'

'Sorry, sir, but it's a bit-'

'- And look what Jeff gets threatened with.' Batten scanned the letter...'*the fruits of your sin shall be denied you.* Well, we haven't turned up any fruits to deny, have we?' Remember how hard we looked?'

Hick did. He'd done most of the looking.

'No, I think Veech made a mistake, and got his letters mixed up. If you'd already sealed them, side by side, there's any number of ways it could happen. It'd only take a gust of wind.'

Hick dragged out the file of photocopied letters and jerked his eyes across them, one by one.

'It can't work, sir. The letter sent to Jean Phelps, it's meant for her, all day and backwards. And, hell's teeth, the one sent to - .' What passed for decorum stopped Hick in his tracks.

'You're allowed to say it, Hickie. The one sent to Mrs Kemp and Sian?'

'Sir. Well. That's no cock-up either, is it?'

True. A bloody bull's eye, that one.

'In which case, sir, Jeff's letter is...well, it's Jeff's. Can't see any other way.'

'There is another way, Hickie, plain and shiny-white as these three envelopes here.'

And plain as the unfinished sampler in Terence Veech's house. Batten waited his usual five seconds for Hick to catch up. It took him less.

'Bugger me, sir. There *is* a fourth letter?'

A nod, smug.

'And Jeff should've got it? Instead of what he did get?'

'It's a theory.'

'So who got Jeff's?' Hick instantly knew. His finger twitched towards Interview Room One. 'Young chummy, in there?'

Batten's nod said Q.E.D.

Hick recalled Andrew Priddle's eyes and lips, snailing through his witness statement.

'Bet he's still trying to read it then, sir.'

'Maybe so, Hickie. And if he hasn't chucked the bloody thing on the fire, we might be able to help him, eh?'

What do I say? Andrew Priddle asked the metal table in his very own Interview Room. The tall detective was still going on about that letter. *Should've got rid of it!* Andrew hissed silently at the vinyl floor. Neither floor nor table could comment. *It's why we came back*, he told his hands. *To clear the place out!*

Someone else's hands, on the doorknob. *More questions*, he told the vinyl floor. The What's-his-name mask slid into place as Batten and Hick sat down again.

'I'm not much of a reader', he lied. 'Letters, nor anything else.'

He answered all their questions like that.

By the time the search warrant came through, Batten was a rainstorm on an iron roof. The Magistrate thought long and hard before signing it - *a search is likely to reveal...illuminate a related murder case...the house in question will soon be demolished...*

But sign he did, and Batten switched the team into high gear. When the process was explained to Andrew Priddle he barely blinked.

'Make sure the man-child gets a good meal', Batten told the Duty Officer, before he and a refreshed Sergeant Ball climbed into the Ford Focus.

Thirty seven

Batten wanted to wash. Perhaps the clean memory of a hot shower might armour him against this alternative universe of filth. An accumulation of old ordure and weak disinfectant, wood-rot, rancid drains and tarry tobacco drilled its way past the protective mask strapped over his nose. He brushed aside a brown, stained newspaper, feeling its coating of grease and grit even through crime-scene gloves. The badly-painted front door had felt the same, when he'd reluctantly pushed it open.

Andrew Priddle's dwelling had once been a cottage, similar in size to Batten's own hamstone house near Ashtree. His was clean, well-maintained, its garden painstakingly reclaimed from weeds and its lean-to garage re-roofed. The Priddle home, by contrast, had not long to live. Were it built on softer ground, Nature might already have repossessed it, sucking the crumbling stone and the smashed tile back down into the earth on which it slovenly sat, a dying maggot, a slattern. Beyond the house, a man-trap of nettle and thorn bided its time.

Ball's eyebrows echoed Batten's, but needs must. At least they'd drawn the long straw. Magnus and Hick were upstairs with the SOCOs, searching the bedrooms and, god help them, the toilet too.

'Any chance of one of those radioactive suits?' Hick had asked.

'Get on with it, *Loft*', Ball told him, short sentences and closed mouths being the order of the day.

The 'sitting room' was largely ironic. One sofa had burst its banks, horsehair and springs spilling out and flowing onto a reservoir of unspeakably-stained linoleum. Batten struggled to remember if he'd ever seen as filthy a floor. New dirt had run out of places to go, and lay there on top of the old. A second sofa was half-covered in dead copies of the Radio Times, and faced the newest item in the house, an incongruously large and brand-new flat-screen TV, the only thing in the whole place not covered in dust. Hick's plausible suggestion that Keith Mallan had nicked it and sold it on was squashed by the receipt found in Andrew's grubby pocket when he was searched.

'Dad left a big wallet of money in a drawer. So I bought the telly and an old car,' was all he said.

Should've bought logs instead, Zig. An empty woodstove was the only source of heat on the ground floor. Heat, Zig? The place was colder than stone.

Upstairs, Magnus had her head through the wide-open landing window, breathing marginally fresher air than that in the toilet. Two minutes searching amid the fetid stench was plenty. Hick took a turn, while Magnus dealt with the main bedroom. The stained bed had been stripped and there were marks on the encrusted carpet where objects had been removed, leaving a barely less filthy outline. A bedside table had been smashed into splintery shards.

'Probably for firewood, Nina', she told herself. Even in her padded parka she was ice.

Hick didn't last long in the Priddle loo.

'You could die in that bog', he told Magnus. 'You'd need a gas mask just to have a pee.'

'Find anything?'

'Yeh.'

'What?'

Hick twitched an answer.

'Germs', he said.

Downstairs, Ball found something other than bacteria.

'Look at this, zor.'

He pointed at a grimy sideboard. An accumulation of dust had been smudged from around the keyhole of its only door. Ball tried the handle - locked. He jiggled through the bunch of keys taken from Andrew Priddle and produced a piece of rust of about the right shape. The lock was a surprise, yielding smoothly.

'Oiled', Ball said, as he clicked open the door.

Three objects gazed up at them. Ball flicked through the first, a house rental agreement, signed in all the right places.

'Southwold, zor. Where Andrew's headed, I suppose, before the bulldozers move in? Isn't that in Suffolk?'

Batten nodded, his attention focused on the second object. It was a bible. A childish hand had written in the flyleaf: *This bible belongs to Sophie Priddle, aged nine and a half.* Some of the pages were loose, a few missing. It was the only book in the house. Ball watched, as Batten's long fingers turned the pages carefully, from Old Testament to New. Batten sensed Ball staring at him, caught his eye.

'Looking for work, Ballie?' He softened the gibe with half a smile.

Ball failed to disguise the concern in his voice. 'We're all looking for something, zor.'

They both stared now, as Batten turned more pages, and there it was, The Book of Revelation.

Batten scanned the verses, breath held, as if for pencil marks. In this particular copy, not a single word was underlined. He whooshed out stale air. Ball followed suit.

'Completely clean, Ballie.'

'Yes, zor. Only thing in the entire place that is.'

When they turned their attention to the third object, their interest in Andrew Priddle soared. Stuffed in the back of the sideboard was a familiar ice-white envelope. Batten eased it out. It was blank, like the others. Turning it over, he saw the grubby seal had been roughly torn.

'Letter number four, zor? And young Andrew's the lucky lad?'

'Seems so, Ballie. But maybe not the letter he was supposed to get.'

'So why would he say he never got it?'

'Why indeed?'

Guilt, pure and simple? Or a lack of understanding of the letter's meaning? Maybe a submerged sense of pride - not wanting to seem...challenged? Is that the modern euphemism, Zig?

Ball watched as his Inspector slid out the flimsy single sheet - reluctantly, but not because of the grime.

Andy Connor's face and mood were in harmony. Both said 'ugh'.

'The staircase is a staircase, Zig, and nothing else. No sign it's been fiddled with, no trip-wires, man-traps or ejector seats. It's filthy and clapped out, though, and there's wet-rot in at least five places, top and bottom. From *that*.' He pointed up at the blackened ceiling, where a sieve of a roof had soaked the plaster.

'Well, thanks all the same, Andy.'

'Feel free to point at something clean, and I'll have a delve. Never seen so much muck in one place before. Not where people *live*.'

'Bag this then, Andy. It's a bit cleaner.'

Connor carefully took the letter from Batten.

'Laundry bill?'

The smile was not returned.

'Ah. Right. Number four?'

A nod.

He scanned it.

I am the watcher, the chosen one. Only the watcher may choose.

No creature shall be harmed, unless the watcher decrees.

The watcher has observed. You have killed a creature and I shall have my revenge.

Beware, for the watcher's wrath shall strike. The fruits of your sin shall be bitter on your lips and tongue.

Prepare yourself.

'This the letter you think Jeff Wynyard should've got?'

Batten nodded, sure of it now. He re-lived the bitterness of Jeff's lips and tongue, what was left of them, black with blood on a cold orchard floor.

'Do the usual, Andy. We might get lucky.'

He didn't think they would. He was thinking more about the letter that Jeff did receive. The one intended for Andrew Priddle, And thinking about what it meant.

Thirty eight

Though less harassed this time, Doctor Roland Pym's smile was no less false. To Batten he was still Doctor Grim.

'Ah, Inspector. The case of the stolen Doctor's note, again?'

No. Pym was Tom Priddle's doctor, the one who'd pronounced him dead.

'Quite frankly, it was a blessing. He was a bag of bones. Had he been less stubborn - less cussed – he would have sung in the heavenly choir far sooner than he did.'

'What was wrong with him?'

'Were you to randomly open a medical dictionary, Inspector, one of old Tom's ailments would doubtless grace the page. What was about to *kill* him was MND. Crippling, fatal.'

'MND?' For some reason, Weapons of Mass Destruction popped into Batten's head.

'Motor Neurone Disease, Inspector. A sudden, vicious wolf. Old Tom's version was the worst. And before you ask - yes, even doctors wonder if vicious men deserve a vicious illness.'

What about *non*-vicious men, Zig - and women? The ones who live a good life but still get rewarded with a vicious illness, or a murdered spouse or a splattered car? He thought of Di Ball, Scilla Wynyard, Jean Phelps. But he couldn't find an answer. Call yourself a Yorkshireman, Zig? You of all people should be able to find true north on a moral compass.

Batten hit fast forward. To *did he fall or was he pushed, down the winding staircase of death?*

'But MND didn't kill him?'

'Technically, no. But he could not walk unaided, and the stairs - well. All the available help *was* offered, and tersely refused. Social Services were at the ready - my conscience is pure and clear in that department.'

I bet Dr Grim-Pym's conscience is always pure and clear, Zig?

'I can tell you precisely what old Tom said, if you wish?'

A nod.

'Sewcial bloody Surrvices? Wha'ya think bloody *Aandrew*'s forr?' Pym did a passable impression of the local twang. 'Old Tom rarely wasted a complete word, Inspector, when half would do.'

Batten bit back a retort. 'No concerns, though, when you saw the body?'

For the first time, Doctor Pym paused before speaking.

'I do see what you are asking, Inspector. Neither myself nor indeed your colleagues had the slightest doubt. Andrew came home in that awful van and found Tom dead, at the foot of the stairs. There was an autopsy, as doubtless you know. Broken neck. Shock. Tom had been a dead man walking - barely walking, even with a stick - for quite some time. Young Andrew was in pieces. I had to sedate him.'

'Did he say anything?'

'Does he ever, Inspector? Old Tom's stick beat a hard silence into him, and he learned it well. Had I been allowed, I might have written 'a blessed death' on the certificate. 'Accidental' was the truth, but it failed to catch the nuance. No, my concerns were more for the boy left behind. Bad enough that young Andrew lived and toiled for as long as he did - thanklessly - in that stomach-churning cess-pit. But to live there entirely *alone*?' Pym shuddered. 'I spotted a 'Sold' sign, when I drove past the other day, and I confess I felt relieved for him. Though fearful. Heaven knows where he will go.'

He'll go to Southwold, Zig, with the 'rewards of his sin' - the inflated sale price of a half-acre, crap-infested building plot. Unless we find a recently-fired .410, buried somewhere in that stomach-churning cess-pit. And a piece of paper with Terence Veech's address scrawled on it, in a distinctive loopy hand.

Batten headed back to his car, with loners on his mind. Andrew Priddle, who learnt a hard silence. Terence Veech, who imposed his own hard silence on others. The lonely silence of Di Ball. Jean Phelps, alone but no longer private. Scilla Wynyard, with just sheep now for company.

And what about Zig Batten, Zig? *He* lives alone. Yes, but he has a relationship. He *did* have, Zig, till a loner called Veech buggered it up for him. And now someone's buggered up Veech, eh?

He drove away. What will you do, Zig, if *someone* turns out to be Andrew Priddle? Beat the poor sod with a cack-handed walking stick called 'the law', or do what Hick keeps suggesting, and give him a medal?

Batten did not go back to Parminster, to HQ. Nor back to Stockton Marsh and Andrew Priddle's house. But back he went nonetheless, to the far fringe of Ball's village, back to the sealed house of Terence Veech. You're like a walking bloody Equinox, Zig! What's wrong with going forward? Why does it have to be *back*?

No sooner did he enter than he instantly wished he was in The Three Bells at Ashtree, surrounded by revellers on a busy summer's night. The boiler had been switched off and the whiteness of the house - well, it's not all white now, Zig - made it feel twice as cold. But a man's home tells a story, doesn't it? The Priddle house had spoken, and Veech's mausoleum still had tales to tell.

The kitchen was sterile enough to be an operating theatre. Or, God knows, Zig, a morgue. He wandered over to the shelves of cookbooks, where Ball found the bible. Yes, a strange place to keep it. Batten looked at the scrubbed kitchen table. The gun-cleaning kit and the newspapers had been commandeered by Forensics, and a pristine surface glared up at him now. He imagined Veech tapping at a Remington here, composing lines of bile, sliding the hard letters into soft envelopes and - what? Smiling?

Explains why the bible's in the kitchen, Zig. Veech's version of Google. Ball's curious hesitation was understandable, I suppose, when the bible turned up?

Not why you came here, Zig. Get on with it.

He crossed to the kitchen cupboard where the plates and dishes were strictly arranged by size and colour and function, looking for the one object still niggling at him from the previous search. The Priddle/Wynyard letter made it more than a niggle now.

The watcher has observed. You have killed a creature and I shall have my revenge.

The dog bowl was a large round dish, some sort of shiny metal, with a hollow base you could weight with sand, so a hungry dog's tongue didn't spin the bowl round the kitchen every mealtime. Chris Ball had a similar bowl at his house, for Gus, the Labrador. Batten flipped the bowl over, found the screwdriver on his Swiss Army knife, and unscrewed the baseplate, tongue between his teeth in expectation. The screw rattled out, the lid clattered off - but the cavity was empty. The hiding place Batten had conjured up was a dud. If anything had been hidden there, it was gone.

Neither was it full of sand, to weigh it down. There's no need for sand, Zig. Terence Veech has a dog bowl, yes.

But he doesn't have a dog.

Hazel Timms was trying to stop herself looking at the Parminster CID clock. Not time yet, Hazel. And if you overrun, you'll just have to pay the carer overtime, using cash from your overdraft that you'll then pay off with your unpaid overtime.

When the phone rang, she was marginally closer than Magnus.

'Hazel?'

'Sir?' She got that feeling again.

'Is Magnus there?' Ah, relief.

'Yes, sir.' Thank god.

'Great. You and Magnus get over to Scilla Wynyard's will you? Ask her if Jeff ever shot a dog, you know, one bothering his sheep or somesuch. And check again if anything's on file about it. OK?'

'Sir.'

Blast. She knew there was nothing on file about a dog. She'd done a thorough job the first time she took Jeff Wynyard's life apart. Unfortunate choice of words, Hazel.

'Your turn to drive, Nina', she said.

And the pair of them got on with it.

Thirty nine

A fair ultimatum, Meg Mallan thought, under the circumstances.

'Cut back on the cider, Keith - and whatever else I could smell, soon's I stepped in here.'

The kitchen was cleaner than last time, but only just.

'I see drunks all day, working in a pub. Don't wan' see one at home, do I?'

Keith Mallan nodded in agreement. Home. She did. Meg called the place 'home'.

'And the whole house needs a clean. A Spring clean, top to bottom. A proper job. You'll have to get professionals in.'

He would. He nodded again. He'd use the cash from selling the venison. Still had it, though he told the cops he'd drunk it all. They'd told *him* he was bloody lucky to get a suspended sentence. Meg spoke up for him, and the beak must have had a good lunch, that day. Chris Ball didn't mince his 'quiet word', though - 'no second chances, Keith. If there's a next time, it's a prison cell for you.' There wouldn't be a next time. Except with Meg.

'I'll get 'em in directly Meg. Keep it clean after, too.'

'You will, Keith.' No need to say more. She wasn't letting him slide. Or herself. She moved from the kitchen to the boot room. Seconds later, Keith's smelly trainers were in the washing machine, and its door firmly closed.

'I'll leave you to switch it on', she said. He didn't protest.

But Meg hasn't mentioned the shotgun, Keith. Will she? Knowing her, she'll have folded the little .410 and dumped it in the River Parrett, or in a furnace somewhere, no questions asked. What did Jeff say about Meg? Resourceful? Was that the word? Barely set foot in the house before she's sniffed out the shotgun and made it disappear. She's unmade it, Keith, he chuckled to himself. Unmade it, like a deer. One minute it's in the hidey-hole by the chest freezer, next minute...

Well, if Meg Mallan can keep quiet about the .410, so can you. Some secrets are best left lying.

And Meg never did like guns.

Just when she's getting on top of the loneliness, those *policewomen* turn up again and ask her about Jeff. Scilla Wynyard gave Timms and Magnus a full ten seconds of sharp silence before flopping into her kitchen chair and hissing out a sigh. And she wasn't inviting the pair of them to sit down.

'When was this supposed to be?' she snapped.

Magnus wasn't sure.

'Fat lot of use you are, then.'

Timms gave Scilla a look, and took charge.

'Doesn't matter *when*, does it? You either remember or you don't.'

She's had a hair-do, Scilla, the Timms woman. About time. Looks less like a dead shrub now.

'Well? He either did or he didn't.'

Did he? A dog? Did Jeff shoot a dog? Remember, Scilla? Three dead lambs and all the palaver? Yes, a stray dog, worrying the sheep. He shot it. She could hear the boom of the shotgun, in her ears, now.

'Twelve months back. A dog, killing his sheep.' Not his sheep, Scilla. Yours. 'Come to arrest him for it, have you?'

Timms let that one go. Scilla Wynyard was in trouble enough, having waved a loaded gun at a pub full of innocents - two of them CID.

'Did he claim on the insurance?'

Scilla paused, and shook out a 'no'.

'What did he do with the carcass, then?' There was nothing in the records. No microchip, no owner's details, no police report.

'No idea. He'll have burnt it, knowing Jeff. K.I.S.S. That's the way he did things.'

'K.I.S.S.?'

'Keep It Simple, Stupid.' Ooh, look, Scilla, you made a police-lady's face turn pink and her eyebrows flick together, just like the tall detective's. 'He read it in a farming magazine. Used to say it all the time, did Jeff. K.I.S.S.'

Used to.

'Maybe you could arrest him for that as well,' she sniped.

Timms gave Scilla Wynyard another glare, before pointing an eyebrow at Magnus. Magnus tried to point one back, but couldn't. Instead, she gave a tiny shake of the head. Jeff shot a stray dog, yes; microchip, no; insurance report, no. One out of three is better than the norm, in this house. They left.

With only part of the truth. These last few weeks, Scilla, half-truths are mounting up, aren't they? Jeff told you he *had* claimed for the lambs. But he hadn't. When you went through the paperwork you couldn't find the insurance certificate. Because there wasn't one – and there still isn't. Can't pay the premium. If anything happens to the sheep...

She made up her mind. Grit your teeth and visit Mr Goode, solicitor and farmer's friend. At a price. Tomorrow.

And say, 'I'm selling up.' Once the police finish with me. 'I'm off.'

Scilla Wynyard had no idea where.

'Sir?'

'Yes, Hickie?'

'Don't get me wrong, sir, but it feels like a waste of time.'

'What does, Hickie?'

'This, sir.' Hick waved at the pile of paper on his desk. 'Postman Pat, sir. Veech.'

Batten had a soft spot for DC Eddie 'Loft' Hick. Sometimes, though, the soft spot was Hick's brain.

'*Veech* is a waste of time?'

'I mean, nothing'll bring him back, will it, sir?'

Bloody hope not, Zig.

'Yet we're spending all this time on him?'

The morning briefing had spent time on a lot of things. Veech was one of them.

'You must've wanted to throttle the bugger yourself, sir? And now someone's throttled him for us, right? And here we are, flogging dead horses, looking for the someone?' Hick paused for breath. Long sentences did that to him. 'We should be giving *someone* a medal.'

Batten took a long look at 'Loft' Hick. An enigma? A cop with a thought-process that defies logic? Or a man speaking thoughts *you're* not even allowed to think, Zig?

'Come on, Eddie, try and remember what we're for. And there's a rogue gun, still out there. What if it takes a pot-shot at *you*?'

Hick gave Batten his best 'like to see it try' look.

'If the police don't care about the law, Hickie, why should the criminals? When public order gets frayed at the edges, you and me are supposed to tie up the loose ends.'

Hick shrugged, cocked his pencil. Sounding off, but getting on. All in a day's work, Zig?

'Wish we were short of loose ends, sir.'

Hick flicked a paperclip at a bulging filing cabinet, so full of loose ends they were climbing out of the drawers. Batten followed the arc, heard a *'ching'* as it hit.

'Someone has to tie them, Hickie. Who'll do it if we don't?'

No reply. Batten thought back to this morning's briefing, where Hick had ploughed the same furrow...

'I keep lifting stones, sir, but there's bugger all underneath. This Veech bloke - he's got 'cold case' scrawled all over him.'

Batten wasn't going there, and he wasn't letting the team go there either.

'Not your decision, DC Hick. What about the rest of you? Anything?'

Ball put in his penn'orth.

'Not a squeak from the media appeal, zor, from Twitter, from the flyers. And sod all of any use from Veech's biog.'

Terence Veech went from children's homes to a half-way house and then to a postman's life with the Royal Mail.

'Eighteen years a postman, zor. Six different depots, all over the country. And every place he goes, there's rare birds to watch.'

'Can't be the only reason?'

'Well, if he was good at putting people's backs up, his supervisors were just as good at not sticking it on his file. We're still digging, zor. He managed five years here, in Somerset. His longest stint.'

'Our bad luck, Ballie.'

'Or maybe Somerset should take credit, zor. The Levels, green hills, apple orch- .'

Ball stopped himself. His mind's still a yo-yo, Zig. Batten turned to Nina Magnus.

'Any gems in the crime figures, Nina?'

'No threats and murders in his wake, sir. All cross-checked. And no criminal record. Not so much as a caution for kicking a dog.' She shook her head. 'Nothing. Till he came here.'

Ball watched his Somerset theory crash and burn.

Batten had warmed, though, to the theory Timms was pushing - that a further anonymous letter was still out there. And that an unknown recipient blew away Terence Veech's face, in response to the letter's contents. Whatever they were.

'I mean, our mystery killer's hardly going to turn up at the nick and say 'here's the missing letter and the missing gun', is he, sir? So we can say, 'and here's a missing police cell. We've had it wallpapered, specially for you'?'

'If only, Hazel.'

After that, ideas dried up. Batten was left with the thankless task of counting off the negatives on his fingers.

'So. No murder weapon. No .410 cartridges. No gunshot residue. No fingerprints. No trace evidence worth having.' You've run out of fingers, Zig. Don't use your left hand too - it's bad for morale. 'No CCTV. And no witnesses.'

'S'what I keep saying, sir,' muttered Hick. 'Cold case.'

With stubborn professionalism, Batten returned to Andrew Priddle.

'Have we a double-killer here, then, unlikely as it might seem? Old Tom Priddle first? Then Terence Veech?'

Ball took a turn at the negatives. It's what Sergeant's are for, Zig. If he ever returns to his old self, get him to do it more often, so you don't have to.

'Last time I saw old Tom, zor, he was a stick of spaghetti. If I'd sneezed he would've snapped in two. And we've all seen the staircase in that cesspit of his. Accidental death sells it to me, zor.'

Magnus chipped in. 'I spoke to the Doc, sir, as you asked.' She shook her head again. 'Grounds for exhumation - nil.'

'OK. What about young Andrew as our Veech-killer, then?'

A team silence. If they turned up evidence, they'd reconsider, but for now...

Batten gave them a penetrating stare, and did his job.

'News just in', he said. 'This isn't School, and we're not electing Prefects. We're investigating a *murder*. It's not a new idea. There's a victim, and a killer, and I couldn't give a monkey's tit if you don't like the cut of their jib! So wake up! And GET DIGGING.'

With a noise like a gunshot, Hick cracked his knuckles. He'd been digging, solid, for the last four hours. The sound cracked Batten back to the essentials of life.

'You've not kept an eye on the clock, Hickie.'

'Clock, sir?'

'It's an age since bacon sandwich time. Need to double up our calorie intake, this weather.'

It was still brass monkeys. Batten hadn't eaten and it was gone three. He rasped a defiant ten pound note from his wallet.

'Tell 'em to slap a fried egg on mine. White bread today. And a dollop of brown sauce.'

Forty

Not a lot to show, for all the work, eh, Zig? He pushed the evidence summaries aside. If you can see your desk, Zig, you can see your way, isn't that what you keep saying?

As it happens, Zig, I'm at home, it's my day-off, it's getting dark, and the stuff's all over the coffee table. There's some on the floor and the rest is smeared across the sofa where my socks are supposed to go.

Well, Zig, the woodstove's crackling away. Why don't you just open the door and burn it?

Murders. You could build a bonfire with the paper they spawn.

As a detective, he was narked at how little they knew of Terence Veech.

Motives? *Blank.*

Intentions? *Vague.*

Plans? *Unclear.*

Glad, yes, that Veech's vague intentions would never be carried out. But detectives need an answer, and D.I. Batten didn't have one.

As a man, though, and a man living in hope of an enduring relationship, Batten was barely narked at all. The less detail, the less to be publically dissected when the Coroner set to work. And the less gruelling for Erin Kemp - and her thirteen year old.

He shuffled the weight of paper into some kind of sequence and began again. Till the door-bell clanged, like a stick on a broken saucepan. The cold weather was distorting the ringer. And if it's a postman, Zig...

It was Sergeant Ball.

'Ballie. What brings your merry legs here? Not the joy of a freezing cold twilight on this alleged Spring day?'

Ball was silent. He stood on the hall carpet, a Jehovah's Witness so surprised to be let in he'd forgotten what to say.

'Glass of cider?'

Ball shook his head. Batten's eyebrows went into shock.

'Perhaps if we could sit down, zor?'

The sofa was a paper-chase, but Ball had already moved to the dining table. A puzzled Inspector sat one side, a stone-faced Sergeant the other. Ball added still more embarrassment to the mix.

'Give me your hand, zor.'

'*What?*'

'I said give me your hand, zor.'

'My *hand?*'

'Zor.'

'*Why*? You've got two monsters of your own. You've got enough left over to make a third!'

'Humour me, zor. Please.'

Ball's face had no humour in it.

'Er, OK. Which hand?'

Sergeant Ball in serious mode was not new to Batten. But he'd only ever been beside or behind him, at a tricky interview, a confrontation, an arrest. Never opposite. Ball ignored the question. He took Batten's right hand in his own, their two fists ending up not as an English handshake but in the North American cross-thumb grasp favoured by professional footballers. Funny bloody time for an arm-wrestling contest, Zig - and if that's what it is, you've already lost. Ball's grip was so strong Batten's veins began to pulse.

'Ballie, if this is that blood-brother thing, then go careful with the penknife or I'll splatter the walls.'

A weak smile was Ball's only response. He looked directly at Batten and cleared his throat.

'I'm holding on to blood and bone here, zor. It's the only way I'm able to do this. I'm not a religious man, I think you know that, but this is a sort of prayer. It's my confession, zor.'

Batten opened his mouth but Ball's formidable free hand cut off the words.

'I know a few people, in the force. But I've put my mind to this and there's no-one else I can confess to, you see. It's not only that you're...appropriate. It's that you're - well, zor, the others are good men and women, but you're a man of understanding, that's what it is. A man of understanding.'

Batten's embarrassment was dispelled by the slow pulsing throb in the blade of his hand where Ball's giant fist squeezed a strong connection.

'I've always been straight, zor. Proud to be. I've worked with others who've bent the rules a touch, and one or two so bent they disappeared round corners, if you see what I mean.'

Both men remembered DC George Halfpenny, who sold out his own CID team, barely twelve months ago, for a thousand pounds a time in used notes. He was inside now, and by all accounts not enjoying it.

'But I've broken my own rules, zor. That's the problem.'

Ball's grip on Batten's hand became impossibly tighter.

'I know why I need to tell you, zor. I need to go back to truth, you see. It's been very bad, at home, these last weeks, months now, I suppose-'

'I know, Ballie. There's-'

'No, no, zor. You don't. Beg pardon, but you don't know. You know only what we've let you see. Me, Di, Belinda. Truth is, it's been far worse, zor, than I can ever say. Nor will I. You're a man of understanding. You don't need to be told.'

All Batten could do was nod. *Thank Christ he's only holding your hand, Zig.*

'I thought for a long while I might never get Di back. And she's my strength, zor. To see her as you did, at Gemma's grave, clawing at the stone-cold ground till her fingers bled, digging into the soil, trying to...What would she have done, zor, had you and me not found her? You saw the strength of her, and it's that same strength I thought had gone from me.'

Ball cleared his throat once more. *My God, Zig, don't let him cry.*

'When we lost our baby, lost Gemma, it was Di who said we had to hold on to our strength. She was full of nothing but grief, but she capped it off. And she was wrong, I know that now. We didn't grieve enough, I'm sure of it. Or maybe we grieved long and thin, zor. I think we've grieved too long and too thin ever since, if you see my meaning?'

Ball had lost his way. But not his grip. Batten could barely breathe.

'I'm getting to what I need to say, zor. Just bear with me?'

Batten saw a lump rise up in Ball's throat, could feel it, across the table. *Please don't let him blub. You can't do blub, can you, Zig?*

As if noticing the silence, Ball swallowed and carried on.

'It's when the wrong things happen to the wrong people, zor. Di, she should be a mother, no-one better. You can see that. We all can. Much pain she's carried already, and done nothing in her life to deserve it - no exaggeration, zor, nothing. Help others, be willing, that's all she's ever done. And when it has to be her, in the orchard that day, to find Jeff Wynyard, with his face...well, you saw, zor. But me, you, we're trained, aren't we, for what it's worth. It's the job. Not Di's though. So why should it have to be her?'

Even if Batten knew the answer, his desert-dry mouth would struggle to form the words.

'Over the edge she went. Into a pit of silence. So deep, so...*empty*, I thought she'd never climb out, not with all the help, all the love... Maybe it's the mourning we should've done, before.'

Ball closed his eyes for a moment, as if to ensure this thought, however painful, found a lodging place in his memory.

'Perhaps good will come of it, Ballie?'

'No, no, zor, that's the problem - good coming about because someone's does evil? I can't be having that anymore. It won't sit well with me. Feels warped, zor. Plain wrong.'

Batten's hand twitched in Ball's pincer of a fist.

'I'm almost there, zor, almost there. It was when we searched his house, Veech, the postman. Gave me the creeps. Oh I've had them before, I know, but...It was picking up that bible. That's what did it. To call it the good book, after what he used it for? And I thought of Di, doing good for others, volunteering, getting things *done*. But it's Veech's evil poison she stumbles on. I wasn't going to let him poison anyone else, zor. I've done a wrong thing, I know. But I've done it to make things right.'

Ball's spare sausage fingers were scrabbling in his pocket. Batten waited for a giant handkerchief to appear - because anything smaller would look ridiculous in his giant hand. But it was a jumble of folded papers that emerged. Ball dropped them on the table as if they were burning his fingers.

'I saw you puzzling over the dog-bowl, zor, in Veech's house. I puzzled over it myself, because we've got one like it at home - for Gus.' Gus was the Balls' black Labrador.

'I got there, Ballie. But not as fast as you, eh?'

'Well, you're not a dog-owner, zor, so...'

Batten stabbed a finger at the papers on the table. 'These the contents?'

'Yes, zor. Hidden in the base. You'd normally fill it with sand, to stop the d-'

'I know. I unscrewed it. But no sand and no papers, by the time I got there.'

'It's mostly copies, of the letters Veech sent. You've seen the originals often enough, zor.'

Ball's free hand swept four folded letters to one side, pulling the rest of the papers towards him.

'He'd kept these, though, as well.'

Awkwardly, he unfolded and smoothed four photographs, all neatly clipped from The Western Gazette. Batten recognised the fur cloak and hood of Sian Kemp, a pretty Wassail Queen, pouring cider from a jug onto the roots of the oldest apple tree in Stockton Marsh's orchard. A second showed her being lifted high on the shoulders of Norm Hogg and Joe Porrit, the two 'official' shotguns. In a third she was in close-up, fur hood raised, smiling at the camera. Ball had his hand over the fourth image. He turned it over.

'And this one, zor.'

It was a photo of the two shotguns firing blanks into the upper branches of the tree, to scare off 'evil spirits'. In the background, Batten himself was smiling, gloved hands protecting the ears of a laughing Erin Kemp.

Someone - Veech, presumably - had taken a marker pen and drawn a circle round their faces. Underneath was written, '*My Queen needs no fornicators. Inspection pit.*' Batten closed his eyes. One more private detail, to be publicised by the Coroner.

'So that's what he'd planned for me and Erin, Ballie? We'd be defined as collateral damage, I suppose. But it's not much of a grave, is it, a pit in a garage?'

'Unused, though, zor. Thank god. And no oil on the floor.'

'Yes, wouldn't have got our clothes dirty, would we?'

Neither man smiled.

'I wish that was the worst of it, zor.' He fumbled out a final piece of cheap white paper. On it was a neat pencil drawing of Veech's large garden pond, with a circuit diagram showing how the pump and lighting would work.

'He'd almost finished the whole thing, had Veech. Couple of wires to connect, that's all. I finished it for him. Curiosity, zor. Don't they say it's a wonderful thing in a policeman? It lit up, soon as I plugged it in, the pond. Deep blue.'

Batten understood. Veech's very own sea. 'He'd stitched a blue sea, or something like it, into the sampler we found, remember?'

Ball nodded, and flipped over the white paper. Batten read the few words, written in a cold, precise hand.

Our final trip, Queenie and I, to the sea.

'It's a very deep pond, zor. For no reason I could figure. I jiggered around with a long-handled hoe and it didn't touch the bottom.'

They both knew why Veech had dug himself a deep sea, but neither wanted to voice it. Ball cleared his throat.

'Deep enough for two, zor, sadly.'

The final words of Erin's letter pierced Batten. 'Not for two, Ballie.'

He had to close his eyes, to block an image of a blue-faced Sian Kemp.

For the watcher and the Queen shall be One.

Had she ever liked sheep? She'd liked *Jeff*, and he liked sheep. Scilla Wynyard couldn't recall a time when Jeff didn't smell of the beasts. Jeff *was* sheep.

But now, each sheep was Jeff. The smell brought him back, then the wind blew Jeff away again. Without thinking, she opened the kitchen window, despite the cold.

She'd agreed a price for the sheep. And the converted cowshed, and whatever else. She totted up the bills from the cardboard box on the table. Could be worse.

'Pay your debts, Scilla, and start again.'

Where?

'Somewhere without sheep!'

Oh yes?

'A city. Not many sheep in a city.'
Where then?
'The bigger the city, the fewer the sheep.'
Ah. London?
'London will do.'
'Do for what?
'For living in.'

It was not the absurdity of his hand being clamped in his Sergeant's pincer-fist that disturbed Batten, it was the pain. But Ball had his reasons for not letting go. Photographs and letters lay between them on the dining table. Ball's free hand pushed them into a single pile.

'What happens now, Ballie?'

'Now, zor? This.'

Before Batten could move, a nimbler-than-he-looked Sergeant Ball scooped up the pile and crossed to the woodstove. Asbestos fingers flipped open the door and threw the suborned papers at the flames. Batten could only watch. The pages fizzed - with hate, Zig? - as the white papers turned brown. They twisted and curled into blood-red and blue, till there was nothing left but the pale grey of ash.

Smoke from the log fire filled the room. Batten always used the same logs. Apple-wood.

He wanted to shout, '*you bloody fool, Chris!*' All he could manage was, 'I can barely feel my hand.'

Ball could feel his. He used it draw from his coat pocket a see-through plastic evidence bag. It landed on the table between them. Batten recognised the torn, marked pages from Terence Veech's copy of *The Book of Revelation*. You've been seeing them in your dreams, Zig. But at least these are already in evidence.

'They should be in separate bags, Ballie, and paper ones. Sloppy work, Sergeant.'

Batten reached for the plastic bag but Ball pulled it out of range.

'I'm well aware of that, zor. And well aware it makes no difference. Best if you don't handle them again. Best if you'd never seen them, in truth. I tried to make sure you wouldn't. When we searched the first time,

I hid the bible where only I could find it. Got a shock when the second one turned up. And when you spotted it, zor, well, what choice did I have?'

Before Batten could remind him it was the law that made the choices, Ball was shaking the torn pages onto the table and putting them in order. Batten could read the underlined words clearly enough, but had no need. He knew them by heart. By heart, Zig? *Heart*? Will you ever get your words sorted out?

Verse 20 ...*that woman Jezebel...to commit fornication.*

He saw Erin's face, at the Coroner's Hearing, listening to the words read out for everyone to hear. And reading them herself, afterwards, in a transcript. In a newspaper.

Verse 21 ...*and she repented not.*

Verse 22 ...*Behold I will cast her into a pit, and them that commit adultery with her, into great tribulation.*

Well, you could hold her hand, Zig, at this point in the Coroner's proceedings - since you're obviously implicated. Reassure her: you're not even *technically* an adulteress, Erin. And chin up, you're still alive. We both are. No harm done. None at all.

Ball watched Batten's eyes rove along the underlined words.

'It's the last page, zor, that sent me over the edge. How can we let Sian read that? How can we?'

Batten was still struggling with the thought of *Erin* reading it. He'd suppressed the idea of Sian reading it too. Ball grabbed the page, and as quickly flung it down. The underlined words landed face-up, burning the room and the two men in it.

Verse 23 ...*And I will kill her children with death.*

Final rehearsal. Erin Kemp dreamed she was elsewhere; dreamed she was never a singer, that she had never said 'yes, I will'. *A Child of Our Time* was somebody else's dream, not hers.

The chorus, a full fifty tonight, in three ranks behind her, wore black suits, white shirts and gold ties, or smart black dresses with a sash of cloth of gold. She could feel a hundred eyes burn through the back of her gold shawl and purple dress, and drill into her heart. If she still had one.

'Is everybody ready?' Michael, the Leader, asked the Chorus.

Erin heard fifty voices mumble 'yes' behind her. The Leader's hand asked the Orchestra and twenty more voices said 'yes'. Her fellow soloists nodded one by one as the hand gently questioned.

Soloist. That's you, Erin. A person who sings alone. Time to stand up and sing alone. Yes?

'*No*,' said her heart, and the word moved into her throat. '*No!*' drilled its way from throat to teeth. Michael's eyes opened wider, a direct question.

'No, I can't do this'. Erin Kemp felt the words form on her tongue.

'*Yes*', said her lips, in hope.

Although he sat at his own dining table, near his own woodstove, in sight of his own paper-strewn sofa, Batten was in the Coroner's Court. He heard the evidence being unpicked, felt the shock of private worlds being publicly displayed and dissected. Neutral, workaday, for the professionals. Acid in the heart for the rest - man, woman, or child.

He threw a sad finger at the scraps of bible. 'It doesn't matter what you and I think, Ballie. They're already in evidence. Pointless burning them. And there's more than one copy of *The Book of Revelation.*'

Ball looked squarely at his Inspector. Not difficult, they were barely two feet apart.

'Ah, zor. It's not pointless, you see. That's another thing I've done wrong, to make things right.'

'Ballie, there has to be a consequence. There'll be-'

'You and me, zor, we're the only ones to see these pages. Apart from Veech. I made sure the SOCOs didn't, and our lot were too busy with the rest of that nasty house. I pretended to record them, and the second bible too, but I never did. They'll end in fire.'

'Stop, Chris. This has to stop. *Now*. There'll be consequences.'

It was as if Ball could speak, but not hear.

'You see, if Gemma had lived, she'd be around Sian's age, give or take. And me and Di, well, Sian's a bit like one of the family now. Uncle Chris, she calls me. You've heard her. If Di had found her voice, at the time, I know what she'd have said. End it in fire. Burn it.'

Batten's hand - his Detective Inspector hand - shot out to grab the torn pages. But Ball was faster. A giant hand slammed down on them, the other at the ready. Both men rose from their seats, shoulders set. My god, Zig. Has it come to this? A robust stab at restraint techniques, on my own Sergeant? In your dreams, Zig. He's built like a bull.

'Ballie. Please see *sense*.'

When his Sergeant spoke, it was a harder voice that emerged.

'It's going in the flames, zor, and you'll not stop me. You can tell the Coroner if you like, but I'll not corroborate your story. And you'll be the fool, without evidence.' With a noise like rats scrabbling in a drain, the pages disappeared into Ball's massive fist.

'It's not what we do, Chris. It's not *right*.'

Oh really, Zig? Never fiddled at the edges yourself?

'*Right*, zor? Right is the word I've struggled with. I've made it right, in my way.'

In an instant, for a second time, he flipped open the woodstove and cast the offending pages into the flames. Seconds later, they were nothing but smoke.

Defeated, Batten's head sank to the table. When he opened his eyes, all he could see was an empty plastic evidence bag. The white strip where crime is supposed to be recorded, was blank. Ball sat down, quietly, the relief on his face turning to realisation, then sadness.

'Consequences, zor. I'm ready for them now.'

'Chris-'

'I think it's best if I resign. I'll say it's on account of Di - and in a sense it is. And that way, zor, you'll not be explaining things to the Coroner, or the Area Superintendent. Or them.' He raised his finger towards the ceiling.

'Or to my conscience, Ballie?'

'Now, now, zor. Your conscience is your business. I can only talk about mine, and mine's done its explaining. Yours? Well maybe yours might have to. If it chooses to speak.'

Batten stared at the flames in the woodstove, but didn't like the pictures they made.

'Steady down, Chris. Look, evidence gets lost - genuinely, I mean.

We're not robots.' He picked up the empty bag. 'We'll say you were under pressure. God knows, you've had plenty of that-'

'Zor. Stop. I've included Di in my reasons for all this. But she's not an excuse. And I won't let her be one.'

'But to resign? It's *wilful!*'

'*NO*, zor! It's *DOUBT*! I've doubted the law, zor. Dangerous waters, don't think I'm unaware. But you said it yourself - we're not robots. Sometimes good needs to be left alone - to *be* good - and not have someone else's evil smeared all over it. If I somehow turned back time, so the evidence is still here, not in the fire but on this table, now, what's the law going to *do* with it?'

'Ballie-'

'Going to dig up Terence Veech, is it? *Huh.* Going to wag a legal finger at his corpse and say, 'it's a good job you're *dead*. Because if you weren't, the law would make damn certain that after many a lonely year you died in Broadmoor!"

'*Chris-*'

'And when the law's finished with Veech's corpse, it'll say, 'Ah, Mrs Kemp, let's just pick through what Mr Veech had in mind for you and Inspector Batten. Oh, what lucky escape you've had. No pit of great tribulation after all, so once these highly public proceedings are complete, feel free, the pair of you, to resume your fornication in private!'

Batten shook his head at Ball, wanting him to stop. He raised his hands in surrender, but Ball was burning with words now.

'And let's not forget - that's what the law will say - let's not forget young *Sian* - oh, what a lucky escape you've had too! Oh yes, you might just as easily have been kidnapped, raped and drowned! *What a lucky, lucky escape you've had!*'

Ball's face was reddening beyond its normal ginger-red, into a bloodred, a fury-red, that shook with the rest of him. He could barely finish what he'd begun.

'Let's not forget - no, no, you'll not forget! Thirteen years old but you'll remember all your life. Oh, it's bound to scar you, yes, but we have to explain these things, you see. You'll have nightmares, but the public must understand, you see. You'll look over your shoulder at the shadows, all your life, but every detail has to be recorded. The law *demands* it, Sian, on your behalf, YOU LUCKY GIRL!'

Batten felt the table shudder as Ball's sledgehammer fist slammed into it. Face burning, he rose to his feet, a medium-height giant of a man. His out-of-nowhere yells were not new to Batten, but he had never heard Chris Ball use strong profanity before, never heard his voice pierce stone walls and jolt them.

'AND I'M NOT FUCKING WELL HAVING IT!'

Forty one

If only a conscience could be buried like a corpse. Batten's internal struggle was leaking through every pore. Erin Kemp noticed, quickly enough.

'It doesn't go away, Zig, does it?'

'What doesn't?'

'*It*. All the...disturbance.'

What could Batten say? That some things do go away? That they go up in flames? His attempt to ease Chris Ball back onto undisturbed tramlines had yet to succeed. Your heart was elsewhere, Zig, eh, when you gave him your big speech about boundaries?

'The law is what we do, Chris, it's why we're in the job. You can't knock over the bits of law you don't like. Once you start, a bit more crumbles, then a bit more still, and then there's a big gap in the fence, and the bull charges through and gores the guts out of you. And since nobody gives a shit anymore, you bleed to death.'

All he got from Ball was a vague nod of acceptance.

Erin Kemp sat down next to Batten on the sofa, curled up to him, in front of the woodstove. It was her first visit to his cottage in a while. They both knew her *West Country Choral* rehearsals were only part of the reason.

'Why do I feel guilty, Zig?'

'About Veech?'

Erin gave a sad nod. 'To be relieved, that a man is dead? I felt dirty, from the letter, when he was alive. But now...I don't know what I feel any more.'

Wait till you find a real body, he wanted to say. Like Di Ball did. Or professionally, like Chris and me, who have to study them, unpick their history, bring them justice, when the brute truth is the life's gone out of them. Batten was on body number nine. He still saw skin like cold wax. Saw dead eyes. Life may have gone out of the bodies, Zig, but the bodies haven't gone out of you, have they? Unwanted resurrections, every one of them, every time.

Pack it in, Zig. Next thing you know, you'll be trying to eff the ineffable. And you know what an effing waste of time that is.

'It does go away,' he told her.

Fine, Zig, tell Erin a lie, to preserve a kind of truth. But don't do it too often. Reaching into his pocket, he waved his ticket for *A Child of Our Time*. The first performance was tonight.

'Can't wait to hear you sing solo.'

'Subject clumsily changed, as ever, Zig.' She smiled and leaned into him. 'I'll try to let it all go away.'

Was this the right time to mention the other tickets, and the other 'going away'? He'd bought three airline tickets to Crete, given Grigoris the dates, made the arrangements.

All he need do now was tell Erin and Sian.

Andrew Priddle stayed at the old man's house one final night. The central heating of his Blackdown Hills home had softened him up, and he felt the chill as soon as he opened the rotting door. Dragging in a bag of logs from the car, he broke up the remains of the smashed bedside table as kindling. Old Tom's heavy stick made a handy poker. He stood in front of the woodstove. There was nowhere else in the house he was prepared to go.

Upstairs was a chronicle of ghosts - the staircase not a ladder but a snake. Tonight, he would sleep on the sofa, close to the fire. The TV was in Suffolk, with whatever else could be salvaged from the wreck of his home. After the police discharged him, he made swift plans - and as swiftly rejected them. The Stockton Marsh cricket pavilion had failed to burn. Too risky to set fire to it again. And torching Scilla Wynyard's house would have the police all over him. He heard in the shop she was selling up, in any case.

'She better stay away from Suffolk,' he told the woodstove. 'Or I'll burn *her* down.'

He'd come across a sheep carcass in the hills and planned to shove it in the van and dump it in the brook that flowed through Stockton Marsh, to foul the waters. But the van was already sold.

'Good job we don't need the money,' he said to his shoes, up on the dirty sofa now. 'Got sod-all for the old brown van.'

His final decision was to be away, well away, from this stinking sofa and this stinking village when the bulldozer knocked stinking Priddle Castle to the ground.

That was happening at first light tomorrow. But here he was.

The Hall lights dimmed, and all Erin Kemp could see was a grey mist of audience faces and a light above the Leader's rostrum. Dark and light. Shadow and light. Could she do this? The leader's baton was still, his eyes checking, readying the orchestra. She should withdraw, now, before the first notes sounded, before the trap-door closed.

But Michael's baton moved, the tiniest flick, and the sound began.

Too late to withdraw. She must sing. She had committed to it, but inside...Her throat, prepared mere minutes ago, was dry and dark as soot. An unwelcome visitor named Panic had burst in, ticketless.

She looked beyond the light to those who had paid to be here, to the shadowy audience. She knew where Sian was, next to Zig, behind her parents, her friends. Then all too soon the leader's hand, palm up, fingers gently curled, drew her to her feet and she was standing, remembering Michael's dress-rehearsal words.

'You have a fine voice. Set it free. Sing the shadow, and sing the light.'

And the strange mixture began. Instinct, practice, skill, the power of the music, all finding their balance as the catharsis of song slowly purged weeks of dismay - though the words she sang said otherwise.

How can I cherish my man in such times? How can I be a mother in a time of destruction?

Erin Kemp could almost feel words of dismay flow from her lungs into her throat, coating her lips - less kissed of late - and float into the air above and around her. Up it went, the dismay, into the hall's high ceiling, dismay ringing against the windows, trembling at the doors in search of an exit. And finding a crack, a chink, and filtering through it, to re-join the darkness beyond.

She heard fresh words - *Her face will be illumined like the sun.*

Shadow and light merged within her turning world, and merged in turn with the hum of strings and the harmony of voices, her throat relaxing and the sound transmitting to strangers and friends, to the hall of eyes and ears. She felt connected to every one of them.

Erin Kemp's soprano voice joined fifty voices, joined the woodwind, brass and strings as the leader's hand and baton soothed and wove.

The moving waters renew the earth, said the voices.

Erin Kemp had her daughter back. She was safe. Zig was safe.

She had never sung so well.

A Child of Our Time helped Batten make his mind up too. Instead of struggling to forget his troubled conscience, he decided to permanently remind it. Terence Veech had no family, no next of kin, no identifiable friends to bury him. The money to pay for his 'pauper's grave' came from the sale of his property and possessions. The State would get the ample remainder.

'As I'm sure you know, Inspector, we call it a Public Health Funeral, not a pauper's grave.'

Mr Coombes from the Council had a dignity Batten warmed to.

'And no, a headstone is not the norm, I'm afraid. For a number of reasons, a cremation or an unmarked plot is the order of the day.'

Batten knew there would be folk in Stockton Marsh who'd not thank him for it, but he quietly arranged with Mr Coombes for a small and simple headstone to be erected in the churchyard there - with Veech's full name, and the relevant dates. A person deserves nothing less.

Mr Coombes was the only 'mourner', when the coffin was interred. Batten watched from his car, in the lay-by where Jeff Wynyard had parked his bright red pick-up, weeks ago.

The little headstone was white. Batten paid for it from his own pocket.

With the white reminder still in his head, Batten drew an unsmiling Ball into his cubby-hole office at Parminster. The rest of the team were out, failing to tie loose ends. Without warm bodies to soften them, the pale brown walls of Parminster CID looked worse today.

'I'll come to the point, Chris.'

'Zor.'

'If you resign, I'll shop you. And you know what that'll mean?'

Ball knew.

'Pension problems, zor. Very considerate.'

'I don't recall you considering *me*, before you burnt Queen's Evidence?'

Ball might have said he burnt it very much in consideration for Zig Batten. And for Erin, and Sian. He used his eyebrows to silently return his Inspector's words.

'OK, Chris. Fair enough. But nothing's changed. Resign, and I'll shop you. That's *me* considering *you*, by the way.'

Another half-lie, Zig. It's not that you don't want to lose the best Sergeant you've ever worked with?

Ball appraised his Inspector, and appraised himself, cogs turning.

'Can I think about it, zor?'

'I fly to Crete tomorrow. You've got till then.'

Forty two

They were sticky from gathering wild herbs on the hot hillside. Arms full of greenery and scent, the four children made their way back down the dusty path. The three Cretan girls wore simple t-shirts, leggings and sandals. The fourth girl was dressed in brand-new clothes bought last-minute in Primark and H&M in Yeovil, for a first ever visit to foreign soil. She didn't quite fit in, the fourth girl.

When the Greek children deposited their spoils in the cool stone kitchen, the fourth hung back, waiting to see where her armful should go. Once seated at the table, all four reached into pockets and drew out mobile phones. Experienced thumbs searched for texts, photos, apps. Three screens lit up in the Greek alphabet.

The fourth screen, an English phone, said 'No wifi signal'. Sian Kemp's disappointment was vocal. Mrs Grigoris has shown her the little card with the wifi code written on it. It was in Greek, and she didn't understand what to do. As the others giggled and swiped, she felt more and more alone. Mum and Zig were away helping 'Uncle' Makis with the wedding preparations, and she was stuck here, picking smelly herbs whose names she didn't recognise, and listening to three girls she hardly knew babbling a load of Greek pants. Bullied by peers in England, she was bullied now in Crete, by circumstance.

The eldest daughter, Nina, had been told to 'look out for Sian' by her father, but she kept forgetting. And Sian was fed up of being called 'Sawn', by all of them. She hadn't wanted to come but mum said 'it'll be good for us.' Good? Even rainy Stockton Marsh was better than here.

Nina looked up from her phone, saw the dismay on Sian's face, and remembered.

'Oh, Sawn,' she said, 'you give me please?' And she held her hand out for the phone. Quickly, she fathomed where the code should go and touched 'Connect'.

Sian Kemp watched her screensaver blink and the photo smile back at her. She was wearing a brown fur cloak, and her backdrop was flaming torches and apple trees. She was the Wassail Queen. Nina leaned across and clapped her hands when she saw the image.

'Send! Send!' she cried, taking Sian's phone and swiftly messaging the photograph to three more phones. All the girls screeched with excitement as the image arrived. Nina took a selfie of the four of them, all a-giggle, squeezed together in the cool of the herb-scented kitchen.

'We sisters now', Nina said. 'We all Queens!' And she clapped her hands and laughed.

'Four queens', smiled Sian. She took a photo of her Greek 'sisters', and shared it with her Facebook friends in England.

'Come', said Nina. 'We go swim.'

Andrew Priddle still didn't know why he'd stayed to watch the walls come down. It didn't take the bulldozer long to topple them.

'Only held together with muck and brambles.' That's what the man in charge said.

When everything was flat, Andrew got in his little car and drove to the rented cottage in the Blackdown Hills.

'Paid a full month's rent,' he told the windscreen. 'Might as well get my money's worth.'

He wasn't aware he sounded like old Tom. He spent the days saying a slow goodbye to Somerset, uncertain of his imagined life in Suffolk.

After he returned the keys, it was not the road to Southwold he followed, but the road to Stockton Marsh - for a final look at the ground where he was born. He wasn't sure why.

They had worked fast, the demolition crew. The rubble and weeds were gone and the earth was almost clean. Diggers were excavating deep trenches for the foundations of a 'five bedroom luxury detached.'

He watched till it became too painful, then turned to go.

That's when the workman shouted.

The bride shone with joy. Joy shone from her eyes, from her dress of hand-made lace, her flowers, her bright-white smile that had boosted the sun and now gifted light to the moon.

Batten wiped a discreet handkerchief over his neck and brow, as the hot day merged into an evening of dancing and wine and sweat.

'All too much for you, Zig?' asked Erin Kemp. Her smile was back.

'If I clink my glass one more time it'll shatter,' he said. 'Or I will.'

Another round of celebration interrupted them, spoons rattling against plates, and glass clinking against glass.

'*Na zisete!*' rang out - *long life to you!* - as more guests sang their blessings to the bride and groom.

Erin gazed in admiration at Eleni, the bride. 'Makis told me what 'Eleni' means.'

Batten's head cocked a question.

'Light', she said. 'Eleni means light. I thought he was making it up, but it's true.'

Batten chose not to add what Makis said the groom's name meant.

'He has my name, Sig - his first name. Of course a family name, yes? He is called Gregoris. I tell you what it is, what I and he mean.'

Grigoris paused proudly, his thick moustache pulled left and right by a monster smile.

'*A Watchman*, Sig. That is what we mean, our names. And *he* is not even a police! But my nephew, Gregoris, he will look after her, yes, watch over Eleni?'

The smile grew bigger, dispelling Batten's brief memory of another 'watchman' whose eyes saw only darkness and whose fingers jabbed black ink into cheap white paper.

Erin's fingers jabbed him lightly in the ribs.

'Oi, you nearly spilled my wine', he said.

'Better for your liver if I do.'

'Yes, but it's considered rude. You know, throwing wonderful Cretan kindness on the floor.'

'Yes, and it's considered rude to drift off to Zigland.'

'Was I?'

She flicked a smiling eyebrow. She'd mastered the trick, after much practice. Batten saw only eyes. Erin Kemp's green eyes were back, and they shone.

Should Chris Ball ring Batten? He wasn't sure. His boss liked to be kept in the loop - insisted on it. But he was on holiday, with Erin and Sian in Crete. Ball picked up the phone. And put it down again. Was Batten going to cancel his leave? Get on a plane? Screech his tyres across the car park and dash into Parminster CID in a Hawaiian shirt and flip-flops?

No need. There was nothing Batten could do. As far as Chris Ball was concerned, justice had already been done.

'Sarge?'

'Yes, Hickie?'

'He keeps asking for the boss. For 'Mr Batten'. I've told him Mr Batten's away glugging ouzo but he just gives me that blank look. What shall I do?'

'I'll have a word, Hickie. You chase up Doc Danvers - see if there's anything confirmed.'

Some guests said it was called *the butcher's dance*. Some said *no, no, no, it's called the sailor's dance*. Call it what you like, Batten couldn't hit the rhythm, legs and arms going in all the wrong directions, at war with the music ringing out from the bouzouki.

Get a grip, Zig. You're dancing like Eddie Hick!

He sat down, defeated by the music, the raki, the wine. The music slowed, and he saw an elegant circle dance form and grow, till an entire village swung their bodies as one, left and right, arms on one another's shoulders, smiles and laughter following the easy rhythm of their feet. Makis and his wife, Afroditi, led out the younger guests as the dance spread across the village square. Erin and Sian were grinning for England amid the throng of Cretan dancers.

Batten's glass was empty and he pushed it along the table so it wouldn't be instantly filled. He watched, already bleary with alcohol, heat and euphoria. Erin joined him, leaving Sian happily dancing with Nina and her sisters.

'You'll never guess what I've just learnt about the bride's bouquet', she said.

'It's got flowers in it?'

She nipped him.

'Ow!'

'Serves you right. No, if a guest-'

Then she gripped Batten's arm in fear, and Sian was sprinting back, disturbed, and clinging to her mother's waist.

BOODOODOOM!

Shotguns!

BOOOM!

Again.

BOODOOM!

Every Cretan villager cheered and roared as celebratory guns crackled at the sky and echoed across the square. All were oblivious of the three English wedding guests.

For them, gunfire would never again be a celebration.

Ball explained that 'Mr Batten' was on leave. 'Mr Ball' would have to do.

'You remember we talked about DNA, Andrew?' he said. 'Do you remember what it is?'

Course I do, Andrew told the walls of Interview Room One. *Seen it on the telly.*

'Yes, Mr Ball.'

'And you understand how we take a sample of it, yes?'

Seen that on the telly, too.

'With a swab thing. Like at the dentist?'

'Sort of, Andrew. But no drills, eh?'

'No, Mr Ball. Don't like drills.'

Would Andrew like the reason why the police needed his DNA? Ball wished 'Mr Batten' was here, instead of him.

Hick couldn't fathom Doctor Benjamin Danvers, especially on the phone. Sounds like one of those posh London actors, Eddie.

'I can certainly confirm my early speculations, Constable, as communicated to your Sergeant. Mr Body is definitely female, and definitely adult. *Ms* Body, then, I suppose? And, yes, she has given birth at least once. I can quantify no more accurately than that, alas.'

'How long?' Hick was immune to long words.

'How long has Ms Body been in the ground? Mm, more tests, more tests, of course. But indicatively?'

Hick grunted a 'yes'.

'At least thirty years. Probably more.'

'One more? Ten more?'

'I would suggest ten is more likely than one.'

'And the other stuff?'

'I take it you mean the damage to the skull?'

'Yep.'

'My nine year-old could waltz through the analysis of *that*, Constable. Classic blunt instrument trauma. Some damage to the cranium - not necessarily fatal - but considerable damage to the upper vertebrae and the base of the skull - which certainly was. Someone 'knocked her block off', as your Inspector Batten might say, no?'

'With?'

'Ahah, the murder weapon. Now, Sergeant Ball will be thrilled. Fragments of metal lodged in the skull and faint traces of hardwood - ebony, I'm told. And the metal is silver. I cannot be entirely certain, but the pattern of marks on the skull may suggest a stout, silver-tipped walking stick? Or somesuch?'

Zig Batten and Erin Kemp spent the day after the wedding in the dappled shade of vines that clothed a rickety pergola tacked on to the Grigoris family home. Makis offered ouzo.

'It for the stomach. To settle you.'

They declined, drank water, nothing else. After a few morsels of Cretan salad they slept early and long.

Next day, Batten needed the walking cure. He accompanied Grigoris on a trek through groves of olive and almond trees down into Panormos, then beyond the village and up a winding path lined with what might have been tamarisk. Not too good at tree-identification, are you, Zig, if it's not an apple?

The path ended at a well-kept little church and cemetery overlooking the sea.

'My...great-grandfather? It is correct?'

A nod.

'He is here.'

Grigoris pointed gently at a marble grave like a small cenotaph. Inside a glass case, an oil lamp illuminated a photograph of a dignified man in an old-fashioned military uniform, and sporting a familiar moustache.

'My father, also. I come here much, but after a wedding, always. You see?'

Batten saw. He watched Grigoris refill the lamp and brush dust and grit from the memorial. On the surrounding hillsides, he counted seven half-finished groups of villas or small hotels, and over to the west a large unfinished blockhouse shaking its grey fist at the clouds.

'The developers are moving in on Crete, Makis. You'll not recognise the place in ten years time.'

'No, no, Sig.' He re-lit the oil lamp and watched the flame gather. 'Where your family are born, and where it die, you recognise always, yes?'

Batten thought of his own non-existent 'family', and his early days in the old streets of Leeds, streets buried now under new concrete, lit mostly by car headlamps and the iced white of neon.

'Maybe, Makis. Maybe.'

'These new things, Sig' - Grigoris swept a hand at the empty breezeblock chambers on the hills beyond - 'if I regret them, what can I say to this village? Do not beg the owners for jobs in these new hotels, in these bars, in the shops where, we hope, the new tourists bring euros? Go back, go back to scratch the dust, do not pay debt, do not eat, do not live?'

Batten was reminded of Keith Mallan banging on about the unmaking of the deer, the butchering of the carcass, with the best cuts going to 'the owners', as ever. He wanted to ask Grigoris who got the best cuts of Greece, when it was butchered. He knew Grigoris well enough to opt for silence.

'Or perhaps, Sig, you pay my people euros without they work, yes? *Then* the green hillside it stay green, because you are kind, because you are rich and pay all the people?'

Grigoris gave a hint of a smile. Only a hint, his moustache barely stretching his mouth, and the familiar gleam of life's joy not quite lighting up his eyes.

'We will build, Sig. Greece is an olive tree. Grow slowly, twist may be, but grow. And then, after much time, the harvest.'

Batten nodded, and turned to take in the long sea view - white ripples of foam at the shore, blue-green water in the bay despite the clouds. He scanned the harbour and the terracotta rooftops and the offending hillsides with their breezeblock squares and rods of reinforced steel pointing at the sky like unfinished crosses. Were they mocking the carved marble crucifixes in the trim cemetery where he and Makis stood?

There's a price to pay for everything, Zig. We all sell something to the devil. He thought of Chris Ball, Terence Veech, Andrew Priddle, the Wynyards, poor Jean Phelps. And you, Zig. Unless Mephistopheles tapped everyone but *you* on the shoulder, when he last did the rounds?

As he stared down across the cemetery to Panormos village, it was Stockton Marsh graveyard that he saw, and his hand was clicking the latch on the gate leading to the orchards, still soiled by blood and bad memories. A human hand pulled a trigger there, twice. And on the village fringe, another hand and another gun blew more life away. What did they sell to the devil, those human hands? What temptation did Mephistopheles whisper, in triumph, as he sauntered by?

The police returned Andrew Priddle's bible, and he kept it in the glove compartment of his little car. He didn't read beyond the flyleaf.

This Bible belongs to Sophie Priddle, aged nine and a half.

The handwriting was his mother's. It was all there was. Unless his DNA proved the skeleton was also her.

'You're hers too', he told the money, whenever he spent some.

Despite being born and raised in Stockton Marsh, neither Andrew Priddle nor Sergeant Ball knew much of old Tom Priddle. They were far too young to have seen him bludgeon his wife with a heavy walking stick. Nor, once he'd sobered up, did they see him scrape aside a sharp mound of brambles in his foul rear garden and begin to dig a hole. He had no interest in garden ponds. He merely dug, deeper and deeper, over two nights, till the hole was so deep he needed to use a ladder. Then he dug it deeper still.

Andrew Priddle would never remember he was crying - an underfed two-year-old - when his birth mother slid into the depths. He was still crying when the suitcase she'd dared to pack was throw in too, and the grave refilled. He was exhausted into a long silence by the time nettle, ivy and bramble covered her.

An alert DC Hick flipped out another good question.

'I know it's before your time, Sarge-'

'Before my *time*, Hickie? I was barely *born*.'

'Yeh, but when we trawl back through the files, it'll be there, plain as day. I mean, it'll be missing.'

Ball had learnt from his Inspector. He waited five seconds.

'He must have, mustn't he, Sarge? Tom Priddle?'

'Must've killed his wife, Hickie?'

'*No*, Sarge. Well, yes. But what I mean is, how'd he get away with it?'

Ball had his own suspicions, but they were a tad uncomfortable, right now.

'He's coughed up a bung, hasn't he? Must've. Wife disappears without a trace. Husband doesn't. And nobody digs up the garden?'

'Things were done differently then, Hickie. You didn't-'

'Nah, he's slipped someone a pile o' cash, Sarge - plenty of it, too, for hiding *that*.' Hick lowered his voice, though they were the only two in the office. 'Someone in *the Force*, I mean. Someone who made it all disappear?'

There would be an enquiry, Ball was certain - as if Stockton Marsh hadn't suffered enough. He gave Hick an awkward shrug in reply.

When his eyes returned to the DNA results on his desk, the shrug turned into a shudder. He stared at them for what felt like forty years. The piece of white paper would be sad news for Andrew Priddle, and Chris Ball was Johnnie-on-the-spot.

He cursed D.I. Zig Batten, for not allowing him to resign.

Grigoris was making his way down the tree-lined path from the cemetery. Batten took in a final view of the little church and its orderly cluster of marble monuments and family plots.

You've got to put a stop to this, Zig.

To what, Zig?

You know very well what. This hanging around where dead bodies are.

Sure, Zig, tell Murder to behave. Or tell the Force to stuff it, and start a new career in property development. Forget about crime, demolish a green hillside instead. Who'd stop you?

With reverence, he closed the latch of the cemetery's iron gate, and followed the footsteps of Lieutenant Makis Grigoris of the Greek International Cooperation Division, down the stony track to Panormos village, gilded in the late afternoon - thank god - by sudden Cretan sunshine.

At the Parish Council meeting in Stockton Marsh, the vote was unanimous: no Easter Wassail this year. A cold vapour still cloaked the neat streets of the village, seeping into the brook, sitting like sad dew on winter-worn verges and lawns. In the graveyard, new headstones longed for lichen to clothe them, standing out like white reminders against the brown hamstone of the ancient church.

If Norm Hogg was to be believed, the bell-tower clock ticked more slowly this Spring, and the faint breath of 'evil spirits' lingered in the orchard, cooling the winds as they whispered through the colonnades of trees, slowing the revival of the trees themselves.

Beneath their boughs, sheep grazed regardless on the first blades of new grass. The apple-blossom, unconcerned, sniffed the air and felt the pale sun's prompting. Fresh white petals teased their way past brown protective buds.

And began.

Acknowledgements

Huge thanks to Yvonne, Sam, Gwyneth, Joni, Pete, Moya and Marnie for patiently commenting on early drafts, and to all the poor devils who listened to me banging on about writer's block and deadlines. Particular thanks to Richard and Steve for advice about shotguns, and to Mick for advice on police procedure. Any errors are mine, not theirs.

And a very special thanks to the apple-landscape of Somerset.

To the Reader

If you've enjoyed *A January Killing*, please consider leaving a review - for example on Amazon.co.uk, Amazon.com, or Goodreads.

And do keep a lookout for the third book in the series which will be published in 2016.